MOONBLOOD

T.W. FENDLEY

SOUL SONG PRESS, LLC

Published by Soul Song Press, LLC, in St Augustine, Florida, 2020.

www.SoulSongPress.com

ISBN 978-0-9998434-3-7 (Paperback)

LCCN 2020907947

To my grandchildren
Galen, Lillian, Jake, Lucy, Kyla, Juno, Matt and Sarah

Thank you for bringing great joy and love to my life. You are my legacy of hope for a kinder world. May love and compassion guide you!

1

ARI

I raised my face and palms toward the sky along with fifty other blue-eyed, black-haired women who encircled the crescent-moon fountain. Unfettered by clothes, our pale brown skin drank in the moonlight and tanned to rich dark hues. Our bodies fed on the moonsong, created by a subtle shift in the airwaves that changed tempo as the moon climbed higher in the cloudless sky.

Moonbathing pleased us as nothing else did, but even the full moon above couldn't quell my longing for something uniquely mine. I felt invisible, stifled by the sameness.

We'd been here for hours, and I was growing impatient. To keep from looking toward the gymnasium and giving away my plan, I kept my mind busy thinking about moonbeams. Some said they were in our blood. I didn't know about that, but I didn't want to find out what a month without the full moon's rays might do to me.

Older girls used to scare us with tales of women who'd been locked away in dungeons. Or those who'd been touched in "that way" by a Cain. Either could kill us outright, they said. I doubted the truth of such claims, but I still got the shivers. I imagined better outcomes of coming face to face with a Cain or perhaps even an Adam. The Matron said the compound's towering walls were to keep the others out, but they also kept us in.

I almost sighed with relief when caretakers went to the new-moon fountain and escorted the younger girls to their rooms. Finally. The moon became less energizing as it passed the zenith, and the youngest felt its power ebb first. Before long, it was our group's time to leave. I walked toward our dorm behind the others, dropping back until I could slip into the shadows at the building's edge.

Eventually, the compound grew dark and silent. I'd come to know the pattern over the past six months since I first felt drawn to do what we were all warned against. After everyone was in bed, it was the perfect time to walk in the field.

We were forbidden to go there alone at night, so that's where I longed to be. The Matron said homeless Cains sometimes wandered there from the city and others came looking for a place to party, but I'd never seen anyone except our own sentries.

From cloudy days spent exploring, I knew the field's secrets. A stream small enough to step across cut diagonally through the waist-high grass, making a home for frogs and turtles. Two-thirds of the way toward the gravel road that bordered the property, a tiny oasis of sweet clover and wildflowers lay hidden among the taller grass. That was my destination, as it had been so many nights before.

The field had gotten all tangled up with thoughts of freedom. Outside the compound, I didn't feel anonymous. I felt more myself, not just another crescent-moon cadet.

I'd figured out the best way to leave the compound was through the gate near the gymnasium. The sleeping areas were across the courtyard, so if anyone was still wandering about, they'd be less likely to notice me. Conveniently, the gymnasium bordered the field.

I waited until the sentry crossed to the other side of the compound before I pushed against the heavy wooden gate. Iron hinges creaked as I slipped through. I paused for a few seconds and listened. All was quiet. I left the gate unlatched but closed.

Perhaps the openness of the field made the moonlight seem stronger, but I grew light-headed with the rush of moonsong through my veins. I didn't waste any time getting to my secret haven, but I also let myself revel in the moment. I spread my arms and spun through the amber stalks, which brushed soft as feathers against my skin. When my feet finally touched the clover's springy softness, I dropped onto the fragrant earth. Violas cushioned my fall.

A breeze rustled the stalks. I lay on my back and studied the sky.

A falling star cut across the Big Dipper. Did it offer a wish or a warning? I wished to not be invisible any more. I wished to be free.

I thought things would change when I reached maturity and left the new-moon group. But, instead of more freedom, I'd had even less during my ten years with the crescent-moon group. Another twelve years would pass before I would be considered a woman and allowed outside the compound, and a century or more before I'd join the full-moon group.

Once I petitioned the Matron to allow me to train with the older women. Her kindly smile was the only concession. "Only the first century goes slowly," she said. "You'll see." The full-moon women laughed and nodded.

* * *

A squealing sound woke me. Startled, I leapt to my feet. My heart lurched when I realized the moon had set. I must've been asleep for hours.

Car lights cut across the field, slicing the protective darkness and catching me in their snare. A bottle clanked as it hit the gravel and shattered.

"Hey, lookie there!" a throaty voice yelled as a battered car skidded to a stop. "A nekked girl."

"She's just awaitin' for it," another jeered.

Their voices sounded deeper and more menacing than any I'd ever heard. Men's voices. Cain's voices. Now I understood why we'd been told not to come here. It was twice as far to safety from my oasis as it was to the road, but this was not the time to think about that.

Car doors screeched open. The lewd words reached across the field and stabbed me like icy daggers, chilling my blood. "Have I got something for you, girlie!"

I sprinted toward the compound, gulping air as my legs pumped.

"Wanna play hard to get, do ya?" Laughter floated across the field. Footsteps pounded behind me.

My bare feet skimmed over tender clover, then the cutting coarseness of saw grass. I ran faster than ever, but their panting grew louder as the Cains closed in. I reached the pebbled perimeter that spanned the last hundred yards to the gate. I wasn't going to make it.

A calloused hand gripped my bare shoulder. "Gotcha."

I screamed.

"Ain't she a young one," the other said as he clasped my wrist, jerking me to a complete stop. I careened backward. His bearded face scratched against my arm before my right shoulder slammed against the ground, knocking me breathless.

Although I kicked and twisted, the other Cain easily straddled me. How could he be so much stronger than me? He unfastened his belt and unzipped his pants while the bearded Cain pinned both of my hands to the ground with one hand and squeezed my breast with the other. "Perky," he slurred.

"Help!" I cried. "Leave me alone!"

Weathered skin and yellowed teeth hovered above my face, enveloping me with the pungent stench of the Cain's breath. "It's what you deserve, you little prick tease. Runnin' 'round without a stitch on...you's asking for it, sure 'nough."

"Stop!" I pleaded.

The weight of his chest pressed onto mine as he rammed his rough, denim-clad knee between my thighs.

I squeezed my eyes shut. "No, NO!"

A thunk registered over the blood roaring in my ears. The pressure on my hands tightened, then released. With a groan, the bearded Cain toppled against the one on top of me as he fell to the ground.

"What the fuck?" my attacker said. As he lifted off me to push the bearded Cain away, I heard a swooshing sound. His knee jammed into my stomach as he fell backward, grasping his throat and shuddering. The feathered shaft of an arrow protruded through his fingers and blood spurted from his neck onto my stomach. His eyes rolled back, and he gave a final cry as he tipped over. I pushed his foot off my leg and scooted away.

A few heartbeats later, the bowmaster stood above me. She held a bow in one hand and slid an arrow back into the quiver with the other. Sweat covered her long, muscular legs, which gleamed like polished bronze. From this vantage point, her slender body looked seven-feet tall.

"Ari." Layla frowned. Her eyes surveyed me and the man's twisted body. "I should've known it would be you out here. Did he...?"

Afraid my voice would quake, I shook my head. Even so, my chin quivered and tears rolled down my face as what nearly happened hit home. Would I have died?

She sighed and turned toward the car. "I'll need help to clean up this mess." Layla's voice trailed behind her as she left the clearing at a run. "Get the Matron."

I pushed up onto my elbows and scrambled to my feet, but stopped to gape at the arrow puncturing the left side of the other Cain's back. I'd never seen a human felled by an arrow. The bowmaster never missed her target. She'd killed those men to save me. I gagged on the coppery smell of blood mixed with a stench like wet goats and piss. My stomach twisted, but I couldn't pull my eyes away from the crumpled figures on the ground. Even lying there, their size was daunting.

My head snapped up at the sound of a car door slamming shut. Layla ran through the headlight beams to reach the driver's side. She leaned over the hood and pointed toward the compound. "Go!" Anger distorted her face. "Don't just stand there." She got in and slammed the door behind her.

I spun around and ran. As I passed the wooden gate, the placement of bows and loaded quivers along the gymnasium's outer wall suddenly had new meaning. I made a beeline for the Matron's cottage and pounded on her door. "Matron!"

"Who could that be?" someone inside asked.

"I'll go see," the Matron answered. Then the door opened. The Matron swept her eyes over my bloody midsection and cleared her throat before asking, "Ariadne, what happened?"

A flush of shame heated my cheeks. "The bowmaster told me to get you."

"Why didn't she come herself?"

"It's...a long story," I stuttered. My mind raced with a thousand ways to explain what happened, but all that came out was, "I'm so sorry."

She raised her hand to silence me. "Don't make excuses. Is she hurt?"

I shook my head. "Please come now!"

"Tell me you didn't go to the field again."

I lowered my head, but still felt her eyes blazing at me. She knew.

She turned and called out, "Myranda, we need clothes." A few seconds later, we slipped orange caftans over our heads as we ran toward the field. Layla and the car were gone, so I led the Matron to the bodies. She stopped, then turned to me with wide, questioning eyes.

My eyes focused on the man's unbuttoned jeans. "The bowmaster saved me," I whispered.

She grunted. "But you have endangered us all."

Moments later, Myranda and four other women joined us. Matron nodded at one of them and gestured at the Cains. The woman pulled out a palm-sized device and swept it over the closest body. On the second sweep, the body disappeared. She repeated the process on the bearded Cain.

I sucked in my breath, not believing my eyes. "I've never seen anything like that."

She waved the device my way to give me a better look. "It's a Disruptor." It looked like the plastic squirt guns we'd played with as new-moon cadets.

I edged away. What if she accidentally blasted me with it? I didn't want to dissolve into thin air. When I looked back around, the Matron was walking briskly back toward the compound. She didn't slow down as she barked orders. "Wake the others. We leave for the new compound in an hour."

The next hour passed in a blur. When the other women and I arrived at the central plaza, Layla was dressed and getting back into the Cains' car. She drove off as the other full-moon women hurried to their tasks. I followed one to the dorm where two dozen other crescent-moon cadets and I slept.

She took a conch shell off a shelf beside the door and blew it. The deep wail echoed against stucco-clad walls, waking the others. In moments, they stood in two straight lines at the foot of their bunks. As I took my place, I cursed my stupidity at not removing the caftan —only full-moon women wore the loose, ankle-length dresses. The others stared at me, undoubtedly suspecting I was behind the chaos.

The full-moon woman returned the conch to the shelf. "We're moving to the new compound tonight."

An undercurrent of excitement ran through the room, accentuated by a flurry of exclamations from the cadets.

"Gather your things, then go to the courtyard," the woman said. "We'll need help with the youngsters."

Trying to blend in, I pulled the orange caftan over my head and rolled it in a ball. Too late, I remembered the dried blood covering my stomach. Even those who had turned away stared at me again.

"So, you, what's going on?" Piper demanded.

Of all people, she was the one I least wanted to tell. In ten years, we'd never seen eye to eye on anything. Maybe it was because Piper did everything she could to be more like the full-moon women, whereas I just wanted to have their freedom. Piper stood a head taller than me, but otherwise shared the same dark hair and blue eyes as the rest of us.

She shoved me, her fist rock-hard against my sore shoulder. "Well?"

"I don't know," I lied. "I couldn't sleep, so I tried to open a box of tablets for tomorrow's classes. The cutter slipped." I motioned to my bloody middle. "I was in the infirmary when the Matron came in. The nurse gave me this and told me to keep my wound clean until we had time to properly dress it." I held up the caftan, trying to divert their attention as I reached into the chest of drawers next to the bunks. I pulled out a tunic and slipped it over my head before anyone got a closer look.

Piper eyed me suspiciously, then shook her head and walked away. The other girls followed her lead and returned to packing. They bantered among themselves, mostly trying to decide what to take and what to leave behind. Some voices seemed more fearful than adventurous. We'd all expected to move to a new compound soon, but not *now*.

It didn't take me long to pack all the leggings, tunics and underwear that would fit in my duffel, along with a small bag of toiletries. I grabbed my art tote, filled with books, drawing paper and colored pencils, and made it out the door before anyone else.

Memories surfaced as I watched the full-moon women herd youngsters across the courtyard toward eight gray, double-decker vans lined up beside the three fountains in the central plaza. It was just like I remembered from when we arrived here. I was a preschooler then, barely tall enough to see out the windows that circled both levels of the vans. Our old compound had been bigger than this one, but I couldn't recall any other details. From snippets of conversations I'd overheard at the dining hall during the past year, they'd found few suitable places for our future home.

When I reached the van marked with a crescent moon, I lingered outside, resting a gloved hand on its curved side as I watched the girls file into the new-moon van. One already seated on the lower level waved at me, and I waved back. Would their memories of tonight's trip be as powerful for them as my early adventure? Buildings in the Cain city—made small by distance—had gleamed on the horizon like a thousand stars. The image never left my thoughts no matter how many times I was told their cities were not for our kind.

In times past, some Eves had tried to openly join their society, but Cains lived in fear of anything they didn't understand and labeled us mutants. They would never accept women who didn't need men to reproduce, and they'd never forgive us for being immortal. It was better for us to remain a myth, and for full-moon women to enter the cities disguised as Cains.

At least, that's what I'd been told. It made me crazy. Even though we aged more slowly than Cains, thirty-eight should be old enough to be trusted outside the compound walls. No matter how many times I told myself that, I kept hearing the Matron's words: "You have endangered us all."

And then it was like I was back in the field, smothering under the weight of the Cain pressing down on me. Pulling against the rough hands holding my wrists. My breast aching. I shook my head, trying to clear the images from my mind.

Piper's voice came out of nowhere. "A box cutter?"

I jumped. I hadn't heard her walk up behind me. Relieved to have my thoughts interrupted, I was almost glad to see her. Almost.

She frowned and nodded toward my stomach. "Couldn't you come up with something better than a box cutter?"

For the first time, I noticed she really did look more like the full-moon women, while I still had the slim body of a new-moon cadet. Despite her plentiful curves and apparent softness, I knew from previous encounters we were equally strong. I hoped our disagreement wouldn't become physical, but I wasn't going to back down. "I haven't had as much practice lying as *some* people."

"I knew you'd been sneaking out, but I didn't think you were dumb enough to get caught. Guess you showed me."

I threw my hands up in frustration. I wanted to make a scathing comeback, but grew angry at myself for having to agree with her. Still, I didn't want to give her the satisfaction of knowing she'd gotten to me. "I shouldn't have been in the field tonight. But if the Matron gave us more freedom, I wouldn't have been sneaking out." Inside, I felt an emptiness, knowing my carelessness had forced us to leave our home prematurely. I was grateful when Layla walked over.

"Ariadne, come with me."

I started to follow.

Motioning to my duffel, she said, "Bring your things. You won't be coming back."

I gave Piper a haughty grin, hoping she'd think I'd one-upped her in some way, though I quaked at Layla's words. What did she mean, "not coming back?" Was I banished from the compound? I picked up my duffel and tote. As we walked across the courtyard, a van filled with the youngest children pulled away. It looked like the Matron's deadline would be met.

Layla opened the door to the Matron's cottage and motioned for me to enter. She stayed outside.

"Ariadne," the Matron said. "We've decided to give you what you want."

"Matron?" How could she know anything about what I wanted? It's not like we'd ever spoken about it before tonight.

"Going out to the field—I take it that was more than just restlessness?"

That floored me. If she knew what I'd been doing, why hadn't she stopped me? I found my voice and spoke as calmly as I could, despite my thundering pulse. I gave the speech I'd told myself countless times over the past few months, although now the words lacked the same passion. "It was...it *is* about freedom. Staying in this compound, shut off from everything, is like being in prison."

She sighed. "And what would you know of prison? Now that you've gotten a taste of the kind of people who are out there, I'd think you'd be grateful for those years of safety."

I lowered my eyes. As much as I hated it, she had a point. My first encounter with the outside world hadn't made me eager to push my luck. "I owe the bowmaster my life."

"Yes, well, maybe that's what she had in mind when she suggested taking you along on her mission. Some rules even I don't bend, and one of those is not going into the city alone. Still, it will be dangerous." She shrugged. "And I think Layla may see something of herself in you. Frankly, if I could spare any of the full-moon women, I wouldn't consider her request. But, thanks to you, they're all busy with the relocation." She paused and looked at me solemnly. "This is going to be really hard for Layla. Just try to remember what you've been taught."

Puzzled about Layla's mission and the Matron's reaction to the night's events, I stepped out and closed the door behind me. I had expected to be confined to my room for a year or ordered to scrub floors by hand. Instead, the Matron was granting my wish. Freedom. A chill of foreboding ran down my spine.

"Let's go," Layla said.

2

BLAIR

I was such a fool. For months in the same room with a mutant— discussing the class, exchanging notes. I'd even let her borrow a charger chip.

How can I call myself a true patriot if I can't recognize the enemy when they're sitting right next to me? The cold realization swept over me, numbing my core. In front of me, a Con Squad trooper dragged the girl—no, that's not right—the *mutant* toward the door.

Leather-gloved fingers pressed deeply into my classmate's upper arm, and her shoes made a high-pitched screech as they skidded on the polished tile floor.

"What did I do?" she screamed. "There's been a mistake! Someone help me!"

Did they all put on such a show?

Another trooper shoved her from behind. She stumbled forward until she collided with the trooper dragging her. With another rough push from behind, she careened down the hall and out of sight.

A third trooper stayed behind, facing the class. The open face shield exposed ice-blue eyes. Her steely gaze swept the room, slowly examining each of the fifteen students.

I followed her gaze, analyzing my classmates to see if I could identify any other mutants. Most of the seventeen- and eighteen- year-olds shifted in their seats and kept their eyes averted. With my palm up and the side of my right hand against my heart, I exchanged a salute with two guys at the back of the room who wore bright blue CS Reserve armbands like mine.

After several long minutes, the trooper announced in a gruff voice, "Those who have associated with the mutant are required to report to Headquarters within twenty-four hours for questioning. Leniency will not be granted after that time." The visor lowered and the trooper left.

The instructor stood to the side, his face pale and drawn. I wondered if he had any idea what the student had done. He should. As an instructor, part of his job was to notice and report anyone suspicious. If not, we'd be getting a new teacher soon, and good riddance.

My eyes stalled at the empty seat. Even though I racked my brain, I couldn't think of anything unusual to tell them about the woman. But one thing I'd learned in the Reserve was to not underestimate the Con Squad—something I considered trivial might be meaningful in the greater context.

I looked up from my handheld as the instructor shakily walked back to his desk. "Read the next chapter, and we'll resume our discussion tomorrow," he stuttered. "Class dismissed." He turned and disappeared from the room before I'd even shut off my book. I pushed into the stream of departing students. Many tried to elbow their way ahead of me. I shoved back.

I wanted to be the first to arrive at HQ.

I'd always supported the Contamination Squad. They brought order and discipline to an otherwise scary world where people were not always what they seemed. I was glad the Con Squad had finally been granted the legal authority to act against these enemies of the state before they acted against us, though terrorism was still far too common. Sometimes it took extraordinary measures to keep us safe because not all the threats were violent. They stood against our way of life—against humanity itself.

* * *

I jumped as one of the guys with a CS armband ran up behind me and took my elbow. He wasn't even from my unit. I pulled away from him.

"Hey, that was something, wasn't it?" His round, pasty-white face almost glowed with excitement. "A mutant right here in our classroom!" The doors slid shut behind us as we exited the building.

People crowded us on the moving walkway as we headed toward Headquarters. I had to crane my neck to look up at him. "Had you noticed anything?"

He shrugged. "Nay. I would've alerted them myself if I had."

"Me, too."

"She missed a couple of classes lately, so maybe that was how they caught her."

I nodded, considering what that might mean. Had she been meeting with others, planning some sort of attack?

When we reached HQ, I placed my handheld into the scanner and passed through body screening. The pasty-faced guy stayed at the checkpoint to talk with other Reservists, but I didn't know any of them. I walked toward the station desk, glad to leave him behind.

A uniformed trooper watched a display screen as I placed my thumb on the scanner. "Blair Redkin." He looked up at me, his bushy white eyebrows knitted. "From the Botany 201 class. You're the first to report."

I saluted him. "Here to do my civic duty, sir."

"Very good." He returned my salute. "I see you're with Commander Jacobsen's unit."

"Yes, sir."

"Well, this won't take but a second." He smiled and pointed to the left.

I went through an open doorway and sat in front of a large white screen. A moment later, video feeds from the classroom showed me talking with the woman. Three clips showed us chatting, and in one, she handed me a note. How had I forgotten that?

A trooper emerged from behind the screen. "Care to explain?"

"Oh, that's not what it looks like," I said quickly, a trill of alarm coursing through me.

"And what do you think it looks like?"

"We weren't close," I stuttered. "I would never have anything to do with anyone subversive. That note just had her web address."

"I see."

"No, really. I missed a class, and she had posted some information about the assignment on her page."

"So you miss class one day, then she misses other days, and you share your work so no one notices."

"It's not like that at all, sir." I stepped back, gathering my wits. My right hand rested on my armband. "I'm a Reservist. I support the Con Squad. I always have. That's why I'm here. You can look into my background all you want. I'm a patriot."

"So you say..." She smirked and looked at the scanner. "...Blair Redkin." Her eyes met mine. "Maybe we'll do just that."

Before I could think of anything more to say, she turned and walked away. I stood there alone for several minutes until one of my classmates entered. The trooper from the front desk motioned for me to leave.

"But, she didn't ask me anything," I protested.

"You can sign a statement if you'd like," the trooper said in a monotone voice as we walked toward his desk.

"A statement?"

"Confession. Alibi. Informer's statement. Snitch sheet ... whatever you want to call it." He paused and looked at me questioningly. "Well?"

My stomach rolled, but all I could do was shake my head. "Never mind."

He shrugged. "Okay then."

Stunned, I walked out of Headquarters. What just happened?

* * *

I finished warming dinner and sat down to do my botany homework. My handheld vibrated. I tapped it open to a message from Bethany. Though we were in different sections, she'd asked me to work on a term project with her since we had the same botany professor.

"Just heard about the mutant. Your section?"

"Yes."

"OMG. Did you know her?"

"Not really, but went to HQ to cover bases."

After a pause, she wrote: "And?"

Now I paused. I was tempted to share how unsettled the exchange left me, but Bethany wasn't a Reservist. Even bringing up this topic seemed out of character for her. Usually we only chatted about class, the latest novels we'd read, or something equally banal. "Not what expected."

"Any word on kind of mutant?"

"None."

"A loner?"

Was Bethany afraid of mutants? I'd never suspected that. "Probably. Still on for Friday?"

"Want to meet at my house? I'm up at dawn."

"See you then."

She disconnected.

I stared at my handheld a few more beats, then returned to my homework. The day was full of surprises. Bethany and I weren't exactly close, so why had she checked on me when none of my Reservist friends had?

Around midnight, I put away my books and went to bed. I'd hoped to tell Mom what happened at school, but she must have worked a double-shift at the car factory.

* * *

The next day as I walked into class, I overheard a whispered conversation between two women in front of me.

"Her boyfriend turned her in because she was pregnant," the redhead said.

"That bastard!" the brunette said. "He knows she's no virgin—she told me it's his baby."

The redhead sighed. "I know. She thought he loved her."

"You just don't know who to trust. Did you go to Headquarters?"

"Of course," the redhead replied. "How about you?"

The brunette shrugged. "I don't want my name linked to a mutant's. The Con Squad will have to work to make a connection to me."

The redhead sighed. "If you don't go and someone tells them you're friends, it will be so much worse for you. And your family."

"I hadn't thought about it that way. But it's not like we were very close." They exchanged a guilty look. "I guess I will go."

As they passed by the instructor's desk, the brunette saw me watching them. She nudged the redhead and lifted her chin toward me. Both scowled at me as they hurried toward their seats.

I shook my head. How naïve could they be? The Con Squad wouldn't fall for that. Someone wouldn't be singled out as a mutant without real proof that they were a threat. I mean, if that was all it took, my mother could've been accused of virgin birth.

Like many of her generation, Mom wasn't a fan of the Con Squad, but I'd never heard her say anything against them, either. Had they ever questioned her? My father hadn't been around while I was growing up.

* * *

All the way home, I wondered about my missing father. Why didn't I know anything about him? Mom told me he died in an accident when I was a baby. A few years ago when I asked her about the accident, she stared at me and simply said, "He's dead to me. That's all you need to know." But now it wasn't. Was he even really dead? Or had my father dumped us like the mutant's boyfriend?

After dinner, I sat in the kitchen waiting for Mom as long as I could. Eventually, I gave up and went to bed. Later when I heard footsteps in the hall, I tried to rouse myself, but it was like my limbs were made of lead.

Tomorrow. She'll be here in the morning, and we can talk before I leave for class.

I had almost drifted back to sleep when Mom whispered urgently in my ear, "If you value my life, keep quiet!" She shook me with one hand and covered my mouth with the other. "Get up. Be quick!"

I sat up groggily. Something drew my eye across the hallway to her bedroom window. Light glinted off a black SUV parked on the street, and shadowy figures moved toward the house. A trill of fear fluttered in my stomach.

Mom jerked me to my feet and shoved me toward the closet. She opened the closet door and pulled out two plastic bins of clothes.

"What are you..." I protested. Then my muscles spasmed from a jolt of electricity. I slumped into her arms, and she lowered me onto the closet floor. I wanted to ask why she had done this to me, but I couldn't form the words.

She gave my face a gentle caress. "I'm so sorry," Mom whispered. Her forlorn eyes were the last things I saw before she stacked tunics on top of me, blocking out the light. She shoved the bins back into the closet in front of me, then shut the doors.

Cold sweat beaded on my forehead. What was she doing? I struggled to breathe through the fabric covering my face.

"Be quiet!" she ordered. "And stay there. No matter what." From her fading footsteps, I knew she'd left the room.

An ear-splitting crash at the front of the house made me jump. Sounds of men's shouts and running footsteps—a chase from the front of the house to the back—ended with Mom's high-pitched scream in the hallway.

"Let me go!" she yelled.

My stomach clenched. I'd heard bounty hunters could be overzealous and dangerous, but I wasn't going to let them treat her like this. Once her attackers knew a Reservist lived here, they would run like crazy. I struggled to stand, but my numb and tingling limbs refused. I tried to call out, but my mouth still wouldn't respond.

Heavy footsteps approached.

"Yeah, the woman's kid thought she could pull one over on me," a woman said. "She actually pranced into HQ and dared me to investigate her, like we wouldn't just because she's in the Reserve."

I froze, processing what she said. Dared her to investigate me?

"Had you been following her activities?" a younger man asked.

"That's what's so funny...we wouldn't have paid any attention to her mom's record if the kid hadn't come in. That's when we saw the irregularities."

What? A wave of fear washed over me. These weren't bounty hunters. They were Con Squad troopers!

"Check these rooms thoroughly," the woman said. "If we're lucky, we'll catch the mutant's offspring, too, and maybe head off another virgin birth."

Mutant? Virgin birth? I puzzled over her words. What irregularities made them think Mom was a mutant?

"Right, Commander," the young male answered, with a disgusted tone. The closet door jiggled. "These mutants multiply like rabbits."

Anger blazed through me. I'm a patriot, not a mutant.

A moment later, the closet door slid open, sending a shaft of light into the cramped space. Clothes hanging on the rod above rustled as he shoved them from one side to another. The man grunted as he kicked the bins—jamming them into me. The light brightened and realized he must be shining a flashlight onto the clothes covering me. My stomach knotted as one of the tunics covering me rose. Suddenly I wasn't so sure that I wanted to be discovered by a trooper who thought I was a mutant, especially when I couldn't say anything to defend myself.

Another set of footsteps entered the room. "Anything?" a new voice asked.

"Not really." The tunic dropped back onto me as he stepped toward the speaker. "But look at the bed. The sheets are rumpled like someone just got up."

"Or maybe they never straighten the covers," the other man said with disgust. "Let's go. We have another stop tonight."

"Another virgin birth?" the young man asked, his voice fading as their footsteps grew distant.

It had to be at least fifteen minutes before I finally managed to tilt onto my side, cringing as my muscles awoke painfully. Next, I folded into a crouched position with my forehead on my knees, clothes that had covered me spilling on either side.

All the while, I kept remembering interrogation techniques we'd learned in my Reservist training—ones they'd soon be using on my mother. She'd immediately undergo a barrage of tests, some of which could be fatal. Much depended on the type of mutant they thought she was.

Virgin birth and immortality were both hard to discern in the short-term, though that wouldn't stop them from trying truth serums or waterboarding. To test for suneaters, though, required little more than leaving the suspected mutant in the sun without food to see if they survived.

After another twenty minutes passed, I stood and pushed aside the tunics hanging on the rod above, taking care to not make noise. I lifted one of the bins in front of me and placed it on the other side of the closet, then inched open the closet doors. After each tiny movement, I stopped and listened. All was quiet.

I spotted my backpack with everything dumped out of it onto the floor at the foot of my bed. I grabbed my handheld and sat on the floor, out of sight of the door. I needed someone to clear my Mom and me of suspicion, and who better than the commander of my CS Reserve unit? He would get to the bottom of this!

I tapped in the passcode, but instead of opening to the Reserve's landing page, an orange circle with a slash through it blazed onto the screen. I entered the code again. No luck. I submitted a passcode reset request and waited for the update message to appear. And waited. I couldn't deny it any longer—I was blocked. Without access, I couldn't reach Commander Jacobsen.

After four years in the cadre, I found it hard it to accept that I could be marked so easily as a mutant, yet I felt sure that was why I was blocked. If I contacted my fellow Reservists, they would turn me in without giving me a chance to explain. That's what we were trained to do.

Staying here was not an option. Before long, a team of Reservists —maybe even my own unit—would be assigned to go through the house to search for evidence and leads to other mutants.

And I couldn't go back to class. The Con Squad would watch my family members, so staying with my aunt was out of the question, too. I scrolled through the messages on my handheld. Bethany was the only person not in the Reserve who had contacted me since the incident at school, and we had a study date set for tomorrow morning.

I started crafting a plan. First, I needed a few things from the house. Though my muscles were still stiff, finally I could move without pain. I tiptoed into the hallway. Keeping my back flat against the wall, I stealthily moved in the deepest shadows toward the front of the house. From the hallway, I saw the lights glowing in the living room. The front door stood open, with a gaping hole where the lock had been in the wooden frame. My knees went limp as I replayed the sounds of the splintering wood, the men's shouts, and my mother's screams.

Outside, the visible part of the driveway was empty—no black vehicle, no flashing lights, no troopers. I gnawed my bottom lip. No Mom.

Traffic on the nearby freeway hummed steadily. No other sounds broke the stillness. Toward the back of the house, the kitchen sat in darkness.

I inched back down the hall, crossed it, and entered Mom's room. Through the open curtains, I saw someone walk by the house. My heart pounded. Was it a trooper? I crouched down, hoping it was too dark inside for me to be seen. I crawled around the bed. Although my eyes had adjusted to the darkness, everything still looked shadowy. A streetlamp's glow reflected off something glass atop the nightstand. Mom's handheld. I grabbed it and crawled back to my bedroom.

I tugged on a pair of cropped gym pants, a sports bra, and a top, then stepped into my running shoes. Out of habit, I reached for my CS armband. But how could I wear it now? With a sigh, I stuffed it and some clothes in my backpack.

Should I leave now? I looked at the time—3 a.m. I figured it would look less suspicious if I waited until the morning joggers were out. Bethany lived only a few blocks away.

I got back in the closet, restacked the plastic bins, and pulled the door closed behind me. For now, it was the only place I felt even a little safe.

The minutes ticked by slowly, giving me too much time to think. Why hadn't Mom hidden? If only she hadn't been so courageous in trying to face down the intruders. Maybe she thought the men knew someone was inside the house and wouldn't give up until they found us. We both should've run. Had she suspected it was the Con Squad?

I panicked. The idea of never seeing her again punched my gut like a fist. Where had they taken her? Hot tears streamed down my face, and I struggled to keep from sobbing. *I'll see her again, I'll see her again, I'll see her again.*

A loud clatter in the hallway made me jump. Footsteps down the hallway came closer.

"C'mon," a boy's voice called out. "Make it quick."

"All right!" another boy shouted gleefully from the direction of my mother's room. "Got some creds right here."

Why hadn't I grabbed Mom's wallet when I got the handheld? Or maybe it was better this way. The Con Squad monitored credit card usage, so when these thieves made purchases, maybe they'd think it was me. Any diversion could be helpful.

"Hey," yelled another boy, whose hurried footsteps echoed from the front of the house. "Someone's coming. Go, go, go!"

The backdoor screeched open and slammed shut. Seconds later, another voice in the hallway answered an electronic squawk. "Just missed them—looters, most likely. Deploy a drone."

"Copy."

"No sign of the girl. Yet." His footsteps faded from the back of the house.

Now I knew for sure troopers were watching the house. I had to stay alert.

* * *

I jerked awake, bleary-eyed but pumped with adrenaline. Sunrise bathed the room in pink light. Sounds from outside grew louder as the neighborhood awoke. I crawled out of the closet and walked to the kitchen, crouching below window-level. I grabbed the household emergency cash from a container in the freezer, snagged vending machine tokens and snack bars from the cookie jar, and picked up a charger chip for the handheld.

Keeping hidden behind the curtains as much as possible, I peeked through the window. A trooper walked by on the other side of the street, his gaze fixed on our house. I timed his walk around the perimeter a few times.

When I felt confident, I waited until he passed in front of the house, then stepped out the back onto the patio. I left the door ajar, just as I'd found it. I stayed behind the shrubs next to the house. By now, the trooper should've reached the farthest point away from where I was. I darted across the narrow side yard toward the neighbor's garage and scrambled into the shadows. I moved quickly to the side away from my house.

I barely caught my breath before a woman walking three dogs passed by. "Rex, come on!" she said, barely slowing as a black terrier tried to wander toward where I hid.

When they were a few houses away, I jogged to the sidewalk and headed the other direction, toward Bethany's house. About a block from home, a faster runner came up behind me. My throat closed off with panic until he ran past without a glance in my direction. I ignored a few other joggers as they huffed by.

I slowed my pace when I saw Bethany's small, buff-brick one-story home just ahead. A light was on in the kitchen, but the front part of the house was dark. It almost looked deserted, which didn't make any sense.

I was a few minutes early, so I decided to run an extra block and burn off more of my nervous energy. Besides, I wasn't looking forward to our conversation. I didn't know where to start. Who knew how long

I'd have to hide while I tried to clear my name? Would she even be willing to help?

As I neared the next corner, a strange prickly feeling made me wonder if I was being watched. I slowed to a walk. Voices, barely audible, buzzed around me. A lot of them. I hid behind a big oak with a good view of the street behind Bethany's house. About a half-dozen troopers stood beside two black SUVs. They placed a ladder against the fence and climbed over it. Some positioned themselves against the back of her house. One of the troopers took Bethany's arm and escorted her into the house. The rest of the troopers followed them.

I leaned against the tree, my legs weak. How had they figured out I was coming here? Did Bethany alert the Con Squad because she heard about my mom and thought I was a mutant, too? I tapped the Neighborhood Watch icon on my handheld. Sure enough, someone had posted pictures of the Con Squad dragging my mom into the black SUV.

My handheld vibrated.

"Coming?"

If I didn't answer, would they leave here to look for me? "Running late. B there soon."

I put my handheld on the ground behind some shrubs next to the tree and walked away. If they tracked it down, I didn't want to be anywhere nearby.

* * *

I jogged for twenty minutes until I reached a park. With each step, I wondered what I should do. Mom's handheld was full of her contacts. Would any of them help me? Who could I trust?

Catching my breath, I sat on a bench and dug Mom's handheld out of my backpack. A few weeks ago at some charity event, Mom introduced me to a childhood friend who happened to be attending. If only I'd paid attention to their conversation instead of the social feed on my handheld! I'd gotten the impression that Dina was something of a rebel, and that was exactly what I wanted now.

Scrolling Mom's contacts, I found only one Dina. I memorized the address and checked the route to her house. I didn't want to make the same mistake twice, so I decided to not call in advance. I put the handheld in my backpack and set a jogging pace for the four-mile trek.

When I entered Dina's subdivision, I spotted a tall, gray-haired woman who I immediately recognized. Dina walked toward a black Shell car about midway down the block. I broke into a run, reaching the car as it pulled onto the street.

"Wait!" I waved my arms.

The car stopped, and she lowered her window an inch. "Yes?" she said cautiously.

"Dina—remember me? We met at the gala." I panted.

"Blair?" The woman pushed a button, and the car reversed into the driveway. I ran after her. Frowning, Dina ushered me into her home without another word. As soon as the door closed, she asked, "Is something wrong?"

I nodded, still gulping air. "I couldn't think of anywhere else to go."

"What happened?" Dina's eyebrows furrowed. We stood in the foyer of a house twice as large as the one Mom and I shared. A glance told me the furnishings were also much finer.

"The Con Squad broke down our door and took my mom last night."

"You're sure it was the Con Squad?"

I nodded and showed her the Neighborhood Watch clip on Mom's handheld.

The blood drained from Dina's face, leaving her ashen. "How did you escape?"

"She tased me and stuffed me in a closet."

Dina snorted. "That sounds like something she'd do. Are you okay?"

My face heated with shame. "They were looking for me, too."

She motioned toward the living room. "I'm not surprised."

"They called us mutants, which is obviously a huge mistake." My voice quivered with emotions that hit me from nowhere. It was hard to talk. "My commander could correct this, but I can't contact him."

"You're a Reservist?" She frowned.

"For four years." A lump closed my throat and tears welled in my eyes. I had been so proud to be a Reservist. To be part of something so important. But now, I felt more betrayed than proud.

She leaned toward me and took my hands. "Blair, you have a

decision to make, and there's no going back once it's made. You can turn yourself in to the Con Squad, or I will do what I can to help you. From your Reservist training, you know there's no middle ground."

She was right. If I didn't turn myself in, it wouldn't matter that I wasn't really a mutant. If I was captured, I would be treated as one. But they'd already decided Mom and I were mutants before the raid on our house. Really, I had no choice.

"I know it's a lot to ask when you barely know me, but I'd appreciate your help."

Dina squeezed my hands. "Wise choice."

She gestured toward a velvety, beige couch. As I sat, she took a seat facing me on a blue-striped chair with wooden arms. "Okay, let's think through this calmly. I'm sure we can come up with a plan." Dina pulled out her handheld and told it to send a message to her office, indicating she would arrive two hours late.

"You and Mom seemed to be good friends."

Dina nodded. "As she told you the other day, we grew up together." After a pause, she added, "I even knew your father."

I swallowed hard. Then I released a fear I hadn't wanted to admit to—even to myself.

My mom wasn't a mutant.

I wasn't a mutant.

I had a father.

"I'd love to hear everything you remember about him. Right now, though, I need to focus on getting Mom freed."

"That's not going to be easy." Dina looked away and shook her head. "As a Reservist, you know that once labeled a mutant, fewer than five percent of the accused are ever cleared of the charge."

The figure startled me. Could it be true? When I hadn't known anyone accused of being a mutant, I hadn't questioned what I'd been told about the Con Squad's tactics. Now I wondered how many others were like Mom and me.

"But we had no warning," I said. "They came into our home and took her!"

"They'd probably been watching her for a while," Dina said. "Or someone may have accused her."

I told her about the troopers at my school, and my visit to Headquarters.

"It doesn't take much to make them suspicious," she said.

I twisted my hands in my lap. "There has to be something I can do to help her."

"Right now, the best thing you can do is lay low," Dina suggested. "You can stay here for a day or two while I make some inquiries."

"You'll do that for us?"

"Of course—for old times' sake." Dina stood. "You'll have to stay in the basement, in case anyone comes over unexpectedly." She opened a door and led me down carpeted stairs. Windows on two sides and French doors that opened onto a patio let in plenty of light. Bedroom suites opened off either side of a large den, and a fully equipped wet bar ran along the wall opposite a stone fireplace.

It wasn't what I would call secure, but it offered more privacy than the upper floor. And I wouldn't be trapped if someone blocked the stairs.

"I'm not expecting any visitors. If you should hear anyone, stay hidden until I come to get you," Dina said. "Remember, it's better to err on the side of caution."

I nodded, checking the room for possible hiding places. I opened the door to the walk-in closet. It was empty, except for a couple of ankle-length winter coats. *At least someone would have to search to find me.*

As if reading my mind, Dina entered the closet and moved the coats aside. She pressed a seam between two cedar panels, and part of the wall swung forward.

"What?" I said. I followed Dina into a tiny, hidden room with a single bed, a mini fridge, and a small food dispenser. A curtain separated a toilet, faucet and small sink from the rest of the room.

Dina pulled the cedar panel shut behind her, then closed the interior door. "It locks from inside. My lucky number, three times." She pushed 131313. "If you enter the code again, it unlocks." Dina tapped a remote and a monitor above the door showed views from around the house. "You can see if anyone is out there before you leave."

"Wow," I said. "I've never seen anything like this." How had she managed to do all this?

"It's not much as safe rooms go, but I can assure you from previous experience, it's not easy to find."

I swallowed hard, wondering—but not daring to ask—what she meant.

"Over the years, I've tracked down other friends who were taken," Dina explained. "But it's been a while since I contacted any of the people who kept tabs on the Con Squad. I don't know if they're still around."

I pressed my lips together, holding back angry tears. "I feel so useless."

Dina wrapped an arm around my shoulders and pulled me close. "It will be better if I make the calls from work. Hopefully by tonight I'll have a few leads you can follow up on, okay?"

I nodded, but I wanted to scream with frustration.

"In the meantime, try to get some rest. Bear in mind, if the Con Squad is looking for you, staying in one place for long is never a good idea."

That made sense. Finding Dina probably wasn't going to solve all my problems. It was only the first step. I had to find a way to disappear.

"Thanks, Dina."

Dina smiled and patted my hand, then turned and punched in the code.

I pulled the cedar panel back in place after she left and locked the inside door. On the monitor, I watched her walk up the stairs and leave the house.

I paced the small room, pausing at each end to check the cameras. I half expected a trooper to appear. Not that I'd noticed anyone following me, but I'd always been on the side of the hunters, not the hunted.

Although I could hear and feel air moving, I struggled to catch my breath. This room had to be smaller than my closet at home. I reached my arms to either side. I couldn't stretch without hitting the walls.

After a while, I plugged the handheld in to charge and went into the settings. By default, the tracking application was on, so I switched the button to "off." Then I turned off permissions on the GPS for "finding my location."

I opened the tiny fridge and took out a soda, then selected a chicken wrap from the dispenser. I took a bite and sat cross-legged on the bed. As I ate, I queried on the handheld for topics such as "mutants" and "Contamination Squad." All that came up were official sites. Why had I never noticed that before? They spouted the same slogans I'd heard all my life. "Protecting you and the ones you love." "Keeping humanity human." I checked the news, but couldn't find anything about the raid at my house or at school. Of course, I didn't really expect to.

When I'd finished with the handheld, I turned the power off completely and put it in my backpack. I sent my silent thanks to the looters and hoped they were leading the Con Squad on a merry chase far away from here.

Another hour passed with no movement upstairs. The house remained quiet and empty. Slowly the tension from the night before ebbed. When had I ever been this tired? It was all I could do to hold up my head. My eyes fluttered. I slipped under the covers, imagining Mom beside me, and my life as it had been only a day ago. Before my world went crazy.

3

ARI

I followed Layla to another cottage. Once inside, she pointed toward the couch. "Those should fit you."

I'd only seen these kinds of clothes on the vids—black tights, a blue-and-black print skirt, blue gloves, and a belted blue tunic with a black neck flare. The black knee-high boots had three-inch spikes.

I put on the strange clothes, but she dressed more quickly. Layla thrummed her fingers on the doorframe as she waited in her red-and-black skirt with a hooded tunic.

"We're going to the city?" I clipped up my hair and slipped on U-shaped blue plastic shades slashed by the lens' narrow band.

She shrugged. "Someone's got to do it."

"I'm not so sure ..."

Her glare stopped me mid-sentence.

We eyed each other like gunfighters waiting for the other to draw. Despite all my bravado, leaving the compound didn't feel like I expected. Instead of elation at escaping prison, I pictured myself as a baby bird perched on the edge of its nest, looking far below at the forest floor. And I didn't have wings.

Cains lived in the city. Thousands of them. Cains like the ones who attacked me. Would these clothes be enough of a disguise? I checked the mirror one more time. Instead of looking like every other crescent-moon cadet, I looked like the Cain women I'd seen on the vids. It could work. It must. Full-moon women like Layla went into the city all the time, even if they didn't stay there.

"Why aren't we going to the new compound with the others?" I whispered, unsure whether I was more afraid to ask or to not know.

"The Matron told you—I have a mission," Layla said in a strained voice. "And I need your help."

"You mean because everyone is busy?"

"Does it really matter, Ari? Come on. Freedom awaits," she added sarcastically.

I followed her out to the silver two-seater, a Shell car. We traveled the two-mile stretch of gravel road to a two-lane asphalt road.

Looking back in the direction of the compound, I tried to make out any of the buildings. Nothing. All I could see in that direction were rounded hills and trees. An orange "Bridge Out, No Trespass" sign was posted where the gravel road began. Why had the Cains chosen to go down it?

A glimmer of the feeling I'd had before the Cains invaded the field returned. I let myself enjoy my first real taste of freedom.

In less than ten miles, we reached the SuperFlex, and I was awestruck by its ten lanes. I watched the control panel as we entered the queue. It said we were in the northbound express chain. Layla picked our exit from the menu and sat back.

She turned toward me, but I couldn't make out her eyes in the dark slit between the red plastic frames. "Well, kid, now you're out of the prison." She smirked. "Be careful what you wish for."

I smiled, remembering the falling star. Despite misgivings about where this might lead, I wanted to make the most of my newfound freedom. "Why did you ask for me?"

"I figured your curiosity might keep you from being overwhelmed," she said. "At least for a while."

I wondered what she meant, but I did have a lot of questions. "Where are we going?"

"You'll see soon enough." Layla looked away and sighed. Her voice sounded sad, and I wondered if it was because we wouldn't be returning to the compound that had been our home for decades. Behind us, a blue car locked to our bumper, and a red one behind that. As we pulled away, the next train of ten cars was already building. The chain revved up to full speed, and we zipped past suburban high-rises. Although I'd seen vids, they didn't give you the claustrophobic feel of rushing through the shadowed canyons between the buildings' towering walls.

After several minutes, I squeaked, "Just how fast are we going?"

"Close to two hundred miles per hour until we reach the city limits, then it slows to a hundred." She grinned. "You look a little green around the gills."

I sucked in a deep breath, determined to not embarrass myself. My stomach lurched again. "Uh, how did you learn how to drive?"

She laughed. "I'd hardly call this driving." She pointed out the buttons for moving, stopping and voice navigating. "You can't even run off the road or into anyone unless you're on a dirt road, and those are really hard to find. These Shell cars do most of the work, unlike that piece of junk those Cains drove."

The locks released at our first junction, and our car recoupled with another chain with a barely audible click and subtle jolt. Now we followed a silver car instead of a green one, but the blue car was still behind us. The junctions were almost continuous after that as we sped through a multi-level maze of loops that wove through sprawling, many-storied glass buildings. The flashing lights, the speed—it was too much to comprehend.

I forgot all that when we leveled out beneath the famed Waterfalls of Westover. From all sides, water roared from the top floors of towering buildings, arcing through the air into a floating lake. The lake's glass walls created an aquarium viewable on all sides. Shimmering jellyfish the size of trees languidly pulsed through the teal water, and glowing, iridescent fish as big as our car gazed out at us.

I realized my mouth was gaping open and snapped it shut. "I didn't think it was real."

"The Falls are amazing," she agreed. "Who would think someone could make a beautiful wastewater treatment system?"

I kept looking back at it until we took the next junction. Our car again uncoupled, but this time it merged into unchained traffic on a ten-lane divided highway. Everything was happening so fast, I felt disoriented. From the corner of my eye, I saw the blue car also exited. I started to say something, but chided myself. First-timer nerves, no doubt. Layla's attention was on her handheld, her expression both distant and intimate as she gazed at the image of a woman I figured must be her partner. Minutes later, we pulled onto a parking ramp.

Layla got out and I scrambled to follow her. She swiped the heel of her right glove across a meter as we closed the doors, and the moving ramp took the car into an underground garage.

Crossing the sidewalk to enter the building was my first real challenge. Cains crowded shoulder to shoulder in two rivers of humanity moving in opposite directions. No one slowed, including Layla. She walked straight across and somehow didn't run into anyone. Panicked, I followed as fast as I could. Although I was right behind her when she took the first steps into the crowd, I couldn't make it through the openings she found.

The first Cain I ran into was a woman at least a head taller than me. My face brushed against her lilac-perfumed chest, earning me a disgusted look as she moved past. I ricocheted into a sweaty man, whose gray brow furrowed in anger. I soon lost count as I bumped my way across the walkway, stepping on toes and colliding with elbows. My gut clenched at the unfamiliar scents of concrete, glass, and metal, and the overwhelming stench of Cains, whose bodies reeked of the food they ate.

I couldn't even get angry about the smirk on Layla's face when I emerged from the fray. I would've laughed out loud if it had been Piper. Just imagining that made me grin, and my thoughts turned toward home with a fondness that surprised me. Had they made it to the new compound yet?

I hurried after Layla, who went straight to the riser. When we reached the thirtieth floor, we exited into a dark, narrow hallway.

I gagged on a bloody, smoky stench. "What's that smell?"

"Someone's cooking meat," Layla replied.

My jaws tightened and saliva flooded my mouth as the nausea rose. How could people live that way? I cringed at the inefficiency and brutality of it all, so unlike our ability to draw sustenance from moon rays.

Layla knocked on a door and held her gloved wrist up to the ID scanner. The door slid open. A blond-haired man a head taller than her moved aside to let us enter. He wore a black-and-green jumpsuit of the same fabric as my tunic. "I'd almost given up," he sighed. "She's so weak."

The room we entered had barely enough room for a threadbare couch and a mismatched armchair, which was pushed against it. A dark-haired woman covered with a knitted beige blanket lay propped up on the couch. She gently stroked one of two newborns sleeping on the chair's cushioned seat. The woman's weary face lit up with a smile for Layla. "Thanks for coming."

Layla took off her shades and glared at the man, her face contorted in anger. "Did you take her outside last night?"

He looked away from her. "I couldn't leave the babies, and she couldn't make it alone."

"Tibor did his best." The woman's eyes fluttered as she gave him a weak smile. "If he hadn't been here, I would've faced the birthing alone. Besides, it wouldn't have changed anything—the outcome will be the same."

Layla shuddered. "When was the last time you were out?"

"A week ago. I stayed out as long as I could," the woman whispered. "I knew the babies would come at the full moon."

"How are you feeling?" Layla's voice softened as she crouched beside the sofa.

"Like I'm going to die."

Tibor gripped the back of the chair, his face etched with sadness. "Don't say that!"

Layla growled at him, "Yeah, even if it's true."

The woman reached for Layla's hand. "Give it up, Layla. The time for anger is past. My sons deserve a chance to live."

Layla jerked her hand away and scowled at Tibor. "Just what the world needs. More of them."

"Wait a minute." He held up a hand defensively. "At least we don't kill children."

"That makes you so superior, doesn't it?" Layla smirked condescendingly. "But if the situation was reversed, I wonder what you'd do."

I still stood by the door, trying to understand what was happening. I shook my head as it dawned on me why the Matron said this trip would be hard for Layla. The babies' mother was Layla's close friend, possibly even her partner. My heart broke for them both. Even though I knew every Eve would eventually conceive an Adam, I hadn't thought about how it would affect everyone who loved her.

No one knew for sure why males were conceived, although we did have several theories. What we did know was even a six percent mutation rate would catch up with each of us over the course of centuries. If the pregnancy wasn't terminated, the Eve's immune system would turn against itself while trying to eliminate the male fetus. She'd die, and often the baby, too.

I took off my shades and finally found the courage to talk. "So, you're an Adam?" I asked Tibor.

Layla answered for him. "Yes, Ari, he's an Adam. And so are those." She jerked her thumb toward the babies, who mewled like kittens.

"Let them live, Layla, or my death will be for nothing," the woman pleaded.

"You chose them," Layla said coldly. "Their fate rests with their own kind." She glared at Tibor.

"I've lived centuries. Surely they deserve a chance at life." The woman coughed. I didn't think she could get any whiter, but her face blanched.

The anger drained from Layla's voice as she choked out a desperate plea. "Hold on!" She rushed over and gently caressed the woman's face. "Please, hold on until moonrise, then I'll take you back home."

The woman gave a slight shake of her head. Weakly, she said, "I'm sorry." Her arm slipped limply off the couch, her hand dropping to the floor.

Layla sat on the edge of the couch and gathered the motionless woman in her arms. She rocked her back and forth, cooing to her, then gently lowered her back onto the pillows. She placed the woman's hands over her chest and straightened the folds of her knee-length dress. "She's dead," Layla said flatly.

One of the babies started crying. "Shush, shush," Tibor whispered and picked him up. "It'll be okay." A tear slid down his face as he looked at the woman, then he gave me a nod as he left the room.

At first, I just stood there, trying to come to grips with my own anxiety. Could she really be dead? I'd never seen an Eve die. I looked for some sign of life, but the woman wasn't breathing. I kept waiting for her eyes to open or her mouth to twitch, but she was perfectly still. I moved next to Layla and put my hand on her shoulder.

After several moments, Layla brushed the tears from her face with the back of her hand. "Okay." Her voice was husky. She pulled out a Disruptor and swept it over the woman's body. Red lights glowed. "She's really gone."

"I'm so sorry, Layla." I wanted to find some way to comfort her, but she pulled away as if even my hand on her shoulder was too intimate.

Layla pressed a button and did another sweep. The blanket slipped to the floor as the woman's body began to fade. Soon only an indentation remained on the red, flowered cushions where she'd lain. "It's amazing what science can do to dispose of our bodies, yet they can't seem to find a way to help us survive the birth of sons," she said in a wooden voice. Layla leaned over the chair and clicked the device on again.

I lunged for her, trying to pull her away from the baby, but the Disruptor harmlessly glowed green as she pressed it repeatedly.

"Surprisingly, it has a soul," she said. "You know, the Disruptor won't work if the soul hasn't left the body."

"What are you doing?" Tibor rushed back into the room as Layla pocketed the Disruptor.

Shaken, I dashed over and lifted the baby from the chair. I'd held babies before, but never a newborn. And never a boy. His tiny body felt fragile. Why did I feel so fiercely protective of him? Maybe it was the passion of his mother's love that awoke something dormant inside of me. How much would you have to love someone to be willing to die for them?

This perplexing attachment to the newborn bore no resemblance to the cool detachment I'd observed between mothers and their babies at our compound. The feeling was mutual—I'd never known, nor cared, which of them actually carried me inside her body. How different that was from my compulsion to safeguard this helpless young Adam's life.

Tibor's jaw flexed as he watched me warily. I'm sure he was trying to judge whether to trust me. "They're going to need to feed soon," he said. "We better get going."

"We?" Layla spun around and bared her teeth. Grief and fury twisted her face, which reddened as she growled, "Our reason for being here is gone. Or did you think we'd all be as daft as their mother?"

"I see." He reached out his free arm to take the child from me.

I hesitated, wondering how Tibor would manage to care for two infants. Before I could respond, I heard the riser door slide open and the footfalls of several people approaching our room. We looked toward the hallway in unison, all sensing a shift in energy. I held the baby closer. My skin prickled with the ultrasonic probes of sensors like those we used in our training games, but these were much stronger signals.

In a hushed voice, Layla snarled, "Is this your doing?"

Tibor shook his head and grabbed a backpack from the floor next to the couch. He pulled out a canvas sling, slipped it over his head, and put the baby he'd been holding into it. "Someone followed you. I would've thought you'd have been more careful."

I thought back to our trip here. Had it only been coincidence that the blue car exited the SuperFlex when we did?

Layla grabbed me and squeezed my shoulders, forcing my face inches from hers. "I'm sorry I got you into this, Ari. Go with him—he owes you protection."

"No," I said. "I want to stay with you."

Layla's eyes strayed briefly to the empty couch and then down to the baby I held. "Do as you're told," she snapped. "None of us will get out of here without a diversion. I'll do what I can to give you a head start. The Adams know the city better than me or any Eve." She put the Disruptor into my free hand, and I slipped it into my pocket. "Remember, whatever happens, don't let the Cains take any of us. Dead or alive."

My head was reeling. I couldn't believe Layla wanted me to go with this Adam when only moments before she'd seemed ready to attack him.

Tibor jerked me into the adjoining room and opened the window. I put my visor back on to shield against the morning sun, twisted the baby's blanket in a sling around my neck to ensure I wouldn't drop him, and followed Tibor onto an ancient black fire escape ladder. The open grating of the narrow landing gave me a clear view of the city streets far below. Never one for heights, my head spun. I tightened my grip on the child.

Tibor tapped on the window of the room below. A brown-haired man wearing a black-and-green jumpsuit identical to Tibor's opened it and helped us both inside. He pulled out a device that looked something like a Disruptor, but bigger. Holding it with both hands, the man aimed at the ladder. It glowed red hot, then crumbled into dust and fell away.

"What about Layla?" I cried.

A massive crash and shouting in the room above answered my

question. True to her word, she was keeping the Cains busy so we could escape. The man ran into the hallway, then motioned for us to follow. Tibor and I stood around the corner from the riser as the doors opened. The man nodded. We ran to the empty riser, then followed him through the busy first-floor lobby. I kept my face down, trying to ignore the black cars with flashing lights and Cains in dark blue uniforms with mirrored face shields.

Startled by all the commotion, the infants scrunched their faces and angrily waved their hands as they wailed. Tibor placed his finger in one baby's mouth and I did the same with the other, thankfully silencing them.

Unlike my walk into the building, crossing the walkway proved effortless. This time, I matched my steps to Tibor's and the other man's. They walked on either side of me to a green Shell car, which waited for us on the garage's movable ramp. I assumed the Adam had signaled it somehow. The doors opened as we approached. Tibor and I got in. I wondered where the Adam would sit until I saw him heading back toward the building. I kept looking for Layla, even though I didn't hold out much hope. Tibor selected a destination, and we began moving.

As our car left the garage's moving ramp, uniformed troopers came out of the building with a vinyl bag on a gurney hovering between them. Layla's body. Remembering her last words, I aimed the Disruptor across the walkway as we turned the corner and drove alongside the building. I shot twice, and the body bag deflated. With it, my last hope that Layla would escape evaporated, leaving behind an emptiness at my core.

Tibor nodded. "Quick thinking."

I slumped against the seat, refusing to believe I'd never see Layla again. I'd never know why she wanted me to come with her to the city. Did she really see something of herself in me, as the Matron suggested? I kept picturing how Layla looked when she stood above me in the field, bow in hand, like a goddess. Then it hit me—I'd gotten my wish. I was truly alone among the Cains and the Adams. The only Eve. When it dawned on me that I didn't have a clue how to find the new Eve compound, I panicked. What was I going to do?

The gurney must have signaled the change in weight because the troopers stopped. Through the rear window, I watched them unzip the bag and look around to see who had taken away their prize.

Because that's what our teachers said we were to those who hunted Eves—mythical beings whose bodies held the secrets of immortality and virgin birth. Mutants. The troopers didn't spot us as we sped by, but a young woman standing by the riser held my tearful gaze as we passed.

4

BLAIR

I awoke with a start. It took a moment before my surroundings made sense. Dina's house. The safe room.

How long had I been asleep? I propped myself up on one elbow and scanned all the cameras. Every room in the house was dark. I checked the time and jerked upright--nine-thirty! Where was Dina? She should've been home from work hours ago. Had she asked questions of the wrong person and ended up in trouble with the Con Squad, too?

I pushed the covers away and swung my legs over the side of the bed. I paced the small room, counting steps. Eight in length, six in width. I kept my eyes trained on the cameras.

After thirty minutes, I sat on the side of the bed and considered my options. Should I continue to wait? If the Con Squad picked up Dina, they would almost certainly search her home. My fingers wrapped around the pocket taser in my backpack. I still couldn't believe Mom had tased me with it, but I'd be ready if anyone uninvited came down those stairs.

I scrolled down the list of names on Mom's contact list. Where could I go? I could try to make it across town to another one of her friends, but that would be at least as risky as staying here, if not moreso. Frustrated, I sighed and put away the handheld. I could only hope Dina would return soon with some idea of how to help Mom. At least she seemed to have an inkling of where to start.

Then one of the screens above the door showed a light in the living room. I watched as another flicked on in the kitchen. It was Dina! She threw her purse and a couple of bags on the counter, then picked up a remote. With a click, the curtains on all the windows drew closed. Dina put down the remote and walked toward the top of the stairs leading to the basement. A few moments later, I heard the scrape of the cedar panel opening and the keypad's beeping. The door opened slowly, and Dina peered inside so only her eyes and the top of her head showed.

"Everything okay?" she asked.

"I'm so glad to see you! I was afraid something bad had happened."

"Sorry about that." She walked to the bed and sat, patting the covers next to her. I sat. "I made a few calls from work to some old friends, but I didn't want to say too much over the phone. We met for drinks, then some other friends joined us for dinner. They're the ones who have the contacts we need."

"Someone knows how to reach my mom?" I bounced to my feet, excited.

Dina shook her head. "Not exactly. One was a civil liberties lawyer who's quite well known. I just sent you information about him, including his office address. He's expecting you tomorrow before regular office hours."

"I don't understand." I sat, my mood deflated. "What can he do for us?"

"He's the only lawyer I know of who's been able to get people released from the Con Squad," Dina said. "But he said to not get your hopes up. Things that used to work haven't been lately."

I fidgeted with the bedspread, twisting multiple peaks on its smooth surface. "I don't have much money, not enough to pay an attorney."

"Don't worry about that," Dina said. "My friends and I can handle his fees."

I swallowed hard. "Thanks, Dina." I picked up Mom's handheld and looked at the address. "That's in the middle of the city. They'll spot me."

Dina smiled. "I can help with that, too." She rose and walked out the door. "C'mon."

I hurried after Dina, following her upstairs to the kitchen. Dina gestured to the packages on the countertop.

Inside the smallest package were ten small, clear ovals. With a grin, Dina pulled one of the ovals from the package and held out her hand, palm up. "Give me your hand."

Puzzled, I hopped onto a barstool next to Dina's and offered my hand. Dina pulled the backing off the oval, then placed the clear strip over my fingertip. "It blurs your fingerprints slightly, but not enough to be suspicious."

Dina filled two glasses with red wine as I examined the other packages. She'd raided a spy shop, or that's how it appeared. She had sun visors to distort my retinal pattern, a high-fashion tunic and tights that gave me more curves, and a special skin cream.

"It's made of tiny holograms that create a moiré pattern," Dina explained, taking another sip of wine.

"Moray?" I cringed, putting the jar down quickly. "Like an eel?"

"No, like an interference pattern." Dina chuckled. "It distorts images on video and computer screens. My friend said it's the very latest technology."

"Won't that make the Con Squad suspicious?" I took a drink, savoring the bold flavor. I'd had wine a few times before, but nothing as good as this.

"It will look like there's a temporary glitch in the signal," Dina agreed, "but it will clear up too quickly for them to determine there's not a real problem."

"So, I need to keep moving?" I said.

"That's it," Dina said. "Until you get inside the lawyer's office."

I checked the address again. "And you trust him?"

Dina sighed and wrapped an arm around my shoulders. "As much as you can trust anyone. My friend trusts him, so I do, too."

"Did my mom know him?" I asked, leery of reaching out to a total stranger.

"Not that I know of," Dina said. "To protect you, your mom kept her distance from anything that would draw suspicion. That's why we lost touch after your dad disappeared."

"What does that mean—disappeared?"

Dina turned away, avoiding my gaze.

"Did he die or just get up and leave one day?"

Dina shrugged and rearranged the packages. "Knowing your dad, he wouldn't have left you and your mom without a good reason. He was crazy about both of you. But your mom never would say what happened. Not long after that, she moved to the house where you've been living and took the production line job at the car plant. None of us understood it."

"What had she been doing?" I downed the last of my wine and placed the empty glass on the countertop.

Dina looked up. "We did the same kind of work—corporate communications. We'd always done everything together. Then she cut ties with me and all her other friends."

"She used to know a lot of influential people?" I asked.

Dina nodded. "Yes. But when it was just you and her, having a high-profile job seemed to frighten her. She simply wanted to get as far from this life as possible. That's why I was so glad we were able to reconnect a few weeks ago."

Dina picked up both glasses and took them to the recycler. "It's getting late, and you've got a long day tomorrow."

I rose and walked toward the stairs, carrying all the packages. "Thanks, Dina. I appreciate everything you've done."

"I only hope it will do some good," she said. "Truthfully, I don't know where else to turn. Oh, I almost forgot the most important thing." Dina pulled a nondescript flesh-colored band off her wrist.

"What's that?" I asked.

"It's the key to a Shell car that's parked on the fourth floor of Buckeye Garage," Dina said. "I'll drop you off there tomorrow. If you press here"— Dina placed her fingers on both sides of the wristband — "the car will come to you."

"Really?" I examined the flimsy rubber wristband.

Dina chuckled. "Yeah, it was an ingenious solution for people who kept losing their keys before we had things like retinal access."

I juggled the packages and slipped it on my wrist.

"You have driven a Shell car, right?" Dina asked.

"Of course," I said. "That's part of the standard curriculum."

"Well, I'm not expecting you to need it. But, if something goes wrong at the lawyer's, my friends assure me that, in addition to providing transportation, the car is a perfect place to hide. The ads keep anyone from seeing inside, and you can stay on the move."

"Ads?"

Dina chuckled. "Well, after all, it's a pizza delivery car."

I snorted in surprise.

"It's really quite brilliant," Dina said. "Pizza and Chinese food delivery vehicles are the only ones you can't see inside."

I nodded. "I know. You're not supposed to even have dark-tinted windows."

She gestured for me to move. "Enough talk. Let's get some rest."

I returned to the safe room. Despite feeling like the walls were closing in, I locked the door behind me. That was the only way I'd ever feel comfortable enough to close my eyes, although the idea of sleep seemed unlikely. I eyed the packages and tried to keep a positive attitude.

Even though Dina assured me the devices would distort my image, the thought of walking downtown under the scrutiny of so many cameras made me queasy. But I knew Mom would do this much, and more, if I'd been the one taken. I breathed deeply. *Calm down. It will be all right.*

Early the next morning, Dina came downstairs as I attached the last oval to my fingertips.

"The lawyer won't have long to meet with you," Dina said.

"But I'm expected?" Hope and anxiety warred within me as I envisioned walking into the lawyer's office. Could he really help my mother?

"Just tell the receptionist you're Dina's intern."

I nodded.

"C'mon, let's go," Dina said.

I followed Dina out to her Shell car.

"You'll have to walk about ten blocks, but that's safer than me dropping you off in front of the building," Dina said. Minutes later, she stopped in front of Buckeye Garage. "This is where the pizza delivery car is."

I got out.

"Let me know how it goes with the lawyer. Then we'll figure out our next steps."

I gave Dina a quick smile and turned to join the crowd of commuters on the nearest moving walkway as she drove away.

* * *

The handheld's GPS beeped a few seconds before I arrived in front of the building, giving me time to step off the moving walkway and onto the sidewalk. I fought a wave of dizziness as I stood on the corner looking up. I tried to steady myself physically and emotionally. I could do this! A doubting voice in my mind scoffed at me.

Through the glass walls, I watched people come and go from a bank of six risers—three on each side of the lobby. I took a deep breath and forced myself to walk through the double doors, which slid aside as I approached. Although I'd memorized the lawyer's office number, I lingered by the building directory, gathering courage before pushing the riser button. Was I really going to do this?

Shouts behind me caused my heart to beat faster. I turned in what seemed like slow motion. People scattered in all directions, clearing a path for a half-dozen armed Con Squad troopers. Face shields down, they ran into the lobby. My heart clenched. Had one of Dina's dinner companions tipped them off?

"Holy shit!" I said under my breath. What kind of idiot was I, trusting someone I barely knew? I turned and pounded on the nearest riser button. "Open, damn you!"

I glanced behind me at the troopers headed my way. Giving up on the doors opening, I stepped away from the riser and searched for another escape route.

"Whoa, where are you going?" One of the uniformed troopers grabbed my arm and shoved me against the wall.

Jarred by the impact, the sun visor Dina had given me flew off my face and skidded into a corner. *Coming here was crazy! One retinal scan and I'll be finished. And there'll be no one to worry about freeing Mom and me.*

I waited for the trooper to frisk me. Then the riser door opened and he dropped my arm to hold it open while the other troopers entered. The mirrored face shield remained focused on the riser after the doors closed.

Maybe I wasn't the target after all? I checked again for escape routes, but feared if I moved toward the lobby door or the risers, I'd draw the trooper's attention. Not being able to see the trooper's face unnerved me. I remained very quiet and still, like a mouse hoping a cat would forget about it.

I jumped when the middle riser door opened. Two men wearing black-and-green jumpsuits—one dark-haired and a younger one with an infant in a sling across his chest—and a young woman carrying another baby walked quickly across the lobby. Then the farthest riser door opened, and four more people followed the threesome out of the building.

An infant's wail rose above the other noises. The man jostled the baby and shushed it, letting it suckle his finger. Was it my imagination, or did the woman's dark skin grow paler when they stepped onto the sunny sidewalk? I continued to watch as they made their way with the rest of the crowd through a gauntlet of a half-dozen troopers outside. When they reached the parking ramp outside the building next to the walkway, the two carrying infants entered a waiting green Shell car. The dark-haired man disappeared into the crowd.

The trooper in front of me spoke into his headset, drawing my attention. Moments later, the closest riser doors opened, and four troopers guided a floating gurney bearing a navy vinyl bag into the lobby. A body bag.

I recoiled. My stomach churned as my mind played out all sorts of scenarios. I envisioned the troopers breaking down the lawyer's door. He'd resisted, and they'd killed him. Or maybe someone who went to the lawyer for help refused to be taken prisoner? I sucked in my breath. *That could've been me on the gurney.* Or maybe it had nothing to do with the lawyer's office or me. Merely a coincidence.

The gurney wobbled and rose a few feet. "What!" one of the troopers exclaimed, looking around to see if someone had knocked it off-balance.

Another trooper unzipped the deflated bag. "She's gone!"

The body disappeared! How did that happen? Reflected sunlight flashed in my eye. I turned and saw the green car, visible through the glass wall. Was the woman pointing a gun at the troopers? I squinted, trying to get a better look. Our eyes met for an instant, only long enough for me to see tears glistening in her blue eyes before the car careened around the corner.

Troopers spread out across the lobby. A mirrored face shield pivoted toward me as the trooper suddenly remembered I existed.

"Put your hands against the wall! And spread your legs," a harsh voice commanded.

As I turned, I suddenly realized everyone but the troopers had left the lobby. I swallowed hard. Rough hands pressed my cheek against the smooth stone walls, then proceeded to frisk me. Why hadn't I run? Behind me, rapid footsteps approached, then something heavy fell to the floor.

"C'mon," a man's voice hissed. The dark-haired man in a jumpsuit who'd left the riser earlier jerked me aside. The trooper lay unconscious on the floor. "Haven't you got enough sense to run away when those guys show up?"

"But they weren't after me," I protested as he pulled me past the closed riser doors and headed toward the far wall.

"By now, they'll have your ID from the security cameras. Talk about being in the wrong place at the wrong time." He ran in front of me and opened a door to a stairwell I hadn't noticed before. "They'll think you were our lookout."

"You're the ones they're after?" I stopped abruptly. "So you came back to make sure they'd connect me to you?"

"You don't get it, do you?" He grabbed my hand, yanking me off balance, and ran. I struggled to stay on my feet as we took the steps three at a time. I jerked my hand free as we exited the basement's outer doors. Before they closed, the door at the top of the stairwell squeaked open and heavy footsteps headed our way. He took a triangular device from the belt at his waist and aimed it at the door handle. The metal sizzled, leaving the catch a molten lump.

"That won't hold them long," he said. "Let's go!"

"No!"

He shook his head. "Haven't you known people who were labeled a mutant for doing something far less suspicious than you did today?"

"Look, I don't need any help getting the Con Squad's attention," I snapped.

His gray eyes met mine as he spoke. "I wasn't trying to make you look guilty. I could've disappeared into the crowd, but I didn't feel right about leaving you there to take the blame for trouble we caused. But suit yourself." He reached out and squeezed my hand, then turned and ran down the alley.

I hesitated, considering the options. What he said was true. The Con Squad would soon see the lobby security footage and realize who I was. After running away, now it looked like I was part of his group—mutants the troopers were hunting. With shaking hands, I pulled out the handheld and called Dina.

"Blair?" she answered.

"The Con Squad was here," I said.

"At the lawyer's office?" Her voice rose with alarm.

"No, I never got that far. They stormed the lobby before I went up. They were after someone else, but now they know I was here. What should I do?"

After a pause, Dina said, "Until I can be sure no one turned us in, you should keep on the move. Get the car. Call me in a couple of days, and I'll let you know if it's safe to return. If I don't answer, don't try calling again or you may be tracked."

I turned and walked as quickly as I dared toward the Buckeye Garage, trying to blend with the crowds on the moving walkways. From the corner of my eye, I caught sight of a trooper in the alley between the buildings to my right. Ahead of me, I saw another on the left. Both watched me. That hadn't taken long. I would never make it to the car.

"You see them?" asked a male voice from behind me. "If you've changed your mind, just get off at the next intersection and follow me."

As soon as I stepped off the moving walkway, the dark-haired man from the lobby dashed from behind me into an alley on our left. I followed him. At the end of the alley, a driverless white Shell car waited with its door open. He jumped in and smiled at me as the door slid shut behind us. "You made the right choice."

I hoped that was true. I feared my life would never be the same.

5

ARI

"That was a good shot," Tibor said as we pulled away from the building.

"Layla taught me. We called her the bowmaster, but she was good with any weapon." I felt empty inside, like a hole had opened in my guts and let in frigid Arctic air. "We don't leave our kind behind, right?"

"Right. A few Cains still believe some of us survived, but we don't want to give them proof. To most, the legend of Adams and Eves is not much more than a child's tale." Tibor seemed to guess what was running through my mind. "Layla drew their attention away from us, and she paid the price."

I felt sick. I knew now why Matron kept us inside the compound. This was no place for a crescent moon like me with only a few years of maturity. Or for someone like Layla, whose heart was breaking. Any distraction could be deadly.

We got on the SuperFlex. I kept an eye out, but didn't see anyone following us as we made the switch from junction to junction. It wasn't long until we gave in to the infants' demands. Tibor pulled two bottles from a bag beneath the seat and held one out to me.

"Sugar water?" I asked.

He nodded. Apparently Adam babies had some of the same needs as Eve infants. When they were sucking air, we pulled the bottles away. Tibor's mouth made an "O" when their wailing immediately resumed. He entered a query onto the dashboard panel and ten minutes later, the car pulled off at a lakeside park. I followed Tibor to a stone picnic table and helped him remove the infants' clothing so they could soak up the sun. Even the short time in direct sunlight sapped my energy. Tibor removed his shirt and handed it to me.

"Thanks," I said, "but I'll need more cover than that. I have to find some shade." Weak and foggy-headed, I staggered over to another table beneath a large oak where I could watch the Adams. The sun nourished their bodies, turning their skin from creamy white to a caramel color much like mine at full moon. How had those long-ago Eves figured out Adams needed sunlight to survive? I'd never considered it before, like so many things about Adams.

Tibor tenderly cradled the tiny, bare infants against his naked chest. I'd never been touched like that. Eves might give a pat on the back or a hug, but this was something different. I thought back to what Layla's friend had sacrificed for these children and wondered if Tibor loved them as much. How could you be willing to risk everything for someone else?

I kicked a gumball across the driveway as a funk settled over me. Couldn't someone find a way for Eves to bear Adams without dying so we could end all this misery? The whole system puzzled me, especially how the two secretive groups remained connected.

"How did you end up being there when the babies were born?" I asked.

Tibor looked up. For a moment, I thought he wouldn't answer.

"The Patron sent me," he said. "Your Matron alerted him of the need for support, and he provided the address of the safest place we could find."

"Were you there together very long?"

"We spent a couple of weeks together," Tibor said. "It was my first time to be with a birth mother. There's a whole team assigned for each birth in case something goes wrong. Before this, I did surveillance and support."

"Do things go wrong often?" I asked.

"No, but lately we've had some close calls," he said. "We stay with the birth mother for as long as she lives, to honor her sacrifice." He paused and swallowed hard. "Usually that's only a few hours, or a day at the most."

"The birth mother always dies?"

Tibor nodded and looked away. "Always." His voice was hoarse with emotion. The sadness tugged at my heart, too. "Then one of two things happens—someone from the birth mother's compound arrives or one of our group makes sure no trace is left for the Cains to find."

"So you were expecting Layla?"

"I think that's why the birth mother hung on so long after the births—she was waiting to see her partner," Tibor said. "What about you?"

"I've never really been involved with any of this before." I kicked another gumball across the driveway. "No one ever explained how we interact with Adams. I guess you have to be older before they share that kind of information."

"But you knew about us—about Adams?" Tibor repositioned the infants, who had fallen asleep, one on each shoulder.

"I knew the basics, but I'd never thought it through. I'd certainly never been around an Eve who chose to bear sons."

"No, I guess not," Tibor said bitterly. "The whole thing is really screwed up for the birth mothers and the sons."

"And for the Eves the birth mothers leave behind." I added sharply. I couldn't forget Layla's sacrifice. Silence stretched between us for several minutes. I kept moving closer to the tree to avoid the sunlight, which ate away the shade in giant bites. Finally, I said, "I need a shadier place."

"Sorry, I hadn't noticed." He walked over and lowered one of the infants into my arms. "It's time for us to get moving anyway. We've been here almost an hour."

"Where are we going?"

"To our compound."

We walked to the Shell car together. The sun seared my skin until I slid under the car's protective cover with a sigh of relief. Moments later, we were back on the SuperFlex with two sleeping babies.

"Maybe their science could help us," I suggested

Tibor cocked an eyebrow. "Whose science?"

"The Cains."

He squished his eyebrows together and frowned. "Where did that come from?"

I felt my cheeks redden. "We were talking about how screwed up things are for everyone. It's all because we haven't found a way to carry Adams to term without dying. We don't even know why males are conceived."

His face contorted like I'd slapped him. "It's not like we wanted our mothers to die."

Now my whole face burned. "I didn't mean it like that."

"I guess what I've heard about Eves is true. Who'd want to die for an abomination like me? You think it's better to kill us all instead." He gestured toward the sleeping infants. "Their mother's dead, like mine. And our mothers were the only ones of your kind who thought we deserved to live."

I closed my eyes and turned away from him, too emotionally drained to think. Besides, what could I say? It was true. No matter how much I wanted to say otherwise, within my culture, carrying a son to full term was deemed a form of suicide. Eves died if Adams lived. Always. Even a crescent-moon cadet like me knew that much. And he'd confirmed it.

Tibor settled into a moody silence. My emotions were in turmoil, but I couldn't help but be enthralled by the passing sights. Everything was new to me—the spacious fields, the small towns we passed through, the signs on intersecting highways showing distances to places I'd only heard of in vids. Eventually, my lack of sleep the day before and the car's rocking motion lulled me to sleep. I awoke as we pulled through the gates of a compound larger than the one I remembered as a child. Floating sensor discs topped the twenty-foot walls. Inside, the city had multi-storied buildings instead of cottages. Heads turned as we drove into the center of the compound. I quickly realized why. I was the only female—the only Eve in a world of Adams.

The baby I held awoke and squirmed in my arms. He looked up at me with trusting eyes, so defenseless. I brushed his check, marveling at its silkiness.

At Tibor's command, the car stopped in front of a long, narrow building with clear glass walls. The infant Tibor held was still slumped against his chest until we got out, then it whimpered crossly.

Our footsteps echoed on the slick-floored hallway that surrounded an octagonal-shaped nursery.

Inside, a dozen cribs hovered along walls striped with pastel blue and yellow. Some held sleeping infants, and in others, toddlers played with toys or simply watched us with wide brown eyes. An elderly man crossed an expanse of plush golden carpet and reached for the child I carried. I brushed my face against the baby's soft hair and breathed in the sweet smell. The baby snuffled as I released him, and my heart twisted. But what else could I do? He was an Adam, and this was now his home.

The man nodded. "Come back after you feed, but try to keep out of sight." He took the other baby from Tibor and mumbled, "You shouldn't have brought her here."

My hands felt empty as we walked out, but our visit to the nursery had raised new questions. "I had no idea there were so many other groups of Eves."

"Because there are so few Adams born to women from your compound?" he asked.

"Well, yes," I said. "So the babies must come from somewhere else. How do they contact you?"

"You really are a young one, aren't you?" Tibor shook his head. "It's so hard to tell. From the vids I've seen, you all look about the same age to me."

I frowned at him and waited for an answer.

"Your Matron knows how to contact us."

"Oh, thank goodness! With Layla gone, I thought I was stranded here," I said. "So when can I go home?"

"She'll be in touch when you don't return, but don't expect that to happen before the next full moon. It will take all her energy to get the new compound secure. It wasn't ready yet."

"How do you know about the new compound?"

"Who do you think built it?" he asked.

I'd never thought about such things. Now that I did, it explained why we'd never built another dorm when ours became crowded. Adams needed to protect Eves from Cains, and having both groups working together toward that goal seemed like a good idea.

"But why do I have to wait if you know where it is?" I asked.

"It is taboo for Adams to return after the construction is finished.

To make sure, they remove the workers' memories each day. So those who once knew the location don't remember it now."

"How can that be?"

"It's a procedure perfected over many years," he said. "Even if I knew where the Eve compound was, the Matron wouldn't allow you to enter now. You have a lot to learn about your own people."

I didn't believe him. The Matron would never turn me away. Would she?

The moon had already passed its zenith when Tibor showed me to a room with a private courtyard. After he left, I pulled off the tunic and leggings Layla had given me a lifetime ago and walked outside. The moon's rays caressed my bare skin, but couldn't fill the emptiness inside. I felt humbled to remember how this all started, with my romanticized longing for freedom. It would be different if I'd been mistreated. The reality was I could've died from my first encounter with the Cains, but Layla saved me. Then she sacrificed herself to save me again.

Now, instead of feeling invisible among those of my kind, I was alone and far from home. I'd even welcome Piper's gibes, just to see a familiar face. I listened for the moonsong as moonbeams filled my blood.

A falling star grazed the sky; this time, I didn't wish for freedom.

6

BLAIR

The Shell car zigzagged away from the building, merging onto the SuperFlex among five identical white cars that entered at the same time from different ramps and just as quickly exited onto other streets. It was dizzying to watch—a shell game played with Shell cars.

I hoped whoever was watching couldn't guess which car we were in any better than I had guessed where the prize was years ago when my grandfather taught me the twentieth-century parlor game using actual seashells to hide a marble. My eyes teared-up at the memory; he'd always been my biggest fan. I needed someone like that now.

The dark-haired man stared out the windows, undoubtedly watching—as I was—for any sign of the Con Squad on our trail. No troopers were in sight. A few exits after the last decoy car disappeared, we broke from the chain and merged onto another highway.

"Here." The man held a red scarf out to me. "Cover your eyes."

I reluctantly reached for the scarf, second-guessing my snap decision to go with this man—a stranger. A chill ran across my shoulders. "Are you kidnapping me?" I said, only half in jest. "There's no one left who'd care enough to pay a ransom."

His hand lingered on mine, warmth and strength contrasting with the silky coolness of the fabric. "I want to protect you, but I can't betray my people by letting you know where we live."

The hint of a smile lifted the corners of his mouth and sparkled in his grey eyes. I took a deep breath. I should have him stop and let me out, but we were nowhere near Buckeye Garage. I hated to think about making my way there on my own. After today's encounter, the Con Squad was probably hunting me harder than ever. Wherever he was taking me had to be better than being captured by them, didn't it? I tied the scarf over my eyes.

After various U-turns and detours over bumpy roads, we stopped. It hadn't been long, less than a half hour.

"You can take it off now," he said. The door swooshed open and we entered a parking garage with concrete walls and dim lighting. Shell cars of various styles were grouped by color, explaining how they had mobilized the decoy white ones so quickly.

"Do all the cars come back here?" I asked.

"No. Most are deployed from one lot and returned to another one," he said.

"Terence, you made it!" An old man with bushy gray eyebrows approached, giving my escort a friendly shove as he exited the car. "Son of a gun!"

"Have you heard from the others?" Terence asked.

"No, but it's too soon. I hear their compound is a lot farther out, so no news is good news." He combed his fingers through his slicked-back hair and tugged at the seat of his green-and-black jumpsuit as I stepped out of the car. "So, who's this?"

His lopsided grin made me instantly distrust him.

"A deer in the headlights," Terence replied. "I couldn't leave her behind with the Con Squad. Besides, I figured adding another woman to the mix would confuse them even more."

"Maybe so." The man's eyebrows knit together as he studied me from head to toe. "How old are you, sweetie?"

My mouth fell open. I didn't remember anyone so brash as to ask my age since I'd been a tween.

"Well?" he asked. "You look at least eighteen—old enough to be legal, anyways."

I didn't like the sound of that. The only things age usually mattered for were drugs and sex. I ignored him and turned toward

Terence. "I don't know what was going on back there, but I appreciate you getting me out safely."

The old man smirked. "You sure didn't hit the genetic jackpot on survival instinct."

I hadn't been totally comfortable with coming here to begin with, but this man's attitude pushed me over the edge. "Um, I guess I'll be going now."

Before I took a step, the man grabbed my arm.

"Hey!" I cried out, my heart pounding. "What are you doing?"

The man scowled at Terence, who hesitantly grabbed my other arm. "Sorry, but we can't let you leave here. It's a closed tower."

"You didn't say anything about that." I struggled to get free. *A closed tower? It sounded like a prison. Maybe they were slavers? None of this made any sense.* "I only thought I wasn't supposed to know the location."

"So we can't just let you walk away, can we?" the old man said.

"Help!" I yelled, and tried to pull away. Terence avoided my eyes.

The old man tightened his grip. "No one can hear you."

Both held my arms firmly as they walked through a series of corridors between the garage and the main building. I tried to keep track of the turns, but lost count. They stopped at a bank of risers and entered one. On the top floor, we walked down long hallways with more turns until we reached another riser.

"Really, I wouldn't say a word," I said. "If you let me go, the last thing I'd want to do is call attention to myself."

"That's the truth," the old man chuckled. "Guess you have some instincts, after all."

"This is for your own good, as well as ours," Terence whispered in my ear, his voice sounding almost sympathetic.

I jerked away from him. This time I wasn't falling for it.

The old man waved at a security scanner. It beeped and the door slid open to a curved, narrow room with dining tables and chairs on one side, and lounge area with comfortable-looking tangerine sofas and chairs with turquoise pillows. More than two dozen women scattered throughout the room stared at me as the men pushed me out of the riser.

Some of the women gave me a quick smile, but most had blank looks on their faces. A short woman about Mom's age frowned at

Terence. She had smooth skin and thick, silver-gray hair. She extended a hand to me.

I shoved past her, turning to grab Terence's sleeve as the riser door began to slide shut. "You can't just leave me here," I said.

He pushed my hand free. "I'll be seeing you." The door closed.

"But, why?" I said to no one in particular.

"It'll be okay." The woman rested her hand lightly on my shoulder. "It's never easy for those who come from the outside, but you'll find things much better here. I promise."

I spun around and snarled, "Don't act like you know anything about me or what my life is like." If it wasn't bad enough that the Con Squad had taken my mother, now some underground resistance group had kidnapped me. I wanted to lash out at someone or something. "For all I know, you're all mutants."

They didn't react—not a gasp or a chuckle or even an angry grumble. I stepped back until I stood with my back against the riser door. I wasn't going to let my mind go any further down that path. That was simply crazy-thinking.

7

ARI

I reluctantly left the courtyard and returned to my room. Folded neatly at the foot of the bunk was a black-and-green jumpsuit like the one Tibor and the other Adams wore. Had Tibor brought it for me? Did he think it would be better for me to blend in, to not flaunt my "otherness?" Without hesitating, I stepped into the jumpsuit, tugged the zipper to my chest, and rolled up the cuffs. I placed the city clothes I'd been wearing in a drawer, smoothing out wrinkles from where they'd lain crumpled on the floor.

Tibor's voice followed tapping on the door. "Ari?"

I opened it a crack. He was alone.

He cleared his throat. "May I come in?"

I stepped back and pulled the door open. On the other side of the compound, two Adams walked past. They glanced away quickly when they saw me.

I shut the door behind Tibor. Truthfully, I was glad to see him, but that made me mad at myself. If it hadn't been for the Adams, Layla and her friend would still be alive. They were *my* kind, and I owed them, not the ones who cost them their lives.

"I may as well be a prisoner here," I snapped, glaring at him.

Tibor grimaced. He took a seat on a red loveseat, and I climbed onto a tall rush-bottomed wooden stool across from him. In back of me, a waist-high stone bar divided the sleeping and sitting areas.

Thinking back to the crowded crescent-moon dorms, I wondered if all Adams lived so well.

He folded his hands together and looked at them as he spoke. "I know you're hurting because you lost your friend, but you should know what's happening. You see," he looked up, frowning. "We've never had someone like you here, and some of the Elders are upset about it."

I couldn't keep a grin from sneaking onto my face. "Got in a bit of trouble, did you?"

"It's really not funny." His gray eyes pleaded. "If you could try to act grateful for their protection, I think it might help both of us."

"I guess that explains these." I ran my hand over the bulky jumpsuit. "You want to camouflage your unwelcome visitor?"

He squinted his eyes as he replied, "yes," then shook his head. "I mean, no." He sighed and threw his hands up in exasperation. "You don't understand. I'm glad you're here, but the Elders could have you banished."

"Great!" What a relief! I was ready to go back to the compound, even if it meant facing the Matron. Now I had something to compare to my life of invisibility, and being one of many crescent-moon cadets sounded fine to me. "Where can I find these Elders?"

"You don't understand," he said again. "You'd be banished to the city. The Cain city."

A chill settled in my stomach as I recalled how I hadn't even been able to cross a sidewalk on my own without drawing attention. When he looked up, maybe it was the way he bit his lips or how he kept brushing his hair back from his face, but I knew he believed there was real danger. I wondered if he was afraid for me, or if he'd also be banished.

I jumped off the stool and paced as I tried to figure out what I should do. My thoughts churned, like my stomach. I probably walked at least a mile back and forth across the room before I said anything more to Tibor.

"So I'm supposed to hide here until the next full moon and try to not attract attention?" I turned around just in time to see Tibor jump. He yawned and rubbed his eyes.

"Are you sleeping? Seriously!"

"It is the middle of the night," he said defensively. "Well, at least there's a chance keeping a low profile will work."

"Not much of a plan."

"Do you have a better one?" he mumbled.

I turned away and resumed my pacing, working off my anger with him and all the Adams. I reminded myself how Layla's friend wanted to give her sons the chance to live. What choice would I make in her situation? Someday I would find out, if I didn't get myself killed before then. Right now, I wasn't even sure what tomorrow would bring.

When I looked back over at Tibor, I guess I'd lost track of time again because he was slumped over in the chair, asleep. Although night was energizing for my kind, it obviously wasn't for his. My mind continued to spin.

Today I'd found out I really didn't know much about the world, and that was unsettling. But I did know one thing—I'd helped someone who was even more vulnerable than me.

I tiptoed across the room, opened the door just wide enough to slip through, and carefully closed it behind me. The setting moon softly illuminated the empty walkways between the buildings. Glad to be alone, I retraced my steps to the octagonal building. As I entered the nursery, a single chime announced my arrival.

I was glad to see the gray-haired man who'd taken the baby from me earlier that evening. As he walked toward me, he motioned to one of the floating cribs along the wall. I met him there.

"Rayson missed you," he said.

"Rayson," I repeated, wondering who named him. Hiccupping sounds made me think he'd been crying. My fingers hovered above the wriggling blue blanket. "May I?"

The man nodded.

I slid my hands beneath Rayson, feeling his softness mold to my touch. His eyes opened long enough to make my heart squeeze even tighter. Perhaps I imagined it, but I'd swear he recognized me. His hiccupping stopped.

I lifted him and laid the bundle of warmth against my chest. He was as fragile as a butterfly's wing, yet it had taken a strength of will as rigid as steel to give him the chance to live. I didn't know what to make of it all.

Women like us bore children of our body. The creation came spontaneously, though not without a catalyst. Some said the body knew when the community needed new members. Others said fear would cause a quickening in our wombs. Our teachers said procreation by parthenogenesis was rare, only found among a few amphibians. And our kind.

I carefully examined Rayson's perfect, tiny fingers and marveled at their miniature fingernails. As small as he was, he was almost twice as large as our newborn daughters. I wondered if that had something to do with why the Adams' mothers died.

Memories of my own childhood flooded in, how I awkwardly held round-tipped scissors to cut out paper dolls with their hands linked together in a chain. That's how I envisioned our society—each of us one of those dolls, mothers and daughters linked in an unbroken chain.

Of course, it wasn't that simple. Lots of things caused the chain to break. Some full-moon women never bore a child, and many went centuries between conceptions. In a society where raising children was a shared joy, most didn't regret their lack of conception. They could spend as much time as they wanted mothering other women's daughters, who were, after all, genetically like their own children.

Other links were broken when full-moon women left the compound before having daughters. Now I wondered where those women went. Before, I'd thought it was easy to pass from one compound to another, but if my own group wouldn't welcome me back, why would others take me in?

Then there was the fatal link, the one irrevocably broken when an Eve bore an Adam. Yet it created a link I'd never imagined, one forged to a new life in a world separate from ours. Here I stood, holding the tiny, perfect hand of an Eve's son. Hand in hand.

I shushed the young Adam, who nestled his face against my cheek. Was he hungry again already? I put my finger to his lips, which closed around it fiercely.

I jumped when the elder man cleared his throat. I'd forgotten he was here. "I regret abandoning you, but I must prepare for the next watcher." He sounded tired.

"Have you been here all night?" I asked.

"I spend part of most nights here, but tonight I took an extra shift. I knew you would return, and I wanted to be here. Tibor told me how you helped him save the babies from the Cains, and I saw how reluctant you were to leave the little one." He softly stroked Rayson's head.

I smiled at the man, appreciating his gentle spirit. I felt safe with him. I followed him to the crib where Rayson's twin slept. He smoothed the lightweight blanket with a hand as large as the sleeping infant's back. "This is Laylan."

I felt a catch in my throat.

"Tibor said his mother wanted to name him after the one she loved."

I nodded and opened my eyes wide to keep the tears from spilling out. "And your name?"

"Friends call me Fike." A smile danced in his eyes. "The time may come when you need someone to help you. I'd be honored to repay our youngest ones' birth debt to their mother by helping you."

I didn't know what to say. Birth debt. I'd never heard it termed that way, but I could guess what it meant. The Adams knew each of their lives cost one of ours. Maybe that was why they built our compounds, to repay their birth debt.

"You don't owe me anything," I said. "But thank you, Fike."

He dipped his head. "You can visit a little longer, but leave before sunrise. The others will come then to feed their sons. Don't be here to remind them of Tibor's transgression."

"So the Elders are really angry?"

Fike shook his head. "It's more than that. Ours is a society that lives on the outskirts of two cultures. We tread a tightrope between them, and any disruption can throw off the balance."

"I don't understand."

He grunted. "It's like this—every Adam must choose a path in life. It's never an easy decision, and once it's made, there's no going back. If he chooses to procreate, he must mate with a Cain. To keep the rest of us safe, his memories are purged. He loses his past to gain the future. If he decides to stay among us, his opportunities are tied to your kind. We depend on Eves for sons to nurture, to bring meaning to our lives. To continue to exist. And fewer Eves are making the decision to have sons."

I looked down at the newborn, whose birth was so vital to this community and so abhorrent to our own.

"Adams and Eves both hide from the Cains, knowing discovery would mean our end," he continued. "As I said, a tightrope." His footsteps echoed as he walked across the room. He disappeared behind a partition on the far side.

I took Rayson over to a rocking chair. He squirmed and made mewling sounds, but I rested his head on my shoulder and rubbed his back. I hummed and rocked. Each time I stood, he snuffled, and I had to start all over again. Everything but the feel of his warm breath on my cheek faded away.

Finally he was fast asleep and didn't stir when I rose and lowered him into his crib. I was still picturing the sweet curve of his eyelashes against his cheeks as I pushed open the door. I blindly ran into an Adam's rock-hard chest. Strong hands gripped my arms, jerking my attention upward to the scowling face of an elderly, white-haired man. My gut told me this was one of the Elders. I'd definitely waited too long to leave.

8
———

BLAIR

I stood by the riser long after the doors closed, pounding on the button. "Stupid, stupid, stupid," I mumbled. I'd noted the eye-level scanner and assumed the riser only responded to certain people, but I needed to release some of the tension coursing through my body.

I tried to make sense of the bad decisions I'd made over the past few hours that had turned my life upside down.

If I hadn't tried to track down the attorney Dina said might be willing to help me find my mom, I wouldn't have been in the lobby of that cursed building.

If I hadn't frozen while the trooper was distracted, I would've run out of the lobby like everyone else. I would've been long gone before the trooper remembered I was there.

If I'd fought off Terence after he knocked down the trooper, or at least hadn't gotten in the car with him, I wouldn't be trapped in this tower.

But I had, and I was.

If nothing else, today I'd confronted something I'd never known about myself. The old man was right—my survival instincts were nonexistent. What I could do about that, I hadn't a clue. Maybe it was too late to matter.

The tension burned itself out, leaving me exhausted and defeated. I slumped against the wall, wondering what would happen next. A movement across the room caught my attention. It was the silver-haired woman, sipping from a tall, white cup.

I sighed, giving up on the riser for the moment.

"Have a seat." The woman motioned to an orange plastic chair with metal legs, then rested both hands on the glossy black tabletop. A steaming cup of tea waited for me. "I'm Margie."

I sat and fiddled a few minutes with the ceramic cup, noticing its shimmering reflection.

"You're now a Eureka Towers resident," Margie continued in a cheery voice.

I took a sip. It was sweet and strong, a mix of black tea and something herbal. It smelled of cinnamon. I appreciated the woman's kindness, but I wasn't going to make the same mistake and trust someone too quickly. "You know I'm being held against my will."

Margie nodded. "Although the circumstances of your arrival are less than ideal, many of us find the lifestyle very pleasing. It takes a little time to adjust."

"I don't want to adjust." I smacked a fist on the table. "I want to leave."

"And where would you go?" the woman asked, undaunted. "Terence wouldn't have brought you here if the Con Squad hadn't marked you as subversive." She cocked an eyebrow. "Of course, he might not have gone to the trouble if you weren't so young and pretty."

I pictured the crowd of women who filled the room when we entered. More than half were about my age. "So what is this, a harem?"

Margie recoiled and gave me a sideways glance. "Someone in your position might consider using less inflammatory language. This is the women's quarter. No men are allowed on this floor beyond the riser lobby."

"And will I be allowed to leave?" I didn't know if I wanted to hear the answer.

"Yes, you can leave this floor with others after you've shown you're willing to be part of the community."

A chill settled in my gut.

"And calling us mutants or a harem isn't the way to win friends here," Margie continued, her jaw set sternly. "We have feelings, too."

Chastened, I dipped my head and focused on drinking my tea.

When I finished, Margie stood and motioned for me to follow. "You can stay in my guest room for now." Margie stopped in front of the vending machines. "It's getting late, so if you haven't eaten, you should get something."

"I don't have any cash," I said.

"Food is free," Margie said. "Get what you want."

I checked the nearest vending machine and didn't see a payment slot. "So many choices!" I said, as I went from machine to machine before finally selecting a salad topped with sliced chicken, fresh fruit, and pecans. I pushed a metal lever and my food dropped onto a tray. A glass panel slid aside, and I picked it up.

Margie stopped at a different dispenser and refilled our tea, then led me down a curving hallway to another riser lobby. Floor to ceiling windows faced the reddish trunk of the largest tree I had ever seen. I stopped and gasped. "Is that..."

"...a redwood tree?" Margie finished my sentence. "Yes, it's *our* redwood tree."

The trunk was easily wide enough to drive a Shell car through, with room to spare on either side. I put a hand on the glass, imagining the rough bark against my skin. "This isn't possible," I said. "I study botany, and the climate is wrong here for this species to grow to full height."

Margie snickered. "Eureka Towers may have a few more surprises for you. Just keep an open mind, okay? It's not perfect here, but it's been a better life for me than on the outside."

For the first time since the troopers stormed into the lobby, I felt a little hopeful. I hated not being able to leave, but freedom had its own consequences—the Con Squad would be watching for me.

I was reluctant to leave the window, but it turned out Margie's apartment was around the next curve. A large living room comfortably furnished in blues and greens separated two bedrooms. Poster-sized photographs of different kinds of trees covered the walls, giving it a forested feel.

"That will be your room tonight." Margie motioned to the right.

It was a small room, with a desk below a bunk bed. I placed the salad on my desk and took the tea from Margie with a smile. "Thank you."

"You're welcome," Margie said. "I know it's been a hard day for you. We'll talk more tomorrow. Or I'll be up for a while longer, if you feel like some Nadux-style entertainment. The main unit is in the common room, but each of our apartments has access to the basic features."

"Okay." I closed the door behind me and sat at the desk. I took a few sips of tea before opening the container. I absentmindedly fiddled with the dark green lettuce, which looked fresh and crisp. I hadn't thought I was hungry until I took the first bite. When the bowl was empty a few minutes later, I felt satisfied.

I found an oversized blue silk nightshirt in a small chest of drawers next to the desk and put it on, then took off my boots and climbed the ladder. I felt like stooping, but found I could sit on the mattress without hitting my head on the ceiling. I lay down and took a deep breath, willing myself to relax. My thoughts went in circles. The way the old man leered at me had been frightening, but I felt relatively safe here with Margie. Still, I couldn't think of a good reason for all the women to live together on a locked floor. Was it to keep them safe from the men, or to keep them from escaping? Either way, it wasn't comforting.

Again I considered different scenarios. Even if I escaped, I'd be hunted by the Con Squad. Maybe tomorrow would be a better day.

When I reached up to turn off the light, I noticed a piece of paper jammed between the fixture's glass globe and the ceiling. I pulled it down and flattened the sections of a three-inch square, which had been folded accordion-style.

Written neatly in ink was the message: "White is the color of the moon."

9

ARI

"You!" the Elder snarled, and shoved me back inside. A toddler sleeping near the door whimpered.

I backpedalled and stumbled. "I didn't do anything," I insisted, finally coming to a halt near the room's center.

He faced the man accompanying him and ordered, "Get Tibor. Now!"

My heart thundered as my mind replayed Tibor's words. This man, this Elder, wanted to banish me to the Cain city. The scene from the field flashed before my mind's eye, but this time, I imagined what might have happened if Layla had not been there to save me from the Cains. Layla would never be there again. Tears burned in my eyes, but I blinked them back. I felt so alone, so vulnerable, but I didn't want to give any inkling of that to fuel his anger. I shouldn't expect pity from someone who reacted so violently at the sight of me.

A few men stepped up from where they'd been standing by the cribs, several holding infants. I must've been drowsing when they arrived for the morning feeding and hadn't noticed them in the shadowy darkness. I tried to read their mood, but couldn't. They didn't avoid my glance, but no one gave me a reassuring nod or smile either. They seemed to be waiting for a cue from the Elder. They got it. He turned his back to me, as if ignoring me would make me disappear.

In some ways, I had. At least, I'd stopped listening. By his enraged and sanctimonious tone of voice, he was clearly railing about me, but all that registered was meaningless noise. Fear had somehow amplified the grief I felt for the loss of the two women whose thousand-year lives had ended that night. And for what purpose?

In the glow of early-morning light, surrounded by a growing number of hostile Adams, was the first time I'd really acknowledged that my protector, a woman of my own kind, had died only hours before. Even when I'd been standing in the courtyard earlier, letting the moonlight seep into my skin, I hadn't let myself dwell on their sacrifice. They both died so someone else could live.

I longed to somehow tell Layla I finally understood what she did for me, but I didn't know how to penetrate whatever veil separated her from this life.

Layla had saved me twice, but the second time seemed so unnecessary. Why was her friend in the Cain city? Weren't Adams born within our compound? In my heart, I knew better-- until the two Cains appeared in the field, I had never seen a male except on the classroom vid screen.

If Eves weren't permitted here, did that mean Adams were always born in Cain cities? The woman told Layla she would've been alone if Tibor hadn't been with her at the birth. So far, the Adams I'd met seemed more concerned about keeping Eves away from their compound than protecting male babies. It didn't make any sense. Giving birth on hostile ground made it precarious for all involved.

"Well, what do you have to say for yourself?" The Elder jostled my elbow.

"What?" I hadn't a clue what he was talking about.

He frowned and said. "Why are you here?"

As I stumbled for some sort of answer, the door slid open and the man who'd accompanied the Elder returned. Tibor jerked along behind him, his arm firmly in the man's grip. A flash of anger that crossed his face when he saw me quickly transformed to fear; he looked away.

"He was in the guest quarters, sleeping. Guess he didn't know she snuck out," the man said.

I tripped as I backed away from the Elder. Tibor tried to steady me, his touch like electricity on my skin. Then he just stood there, waiting for whatever would happen next. Murmurs grew louder behind me. From the corner of my eye, I glimpsed Fike entering from behind the partition. He looked tired and more than a little irritated. I cringed, remembering how he cautioned me to leave before daylight.

"Patron, this is no concern of yours." The Elder gestured dismissively.

Fike scowled and motioned at the cribs. "Anything that affects our sons is my concern." With narrowed eyes, Fike took the Elder's measure. When the taller man dropped his gaze, Fike addressed the others. "Don't let anyone distract you from your duties to our sons, even the Elder."

The caretakers moved away, leaving five of us in the center of the room.

Fike tilted his head toward the door. "Let's continue this outside. The babies will be fretful and hungry when they wake, and they don't need any added anxiety."

The Elder snapped, "As if it wasn't perfectly obvious what this is about!" He slung his head back defiantly, but didn't argue with Fike. He spun on his heels and the other man followed, shoving Tibor in front of him. I turned to Fike; he nodded at me but didn't meet my eyes. If only I hadn't stayed so long.

The hallway's glass outer walls gave a panoramic view of the waking compound. White stucco buildings still glowed pink in the light of a brilliant sunrise. A half dozen Adams had just arrived, but they stopped in a restless huddle by the outer door when they saw us standing in the hallway in front of the nursery. My skin felt scorched by their stares, or maybe I simply anticipated the touch of sunlight.

Fike crossed his arms and stepped so close the tips of his shoes touched the Elder's. "Now, tell me why you've disrupted my nursery this morning."

The Elder stepped back, but his eyes remained cold and his hands curled into fists at his sides. "My apologies, Patron. I will take the matter elsewhere." He pushed Tibor toward the outer door, then reached for me.

"I did not release the Eve to you." Fike brushed the Elder's arm away from me. "As you well know, those within the nursery have sanctuary."

"But..."

Fike's voice was steely. "I invoke the right of protection for this Eve. Don't bother returning without a signed order from all five Elders."

The Elder's face reddened. "Patron, we've had our differences, but this is going too far."

Fike stood motionless and silent.

"Have it your way!" The Elder spun around. The door barely slid open in time. The other man dragged Tibor after him.

I stood frozen in place. An apology was on the tip of my tongue when Fike said, "Guess it was bound to come to this someday. Might as well be today." He went back into the nursery. I followed him, wondering if he meant an Eve coming to their compound or the standoff between him and the Elder. However he meant it, I was in the middle of it.

Fike walked past the other Adams and the babies, and disappeared behind the partition. When I reached it, I saw the partition separated the nursery from a room designed for toddlers. The play areas were separated by use of color—red, blue and green —with coordinating rubbery floor tiles to cushion falls. The wall perpendicular to the partition opened to a doorway that was already sliding shut behind Fike. As I approached, it opened with a hiss.

I entered a hallway. Fike waited for me at the end, standing in front of another open door. When I reached him, he guided me into the most comfortable room I'd ever seen. The dark paneling should have seemed oppressive, but instead it made the room seem cozy. He motioned at a plush couch covered in forest-green fabric with brass tacks, which faced a stone fireplace. As I sat, I noticed a massive wood desk against the other wall.

Fike sat in an overstuffed chair, and leaned toward me as he spoke. "We don't have much time. The others do what the Elder says. When he returns with the order, I will have to release you to them."

I didn't know exactly what that meant, but I'd rather be with Fike than with the Elder. "What can I do?"

His hand cradled his chin as he sank deeper into thought. When he straightened a few moments later, he said simply, "Run."

My breath caught. "Run?" I said. "Where to? I don't even know where I am." Even if I could somehow find my way back to our compound, the Matron had met her deadline. No one would be there, and Layla hadn't given me a clue on the location of our new home.

His face looked grim. "I could program a car to get you away from here, but then you'd be on your own."

This just kept getting worse and worse. So long as I could safely feed in the moonlight, I wouldn't starve. In a densely populated area, however, I wasn't confident that could happen. And I'd have to find a way to avoid the sunlight. "On my own? You'd banish me to the Cain city, like the Elder?"

"He would never have let you leave here with your memories intact." Fike paused. "If he let you leave at all, which I doubt." He tilted his head and gave me a strange look, then added with more enthusiasm, "Yes, I think you could pass for an Adam if your hair was short."

I reached up to protectively caress my hair, which fell past my shoulders and down my back. "An Adam who feeds on moonlight?"

"That is a problem, but you can't stay here. Remember, I told you how some Adams join the Cain world so they can have families. I could send you through that network. With some luck, you could hide out for a month. You need to return at the next full moon to see if I've had word from the Matron."

"Luck!" I snorted. "The only luck I have is bad, or haven't you noticed?"

"Who's to say what is bad luck and what's simply meant to be. Personally, I don't believe in coincidence."

"You sound just like Matron," I said.

He raised his eyebrows. "Comes with the territory."

Now it hit home. When the Elder called him Patron, it hadn't really registered that he was the Matron's counterpart. "Oh," I said.

"Yes, well, it's not quite the same here. As you can see, our Elders have gained a great deal of power in the past century." He got up and walked toward the desk. "From what I hear, Adams are more like Cains when it comes to rivalry among ourselves. I wouldn't be surprised if I'm our group's last Patron."

Through a window on the outside wall, I caught sight of Tibor being led into another building.

"Look." I pointed, my voice shaky. A red scarf covered Tibor's eyes.

Fike groaned and rose to his feet. "I was afraid of that. He's been banished."

73

"You mean he has to leave here forever?"

"Yes, but he won't remember any of it." Fike walked to the desk and entered a message. In reply, the code 1A55 appeared on the screen. "Looks like Tibor's already been assigned to a handler. Let's get you over there, too."

He pointed to the desk chair and opened a drawer. Before I could protest, I heard the buzz of cutters. My hair fell in long, dark clumps onto my lap and the floor, leaving my neck cold and my head feeling too light and naked.

I stood, catching my reflection in the mirror above the fireplace. I didn't even recognize myself with the uneven wedges of hair framing the angular planes of my face.

He must have thought the same thing. "Yes, this could work out much better than I first thought."

Everything was happening too fast. I inched toward the door, wanting to rush back and hold Rayson one more time. Fike must have guessed what I was thinking. He shook his head and pulled two scarves from another drawer.

"I'll have to lead you over there so the handlers will think you're just another Adam who's made the choice. The good thing is that all Adams are disoriented from the memory purge, so your confusion about who and where you are will be perfectly natural. Expected, even."

He handed me a white scarf and raised his eyebrows as he nodded at my chest. "Maybe you could look more like a boy?"

I felt a blush creep up my cheeks, but I turned my back to him and unzipped the jumpsuit. I wrapped the white scarf tightly around my small breasts and zipped up.

"How's this?" I asked.

He nodded.

My throat constricted with fear as he slid the red scarf over my eyes and tied it. He took my arm and guided me out of the room. As we walked to the building where Tibor had been taken, I stopped in panic. "How will I find my way back if I'm blindfolded when we leave? I mean, Adams can never come back, right?"

"Look for signs to the apple orchard. If you're meant to return, you will find the way."

We stopped again a few minutes later, and I heard another door open. A rush of cooler air carried musky male scents and the sound of whirring motors.

"Wait, I have one more," Fike called out.

Another door hissed and hands guided me into what felt like the cramped interior of a Shell car. Moments later, we were on our way to the Cain city.

10

BLAIR

I refolded the paper and stuffed it between the light fixture and ceiling before I tapped the "off" switch. In the darkness, I considered the words: White is the color of the moon. What could it mean?

I rolled over a few times trying to get comfortable. Leaving cryptic messages didn't seem Margie's style, so whoever left it was probably another captive. Perhaps it didn't matter who discovered the note because we all shared a common plight. It could be meant for me as much as anyone else, couldn't it?

Finally curiosity overwhelmed me. I had to find out who'd stayed in this room. I climbed down from the bunk bed and took off my earrings. I dropped one in the hallway as I walked into the living room, where Margie lay sprawled across the couch watching the Nadux. Holographic fairies from an imaginary world danced between her and the wall.

"Sorry to bother you, but have you seen my earring?"

Groggily, Margie sat up and damped the sound on the Nadux. She squinted at me and rubbed her eyes.

I held out a single golden dragonfly. "I lost one of my earrings."

Margie reached for the earring, but shook her head before inspecting it. "I've been sitting here all night. Let's check this room first." She clicked the lights to full brightness. I followed her toward the door and acted like I was inspecting the carpet, too. It wasn't long before Margie exclaimed, "Got it!"

I took both earrings and hugged Margie. "My mom gave me these when I turned eighteen." Even if the earring hadn't really been lost, that part was true, and remembering it left a lump in my throat.

"Now I'm even happier we found it. I'll get a clasp to help keep them from slipping off again." Margie disappeared into her room and returned with rubbery circles for me to place on the back of my earrings.

"Thank you. I'll let you get back to your show." I waited a moment before turning toward my room.

As I'd hoped, Margie said, "I'd be glad for some company. I can play the Nadux any time."

"Are you sure?"

"Absolutely." Margie switched off the projection. She returned to the couch and patted the cushion next to her. "C'mon. I don't know about you, but it's rare for me to have a chance to get to know someone new."

I gave a half-hearted laugh and settled in next to her on the couch. "Well, lately I've been meeting people—since I started searching for my mom—but it hasn't worked out too well."

"Ah, but that isn't the same as getting to know them," Margie said, "and it's a bit too early for you to know how this may turn out. Tell me what happened to your mom."

"It's pretty much a blur, even though it was only a few days ago." I paused to regain my composure.

Margie grunted. "You're lucky they didn't take you, too."

"They planned to." My voice was thick with emotion. "One of the troopers almost found me in the closet where my mother hid me after she tased me. I almost wish he had."

Margie sighed. "Well, sometimes running is the best thing. It won't help your mom if they capture you, too. Your mom tased you?" She grinned.

"Using my own pocket taser!"

"Resourceful woman. I like her already."

"I couldn't help her—I couldn't even move or speak for a half hour."

Maggie nodded. "And by then, the troopers had left."

"Yes, but I knew Reservists would search the house, so I had to leave," I continued. "I tried calling my commander, but my access was blocked."

Margie tilted her head. "Your commander?"

"I'd been in the Con Squad Reserves for four years—would've graduated after this semester and begun training at the Academy." I had been so close. I still could feel the clear direction of my life. So neat and tidy and safe. Unlike now, when nothing made any sense. "I don't understand it. It took only a few hours for me to be declared a mutant."

Margie cleared her throat. "Well, that had to be a big surprise—to have the Con Squad hunting you."

I told her what the trooper from Headquarters said. "And it didn't stop there—they were waiting at my friend's house yesterday morning. I saw them just in time. And twice more since then—in the lobby where I first saw Terence and after I left the building."

"Then Terence brought you here," Margie finished for me. "Why were you in the lobby? You had to know places like that are under surveillance."

"My mother's friend told me of a lawyer who might be able to help. His office is in that building."

"I've never heard of anyone being released after they're marked as mutant," Margie said suspiciously.

"Yeah, well, I thought it was worth a try, both for my mom and me." I fidgeted with the tassels on a sofa pillow. "Of course, now the options are a bit different than I imagined."

"Give it a little time," Margie counseled. She cleared her throat. "Do you still plan to try to contact your commander?"

I shook my head. "I thought I knew what I was doing when I joined the Reserve. The news feeds were filled with reports of mutants leading terrorist attacks on humans. I believed the Con Squad offered our only protection, and I wanted to be part of it. I'd never seen an actual arrest before they took my classmate a couple of days ago. But she wasn't a mutant, and neither are my mom or me. So maybe mutants don't even exist? And if that's true, it makes the Con Squad something totally different from what I thought. Something I don't want to have any part of."

Margie looked away from me, silent for a few minutes. "I've seen enough of the Con Squad in action to know it isn't there to protect us."

"Then why do they hunt mutants?"

"It's about power." She sighed. "It's always about power."

"Why were the troopers after Terence and that couple with the babies?"

Margie stood and paced in front of the couch. "For you to understand, I'd need to go back—to tell you about why I came to Eureka Towers. It's a long story."

I motioned for her to continue.

"First, try to imagine what I was like years ago." Margie grinned sheepishly. "Sixteen-year-old girls are forces of nature. I thought everything was possible, and I believed everyone was like me." Her gaze was unfocused, as if she could see far into the past. "When I met Raul, he was the most exciting person I'd ever met—tall and handsome, older and sophisticated. He bought me tea and presents; he told me I was beautiful. Today, I'd simply say I was a romantic, and he seduced me."

"Oh no," I moaned. "You didn't!"

She grimaced. "Despite everything I'd been taught, I did. Not at first, of course. He broke things off for a while, told me to date someone else. I didn't want to live without him. So when we got back together a few months later, I knew if we didn't mate, he would find someone else."

"Did the troopers..." I stood, reaching out for her, wanting to comfort Margie for the long-ago trauma.

"No, no, it wasn't that way at all." She shrugged. "I was really lucky, and that's truly all it was—dumb luck. After we found out I was pregnant, he told me his secret: he was a suneater."

What? I'd expected her to say she had been accused of being a mutant, but instead, her lover was one?

"My upbringing had been sheltered," Margie said. "I was a preacher's daughter."

I grunted. "Don't tell me—Arm of the Lord?"

She nodded. "But they'd gotten it all wrong." Margie grinned mischievously. "I never believed suneaters existed, and that's where I was wrong. Suneaters do exist. They're not the evil superhumans the Arm of the Lord and Con Squad fear, but they are different from us."

Stillness opened up inside of me, like the feeling when a roller coaster tops the highest peak and you begin the descent, but can't see the track below. Looking back, I recalled joking with the other

Reservists about suneaters and other mutants. We'd studied ways to hunt them down, practiced ways to fight them, and even learned "interrogation" techniques. Everything I knew came through official channels. But I couldn't recall anyone—not even Commander Jameson—saying they had so much as talked with a mutant.

I watched Margie, who sat patiently, waiting for my reaction. I tried to imagine what it would be like to fall in love with someone— to become pregnant—and only then learn my lover was a mutant.

I leaned back and shook my head. "Well, this conversation sure didn't go the way I thought it would. I figured when you got pregnant, he turned you in to the Con Squad for virgin birth."

Margie shrugged. "You know, I think Raul really did love me in his own way. It wasn't the 'ever-after' kind I thought we had, but he didn't abandon me. In fact, he was thrilled I was pregnant."

"Really?" A twinge of jealousy kindled thoughts of how my father had abandoned my mother—and me—before I was born. "That's unusual. About the best you can hope for these days is a pre-paid paternity contract."

"So true," Margie sighed. "Other men don't seem to get it, but suneaters do. They're afraid they'll go extinct without us."

This conversation was making my head hurt. "Well, men don't get pregnant. If women don't have babies, all humankind *will* cease to exist."

"That's it—suneaters understand that on a visceral level because all their mothers die in childbirth," she said.

"The mothers all die?" I repeated, horrified.

"Yes. And that's where you came into the picture. Terence was at that building this morning to help the suneaters get their newborn sons to their compound."

"Those were suneater babies?" It all began to make sense—the troopers in the lobby. The elaborate escape.

She nodded. "Twins."

"All suneaters are male?"

"That's right," Margie said.

"But you had Raul's son and didn't die," I said.

"Our son isn't a true suneater," Margie said. "They're born from immaculate conception, or what scientists call parthenogenesis— suneaters don't have fathers."

"What!" I threw a sofa pillow at Margie with a nervous laugh.

"You're kidding me, right? You're pulling my leg 'cause I'm the new girl." Then I noticed a tear sliding down Margie's face.

"I wouldn't kid about this." Her voice was thick with sorrow. "I didn't think it would still hurt to talk about it, but it does."

I looked away, giving Margie a moment to catch her breath. Could she seriously believe her mate had been conceived without sex? As a Reservist, I had blindly accepted virgin birth to be possible, but now I questioned all they had told me about mutants. Broken trust is hard to mend.

Margie sat next to me. "I don't know why I'm dumping all this on you. Maybe we should call it a night?"

"No!" I said. "I mean, if you feel up to it, I'd love to hear the rest. What happened to your son and Raul? And how did you end up here?"

Margie picked up the sofa pillow and threw it onto the couch. "There's really not much more to it. The Con Squad did show up, but they didn't want me. They tried to take Raul while he was at work one day. His coworkers said he resisted and was killed before he even reached their van."

"I'm so sorry!" I wrapped my arms around Margie's shoulders as she sobbed.

"I was afraid I'd lose them both." Margie wiped the back of her hand across her eyes and cheeks. "Raul had told me we'd be safe at Eureka Towers if anything ever happened to him, so I came here. They took us in, no questions asked."

"Your son lived?" I asked.

"Yes," Margie said. "I wish I'd been able to have more influence over how he was raised, but at least I kept him safe. Maybe you can help make him the man his father was."

I cut my eyes toward Margie. "Me?"

"Terence is a little rough around the edges, but I can tell he likes you," Margie said.

11

ARI

Riding blindfolded in a Shell car that's hurtling along the SuperFlex at nearly two hundred miles per hour does strange things to your stomach. I breathed deeply. It didn't help. Every time we bumped another car to lock on or disengage, my gut rolled. I conjured up pleasant images to take my mind off how I felt. Who was I kidding? Saliva flooded my mouth and my jaws clamped; cold sweat dripped off my face.

All the while, I kept telling myself to keep calm. Worrying about where we were headed at breakneck speed wouldn't help a thing. Maybe knowing our destination was the Cain city was as much to blame for my stomach's distress as the motion.

Without being able to see, I had to rely on my other senses. Although our escorts didn't say anything, I could hear breathing in both of the front seats. Tibor sat next to me in the back, emanating the scent that always seemed to envelop him. He smelled fresh, with a lightness like I'd only known on the few times I'd ventured out in daylight. He smelled like sunlight. I wondered if I smelled like moonlight to him.

At one point, we stopped briefly, and the escorts changed. The new men breathed more heavily. One had a cough.

At first, I paid attention to turns. When we linked onto the chain, though, it became impossible. We were going fast. Really fast. It made me realize how difficult it would be to find the Adams' compound. Within an hour's time, the possibilities increased by two hundred more miles in every direction.

It was nearing midday when we finally slowed and uncoupled from the express chain. Traveling at lower speeds, the queasiness soon eased, leaving hunger in its wake.

A deep male voice broke the long silence. "Not much longer now." I heard a ping and figured it was from a handheld of some sort. "Here we go..." the man said. "Took them long enough to get the assignments worked out on these two. So, let's see who we have here. Aaron." After a pause, I felt a hand tap my knee. "That's you, boy. Looks like a lot of late-night shifts in your future. Too bad about that."

Inside I grinned. Night shifts sounded perfect to me.

Another pause. "But you, my friend Carl, are assigned to the University." His hand moved toward Tibor's knees. "Must have a head on your shoulders!"

Tibor didn't react to being called Carl. I wondered what he remembered of his previous life if he didn't even recall his name.

The voice from the front seat harrumphed. "Strange. Looks like you'll be bunking together. Usually they like to split up the newbies, but I guess it's because you're both so young."

Not long after that, the car slowed. "This it?" The guy asked, and got a grunt in reply. "You can take off your blindfolds now," he told us. "Welcome to New Humboldt."

I swallowed past a lump in my throat as I reached up and untied the scarf. New Humboldt—the Cain city. I glanced over at Tibor. He held out his hand. "Guess we're in this together."

Not trusting my voice, I nodded and shook his hand. I couldn't see how this was going to work.

We took in the Cain world speeding by outside the windows. Although we didn't get as close to The Falls as Layla and I had the previous day, I spotted the giant aquarium off to the right. Then we made a sharp curve and sped through some of the darkened canyons between the skyscrapers. Unlike the glass buildings I'd seen before, these were constructed more organically. Green interspersed glass and concrete, like a layer cake. From my studies, I recalled this was where most people lived, worked and studied. Each tower was a self-contained community that generated its own food and energy for its inhabitants. Rumor was that some Cains never left the tower where they were born. Playing Tower was one of the favorite past-times of the new-moon girls, though why it caught our imagination, I couldn't say now. Living in a tower wasn't much different from living in compounds like Eves did.

"This is the Outer Loop," the man on the right said, leaning back across the seat to face us. His complexion was darker than mine at full moon, and he had curly, short-cropped black hair. Creases at the corners of his brown eyes and full mouth made me think he smiled a lot. He gave us a conspiratorial grin now, like we were all in on a big joke that no one else knew.

The other man ignored us, totally absorbed with navigating the car. I guess that meant it was off automated control, which was mind-boggling. The eight-lane highway curved sharply and wove between a series of other multi-lane streets layered in every way imaginable into a tapestry of concrete and steel. Were automated controls more easily tracked?

"I'm Nathan," he continued. "I'll be working with you both for a few days until you're settled. I know this must be confusing, but trust me, you'll be fine."

I wished I could ask Tibor what he remembered, then I chastised myself for even thinking of him as anything but "Carl." If being a female Eve wasn't enough of a problem in this mixed-up scenario, I simply knew too much. I told myself to let *Carl* do the talking. I'd learn from him what I should do. The problem was, *Carl* wasn't doing anything except looking out the window, and I had a million unanswered questions.

Several minutes later, the car slowed, then made a quick deceleration onto a parking ramp at one of the towers. The ramp pulled us into a queue. The driver remained in the car as we followed Nathan onto the sidewalk, then he drove away.

The city smells assaulted my tender stomach. I could only guess at the source of most—meat, oil, metal. Buildings' shadows provided cover from direct sunlight, but I was glad we didn't linger outdoors. It felt risky to be out at midday.

I felt more conspicuous than I had with Layla—I was hiding my identity from everyone now, not just the Cains. Fike hadn't said what would happen if the Adams discovered I was an Eve, but I figured it wouldn't be good. I couldn't worry about that now. I had to get through the next hour before I could stress out about the next month.

The moving sidewalk was far less crowded here, and I easily followed Nathan across it without colliding with any Cains. Nathan waved his pinky at a scanner. Polished steel doors decorated with geometric patterns slid open, and we entered a cool, dimly lit lobby.

Nathan nodded at a uniformed man behind a desk with a bank of monitors on the wall to his right side. At first glance, I thought he was like the troopers who'd taken Layla's body, but his uniform was brown, not dark blue. Security, I guessed. We'd been expected.

A mural engraved into translucent sheets of glass rose from the floor to the ceiling, commanding the center of the largest room I'd ever seen. It was easily as big as our compound's central plaza.

Nathan walked us over to the mural's first panel. "This is a unique building with a long history, of which this is all just a chapter." It seemed a strange comment since the mural depicted centuries, from the first buildings on the site to the creation of this community.

A tower was far more like a town than a building. Agri and food production on each of the structure's twenty-four floors took advantage of gravity to help settle the impurities in the "protein" tank. Much like at the Waterfalls of Westover, fish waste nurtured plants, which fed humans. Recycled gray water refreshed the water for the fish, and so on. The diagrams were artfully sculpted in vivid colors, made three-dimensional by the reflecting glass.

I had to wonder about that—in a tower built for Adams who got sustenance from the sun, why was so much focus on food production?

Floors for living space alternated with businesses and schools, with shopping and entertainment areas. Solar- and air-powered generators supplied energy.

In the riser, Nathan selected the ninth floor. Buttons for the top four floors had been replaced with key slots. The riser opened into a spacious room with couches and chairs arranged in small groups around a center atrium. About half were occupied with Adams, who sat reading, watching vids or playing games that hovered between them mid-air. I stopped abruptly as I realized what the mural in the lobby had hidden.

Sunlight beamed through skylights on the top floor, sending golden streams between metal arches that formed the atrium's domed roof. We walked to the brass railing and stared at the gigantic tree in the center. It spanned the building's full height, from the ground floor almost to the skylights. Branches spread into open air where the railings for the highest floors should've been near the top of the dome. The sparse, needled branches allowed light to flood the atrium on our lower floor.

Wooden walkways with rope handrails looped between the branches, and several couples–men and women–leisurely walked on them. Even though Fike said one of the main reasons Adams came here was to be able to breed, seeing other women startled me. They must be Cain women, I reasoned, since they seemed at ease in the sunlight. Maybe that explained the need for food?

Carl and Nathan wandered over to a plaque on the railing, but I stayed in the partial shade, watching the scene above. Even so, I could feel the energy-sapping rays on my skin.

Tibor—*Carl!*—seemed to come out of his trance enough to express some interest. He read the placard aloud. "Sequoia giganteum, Giant Redwood."

I did a double-take on the bark's reddish hue. Could it be? Only a dozen redwoods remained, and our vids said they were heavily guarded in coastal corporate parks. You certainly couldn't walk among their branches as these people did.

"As I said, the building has a long history," Nathan said. "Although it doesn't advertise, this was the first tower. It was built to safeguard the tree, which doesn't appear in any history books. It's our legacy to the children...and now yours as well."

Carl nodded, as if this was something he knew. I found it a complete puzzle, which must have been obvious.

"It will become clear in time, Aaron," Nathan said. "For now, the important thing is you've taken the first step toward your future life by coming here."

Carl and Nathan lingered in the sunlight, feeding on its energy. Thankfully, I had fed last night, so I left the shade and followed them into the bright rays. I told myself it was the bright light of a full moon. After only a few moments, though, my body burned. I couldn't take much more. I walked back into the shade, feeling exhausted, and sat on one of the couches.

Nathan tilted his head and hunched his shoulders. A concerned frown made it clear my actions weren't the norm.

"I'm fine," I croaked, trying to make my voice husky. "I must've fed right before we left." I hoped that made sense. Should I know when I ate? Nathan didn't act suspicious about my bogus comment. He didn't even react to my voice. Since he wasn't expecting me to sound like a girl, maybe I just sounded like a young boy?

Nathan and Carl basked a few more minutes in the sunlight before joining me. "Now on to the rest of the tour." He gave me a sideways look. "You up to it?"

I made an exaggerated grimace and patted my stomach. "Sure. Just queasy after that ride."

He chuckled. "Before we go to your new home, I wanted you to get the big picture. Many of the lower floors are dedicated to community activities such as business, industry, and learning. But this one is special because it was left open. If you look beyond the atrium, you can see the agri units along the south wall, and the tanks along the west wall. That's the pattern on every floor, but it's not so readily apparent."

"Except on the top floors?" I asked.

He quirked a lopsided smile. "Well, that's not a first-day topic." We entered the riser, and he hit the button for the thirteenth floor.

12

BLAIR

I took a deep breath and let the news sink in. "Terence is your son?" The whole situation confused me. I had started to feel close to Margie, but this jerked me back to reality. "Did you ask me to stay with you because he brought me here?"

"Well, not exactly," Margie said. "I've seen how hard it is for some of the new girls, and I didn't want your transition to be that rough." Her hands fluttered. "I know Terence wouldn't have brought you to the Towers if there'd been any other option."

"So you do this for your son—offer the women he brings home a room for the night so they won't give him a hard time?" I heard the harshness in my tone.

Margie shook her head and smiled. "It's not like that at all."

I stood with my hands on my hips. "Then what? You've never done this before?"

"Don't be silly," Margie said. "We don't get that many women from the outside, but quite a few have spent their first night at Eureka Towers with me. In fact, I had a guest a few days ago. Seems like newcomers arrive all at once."

"Last week?"

"Yes," Margie said and laughed softly. "A very nice girl named Piper. You'll get to meet her and some of the others tomorrow."

"What's so funny?"

"Nothing, dear." Margie patted my hand. "You see, you're the only woman Terence has ever brought to the Towers. I wanted to see what made such an impression, and now I know."

"What do you mean—the only woman?"

"Only that you've touched my heart," Margie said. "I don't talk with just anyone about Terence's dad."

I felt redness creeping into my cheeks. Maybe I hadn't misjudged things as badly as I'd feared.

Margie stood and gave me a quick hug. "Besides, you're feisty. And feisty is one of Terence's favorite things about a woman."

I grimaced. "Puh-lease!"

"Seriously, I know it's been hard for you, but now things will be better. Trust me," Margie said. "Let's get some rest. Tomorrow's going to be a big day for you."

I went to my bedroom and Margie to hers. Alone again, I chided myself for not finding out more about the women who'd stayed here with Margie. I was no closer to understanding the message, but at least now I had a name—Piper. I'd just have to wait until tomorrow.

I climbed up into the bunk bed. No matter how many times I tried to concentrate on what my next step should be, all I saw in my mind's eye was what had already happened—the troopers rushing into the lobby, the couple with infants leaving the building before the riser opened with the body that disappeared from the gurney. Then Terence returning for me. Escaping.

You chose to come here. He didn't force you. How could I have made a better decision when I didn't know where he was taking me? If I'd stayed behind, would the Con Squad have taken me to where Mom was? My stomach knotted with regret and uncertainty. How could I find and help my mother if I couldn't even help myself?

13

ARI

The thirteenth-floor lobby had only a few couches and chairs. Instead of a single brass railing surrounding the giant redwood at the center of the atrium, a series of balconies separated on each side by smooth, white walls encircled most of the space. On the far side, I could see into some of the rooms, but curtains or privacy panels blocked the others. We walked down the hallway along the outer perimeter, and I realized the corridors created a square around the circular atrium.

About halfway around, Nathan stopped in front of a silver door in the center of opaque black glass walls. Across the hall, the fish tank completely filled the wall from one corner of the corridor to the next. The unbroken expanse of blue continued to the floors above and below ours. Shafts of sunlight lent movement to the light and shadow, and fish of various sizes and colors swam leisurely among long, thin tendrils of seaweed.

"You're lucky," he said. "Rooms facing the tanks aren't available often."

"It's so peaceful," Carl said.

"It reminds me of the tanks beneath The Falls," I said.

"For good reason." Nathan pressed a button and the door slid open. "Westover did these as a prototype for The Falls."

"That makes sense." I walked inside the room and stood

awestruck at the view. Through the tinted one-way glass, the tanks across the hall looked like a night sky filled with ghostly sea creatures. It was beautiful.

I turned back around and scoped out *our* room. I was used to living in a dorm with a dozen or more Eves, but sharing a room with a single Adam felt crowded. If I had any chance of keeping my identity hidden, I'd need some space of my own. I breathed an internal sigh of relief when I saw two tiny bedrooms. Each held a bunk bed with a desk nestled beneath it. They straddled a central room with a gray couch and two chairs. While it wasn't as private as having a whole guesthouse to myself like at the Adams' compound, at least it wasn't a dorm.

Drawn by the nourishing rays, Carl and Nathan crossed the room and opened clear glass doors onto a sunlit balcony. They took the two seats closest to the brass railing, leaving two in partial shade. The plush red chairs faced a square slate-topped table.

I stalled just inside the doorway, observing how the staggered balconies on each floor allowed sunlight to bathe the area. I imagined the same would be true of moonlight—at least, I hoped so. It would make it much easier if I didn't have to leave our room to feed.

Nathan misinterpreted my reluctance to join them on the balcony and gestured at his chair as he stood. "C'mon, take this one."

"In a moment." I tilted my head to the left.

The bathroom was a seamless sheet of white polymer, which morphed into the shapes of a toilet, sink and refresher. A chest-high screen inside the refresher displayed symbols for various toiletries. When I left, the lights dimmed and a purple beam sanitized the room. Our compound didn't have anything like that.

I remembered with a start the Eves were already at the new compound. If it had some modern amenities like this, Piper would have one less thing to harass new-moon cadets about. Right now, I'd volunteer to scrub refreshers for a month if it would get me back home.

Nathan and Carl joined me as I entered another tiny room directly across the living area from the bathroom. The thin blue tornado-shaped Nadux symbol marked each of a series of gleaming black panels, which covered the walls from floor to ceiling. I turned my palms up, puzzled.

"We call it the Nadux Room," Nathan said. "All these concessions

—including the Nadux game world—are our own designs, and some are still being tested."

The Nadux game world had been the first of its kind, which made it worthy of study in my 21st Century Dynamics class. They'd gone on to create a technology empire that even extended into our compound. I'd learned the alphabet on an nPad reader and taken chemistry in an nDeck holographic lab. I had no idea Adams were the creators of Nadux. I was impressed.

"Here we have an assortment of drinks." He pointed at brightly colored images of hot and cold beverages. "Just press the icon and get your drink here." A moment after he selected a tea, a steaming cup materialized in a niche. "It's a quantum 4D system, so there are no moving parts to clean. All the patterns are encoded, so it creates— and recycles—energy."

He placed the full cup back into the niche and pressed a different button. A semi-solid transparent sheet covered the opening for an instant, and the next thing I knew, the cup was gone. I stood transfixed, trying to figure out how it had happened. Nathan moved on to the next panel.

We followed the curve of the black panel into an indention large enough for Carl and me to stand comfortably inside. We faced clothing icons and a slot for recycling worn garments. "The Tailor always gives you a perfect fit, and you can adjust the hue and pattern here." He reached in and touched a color wheel icon, which expanded on the screen.

I examined the selection, puzzled to find only jumpsuits. How would the scanner interpret my body? Had it ever scanned an Eve? Again, Nathan didn't linger.

"And this is your E&E center." He waved his hand over another screen, revealing more icons for educational and entertainment resources than I ever imagined. He touched the blue tornado, and then ushered us back into the central room. Holographic images of Nadux's entrance gates replaced the wall facing the couch. "We have a limitless contract," he said, "but privileges are suspended if you don't meet your work quota."

Carl gave me an excited "thumbs up," which I mirrored. If I had any strategy, that was it—act like Carl. It wasn't much of a plan and I knew it, but it was a start. Maybe as the day progressed, I'd find some clues on how to rejoin the Eves and avoid being abandoned in the Cain city.

Nathan turned toward me. "Things happened so suddenly today, I didn't have time to finalize all the busy work that accompanies transfers. Why don't you both get settled in? I'll be back soon."

As the door slid shut behind us, I followed Carl toward the balcony. The earthy fragrance of green and bark, balanced by the fresh scent of sunlight, were at odds with our high-tech surroundings.

"It's all happened fast," he said.

"Yeah, I can hardly believe it," I added.

"I'm glad there are two of us—it would've been even stranger to be here alone." He gave me a sideways glance. "Do you—I mean, it's odd to know some things, but not know how I know them."

I sighed. "I'm glad it's not just me. You seem so confident, but I'm feeling lost."

He laughed with obvious relief. "This place is unbelievable, isn't it? It looks like you can make almost anything in there." He pointed to the Nadux Room.

I grabbed one of two red gloves from the ottoman and plopped down on the couch. "Even playing a simple game seems foreign." That was an understatement. I'd never even touched a real Nadux game unit before.

"That's good news." He smirked and slid on the other glove as he joined me on the couch. "Beat ya!" He tapped his thumb and forefinger together and a life-sized character outline appeared. I did the same, following each step he took until our avatars were fully equipped to enter Nadux. Carl's was outfitted in flexible armor, a golden cape and carried a staff. My tall, slender warrior had a dark-blue cloak and a sword that sparkled with magic. The lotus spinner stopped and the gates to Nadux opened to a world filled with clouds.

"Sweet!" Carl said. He swept his gloved hand in the air and his character disappeared into the mist. "The Quest of Titans."

I tried the same gesture and my warrior fell flat on his face. A puff of black smoke indicated his demise.

Carl snorted. "You really don't remember any of this, do you? Titans is a game of opposites. If I sweep upward, you have to bring the world back into balance with a downward move. Otherwise, depending on how far you are into the game, you die or the world ceases to exist."

"Oh." I hoped my ploy of mimicking him turned out better in real life.

Carl continued playing. For a while, I tried to decipher the connection between his moves and the game. Finally, I gave up and went into the Nadux Room, wishing for some privacy. After a few nervous moments, I decided Carl was too busy to care what I was doing.

I stepped into the niche and selected a jumpsuit style identical to mine. I tapped the color wheel, selecting the forest-green color Nathan wore. I held my breath and pushed the scan button. The Tailor whirred and air puffed around me.

An image appeared in front of me; the lines and grids displayed proportions that were clearly female. The screen responded when I touched it. I could edit the image. I choked down a sigh of relief as I made it bulkier at the waist and less rounded through the hips. I saved "Aaron's" dimensions. A neatly folded jumpsuit fell into the niche at my right.

"Couldn't wait to try the Tailor?"

I turned around, surprised to see Carl standing in front of the E&E panel. I hadn't heard him enter. He clicked the Nadux off and went to the drink dispenser.

"Uh, I thought I'd freshen up in case I have work tonight."

"I hadn't thought about that—I guess you'll at least want to see what you'll be doing. I'm curious, too, but it's too late to check out the University today."

"Yes, it'll be sundown soon." It was still too bright outside for my liking.

He sipped his drink and took a seat on the balcony, which was now in full shade.

"Not bad. Orange and fizzy."

"I'll try it later." After the bathroom door slid closed, I fumbled around until I found the lock. I shed the black-and-green jumpsuit and untied the scarf binding my breasts, then stepped into the refresher. I tapped the screen and selected shampoo. A light shone inside the niche. When I held my hand beneath it, white goo squirted out.

Now all I had to do was find out how to turn on the water. I didn't expect anything as straightforward as a faucet or showerhead like we had at the compound, but I didn't see a likely button, switch or icon.

Hoping for a motion detector, I waved my one free hand at the wall. I made supplications with rainlike motions of my fingers. "I give," I mumbled. "How do you get water around this place?"

A fine spray jetted from three sides and the ceiling, drenching me from head to toe. Fortunately, the temperature was perfect, because I had no idea how to adjust it. My fingers slipped too quickly through my much-shorter hair, which took less than a minute to shampoo. After a good sudsing, I said, "Stop water." Nothing happened.

"No water." It still kept coming.

"Towel?" I cried.

"All right already, how do I get dry?" I complained. The water shut off and warm air swirled around me for a few minutes. It sensed when I was perfectly dry and turned off.

I wrapped the scarf around my chest and zipped up the jumpsuit I made. I didn't have to roll up the cuffs—it was a perfect fit, even with the extra inches I'd added at the waistline. I glimpsed a reflection from the corner of my eye and caught my breath. Someone else was in the room—a young Adam. Then I smiled.

I marveled at my drastically altered look. My short, tousled hair accentuated the strong lines of my jaw and cheekbones. Some Eves favored pierced ears or lips, or other adornment. I was glad that hadn't been my style—and my crescent-moon tattoo wasn't visible.

I scowled and tried to act gruff like the Elder, then tried various other expressions to see if they looked convincing. When I'd gone through my repertoire, I felt pretty good. Except I smiled like a girl.

Although my antics had taken only a few minutes, I felt my energy rising. It wouldn't be long until moonrise. I could hardly wait.

It was noticeably darker when I left the refresher. Carl lay on the bed in the room adjoining the Nadux Room with his eyes closed. I went to the other bedroom and sat at the desk. This couldn't have worked out better. With a few private moments, maybe I could get a message back home. Our compound could access outside systems, so surely I could get a message to someone. Sadly, the only email addresses I could recall were Layla's and Piper's, which left me with only one option.

I toyed with the small hologram projector, similar to the one we'd used in our classes, then noticed another screen outlined on the ceiling above the bunk bed. That seemed a little more private, so I crawled up the ladder and lay down. I said "log-on" to activate the system. I waved my pinky at the DNA reader.

"Ari..." I stopped myself before finishing. My heart pounded as I realized my password was linked to my real identity. That was a close call. Surely someone would be monitoring activity, particularly for newbies. But not having access to the web was inconceivable because everything required it. If I couldn't use my real name, was there another way to gain access?

Since they went to all the trouble to give Adams new names when they left the compound, they must have taken additional steps to make their identities workable. Otherwise, Carl's password would begin with "Tibor" just as mine began with "Ariadne." But would his conditioning before he left the Adam compound have included the new code—conditioning I was only faking?

If Carl knew his password, it would immediately draw attention to me if I couldn't log-on. Attention was the last thing I wanted.

How could I guess my password, assuming Fike had created one for me? He would have no way to know the symbols that came after my name, and I doubted those would've transferred anyway. Still, it was worth a try.

Trying to be more security-conscious, I turned off the voice translator and typed in my old password with the characters hidden, but started with "Aaron" instead of "Ariadne." I wasn't surprised it didn't work.

I was hyperventilating about the implications of all this when I heard a ping. A moment later, the door slid open and Nathan called out, "I'm back!"

I couldn't help but wonder how long I could keep up this ruse when the first thing I'd need on any job would be web access.

14

BLAIR

I awoke to Margie's voice, muffled by the closed door. "I don't know what to do now. I wish Terence hadn't put us in the middle of this."

I craned my neck, trying to hear better.

"He has a good heart. Besides, how could he know the Con Squad would make an issue of it?" another woman replied, her voice husky. "And who ever heard of The Covenant? It's a mess, that's for sure. We just have to make sure nothing draws attention to us."

"True," Margie said, "but with the Con Squad's surveillance system and computer power, they may be able to unscramble the Shell game and follow the trail here."

"Well, it wouldn't be the first time they tried to infiltrate the Towers," the woman said.

"We've always managed to find something to throw them off track, even if it meant someone had to spend time in custody," Margie said. "I'm afraid this time may be different. There's been too much publicity."

"What could they find? Every tower has its own social system— they haven't abolished all our rights yet. From what I've seen, Eureka Towers isn't much different from the others."

"I guess you're right. You can't tell some of the men are suneaters just by looking at them." Margie paused. "But for their safety and ours, Terence and Blair can't stay here."

"Don't sweat it, Margie," the other woman said. Footsteps headed toward my room. "Terence will figure out something. He wanted you to meet him by the riser as soon as you can."

I had slipped down from the bunk and started to remove the borrowed nightshirt when Margie knocked.

"Blair, are you awake?"

"Yes." I adjusted the top.

Margie peeked in. "Then you know we need to get ready to meet Terence."

I nodded. "What happened?"

"The Con Squad released your photos and claimed you're mutant leaders of a terrorist group called The Covenant."

Inside I cringed, but I responded with a derisive snort. "Never heard of them." Of course, that didn't matter. Being the focus of a Con Squad publicity blitz was about as bad as it got.

"Me, neither," Margie said. "But they claim The Covenant poisoned the Westover water supply five years ago. Biological warfare, weapons of mass destruction, and all that."

"Good one." I tried to ignore the sinking, hopeless feeling in my stomach. "That will get people riled up." Now everyone would be looking for me, hoping to gain the Con Squad's favor. "I guess they were saving the water supply terrorists to make a special case, like this one, since everyone was affected."

Margie grunted. "I don't think anyone in the government even knows what truth is any more."

She disappeared from the doorway as I tugged the nightshirt over my head. I didn't know how things kept getting more and more out of hand. A few weeks ago, I'd been an ordinary student living with my mom. Now my life was like a whirlwind being sucked into a very dark and dangerous vortex. My teeth snagged my bottom lip, worrying it as I slipped on a tunic and orange tights I'd found in the room and pulled on my navy knee-high boots. After a brief trip to the refresher, I met Margie in the living room.

"Here, have a quick bite." Margie motioned to the chair across from her. On the side table sat a steaming cup of tea and a small plate with a bunch of grapes and a breakfast roll. "You may have to leave the Towers soon, and it's better to have something on your stomach."

Her thoughtfulness reminded me of my mom. Feeling more than a little homesick, I obediently sat and took a bite of the roll even though I wasn't hungry. It didn't take long for that queasy feeling to be replaced with stabbing fear.

The Nadux showed the terrorist alert in an endless loop. One of the building cams must have been trained on the riser lobby where I waited yesterday. Terence's immobilization of the trooper followed by our escape through the side door bled into familiar footage from the terrorist attack five years ago—placid scenes of the Westover waterworks' settling tanks and shots of test tubes filled with a bright blue liquid.

I'd only been a high school freshman then but I'd always remember that day. I'd come down with the worst-ever stomach virus, but Mom had required an infusion to replace fluids. We had been lucky. The Blue Death claimed more than ten thousand lives in one day and showed the world how vulnerable we were. Like many of my friends, I joined the Reserve.

We cheered when the Con Squad made arrests in the following weeks, but they said those were only the henchmen. No group claimed responsibility for the act, and the mystery continued to be debated on each anniversary. Until now.

Margie clicked on the volume as grainy mug shots obviously pulled from video footage filled the screen. "If spotted, do not attempt to approach. They are armed and dangerous. Press your CS icon and a team will be sent to your location."

Seeing my wall-sized photo beside Terence's gave me the strangest feeling. A silly thought crossed my mind—we made a cute couple. Then I pictured us five years ago. A nervous chuckle escaped.

Margie gave me a sideways glance and raised her eyebrows.

"Oh, it's nothing." I gulped down a bite. "My fifteen minutes of fame. At least they didn't use the picture from my ID. That would've scared small children and dogs."

Margie chuckled. "Whew. I thought for a minute you'd gone bonkers on me."

"Well, there's that." I grinned. "But I thought crazy was the new norm." I paused. "You wouldn't think they'd claim a couple of kids could've pulled off something as sophisticated as the Blue Death attack. We're young now, but five years ago, I would barely have been a teen."

Margie shrugged. "Most people won't stop to think about that. They're just glad their water is safe to drink again." With a grunt, she rose. "We'd better get going."

I had mixed feelings when I saw Terence by the riser. I didn't know whether to be angry or hopeful. I wanted to believe Margie's son had my welfare in mind when he brought me here, but the rough handling I'd received from the old man when we arrived made me think otherwise. Yet even the woman talking with Margie this morning said Terence had a good heart.

Terence wore a green-and-black jumpsuit—the same one or at least very similar to what he'd worn the day before. He paced, his back to us as we approached.

"Son," Margie said, "we're here."

Terence leaned over to kiss Margie's cheek. "Looks like I've done it now." He gave me a look I couldn't decipher. "As they say, no good deed goes unpunished. Guess you were more than an innocent bystander."

"You're blaming me for this?" I screeched. "I'm not the terrorist. The Con Squad wouldn't have even been there if it hadn't been for you and your friends. *That's* what got their attention, not me. Did you kidnap some diplomat's babies?"

Margie took a deep breath and released it slowly. I hadn't noticed the background noises until they were gone. In the silence, I saw we weren't alone. Women sat in groups around the room and lingered near the vending machines. Everyone focused on us.

Terence realized it at the same time. He motioned to some chairs and took a seat. "It would be better if you'd just forget about that," he whispered to me.

"I'll forget about it when my life returns to normal," I said, "which probably means *never.*"

Margie cleared her throat. "Okay, you two. It really doesn't matter why the Con Squad chose to go public with the search. We need to focus on what to do now. Is there a plan?"

Terence nodded. "It will take some time to make arrangements, but we'll need to go to a safe house until things calm down. It's too risky for us to stay here in case the Con Squad decides to sweep the place."

Margie nodded. "I figured it would be something like that." She rose and turned to Blair. "I'll get a few things together for you.

I watched as Margie walked away. I wanted to lash out at Terence for his arrogance, but the anger still boiling inside was now tinged with fear. I'd been so focused on my own predicament, I hadn't really thought about what I'd seen as I stood by the riser. What were they doing with the two infants? Shouldn't the woman who'd driven away with the other man in the green Shell car be here? I looked around the room, searching for those haunted eyes. I'd recognize them anywhere.

Terence mumbled something under his breath, then said, "Okay Blair, you're right. I shouldn't have said that."

I scrunched my mouth into a grimace and glared at him. Mom taught me to accept an apology when it is offered, but Terence's words only made me angrier. "Yes, I am right. You *kidnapped* me! You owe me an apology for that, too. And if you think I'll just go along with your plan, you need to think again. This time I want to make an *informed* decision."

He threw his hands up, his voice edgy again. "You act like there's a choice. Fine, I'll tell you everything I know, but that doesn't change the fact we're leaving here. I haven't got a clue yet where we'll go, but we'll be together, and I'd rather not spend the next however-long fighting. So would you quit being hormonal and focus on the issues?"

"Hormonal!" My yell drew stares again. I pointed toward the riser. "Since I'm a prisoner and can't leave, I suggest you go now before I show you what 'hormonal' looks like." My fingernails scratched against my tights.

Terence looked at the women's faces around the room, then stood. "Just be ready. And do something with your hair so it's not so...blonde."

My hands flew to my hair. "No problem. And you should take your own advice. Any change would improve your looks tremendously."

I jumped to my feet, frustrated at my lame comeback, and stomped away. I didn't get to be eighteen without dealing with assholes, but no one had ever called me "hormonal." Now I was supposed to team up with a misogynist pig and hide from everyone else in the world? I'd rather take my chances on my own.

The more I thought about it, the more that seemed like a reasonable approach. The Con Squad was looking for two people. Surely I could convince Terence if we split up, we'd be harder to find.

But then what? With my photo on every Nadux screen, I wouldn't be able to walk across the street without being spotted. Things were happening too fast—I hadn't even gotten my mind around being at Eureka Towers, and now I had to flee with the man who brought me here. A man who only thought of me as a liability.

When I stopped, I found myself in front of a vending machine next to a woman with brassy red hair.

"Terence can get on your nerves, but don't take it personally, honey."

I recognized the husky voice from this morning.

"He's still Margie's son, and that makes him a good man. People don't get any better than Margie." She extended her hand. "I'm Abigail."

I had always thought my grip was firm, but the woman's strength surprised me. "I'm Blair, the hormonal bitch."

Abigail's grin turned into a chuckle, and I joined her. "I couldn't help but hear the 'discussion' about changing your appearances. I run the salon, and there's nothing I like better than makeovers." She winked. "Just last week, I was a green-eyed blonde."

Checking out her blue eyes, I said, "Contacts?"

"Of course." Abigail linked arms with me and led me down the hallway. "This is one heck of a way to spend your first day here. I hope you can return soon so we can get better acquainted."

I looked from the corner of my eyes, trying to judge if Abigail was serious. "Ah, sure." In a pig's eye. If I managed to escape, coming back to Eureka Towers would be the last thing on my agenda.

15

ARI

Nathan grinned. "Looks like you got the Tailor figured out."

"It's great." *If you like jumpsuits.*

"That's one of the prototypes," he said. "I think it will be a huge success. It only offers limited choices now, but I expect that will change as soon as the techs turn it over to the marketing and design folks. Even I'm getting tired of these jumpsuits."

I almost laughed. Apparently I wasn't the only one who thought the selection was too limited.

Carl joined us, frowning as he motioned toward his desk. "I logged on and there's nothing there except my profile. What happened to all my files?"

With his altered memory, I wondered what kind of files he expected to be there.

Nathan shrugged. "Sometimes that happens. There's really nothing we can do, but you won't need them here anyway. You'll see."

Carl threw his hands in the air. "They didn't say anything about having to start my project from scratch," he muttered and walked away.

His comment puzzled me, but it made one thing clear: I should be able to access my account. I was screwed.

"I hate that." Nathan winced and motioned me toward the door. "How about you?"

"I haven't gone online yet." Even telling a white lie made me squirm. Any time I'd tried, Piper said she could read me like a book. Judging by the Matron's and Layla's comments, I wasn't too successful at being sneaky either. My confidence slipped another notch. What was I thinking, trying to pass as a male?

"Well, I hope you have better luck." He walked a few steps and the door slid open. "We'll make this a short visit, just a few introductions—we've all had a long day." He paused in the doorway and shouted, "Oh, and Carl, I'll come by early tomorrow to take you to the Registrar's office—say around nine?" He didn't wait for a reply.

Anxiety nipped at my guts as we walked down the hall. I'd be spending most of my waking hours at work, so I had to keep from raising suspicions. I only wish I had some idea of what I should already know. "Where exactly are we going?"

"To the most exciting place in the whole complex. But don't tell your roommate I said that," he said. "It would be the most sought-after assignment...except for the hours."

I wasn't going to admit I preferred the night shift. I figured that would put me on the weird radar for sure. "What makes it so exciting?"

He hesitated. "Forget I said that—they really don't like us to talk about the project. Once you've been there awhile, maybe you can tell me if you feel the same, okay?"

I followed Nathan back to the riser, and he surprised me by turning a key in the slot for the twenty-fourth floor. The door opened to a narrow walkway bordering a white, solid-metal exterior wall. Even without windows, skylights made the corridor almost as bright as outdoors. The green needles on the redwood's highest branches filled the atrium, leaving no space for rooms of any type.

When we'd gone a third of the way around, Nathan stopped, faced the exterior wall and swiped his pinky across a scanner. I didn't notice the door until it slid open. A warning light glowed red again as soon as Nathan stepped over the threshold into a room attached to the tower's exterior.

I swallowed hard. He must've read the uncertainty on my face.

"Go ahead. You won't set off any alarms—I entered your SecureID clearance this afternoon."

I'd been mulling over the password dilemma ever since my failed login attempt and Carl's success. If Nathan could access some sort of profile, that could only mean Fike had configured mine. I'd come up with only one likely password, and even that could be entered various ways.

The scanner blipped green as I flicked past, then red again. The room beyond the tower's shell was twice as deep as the corridor where we'd been walking. The see-through grid of white metal stretched in both directions, giving a dizzying view of city streets far below. The true exterior wall was a continuation of the glass dome that arched over the atrium, completing the feel of an observation deck. Workstations hugged the white wall in single file.

The lights of New Humboldt stretched around us. You could sell tickets for a view like this.

I tried to imagine where the Eve and Adam compounds were located, but didn't have a clue. An eight-lane highway packed with Shell cars circled below us. My eyes tracked what I figured was the Outer Loop to the right. I pointed to the one landmark I recognized, an area where lights seemed diffused and shimmery.

"Is that where the Falls are?"

"You have a good eye," Nathan said. "I can see why you were chosen for this project."

Behind us, a deep voice boomed, "So you must be Aaron?" A light-skinned man approached with his hand outstretched. I tried to match his firm grip like I figured any guy would.

"I'm Jed, research supervisor." He wore a forest-green jumpsuit, topped with a white lab coat.

He greeted Nathan and cocked his head. "You can imagine my surprise when I arrived and saw our request for an assistant was granted. That's a first."

Nathan shrugged. "Today's transfers were unexpected. All I can say is someone must believe Aaron has the right qualifications for your project."

Jed grimaced, and then told me, "So few of us can handle this shift. But if you can adjust, I promise you'll find it worthwhile. Just don't expect to get used to night work immediately—it takes a few weeks. We'll help you through the transition with shorter work hours and all that."

He patted me on the back and guided us toward his cluttered desk. It was good to feel welcomed, even if I doubted I had anything to offer. I figured the greatest difficulty would be to act sufficiently tired when, in fact, the night energized me.

"You can sit there," he pointed to a pristine desk behind where he sat. "The shift manager, Seldon, will meet you on your floor by the riser at sundown tomorrow. Shift hours are posted to your profile page. Why don't you check it now? Nathan, could I have a moment alone?"

"Of course." He took a seat by Jed's desk as I wandered over to mine.

The motion-activated computer switched on as I sat. An overwhelming array of icons filled the screen, bringing home just how limited our system at the Eve compound had been. This undoubtedly was Nadux-driven, and state-of-the-art like everything else I'd seen. At least the Home symbol was the same. I tapped it, and the security sequence initiated. I knew I had only a few seconds and no more than three attempts before they'd know I wasn't who I said.

My heart raced. Fike didn't know much about me, and my passcode would have to be information we both knew. When we'd seen Tibor being escorted out with the red scarf around his eyes, Fike said he'd already been assigned to a handler: 1A55. That must be Nathan. I hoped my best guess was good enough. I typed: Aaron1A55Rayson. An error message popped up, red and glaring. I gulped.

"So, are you missing files, too?" Nathan was heading my way, but maybe he couldn't see my screen.

I tried again: Aaron1A55

Again the security warning advised me I had entered the wrong code. I was out of ideas and out of chances. Except one—could it be that simple?

I typed in: Aaron.

Afraid to see that I'd locked it, I closed my eyes.

"Well, are you?"

I jumped at the sound of Nathan's voice right behind me. My eyes popped open. "Uh, no. Nothing important," I stuttered. What I wanted to do was shout with joy...I was in!

I quickly switched to the Profile page, hoping Nathan hadn't noticed I had a new message waiting.

Jed joined us. "Good. I see you found the schedule."

"I'm starting with a two-hour shift?"

Jed nodded. "It really is hard for the body to adjust. Be sure to get more sunlight than usual, too."

Noting my title of research assistant, I asked, "What do you study here?"

"Partly lunar astrophysics research, and partly biology." He pointed to a stylized icon of the full moon on the top bar. "That includes running tests within a simulated lunar environment—a vacuum chamber. You'll learn all about that soon."

I clicked the icon and pulled up a page filled with images taken in a white metal-and-glass lab and numerous graphs. My nerves zinged with anticipation. For years, I'd heard rumors of a low-orbit lunar satellite, but the Cain media said all off-world exploration and related research had halted when NASA was privatized in the mid-'20s. What if the work of the Lunar Science Institute had continued?

Even if it had, what would it matter? Dejection swept over me, totally quenching my initial excitement. I was here, cut off from everyone and everything I knew. A better understanding of electromagnetic radiation, or even how it related to energetic healing, would be of no importance without the guidance of the full-moon women.

Nathan yawned and stood. "I know you're eager to get started, Jed, and I'd love to hear what's happened since my last visit, but it's going to have to wait until tomorrow. Come on, kid, let's get some sleep."

"See you tomorrow," Jed said. "It's going to be a big day for us!"

I nodded and followed Nathan back out the way we came. From my quick glance around part of the deck, I estimated thirty desks. At the riser, I asked, "Why is security so high in this area?"

"We had some trouble a few years back and the Patron decided we needed to take some precautions," Nathan said. "Personally, I don't know why lunar research deserves more security than our solar projects, but no one asked me."

Mention of the Patron snagged my attention. It surprised me that Nathan would refer to anyone from the compound when they'd gone to such lengths to remove those ties from Carl's memory. If Fike had taken a special interest in the lunar research, perhaps he hadn't sent me here simply to hide from the Elder. My list of questions grew.

"How many people live in this tower?" I asked. The riser doors slid open on the thirteenth floor.

"And I thought you were the quiet one." He chuckled. "Last I heard, we had about a thousand residents. We have some turnover, but generally, once a Eurekan, always a Eurekan."

"You mean some people live their whole lives here and never leave?" I asked.

"I'd say most do," he said. "The exceptions are those like us, who transfer here to find a better life. You'll find we're a close-knit group, but we're only a fraction of the total population."

If they weren't all Adams, what were they? My stomach gave a queasy lurch, remembering my earlier encounters with the Cains.

When we reached the silver door, Nathan paused. He brushed his hand through his hair, and his face sagged wearily. "We'll wake you when we return from Carl's orientation, and I'll go over some of the things you'll need to know as a Eureka Towers resident."

"Sounds good." I wondered how often he introduced an Adam to his new life here. I watched him leave, surprised when he entered a room four doors down.

I turned and walked into darkness, except for ghostly figures writhing on the wall. The Nadux was on, but the only sound was Carl's heavy breathing on the couch. He slept with one hand over his eyes and the other still wearing a gaming glove. He looked innocent, not like someone who'd risked his life to save two newborns from the Con Squad. I hugged myself, remembering how Rayson felt in my arms and trying to make sense of how he'd come to be born in such circumstances. I hoped Fike was caring for both infants now that we were gone.

A glance at the balcony confirmed what I already sensed—it was too early for me to feed efficiently. And I probably wouldn't get a better chance to check my mail in private. I climbed into bed and waved my pinky for access.

I opened the Anonymous message, expecting some guidance from Fike. Instead, it said simply, "White is the color of the moon."

What? I banged my pillow in frustration. I could've used a little information instead of this cryptic message. I couldn't think of an appropriately snarky reply, so I let it go.

I needed to reach someone at the Eve compound, to find my way home. The only address I could conjure up was Piper's, but I got an immediate "undeliverable message" reply. Did the Eves have a firewall to block incoming messages or did I not have the whole address? I noticed the Anonymous message and one I sent from here had a "nadux.2" extension, whereas ours at the Eve compound had none at all.

When I left my bedroom, moonglow brightened the balcony, drawing me as surely as the sunlight had earlier called to Nathan and Carl. I stepped quickly across the room and opened the glass doors to the balcony. I wanted to shed my clothes so all my skin could bathe in the rays, but I didn't dare.

It was a clear night, and the moon felt almost as strong as it had at the full-moon peak. Joy filled me as I stood in the rays. I always had the sensation when I fed that my skin became plumper and even glowed, though I'd only noticed its darkened hue at this time of the month.

I checked the balconies, then watched Carl's chest rise and fall as he took a few deep breaths. He was still sound asleep. I rolled up the legs and sleeves of my jumpsuit to expose as much skin as possible. I lifted my face to the moon, closing my eyes in ecstasy as its energy filled every cell in my body. I let my mind wander and tried to push aside the nagging worries about what tomorrow would bring. It was like being on trial without knowing the charge. Anything I did or said could betray me.

A peculiar coolness drew my awareness back to the present. The air smelled like rain and my skin felt dewy. Suddenly certain I wasn't alone, I opened my eyes, but all I saw was swirling fog. I took two steps to the balcony railing and reached my hand into the gray mist. Instead, I hit an invisible bubble-like shield, which confined most of the moisture to the atrium. Huge droplets clung to each and every needle on the massive tree.

Now it was making more sense. Whoever designed this building must have devised the tree's artificial environment hundreds of years ago to simulate the more temperate and foggy coastal regions. Otherwise, the harsher Midwest climate, with its seasonal droughts and subzero winters, would have kept the redwood from thriving.

By the time the moon set, I felt completely refreshed. Morning was still hours away, and the atrium was in total darkness except for starlight. The fog had mostly cleared. I hadn't seen anyone and couldn't explain the feeling I'd had earlier of being watched until I turned to enter our room. That's when I spotted it—someone had tied a white scarf to the balcony of the room directly across from ours.

16

BLAIR

bigail kept chattering, which didn't surprise me. Every stylist I'd ever known was a talker. "When I first came here, I was plenty pissed, too. I'd gotten into trouble with the Con Squad because I've always looked young for my age. Part of that was due to my skill with hair and makeup, but the truth was no defense. Unless you led a really sheltered life, I guess you found that out at some point, too."

My heart ached. Until the Con Squad's raid, somehow Mom had managed to protect me from all this. Then our luck ran out.

"No one would confuse me for an immortal now," Abigail said. "Sooner or later, age catches up with you. But I've had forty good years here thanks to epic skin and a man much like Terence, who snatched me away from the Con Squad when I was thirty-nine."

I took a closer look at Abigail. She looked about the same age as my mom and Margie. "You're almost eighty?"

"I love when people do that," Abigail crowed. "As I said, I've got good genes. These days, that's a mixed blessing with all the lunatics running around with their panties in a wad about immortals and all. It's such a nuisance."

"So, you were here when Margie arrived?" I asked.

"Yes, then I was pretty much in charge of things in the women's quarters," Abigail said as we stopped outside a door with silk flowers arching over it. Laughter escaped the room and filled the hallway.

"We've been friends ever since. I've watched Terence grow up and know what he's made of. He's a bit self-absorbed, but no more than a lot of women and a lot less than most men. Margie managed to pass along some of her gentle spirit, as well as a good dose of common sense."

"Did you know his father, Raul?"

"I did," Abigail said. "Terence looks a lot like him—tall and handsome. Before Margie got here, Raul's father and I had a son together. He was killed by the Con Squad."

"Oh." I said. "I'm so sorry."

"I've always considered Terence the grandson I never had." Abigail motioned for me to enter. A subtle scent of cinnamon filled the air as the door slid open.

The laughter stopped as we stepped into the room. Women sat in the three stylists' chairs and a few others were seated along the wall. All eyes turned my way, and my face grew hot with embarrassment. Either they'd seen the terrorist alerts or the scene by the riser, or both.

"Come on, ladies," Abigail said jokingly. "It's not the first time young couples have bickered in our lobby. Give the new girl a break."

"Yeah, don't take that 'hormonal' crap from him or anyone else," said a gray-haired lady in a stylist's chair.

I gave her a tentative grin, surprised by her support.

"That's right," said a teenager in the chair to my right. "He just can't take what he dishes out. So typical!"

She looked so young, I couldn't help but wonder what someone her age could possibly know what was typical for men.

"Absolutely." Abigail patted the girl's shoulder. "Men are *clueless* when it comes to women. Terence isn't going to know what hit him when Blair gets through with him."

To my amazement, the women actually cheered. I smiled with relief, feeling a sense of belonging I never would've expected under the circumstances. I was, after all, being forcibly held in Eureka Towers, and was now in danger of being banished from it with a man I abhorred. But in this moment, I was happy to be accepted as one of their own. I had to wonder, if the women were this feisty, was it really the prison I'd thought it was? I almost wished I'd have more time to find out.

I followed Abigail through a multi-colored bead curtain that clattered as we passed through an arched doorway into a smaller, private area. Abigail motioned for me to sit in the empty stylist's chair across from a sink.

"Hmmm." She pulled up my long blonde hair to make it look short, then parted it to one side. "Maybe we should start with the eyes, then do the hair." She opened a drawer filled with contact lenses.

My eyes popped wide open at the variety: jade, violet, baby blue, amethyst, gray, honey, sapphire, turquoise, hazel, brown, green, summer, winter, fall, spring. I pointed at a box. "Jaguar?"

Abigail smirked and raised her eyebrows. "Sometimes I feel catty."

I groaned.

"We could have so much fun." She sighed. "Another time. Now we need to concentrate on making you blend in. We have to find a combination of hair and eye color that makes you fade from memory —not an easy task for such a pretty girl."

I felt myself blushing. I didn't really think of myself as pretty, and I certainly wasn't used to having anyone but Mom say it to me.

Abigail pulled out a couple of boxes and handed them to me. "Have you ever worn contacts?"

"Sure, for Halloween and Zombie Runs."

"Good." Abigail walked over to a cabinet. "Take one from each packet so we can compare the colors. They're self-lubricating."

I put a hazel lens in my right eye and was placing a brown one in my left eye when Abigail returned with hair extensions. She held up a light brown switch and another slightly darker one next to my face.

"What I've found when it comes to disguises is, less is better." Abigail put the light brown hair beside the hazel contacts. "Most people would expect a blonde to try to disguise her hair by making it as dark as possible. Instead, we'll go mousey. We'll leave a few highlights so the roots won't be as obvious when the color grows out."

Abigail ordered the dye from a wall dispenser and began applying it on my hair in thick smears, using foil to separate the "low-lights" from the lighter brown. Other strands were covered to retain their natural color. "A brief run through the tanning booth will dull your pale skin. Now we only have to decide whether to keep your hair long and straight or make it short and curly."

"Mom wears hers short and curly." I looked in the mirror, trying to imagine her hair superimposed over my face. "People say we look alike. It might actually make me easier to catch if they've seen pictures of her."

"Well, that settles that," Abigail said. "Can't have you looking like your mom, can we?"

A shiver raced up my spine at the thought of looking in the mirror and seeing my mom's image instead of my own. On so many levels, I didn't think I could take it.

After my hair was a solid mass of dark brown goop, Abigail pointed to the other room. "Out you go. Come back in fifteen minutes."

"You want me to go out there like this?"

Abigail made swooshing motions. "Go. I've got to check with Margie about your clothes." She left through a door I hadn't noticed.

I wove back through the bead curtain into the outer room, which now was less crowded. No one else's hair was filled with goop, but they seemed preoccupied with other things. I spotted a couple of empty seats facing Abigail's room. Before I reached them, however, the teenage girl who'd spoken to me when I arrived motioned to a seat beside her on a tan loveseat. Her brown hair was streaked with red and blue.

"I've been waiting for you," she said.

"Nice hair," I said.

The girl's mouth twitched. "You, too." We both giggled, then the girl's face grew serious. "You're my ticket out of this place."

I scooted as far away as I could on the loveseat. "How do you figure that?"

"They won't be looking for three people, so it would help keep you safe."

I shrugged. It wasn't so different from my thought about traveling alone, but with the girl along, there would be more ties to this place. I didn't want that. "It would put you in danger. Besides, your mother would never agree."

"Please, you don't know what it's like," she said. "I've lived my whole life inside these walls, and most women never leave. I want my freedom."

"This isn't the way to do it. Do you have any idea what will happen if the Con Squad catches us?" I said. "They've branded us as terrorists, not just mutants. It doesn't get much worse than that."

"I'll take my chances," she said.

I bit my lip, trying to figure out how to discourage her and avoid this complication. But I knew exactly how the girl felt; how could I deny someone else freedom if I had the power to help?

"To go outside, I have to have a reason—something that will help the Towers," the girl said. "Together we could convince them."

"I don't know," I said. "I'm not really in a position to help myself, so I doubt anyone would listen to what I have to say."

The girl looked down at her lap, where her folded hands twisted the bottom of her tunic. A single tear splashed on her leg. "Look, there's an old guy here who won't leave me alone."

I straightened, feeling suddenly protective of her. "What do you mean?"

"He's always watching me, wherever I go," she said. "It scares me."

"He hasn't tried to touch you?" I asked.

The girl fidgeted and looked away. "He almost trapped me in the room next to the riser the day you arrived. If Terence hadn't called for assistance, I don't know what would've happened."

My stomach wrenched to think of that old man stalking the young girl. Why hadn't someone protected her from him?

She continued, "I'm going to be old enough to be mated soon, and I know he's going to want to be the first. I can't bear that."

"Have you told your mom how you feel?" I asked.

"There's not much she can do," the girl said. "I can refuse him a few times. But if someone else doesn't choose me, sooner or later, I'll have to accept."

"Okay, okay. We can try, but no promises," I said.

"Thank you!" The teen grabbed my hands and jumped up from the couch. "You won't regret this. I'll get my bag and be back before Abigail finishes your hair."

"Wait," I called out. "What's your name?"

"Jane."

"How can I find some of the women who've come from outside like me?" I asked.

"Ask her." Jane pointed to a dark-haired woman sitting in the center stylist's chair. I wondered how long she'd been watching us. It gave me the creeps.

"I didn't mean to eavesdrop, but I couldn't find a good time to interrupt," the woman said. "I'm Piper."

"I'm Blair." I swallowed hard, remembering the name.

"I arrived a few days ago, but thankfully under far less dramatic circumstances," she said. "Anyway, you won't see me on the Nadux."

I couldn't believe my luck. "You stayed with Margie?"

"I did," she said. "I wondered if you'd noticed it."

"You left the note?"

Piper shook her head. "No, but I know what it means."

I cocked my head and waited, both disappointed that Piper wasn't the one who wrote the message and intrigued that she'd unraveled the puzzle.

The woman checked the room, and I followed her gaze. The stylists gathered around a vending machine in the far corner with drinks in hand, chatting. No other customers remained. The beads spanning the doorway to Abigail's room shook as someone entered through the other door.

"Looks like Abigail is back," I said.

"I won't be far from where you are, so find a way to slip away and we'll talk," Piper said.

None of the other women were paying any attention to us, which made me wonder why Piper was being so secretive. Still, I did want to find out more about the note.

"Please, it's important," Piper said earnestly. "Especially since you're going back out into the Cain city."

I'd heard New Humboldt called many things, but never by that name.

"Blair, let's get to it." Abigail stood in the doorway with the beaded ropes hanging around her, motioning for me to come.

I stood and gave Piper a nod. "I'll try."

It took more than an hour to finish the process, then Jane accompanied me to a tanning booth. I dialed in the settings Abigail gave me. Thirty seconds later, I walked out a few shades darker.

I froze when I caught sight of my reflection in a window. I didn't exactly look bad, but not good either. My shoulder-length hair was gone, replaced by a style popular decades ago. Long, straight bangs blended into a curving, chin-length sweep of hair; the back was stacked in short, thick layers. With tortoise-shell-rimmed glasses over hazel eyes, I looked nerdy—perfecting the older persona I was trying to project.

"Well, did we do it or what!" Abigail said when I returned to the salon.

"What, make me a mouse? Yep, we did it." I grinned at Abigail's enthusiasm. "Can't say I like it much, though."

"Well, no, it's not a good look for you at all," Abigail agreed, "but it's a great disguise."

With another glance in the mirror, I had to agree. I didn't think my own mother could pick me out in a crowd.

17

ARI

Carl stirred on the couch. As he repositioned, the game glove activated the Nadux world's ghostly images. An ancient battlefield filled the wall, complete with screaming horses and armored warriors clanging swords. I paused in admiration, and flinched as a shining blade thrust my way. They'd spared no expense to achieve realism.

Carl jumped to his feet. "What the...!" He fumbled, trying a few sweeping motions before finding the right commands to silence the blaring hologram.

I laughed, which earned me a glare as he dashed into the Nadux Room. The images disappeared, but his frown was still in place when he emerged. "Why did you leave it on all night?"

"What? And miss another chance to see a master at play?" I taunted. "Besides, Nathan said we have an unlimited account."

He snorted.

I shrugged. "Anyway, I'm not the one who fell asleep in the middle of a game."

He gave me a sheepish grin, then looked down at the floor as if wanting to disappear. Eating crow was the least he could do after trying to blame me for the Nadux remaining on.

"Well, yeah. I was beat. I never even got up after you left with Nathan yesterday afternoon," he said. "How did it go?"

I wished I could share how excited I was about the project, but all I said was, "They're doing lunar astrophysics research. Can you believe it?"

"Yuck," he said. "Maybe Nathan can get you out of it."

"No!" I said, a little too forcefully.

Carl tilted his head and shrugged. "But night shift sucks."

"Yeah, it does." What else could I say to that without sounding crazy? "But when we learned in history class about the Lunar Science Institute and other NASA programs, they seemed to have such promise. And nothing's really happened since then."

"Exactly," he agreed, "because no one wants to stay up all night. Well, if things don't work out, maybe you can join me doing solar research."

I raised my eyebrows at him.

"I'll be working in the solar lab while I take a few more courses to complete my degree," he said.

"How do you know that? All you've done since we got here is sleep."

"Not true." He pointed to his bedroom. "I checked my profile. Guess I'll find out more soon."

As if on cue, Nathan beeped and entered. I wished he'd been a couple of minutes tardy. I still wanted to ask Carl about his missing files, hoping it would give me some idea of the type of information I should remember.

"Good morning," he said. "Ready to get started?"

"Sure," Carl said.

"We probably won't be long, Aaron, then I'll show you both more of the Eureka Towers' history," Nathan said.

I yawned. As soon as they left, I dragged into my room and climbed into bed. It seemed like I'd barely closed my eyes when Carl jabbed me in the ribs.

"Stop that!" I snarled. I didn't know how long I'd slept, but it wasn't anywhere near long enough. I punched my pillow, taking out my frustration for Carl waking me.

"And you talk about me sleeping," he said. "C'mon. Nathan can't waste all day while you snooze."

I stretched, swung my legs over the railing and jumped down. Already I could see it wasn't going to be easy to live around people who spent most of the day awake. I didn't require much sleep—

usually five or six hours—but I would've been in real trouble if Fike hadn't given me a reason to be on a different schedule.

"We need to get moving," Nathan said, "but I'm glad to see you're getting some rest before tonight. That's very smart."

"Uh, thanks," I said groggily. "Carl said you've been waiting. Sorry about that."

"No problem," he said. "Our time together will be more limited after your first week here, so I want to answer as many of your questions as I can."

"And after that?" I asked.

"You probably won't reach me, but others will help. I only got involved in your briefing because I'm between jobs." He paused and looked at me. "You'll find out soon enough. I was involved in the lunar research project until a couple of weeks ago."

"What happened?" Carl asked.

"Couldn't handle the hours," he said. "It was affecting my health. And my family."

I sucked in my breath. "Your family?"

"My mate and I have three children," he said. "Two boys and a girl."

My thoughts were coming so fast I could barely focus on any of them. An Adam had a daughter? Did that make them Cains? I wanted to ask him all of these things, but I looked to Carl for some clue to what Nathan would expect from us. Carl fidgeted with a handheld, totally unaffected by the news of Nathan's family.

When I couldn't stand it any longer, I worked on phrasing my question as innocently as possible. "How will we go about finding our mates?"

Both frowned, but Nathan recovered first. "Ah, sometimes the orientation doesn't work as well as it should, which seems to be the case for you, Aaron. If it continues to be a problem, I can get you another session. But the simple answer is our mates are residents of Eureka Towers who came from the Cain city."

"New Humboldt?" I asked.

"Generally, or sometimes from a nearby town. But they're permanent tower residents."

"And your children?" I asked.

"When they're grown, some of the children take responsible positions that require them to make brief trips. Otherwise, only suneaters like us leave Eureka Towers, but few of us do so except on assignment. It's just not safe."

"So the couples we saw yesterday on the wooden walkways on the top floors—they were suneaters and Cain women?" I asked.

"Yes," he said. "That's part of the courting ritual. The Cain women accompany us as we feed, and we do the same."

Nausea swept over me as I remembered the Cains' stench. "You're there while they consume flesh?"

From the corner of my eye, I saw Carl's shocked expression.

"It's not as bad as you think," Nathan said, adding slowly, "after the first time."

I had wondered why the building was designed to provide Cain food, and now I knew. I'd be living with Cains. A horrifying thought crossed my mind—would I be working with them, too? And mating? My thoughts couldn't go there without making me retch. Surely that was far in the future.

"Since you're obviously interested, why don't we start today with the mating protocol? Tomorrow I'll go over the usual second-day orientation about your community service obligations."

I swallowed hard and took a couple of deep breaths. I wanted to know how their mating system worked, but I didn't. I'd seen vids of animals mating, but I couldn't imagine doing anything like that myself. Not that it was an issue, anyway. It's not like I could procreate with another female in the usual way. I almost giggled.

Nathan gave me a puzzled look. "So, the process of finding a mate starts here." He walked into the Nadux Room. Suddenly, the living room was filled with women. Carl and I jumped back from the holographic images. They looked as real to me as Carl did, and from his wide-eyed, open-mouthed expression, I figured the same was true for him.

Nathan chuckled. "I couldn't resist it. I figured you were still getting used to our improved Nadux system. It's like they're really here." He swept his arm around the room. "They're all lovely in their own way, as you'll come to appreciate. You don't have to stay with one —in fact, you're encouraged to meet several before deciding which to mate. We find it makes for more harmonious pairings."

The women were of all shapes, sizes and skin colors, but all were young. I didn't see any old enough to be full-moon women, except, I reminded myself, these were Cain women and not Eves. I couldn't shake the feeling that something was wrong with this. Instead of names, each had a designated number.

It didn't take Carl long to make his first choice—a tall, blonde beauty with slanted black eyes. The contrast of her features was striking and bold. I felt somewhat slighted that she didn't look more like me. The thought caused a wave of confusion—why should I care what Carl thought about me?

"I like her." I pointed to a dark-haired girl who looked a great deal like me.

Nathan punched their numbers into his handheld.

Right after I spoke, I noticed the girl next to her wore a white scarf around her neck. It looked like the one Fike had given me—like the one I'd seen draped over the balcony. She was also dark-haired, but her skin was lighter than mine.

"Wait," I said. "I think I'd rather..."

"Too late," Nathan interrupted. "They've already been notified. You'll have to go through the initial meeting before you can choose another."

I made a mental note of the other girl's number.

"I'll set up your first meeting for tomorrow." He gave me a pointed look. "In case you don't recall, this is a three-step process. First you determine your compatibility. In fairness to the one chosen, you offer them at least a week of your time. Then you either move on to courting or select another."

"And if we move on?" I asked.

"You get private time," Nathan said. "Eventually you're given access to the walkways on the top floors. We call them Lovers' Lanes. It's really a special week," he said wistfully. "If the chemistry is good, you may wish to proceed toward having a natural pregnancy."

"Ah," I stuttered, looking at Carl, who merely nodded.

"Or, of course, you can opt to artificially induce, if you find her repellant," Nathan said. "It doesn't happen often, but occasionally that's preferred."

A chill raised the hairs along my neck. "What if she doesn't want to get pregnant?" I blurted.

"Doesn't want to...?" Nathan shook his head. "Where do you get such ideas? It's not like we can bear children without them, you know." He laughed at his own joke, and Carl joined in. "That's what women are for, to have children."

I bit my top lip to keep from yelling. I'd grown to like Nathan in the brief time I'd known him, but now I realized I didn't really know much about him. Did he think women were simply brood mares? That couldn't be right. I tried another approach. "So, these are women who've volunteered to have children?"

Nathan sighed. "Really, Aaron, I think we're going to have to schedule that orientation reboot sooner rather than later."

He pointed to the couch, and I sat. The women's holograms towered over us.

"Eureka Towers offers them a much better life," he said. "Look at them, how lovely they are. Women are too weak to survive on their own and raise the children."

How dare he say such things? I knew women were strong enough to survive for centuries without men; our children thrived. But if I shouted out what was on my mind, it wouldn't take him long to figure out my secret. Then I would be just like the other women to him— except even worse, since I wasn't even suitable for breeding.

"It's a much harder life for them on the outside," he continued. "When they get pregnant, Cain men abandon them. Only one in three of Cain children survive the first year, but here, most live full lives. Our population remains stable because we all do our part."

No matter how he tried to dress it up, the facts didn't change: women here were viewed as little more than sex slaves. If I had any doubts, they were silenced when I went to my computer after Nathan left and opened a numbered file for the woman I selected. She wore a thin blue gown in the first shots; the next photos left nothing to the imagination. She was a beautiful girl, barely of child-bearing age.

I closed the file, and wondered what Carl thought about the photos of the woman he selected. I brushed my hand along my flattened breasts and felt a pang of envy for the curves I knew she must have. I would look like a child compared to her. Then I got angry with myself. This wasn't what I wanted. It wasn't what any woman wanted.

I knew I didn't understand the Adams who remained at the compound, but how had this happened? How had things gotten so out of balance at Eureka Towers?

18

BLAIR

When Abigail, Jane and I walked back into the main lobby, Margie waited alone at a table near the vending machines "It's about time." Margie talked louder than usual to be heard over a noisy crowd a few tables over.

Abigail looked at the wall clock above the riser. "Less than two hours for this?" She gestured toward me, her hand sweeping from head to foot.

Margie did a double-take. "I didn't even realize it was her. That's amazing, Abby."

"That's more like it," Abigail said. "Now, hon, what's got you all excited?"

"Two of our girls have been chosen," Margie said.

Abigail's eyebrows arched. "Two?

"I know–it's been months since we've had one," Margie said. "But yes, Natisha and that other girl." She motioned with her head.

"What do you mean 'chosen?'" I asked.

"It's part of our mating ritual—how potential partners meet," Margie's tone was almost hushed, as if she didn't want the others to hear.

"Like an online dating service?" I said.

The two women exchanged a look, then Abigail snorted. "More like the lottery—or pimp-o-rama."

The bite in Abigail's voice surprised me, although I found Abigail's description of the process amusing. Maybe everyone wasn't as accepting of their situation as they seemed.

Margie scowled, but before she could reply, a tall blonde woman screeched, "Oh, he's cute enough to be a girl!" She grabbed a handheld from a dark-haired girl with large brown eyes. "What's his name?"

"Aaron." The young woman grimaced and snatched her handheld back.

"You know, you two could be siblings," the blonde said before turning to the other "chosen" girl and grabbing her handheld. She held it up for all to see. "But this one's *really* something. Good going, Natisha." I caught a glimpse of the screen–blond hair, sun-bronzed muscles, and a ruggedly handsome face–a pale version of Terence.

"I know," Natisha said. Her flashing black eyes had an Asian tilt. I wondered at her exotic genes—or maybe a good stylist just lightened her hair?

The blonde laughed and linked arms with Natisha, the proximity accentuating their similar height and coloring. "Carl and I are meeting this afternoon," Natisha said as they wandered off. "You've got to help me find something to wear."

About half the women followed them, and the others remained with the young woman Aaron chose. "I don't get to meet him until tomorrow. He's working tonight." She turned questioning eyes at Margie, who'd walked closer to her.

"Don't worry. He must have special skills to work at night. I'm sure he'll tell you more," Margie said. "He's a handsome young man."

When I looked at the handheld, Aaron's piercing blue eyes took my breath away. I knew those eyes. I'd seen them as the green Shell car sped away—the haunting eyes of the woman whose dead friend had been on the gurney. But that didn't make any sense.

"Well, you'll certainly want to look your best, too," Margie told the young woman. "Any ideas, Abigail?"

"Always," she replied. "It will be fun. But first, we've got to see to these two." She pointed a finger at me and her thumb toward someone behind me.

Jane, who'd been watching the other women with a bored look on her face, spun around and exclaimed, "Look at that!"

Sure enough, when I looked, I sucked in my breath. Terence had a bald pate, and tattoos snaked up his bare arms. The jumpsuit was gone, replaced by tight jeans and a black, short-sleeved tee that hugged his muscular torso. A thin band of silver pierced his lower lip and he wore mirrored shades. He looked...dangerous. He looked...right past me like I wasn't there. My heart sank when I remembered what I looked like. If only Abigail had chosen some look for me other than mousey, but it was too late now.

Margie led the way toward the riser lobby where he waited, with me bringing up the rear. I kept telling myself this disguise gave me the best chance for freedom, but right now all I could think of was I really didn't want him to see me like this. I didn't know why it mattered so much—it just did.

The moment he recognized me, Terence's eyes widened. He gave me a big smile.

"Great disguise." Then he turned to Margie. "No offense to you, Mom, but she could almost pass as my mother."

The words pierced my heart, but my snark was on automatic. "Thanks ever so much. Being bald is a great improvement for you, too."

He smirked.

"I could be your kid," Jane added, looking innocently at Terence and me. Our mouths fell open in shock.

Margie and Abigail doubled-over with laughter. When they looked up, tears marked their red faces.

"What? This isn't funny," I said. But when I looked at Terence and Jane together, I could see how they could pass for father and daughter. Did I really look that old? "This is a disaster."

"No, honey." Abigail gasped for a breath between cackles. "It's perfect. The Con Squad will be looking for two lovely twenty-somethings, not some teen's hum-drum and badass-wanna-be parents."

Well, I knew which I was. Grudgingly, I conceded the logic. Aging a decade in a day wasn't my idea of a good time, but if being "hum-drum" kept me safe and regained my freedom, who was I to complain? "All right, then, I'm in. What happens now?"

"Wait just a minute," Terence protested. "I didn't sign on to babysit a girl and a granny."

Margie gave him a stern look and put her finger on his chest. "Watch what you say, son. These are two intelligent women. Our way of life is in jeopardy. You'd do well to follow Blair's example and make peace with this awkward situation."

He sucked in a long breath, frowning all the while at me. "Fine. I've arranged for transportation after it gets dark tonight so we can avoid some of the surveillance cameras. I'll be back for you–both–after dinner."

Jane jumped in place and clapped her hands. "Yes! I'll be ready. You'll see...you won't regret this."

I shook my head and wondered if I'd ever been that giddy. This trip was going to be a stretch, even if the Con Squad never got on our trail.

Margie wiped the tears from her eyes with her shirtsleeve and turned toward me. "I'm going back to the room. Want to come?"

"I'll be along later," I said. "I need some time to think."

Margie smiled and shrugged. "I'll leave the door unlocked so you can get in. You may want some downtime before you leave. I'm sure whatever Terence has worked out will have some element of drama. He is a man, after all. But I think you've noticed that."

That was enough to set her and Abigail off again. They laughed hysterically as they walked down the hall. I only caught bits of their conversation, but it was enough to know I didn't want to hear more. "So glad I could amuse you," I mumbled.

I spotted Piper waiting at one of the tables near the vending machines with two steaming cups of tea. As I approached, she motioned to an empty chair.

"Thought you could use some calming herbal tea," Piper said. "I know my blood pressure would be spiking about now. What a mess!"

"Exactly!" I said. "I'm so glad someone understands."

Piper examined me closely. "I must say, though, it *is* a brilliant disguise. Abigail knows her stuff, but then she's been at this for a long time. Has she told you how old she is?"

"I couldn't believe it," I said. "She doesn't look any older than Margie."

"Well, don't let her fool you," Piper said. "There's an explanation for it, and that's one reason I wanted us to talk. First, though, I have to know what you want to get out of all of this."

I hesitated only a moment, then decided to take my chances with her, the other new girl. I gestured at the room in a sweeping motion.

"I want to escape this place. I don't want to be a sex slave, or any kind of slave at all."

"Then what?" Piper tilted her head, waiting for an answer. "Where will you go? How will you earn a living? Surely you don't think the Con Squad will simply forget about you."

I gave a frustrated huff. "I haven't thought it through. But what about you? You're in same predicament. Are you going to stay here and be used by those men?"

"No, and I'm not defending the system. But I can tell you're reacting without all the facts," Piper said. "True, I only know what Margie and some of the others have said, and what I've observed in the short time since I arrived. While the women's main purpose here at the Towers is to have children, they have a lot of leeway in selecting their mates. If all else fails, they can deny physical intimacy and opt for artificial insemination."

"They should have control of their own bodies," I said. "Whether to bear a child is a woman's decision, not a man's or society's."

Piper pressed her lips thin. "I agree, but what's at stake now is even more threatening, and could make all the women here into sex slaves in the true sense of the word. They'd have no choice at all."

I gasped. "What do you mean?"

"That's what the message was about," Piper said. "'White is the color of the moon' is a rally cry for women to unite against this threat. And we need your help."

"I don't even know what you're talking about, so how could I be of help," I said.

"Come with me." Piper rose.

I took a last sip of tea and followed her to the riser. Piper held a grey plastic object that looked like a flashlight in front of the sensor. The riser doors opened.

"How did you do that? I thought women couldn't get off this floor without a male escort."

Piper selected the thirteenth floor. "Abigail gave it to me. It's some sort of scrambler that jams the signal." When the riser doors opened, we walked through a lounge area filled with men in jumpsuits. This was a men's floor! The tree's reddish bark glowed in the center atrium's noonday sun, reflecting its light around them.

Piper didn't pause, and I followed close behind her. Some men seemed curious, but no one tried to stop us. About halfway down the hall, Piper stopped in front a door and knocked. "It's Piper."

"Come in," said Abigail's husky voice.

A man stood in the middle of the room dressed in a forest-green jumpsuit. His back was toward us, and a red wig lay on the tea table. When he turned around, an inch-long buzz cut and no make-up made Abigail's features look stern and masculine.

"Glad you could join us, honey," he said with Abigail's voice.

19

ARI

I left my room in a hurry, without any idea of where to go. I just wanted to escape the thoughts flooding my mind. I wondered what Carl would think or if he'd even notice I was gone. It didn't matter—let him think what he would, I had to have some time alone.

I fled into the hallway, rushing past the seascape that filled the wall, and headed to the riser. I got off on the ninth floor and went straight to the railing.

Midmorning sunlight bathed the area. My skin tingled uncomfortably, but I stayed there and breathed in the redwood's earthy, evergreen scent. It felt more open here than on our balcony. More free.

Thoughts strayed into my awareness despite my desire to shut them out. Although I had only spent a day with Tibor before his change to Carl, he was much different now than the man who saved the twins from the Cains and hid me from the Elder. Like the other Adams in Eureka Towers, he had been brainwashed not only to forget the compound where he'd been raised, but to accept this lifestyle. Nathan's comments about my failed orientation made it clear that anyone who questioned the status quo was cured with another dose of indoctrination. Their worldview was reinforced whenever it wavered.

I finally calmed down enough to listen to my body's clamoring.

The nausea and weakness lessened as soon as I moved away from the railing and out of the sunlight, a sensation I'd noticed before. I became aware of the sounds and movement around me; no one paid me any attention. Men of all ages sat at the tables and lounged on couches. I stifled a snicker when I realized they all wore jumpsuits—different styles and colors, but a uniform look nonetheless. As Nathan said, an upgrade for the Tailor was long overdue.

I spotted an empty table in the shadows and took a seat. My thoughts rolled over the situation once more, trying to puzzle out why they would establish a caste system that subjugated women in this way. Obviously, anger toward Eves for aborting most male fetuses played a part. I didn't think that explained it, though. After all, the women here were Cains, not Eves. It seemed more convenient than punitive.

I wanted to talk with Fike, to discover what had inspired the founders. What did the Adams want to accomplish at Eureka Towers that they couldn't do at the compound? Of course, like any system, it would change over time and might bear little resemblance to what had been planned. You saw that all the time in the history of revolutions, where the revolutionaries became just like the dictators they overthrew.

In school, I'd been taught patriarchal systems overthrew matriarchal ones due to the shift from hunter/gatherer to agrarian culture. As warrior and priest castes rose in prominence, Cain women became relegated to more menial roles.

Had the founders of Eureka Towers viewed subjugating women as some sort of agrarian version of human reproduction? Perhaps they had looked for models and decided harems provided a more efficient method for producing children than the matriarchal hunter/gatherer model, which left females with some control. Cain history had its share of cultures built on slavery, but I wasn't aware of any in which the main intent was procreation. Usually slavery evolved around a need for cheap labor to produce crops such as cotton or sugar cane.

The question was what the founders had intended. The Adams' prohibition against women at their compound seemed to originate from the same belief system that spurred the creation of this separate community. I just couldn't imagine what it was all about.

After a few minutes, my heart had slowed to a normal pace, and I felt less angry and claustrophobic. I only had a few hours until sundown, when I'd begin my new job. I needed to do better at fitting in than I'd done this morning or I'd find myself next in line for an orientation reboot.

I had no idea if the memory serum, brain scan, or whatever they used would even work on my body chemistry. Certainly, Eves had similarities to Adams since they were our sons, but their genetic code was foreign enough our bodies vehemently rejected it. The more I thought about, the more convinced I became that orientation would kill me.

Now that I'd faced the dilemma, the path became clearer—no matter what my personal beliefs, I needed to act like the caste system here at the Towers was okay. Bile rose in my throat at the thought.

The sun had inched its way across the table and was already sapping my energy before it touched my body. It was time for me to return to our room and see if I could smooth any ruffled feathers from my disappearance. With any luck, Carl would be gone or asleep.

As I walked toward the riser, I wondered how I could find the woman with the white scarf. Maybe the one I chose could help me find her, though asking about another woman seemed crass and likely to result in hurt feelings. But I didn't want to wait a week, either. Maybe I'd figure out something before we met tomorrow morning.

I was almost envious of Carl for his meeting tonight, but I was also excited about returning to the lab. I hoped Nathan was right about my SecureID working, although Jed said someone would be there tonight to meet me by the riser.

As I neared our place, weariness swept over me, replacing the anger. This morning's nap couldn't make up for all the sleep I'd lost over the past few days, plus the constant drain of sunlight was taking its toll. Inside, Carl's bedroom door was open. I called out, "I'm back." When I got no answer, I checked the rooms and the balcony. He had gone out, too. Relieved to not have to explain my behavior, I shut the door to my bedroom and set the alarm.

It rang at 5:30 p.m. Still half asleep, I stretched and hit my hands on the ceiling. I heard the Nadux in the living room and waved to Carl on my way to the refresher. I came out wearing a new forest-green jumpsuit, identical to the one I wore the day before. It seemed senseless to waste time fiddling with details when the end result would be another jumpsuit.

I grabbed an orange drink from the dispenser and sat next to Carl on the couch. I knew something was up when I saw he wore khakis and a T-shirt instead of a jumpsuit. "How'd your day go?"

"Good." He grinned. "Very good. I spent some time with Natisha."

"But your first meeting was supposed to be tonight." I almost whined.

"I couldn't wait, so I sent a message to see if she'd be able to meet me earlier," he said.

He couldn't wait? Something weighed like lead on my gut, but still I was curious. "What did you do?"

"Nathan gave me access to the nineteenth floor," Carl said. "It has separate areas like living rooms where you can have some privacy, and Nadux access if you want to play games or watch something. She was amazed at our selection—they don't have the same access in the women's quarters."

"What's she like?" I asked.

"Nice," Carl said. "She didn't say a lot, just seemed more interested in me and what I'm doing. The time went by so quickly."

While I'd been sleeping, he'd been meeting a woman who may be his future mate. Something about that didn't set well with me. Not at all. I shook it off and stood. "I wish I'd known we could move things up—I would've done that, too."

"I tried to find you," Carl said. "I had the afternoon off since my real shift doesn't begin until tomorrow."

"Yeah, I was feeling a little claustrophobic and had to get out for a while," I said.

"Same here," he replied. "At least you got some sleep. I don't know how you're going to survive this night shift."

I shrugged. "I guess we'll see."

"Here, Nathan left this passcode for you." Carl messaged my handheld. "It gives you access to the nineteenth floor. He didn't want to wake you or to send it without some explanation, so he asked me to tell you."

"How did you know which room to use?" I still couldn't figure out exactly what I was supposed to do on this meet-up, and didn't want to make any mistakes if it was something I "should" know.

"There's a light next to the reader where you enter the passcode. If it's red, it's occupied," he said.

"Thanks," I said. "Where did you get the clothes? I'd rather not look like this on our first meeting."

Carl snorted. "Don't I know! Once a week, you can place a special order on the Tailor. I got my things in about an hour. Natisha said the women make the clothes and keep various sizes in stock. She selected this for me after my order came in."

Before I left, I took a quick look at the Tailor. I hadn't noticed the button on the lower left. "Special Order" was all it said, so what I got would be a surprise. I pressed it, grateful that whatever they sent, at least it wouldn't be another jumpsuit.

I arrived at the riser a little before six. I stepped in, then realized without a key to the twenty-fourth floor, it didn't matter if my SecureID worked. I couldn't access the right floor to use it. I stepped back into the lobby and waited. Time seemed to pass slowly, giving me too much time to think.

Despite the threats of an orientation reboot and my upcoming meeting with a potential mate, I was most anxious about Carl not "seeing" me when we were together. It made no sense, but I longed for his approval and friendship. I'd never felt that way about any of the women in our compound, although I'd been quite fond of many of them. I even missed Piper. When I felt homesick, it was usually for our bickering camaraderie.

I told myself I should stop thinking about Carl, but then I recalled the way he looked when I woke him, with a tawny, tousled mane and sleepy eyes. Something inside me softened. I caressed my hand, remembering the shock of our touch.

I hadn't understood so many things in the past few days. While I appreciated the Matron's caution, I still didn't agree with her isolationist tactics. We were like an ostriches hiding our heads in the sand. Perhaps the full-moon women who worked in cities were doing something to keep us safe. I couldn't see how else our archaic compounds could've survived this long.

I thought I heard someone approaching from the hallway that ran parallel to ours, but then the footsteps stopped. That would be where the rooms facing ours were. The person who put the scarf on the balcony lived in one of those rooms.

I turned around and saw three people standing there, but my eyes were riveted on one.

20

BLAIR

I walked toward Abigail, trying to figure how I'd missed the signs of his masculinity. Sure, Abigail had a husky voice and a strong grip, but a lot of women did. "I don't get it. Are you a man or a woman?"

Piper closed the door behind us and ushered me over to the couch.

"Sorry to spring this on you, but it's the old 'picture is worth a thousand words' thing." He paced in front of the sofa. "We don't have time for small talk, so I'll give you the short version. I'm what you call a suneater, sent here by the Patron to help safeguard the women in Eureka Towers."

"So, you didn't have to escape the Con Squad because they thought you were immortal?" I said, recalling our earlier conversation.

"No, that's just my cover story as Abigail. It's what everyone believes happened because I look so young for my age," he said.

"He doesn't age as rapidly because he's a suneater," Piper explained. "That makes him immortal."

"Oh," I mumbled.

"My task began almost forty years ago—that part was true, " he said, "but it was all to prepare for what is happening now."

"Wait, wait," I said. "You're going too fast. You're a suneater? That's just...not possible."

"Get over it, honey," he said gently, using Abigail's voice. "I'll prove it to you sometime, but for now, you just have to keep an open mind. Some of this could be even harder to accept than me being a man or a suneater."

Piper coughed to conceal a chuckle. I didn't think it was funny. I reeled as my perceptions adjusted. Humankind apparently was far more diverse than superficial differences like skin or eye color, gender, or race. But a suneater? It was going to take some time to really grasp that. "You could start by telling me your real name, and what the heck is the Patron?"

"I'm Seldon, and the Patron is the leader of the suneaters—we call ourselves the Sons of Adam," he said.

"As in Adam and Eve?" I asked.

"That's a good guess." Seldon tilted his head in acknowledgement. "We built Eureka Towers more than a century ago, mainly to give Adams the chance to have sons. You see, we wanted to increase the chances of our genes surviving into the next generation so we're not totally overrun by the Cains—the food eaters."

"Okay," I said, "you mean I'm a Cain since I eat food, not because an ancestor murdered his brother?"

"Well, yes," Seldon conceded. "Although, as you know, there's no love lost between Cains and Adams."

My thoughts jumped back to the Con Squad and their ceaseless search for mutants.

"Technically Cains don't have any direct genetic link to suneaters," Seldon continued.

"So, Terence is not a Cain since his father was an Adam?" I said.

"That's right. Our mortal sons are hybrids who can survive, but not thrive, off sunlight. Our daughters are even less adaptive and must have food to survive," Seldon said. "The good news is that both our sons and daughters enjoy longer lives than true Cains."

"True Cains?"

"Suneaters' daughters can bear sons and daughters, but all their children—male and female–require food to survive. Those are the true Cains. Over the years, those offspring mated with each other. As time passed, the suneaters' abilities and longevity became the stuff of fantasy to Cains."

I tried to process this. "But wait—where did the Adams like you come from? And why does the Patron think the women here at Eureka Towers need protecting?"

Seldon glanced at Piper and took a deep breath before speaking. "Eves were the first humans of any kind, before any males were born."

"There were only women?" I tried to picture it. "But how is that possible?" I groaned when the answer popped into my mind–another type of mutant the Con Squad hunted. "Virgin birth—really?"

"It's called parthenogenesis, and humankind is not the only species that has that ability."

Margie had said that, too.

"Our history says the Daughters of Eve lived hundreds of generations with only females." Seldon again glanced at Piper, but she remained silent. "The 'fall' mentioned in the legends was when the first Adam was born. No one really knows what happened—either then or now—to cause male births. Science has proven that all fetuses carry the potential to be either gender. Some think maleness is a recessive genetic mutation that's activated by a virus, which—if you believe the legend–may originally have been borne by a certain fruit."

"An apple?" I smirked.

Seldon shrugged. "Why not?"

"Having such a different kind of child had to be a shock for the first Eve who bore a son," I said.

He nodded. "I think the Eves would've accepted it if only the children had been affected. Sadly, when they bear a son, the otherwise-immortal mothers die in childbirth or shortly afterward. To save themselves, they began aborting male fetuses early in the pregnancy."

"But how would they know it was going to be a son?" I said.

"We don't get morning sickness unless we're carrying a male," Piper explained, speaking up for the first time.

"We?" I turned toward Piper. "You're an Eve?"

Piper nodded.

"I thought all the women at Eureka Towers were the suneaters' daughters or Cains from New Humboldt." I scrutinized Piper's face and body for any clue, but found nothing unusual in her appearance that would mark her as different from the other women.

"It's a long story," Piper said, "but one of our Eves went missing, and our Matron sent me here to find her. Instead, I found Abigail, or I should say, Seldon found me."

"How? You look just like me–like any of the other women."

"The moon gave me away," Piper said. "Near the full moon, if you know how to look for it, our skin gives off a slight glow in the moonlight. I snuck out to the balcony to feed since I didn't know how long it would be until I had another chance."

Seldon nodded. "I was on my balcony, leaving a white scarf as a clue for Aaron, who got the same message as you found in Margie's guest room. When I saw Piper, I hurried down and caught her before she returned to Margie's room."

"He said he'd help me find our missing Daughter of Eve if she was here," Piper said.

"But I had to be cautious," Seldon said.

"When the Con Squad put your pictures online and issued the alert, Seldon realized he was the one who might need some help," Piper said.

I drew a circle in the air, as if turning back a clock. "Wait, go back a minute. Did you say you feed on moonlight?"

"I do," Piper said. " I need moonlight to survive. Like the Sons of Adams, the Daughters of Eve can eat your food, but it's dangerous to eat too much."

I pointed at Seldon, then Piper. "So, you're a suneater, and you're a mooneater." I threw my hands up. "Mutants are real, after all? I'd begun to think the Con Squad invented mutants to keep everyone scared, like the Boogey Man." I looked up, wide-eyed. "You don't have any other surprises, do you?"

Seldon chuckled. "Well, no Boogey Man, anyway."

I crossed my arms and gripped my shoulders with both hands, giving myself a hug. "I don't see how our societies can live so close together and be totally ignorant of what's really going on."

"I know it's overwhelming," Piper said. "It is for me, too. It's a difficult thing for all the Eves when one of us decides to have a son. It happens rarely–only once in my lifetime so far—and she was sent away before the birth. Before coming here, I'd never seen a male except on the Nadux. I didn't know anything about Eureka Towers, and I certainly didn't appreciate how dependent Adams are on Eves for survival. It's a very delicate balance. What the Elder wants to do would completely destroy us. And eventually, them, too."

"Who is the Elder?" I asked.

"Our elected governing council, the Elders, is led by a man known simply as the Elder," Seldon said. "They aren't satisfied with Adams having only hybrid sons, although they also want more of those. Ultimately, the Elder wants to control all the Daughters of Eve so more pureblood Adams will be born."

"Didn't you say they'd die?" I said.

"Exactly," Seldon said.

"And eventually, every Eve will conceive a son," Piper said.

"Reasonable men like the Patron point out the dangers. Obviously, we can't let that happen or all the Eves will die. But the Elder has worked for years to get the support of the men here at Eureka Towers, including manipulating their memories. You see, to protect the purebloods' compound, the Adams' memories are wiped of information about their existence before they come to Eureka Towers."

I shivered at the thought. "Grown men choose to leave behind everything, even the memories of who they were?" What kind of person would I be if I didn't remember my mom or growing up in New Humboldt? I tried to make sense of what he was telling me, and to figure out how I fit into the picture. "If they don't remember their past, how does the Elder manipulate them?"

"They're given false memories—and the Elder manipulates those stories to ensure men are insensitive to women. Eurekans think women are happy to serve them in any capacity, and that having their children is the highest honor."

I groaned. "But not you. You remember the Patron and the other compound."

"That's right. The Patron needed an ally here, someone he could contact directly as the threat to women increased over the years," Seldon said. "On the books, I'm like any other suneater here, except I have a night job. Only a few of us can handle the night shift–it's been a struggle for me, too. As shift supervisor, I can monitor most things from my room." Seldon pointed to a bank of monitors above a narrow desk. "It's a good thing I don't need much sleep. In the day, as you know, I run the salon."

"So, you've been living a double life for four decades?" I tried to get my mind around it, but couldn't imagine how it could've been done.

"In the past, I helped the young women from outside adjust to their new lives in the Towers–what Margie does now," Seldon continued. "I have my apartment in the women's quarters, of course."

"Does Margie know?" I asked.

"No," Seldon said. "Margie is exactly what she seems to be, a very loving person. But Terence's father, Raul, was another of the Patron's men here."

"And your son?" I asked. "You said Abigail had a son with Raul's father."

"Another red herring. My son was a suneater I brought here from the compound as an infant. He and Raul were killed because of what they didn't know. I'm not making that mistake again."

"Are you telling me this because I've brought the Con Squad to your doorstep, and now you're afraid others will die because of it?" I shivered with dread.

"No, honey, it's not that." He patted my hand, and I couldn't help but think of him as Abigail again. "The Con Squad didn't kill my son and Raul."

"But Margie said..." I argued.

"I know, she thinks the Con Squad killed Raul." He shook his head. "They aren't our biggest threat, although they certainly are a danger, especially to you and Terence. It's the Elder and his followers we need to worry about."

"They killed your son and Raul?"

Seldon nodded. "It's contrary to what the Elder says he wants. He talks about extending the pure bloodline of Adams, yet he had two purebloods who opposed his views killed. That was decades ago, but the Elder can't hide his true colors much longer."

"Why not?" I asked.

"Because of you," Seldon said, "and because there's a Daughter of Eve here in the Towers with us—the one Piper came to find. We must protect her, and get word to the others of what the Elder has planned."

I was ready to ask a million more questions, but then I remembered the woman with the infants in the building where I met Terence, and a piece of the puzzle fell into place. "It's Aaron, isn't it?"

Seldon blanched and sputtered. "How...What makes you say that?"

"Her eyes," I said. "I saw her sad, blue eyes as they left with the infants from the tower where Terence found me. Her holo was on one of the chosen girls' handheld a few minutes ago. And earlier you said you left the scarf on your balcony as a clue for Aaron."

"I also recognized Aaron on the girl's handheld and confronted Seldon about it while you were waiting in the salon," Piper explained.

Seldon sighed. "I hope the Elders don't find it as easy to penetrate her disguise as you both did," he said. "Her life depends on it."

"It's too bad you didn't have a chance to give her contacts like you did me, although her cropped hair and jumpsuit are decent camouflage, if you don't look too close," I said. "But why would the Elder care about me?"

"Because of what I'm going to ask you to do," Seldon said. "I need you to tell the Matron what's happening."

I braced myself, not wanting to take on another burden, but wanting to help the Eves. And the idea of meeting more of these original humans–and an all-female race, at that–was the most intriguing thing ever. Were they really immortal? What was it like to feed on moonlight? Did they fall in love? There was so much I wanted to know about them, but I didn't see how Seldon's plan would help me find my mom.

Seldon left the room and returned carrying a white scarf. "Here, wear this," he said.

I noticed Piper wore one tucked beneath the collar of her shirt. "That's all? Just wear a scarf like hers?"

"To those who know, it brands you as a sympathizer for our cause," he said. "You'll become a target for the Elders, but a magnet for the ones we need to reach—the Eves."

I draped the scarf over my shoulders. "I will do what I can, but my first priority has to be finding my mom."

"Of course," Piper said. "But you have to be safe first. If you go out without any help, you'll just become another of the Con Squad's captives, and you won't necessarily end up wherever your mom is."

"For once, the Con Squad did us a favor," Seldon said. "By making you and Terence targets, everyone agrees you have to leave the Towers. Otherwise, I don't know how we could've gotten the word out to the Matron. With the rest of us in lockdown hiding from the Con Squad, you're the only ones who'll be able to tell the Eves that the Elders are making their move."

"Why are they doing it now?" I asked.

"It won't take the Elders long to realize the Eve could have come here from the compound," Seldon said. "And she will provide the perfect excuse to send an army of Adams here without raising the Tower leadership's suspicion. Once they're in, well..."

"But I thought this was like an extension of the purebloods' compound," I said.

"It's an uneasy alliance, at best. After so many years, Eurekans see ourselves as independent," he said. "Even with their altered memories, most have resisted the Elders' attempts to enforce more control over the women. But some Tower men, especially the younger ones, are beginning to lean that way, too. It's like an illness that spreads."

"What will the Elders do to Aaron if they catch her?" I asked.

"After they interrogate her about the Eves, they'll probably wipe her memory and keep her here as a prisoner," Seldon said. "They could learn a lot from examining a living Eve's body, and I doubt it would be pleasant for her."

Piper made a choking sound. "That can't happen."

"No, we have to be ready to get her to safety, but without attracting attention to the Towers," Seldon agreed. "With the Con Squad on high alert, we'll need the Matron's help to have a chance of pulling it off." Suddenly, he looked panicked. "What time is it?"

Piper checked her handheld. "6:05."

"I'm late!" He waved me and Piper out the door in front of him. When we neared the lobby, Piper stopped so abruptly that I ran into her.

"What the..." I said.

Piper nodded toward a slender young man waiting by the riser. "It's her–Ariadne. I know it is."

As if on cue, Aaron turned to face us.

21

ARI

"Piper?" I said. "Is that really you?"

Piper ran over, hugged me, then rammed her fist into my gut. I hunched over.

"You are *so* in trouble. Matron is going to kill you." Her usual evil grin colored her voice. "Assuming I don't do it first."

"Oh, please. Try it." I straightened suddenly, faking a head butt that stopped short of her chin. I wouldn't be pushed around even if I was glad to see her. I elbowed her in the stomach and sent her sprawling.

Lying on her back, Piper sucked in a deep breath, then propped herself up on one elbow. "Good one." She held her other hand up for a lift.

Cautiously, I took it. Piper surprised me by smiling instead of retaliating.

"Guess we better not make a scene." Piper glanced over her shoulder as a man stepped forward from the hallway behind her. A mousey-looking woman followed him.

Dread rose from my gut to my pounding heart. They had to have seen our fight. What would they make of it?

"I'm Seldon, the night-shift supervisor." He extended his hand.

Now my stomach quivered like jelly. Instead of finding a newbie, my new boss finds me beating up a girl. That can't be good.

"I'm Aaron." I gripped his hand firmly. "This, uh, isn't how it seems."

He gave me a reassuring smile. "Sorry I'm late, but looks like everything worked out for the best. I wondered how I could get us all together."

All together? I looked from him to Piper, who simply smirked. Now I was really puzzled. How could he know Piper, and what else did he know? Was I supposed to know the woman lurking behind him?

Seldon checked the empty hallway, then guided us toward the riser. "Aaron, you and I have to get upstairs or Jed will wonder what's going on. We don't need that kind of attention. But first, we have to escort these ladies back to the third floor."

Seldon turned to the other woman as we entered the riser car. "Blair, in case I don't see you again before you leave, you have to believe everything will work out. And I haven't forgotten your mother, either. Just keep taking the next step."

They continued to talk, giving me a chance to speak with Piper. "How did you find me?" I whispered.

"Somehow Matron knew to come here," she replied. "The others wanted to send one of the full-moon women with experience outside the compound, but Matron said they looked too old."

"She was right." I envisioned the scantily clad photo of the slender young woman I was to meet tomorrow and knew they didn't compare.

Blair gave Seldon a hug as the doors opened. Before they passed out of sight, she looked back at us and waved. It didn't surprise me that Piper didn't glance our way—she wasn't sentimental like that—but just kept walking. I would've liked her to surprise me. I guess I was getting mushy.

Finding Piper here had been quite a shock, and I was anxious to catch up on all the news. I wished I could've gotten off on the third floor with her, but I had to continue to play my role or face the consequences.

Seldon was quiet for the first few floors after we left them, as if something weighed heavily on his thoughts, too. He obviously cared for Blair and, from what he said, seemed worried about her mother, too.

"I feel like I walked into the mid-season climax of a Nadux series," I joked, trying to lighten the mood.

"Sorry to be so preoccupied, Aaron," he said. "I wish we had more time to come up with a plan—any plan—but all we can do is react. And that's what we're going to have to do now. The Patron said you haven't been through orientation, so don't ask too many questions tonight. Jed and Nathan are good men, but they're Eurekan to the core."

"You know the Patron?" I said.

"After so many years, I thought I did, until he sent me a Daughter of Eve and tried to pass her off as an Adam."

He knew! I took a step away from him, wondering what he planned to do about it.

"I'm going to have to talk to the geezer about his sense of humor." He gave me a reassuring pat on the arm and an appraising glance. "You look okay, though, so that shouldn't be a problem. All you have to do is act like you know more than you do."

"I'm not a very good liar," I said. "Nathan's already mentioned a reboot a couple of times."

Seldon grunted. "That's not good."

"It was the mating stuff–I didn't know how it's supposed to work," I said.

"And now?"

"Well, Carl and I chose our first potential mates," I said. "I'm meeting her tomorrow."

He chuckled. "That should be interesting."

I didn't smile. "But there was another girl with a white scarf I'd like to meet."

He looked up, as if he could see the sky beyond the riser's metallic walls. "White is the color of the moon."

I sucked in my breath.

"Don't worry." He turned to face me. "She'll find you when the time is right. Keep your eyes open. We'll talk more later, but in the meantime, don't you and Piper do anything foolish, like try to escape."

It was almost like he read my mind. I had been wondering how soon Piper and I would be able to sneak away.

The riser car stopped on the twenty-fourth floor. Again, I looked through the metal grating of the walkway to the majestic span of the redwood below us. Above, ruffled salmon-colored clouds dotted the blue sky. Sunset. From the sluggishness in my bones, I knew moonrise was still hours away. I couldn't wait to feel the moonsong thrumming in my veins.

Jed looked up as we entered. "I was about to give up on you both." He glared at Seldon. "Tonight, of all nights, I didn't expect you to be tardy."

Seldon grimaced.

"I'm very sorry," I said quickly. "It was my fault." Whatever was going on, it seemed blaming the "new guy" would go better for all of us. "Nathan introduced my roommate and me to the mating protocol, and I...got distracted." I looked at my shoes and tried to look contrite. "I regret making such a bad impression on my first day."

Jed raised his eyebrows and a smile lifted the corners of his mouth. "Ah, to be young again." He faced Seldon. "Well, it's only a few minutes' delay. We can make it up, right, old boy?"

"No problem at all," Seldon said.

I followed him along the outer corridor of the narrow, curving room. Darkness was falling quickly, with only a few persistent streaks of graying pink remaining in the sky. Inside, bright lights reflected off the white, metallic surfaces. When we arrived at the vacuum chamber, Seldon grabbed a couple of white lab coats from wall hooks and handed one to me as he put his on. To our right, two men watched a holo screen filled with tables of numbers and letters that meant nothing to me.

"This is our final simulation," Seldon said. "We've been recreating the moon's spectra within a vacuum to see if we could boost the signal. Usually it's scattered by the atmospheres of the moon and earth."

"Why is that important?" I could see all sorts of implications for Eves, but suneaters fed on sunlight.

"We've often wondered why our mothers thrived on moonlight but died if overexposed to sunlight. Yet moonlight doesn't harm us," he said. "This experiment is to see if suneaters can feed off moonlight if it's amplified."

One of the white-coated scientists moved to the left side of the vacuum chamber to monitor the vital signs of a man lying nearby on a reclining leather chair.

I wondered if I should stand so close to the chamber, fearing my perfect night-shift job could quickly turn perilous. "How much is the signal amplified?"

"It's nowhere near the Sun's magnitude, of course," he said. "After all, the Sun's about 436,000 times brighter than the full moon."

As Seldon continued to talk, he worked with the other man to adjust the output from the vacuum chamber. A bright beam of blue-white light now shone on the reclining man.

"With other techniques to enhance and focus the signal, we've more than doubled the moon's electromagnetic energy while accurately simulating the spectra," Seldon said.

"I'm not following you," I said. "Focus the signal?"

"It's like shining a flashlight on a can," Seldon explained. "If you're really close, the can takes up a lot of the beam, but if it's thirty feet away, only a fraction of the light hits the can because the beam spreads out."

Thirty minutes later, the scientist thanked the man, but frowned and shook his head as he approached us. "No good," he said. "Barely any change at all. It doesn't look like suneaters can use synthesized moonlight, even if it's enhanced."

"Do you think it matters that his skin is so light, while most Eves are dark-skinned?" I asked Seldon.

"Good question." He gave me a head bob and an appreciative grin. "That was one of the first things we checked, but it turns out skin color has no influence on the absorption of infrared rays."

I followed the three men to tell Jed the disappointing news.

"I don't understand," he said. "It should've had some impact. Moonlight is reflected sunlight, after all."

Seldon gave him a more in-depth explanation, concluding with, "Tonight, we've proven suneaters don't respond in the same way as Eves to infrared and visible light rays—it's a significant finding about how our body chemistry is different. Now we need to shift our attention to the other wavelengths—the ultraviolet, gamma and X-ray."

Jed turned to one of the men. "Pull the data he wants." Then he mumbled to Seldon, "It seems like someone would've already found it, though, if that's the answer. Ever since Hasselbalch did the first spectrographic observations in 1911, that's been the primary area of interest."

I made a mental note to ask Carl if the solar lab had done studies.

Jed walked away slump-shouldered, obviously disheartened by the experiment's results. I felt the same. Maybe if enhanced moonlight could sustain suneaters, whatever caused our bodies to reject male fetuses could be overcome somehow, too. Or not. Maybe the rejection had nothing to do with how our bodies were nourished, but something entirely different.

Before I knew it, my two-hour shift was up. Seldon walked me to the riser, talking quietly. "You did well tonight," he said. "Try to keep your liaison tomorrow as casual as possible. Remember, let her do the talking. I'll try to meet with you and Piper afterward, and Blair, too, if she's still here." He turned and went back to the lab to finish analyzing the results with the other scientists.

When I arrived at our room, Carl was online with his bedroom door propped open. He glanced away from the holo screen and grinned. "On break already?"

"Actually, I'm done for the night," I said.

"What?"

"I know, working only two hours is a bit ridiculous," I said, "but I'm not going to complain. Each week, my workday will increase by thirty minutes until I reach the full six-hour shift."

"Hmm, maybe I should look into night-shift work, too." Carl pulled at his chin like he was stroking a beard, making it clear he was far from serious.

"Well, you might not be so flippant if you knew what we're doing." I headed toward the Nadux Room for a drink of water. "Ultimately, they hope to find out why our mothers all die in childbirth."

Carl followed me into the living area. "Really?"

"Yeah, the research involves both astronomy and biology," I said. "They're using a vacuum chamber to simulate and enhance moonlight, then testing it on suneaters.

"And?" he asked.

"It didn't work." I sighed. "Not at all."

"That's surprising," Carl said. "Maybe the simulated moonlight still wasn't strong enough?"

"I wondered the same thing," I said. "Or I thought it could be a pigmentation issue. I've heard Eves have darker complexions than most suneaters."

"With a few obvious exceptions," Carl said.

I would've blushed if I could've.

"And that wasn't true either?" he asked.

"No, they'd already done studies on that," I said. "But I do seem to need less sunlight than most do." *Far less. None would be fine.*

"Nathan and I had noticed that," Carl said. "We're wrapping up a trial at the solar lab this week that looks promising. It focuses on how we get our energy directly from the sun. They believe UVB rays cause our bodies to produce Vitamin D, which is vital to sustaining many of our metabolic systems. It's a balancing act, though."

"How's that?"

"Well, our trials came about as the result of some research the Cains did. Their bodies often don't absorb what they need from the food they eat, so they've created pills to provide additional vitamins and minerals."

Just thinking of what Cains consumed made my stomach cramp. How could their bodies get what they needed from that? I almost felt sorry for them.

"We repeated the Cains' trials and confirmed it only takes about twenty minutes of sunlight for them to get as much Vitamin D as the body can use," he said. "They can't overdose on sunlight, but they can take too many of the vitamin pills to simulate the effects of the UVB rays."

"It seems like taking more would be better instead of worse," I said.

"You'd think so, but excess Vitamin D from pills can cause toxicity," he said. "They experience symptoms such as nausea, weakness and weight loss. They've even documented cases of kidney damage."

"But not from being in the sunlight?" My mind whirred. The symptoms he described reminded me of sun poisoning. I'd only seen a severe case once, but I'd experienced some of the short-term symptoms he mentioned in the past few days.

"Exactly," Carl said. "That's what was so interesting. From natural sunlight, their bodies produced only the Vitamin D needed, but no more. Only the pills caused toxicity."

Now I was eager to hear the results of the solar lab's research, too. If the suneaters had the same difficulties with pills as the Cains, it would blow the theory that had just popped into my head. But what if suneaters could handle *any* amount of Vitamin D, and actually thrived on it in any form? If that proved to be the case, I bet the opposite would be true for Eves.

I kept thinking about skin pigmentation. The predominance of light-skinned Adams had been apparent since I reached their compound. Here it was so obvious I'd privately dubbed this the Ivory Towers. Maybe the color of one's skin didn't matter when it came to absorbing infrared rays, but what if it affected the absorption of UVBs at the other end of the spectrum? This week, I'd discovered two hours of sunlight was the most I could take without suffering afterward. Perhaps Eves' darker skin stretched the twenty-minute window by up to six times. After that length of time, what if sunlight not only wasn't beneficial to Eves, but had similar toxic effects as the pills did for the Cains?

I couldn't wait to talk to Piper to see what she thought about my theory—she always looked at things so differently than I did. We weren't friends in the typical sense of the word, but together we made each other better. I'd always wondered what the Cain saying, "tough love," meant, but now I thought maybe it applied to us. We challenged each other to be the best we could be. We forced each other to think, but we didn't cut each other any slack. It was hard to admit to myself, but of all the Eves, I had missed her the most.

22

BLAIR

As we left the riser, Piper nudged me toward an empty hallway, avoiding a group of young women who'd just entered the vending area.

"Blair, I don't know when we'll have another chance to talk without other people around, so listen carefully to what I'm going to tell you," she whispered.

"I'm listening." I brushed my hair back and repositioned the white scarf Seldon had given me.

"Seldon was right about that," Piper pointed to the scarf, "but it's only effective to a point. If you're walking around the city for very long, you'll probably get noticed by some of our full-moon women who live in New Humboldt. But it won't get you into the Eves' new compound, and that's where you have to go–to see the Matron."

I bit my lip. "How am I going to do that if someone doesn't show me the way? I never even knew Eves existed until today."

Piper looked around nervously. "Look, I swore not to tell anyone, but Seldon's probably right–either the Con Squad or the Adams, or both, are likely to search Eureka Towers in the next day or two. With the increased security, I doubt Ari and I will be able to leave. We and all our kind are in grave danger, so I don't have much choice but to trust you."

Piper reached under the collar of her tunic, pulled a braided black silk cord over her head and handed it to me. A white crescent moon on a smooth, black background embellished a round ceramic pendant as large as the base of a teacup. It lay heavily in my hand.

"If a woman with a white scarf shows up, challenge her with the words 'white is the color of the moon' if she doesn't say it to you first,'" Piper said. "If you ask, she must show her pendant, or vice versa."

"And then she'll take us to the Matron?" I asked.

"Not so fast. Be sure the pendant looks similar to this, but it should have a full moon."

"Got it," I said.

"If she doesn't have a pendant or if the chain is made of metal, make any excuse you have to, but get away from there fast," Piper said.

"And if she does show me a full-moon pendant?"

"She will escort you and Jane to the compound. Tell the Matron where Ari and I are, and what's happening," Piper said. "You'll be safe there, at least, safer than anywhere else for now."

"And Terence?" I dreaded to hear the answer.

"Can't go there." Piper shook her head so forcefully her dark hair whipped in front of her face. "They'll kill him if he tries to follow you, so don't let him try it."

I waved my hands in the air and snapped, "What kind of plan is that? We can't just dump him."

"He's not your responsibility." Piper's voice rose.

"But he saved me from the Con Squad," I said.

"He didn't tell you how women were treated here." Piper put both hands on her hips and glared at me.

Avoiding Piper's gaze, I hung my head. "I have to think his intentions were good."

Piper snorted and flung her hands upward, palms raised. "I don't know why you believe that, but it doesn't change the facts." She took a deep breath, visibly forcing herself to calm. "It's not hopeless–I overheard one of the full-moon women say the Adams' compound is nearby. Apparently they had to build our new compound on part of their property since the Cain population has expanded into rural areas."

"The Adams would take Terence in?" I exhaled softly and looked up.

Piper paused, her forehead wrinkled. "I don't know what other option he has but to try."

I curled my fingers into tight fists, wishing I could pound my way through all the roadblocks in our way. "What if no one notices the white scarf, or the full-moon women choose to avoid me after seeing the terrorist alerts?"

Piper dipped her head almost imperceptibly. "That's why I'm reneging on my promise to the Matron. I'll tell you the way to the compound, but don't tell *anyone* else. Not Jane. And certainly not Terence."

I pressed my lips together and scrunched my eyebrows. I hated making promises, and this one seemed almost impossible to keep.

"Promise?" Piper glared at me.

"All right," I snapped. "But this all makes me crazy."

Piper huffed. "Yeah, it's no picnic for any of us. So, if you go southwest of town, you'll soon run into holo ads for Genesis Apple Orchard." She winced, as if saying it physically hurt. "It's the one with the picture of a smiling snake entwined around the nude figures of a man and woman."

"Seriously?" I chuckled. "I follow holo ads to this secret place?"

"I know!" Piper laughed. "As far as I'm concerned, they might as well have painted a big red target on the place. Maybe that's why the Con Squad doesn't pay it any attention. It's too dumb to be real."

"Amazing," I said. "But if they're so open about it, why are you swearing me to secrecy?"

"Don't take this lightly—approaching our compound alone is a dangerous thing for outsiders. No one has survived it before, but no one carried one of our amulets, either."

I swallowed hard. "So, I can just follow those signs?"

"Exactly," Piper said. "But they get smaller and harder to find the closer you get. And sentries will challenge you.

"There you are," a familiar voice rang out. "Jane and I have been looking all over for you, Blair. It was like you disappeared, and Abigail, too."

"I, ah, didn't mean to be gone so long." I shoved the amulet into my pocket to avoid having to explain it to Margie and Jane. "I guess Piper and I got carried away."

"Piper, my dear, are you beginning to settle in?" Margie wrapped an arm around each of us as she led us back toward the vending area. "And Blair, after chatting with Piper, now maybe you'll believe Terence and I didn't have some sinister plan for the new arrivals."

"I do feel much better," I said.

"Well, Terence said it's still a couple of hours before you can leave, and Jane insists there's something she must show you in the meantime." Margie put her hand on my shoulder. "Don't wander too far. The Con Squad is in the building, but it seems to be a routine inquiry. In case you have to leave in a hurry, here are the clothes Abigail and I chose for you."

The mention of the Con Squad sent cold fire racing through my veins as I absentmindedly took the denim backpack. I hated to think of them being so close, to know they were looking for me. "Thanks." I imagined it was filled with more shapeless garments in neutral colors like the tan pants and gray top I now wore. "But I'll see you before we go, right?"

"Of course." Margie patted my hand. "But it doesn't hurt to be prepared."

"Come on!" Jane grabbed Piper and me by our wrists and dragged us down the hallway.

I had been in towers before and knew they were more like neighborhoods than buildings, but Piper was all eyes. We'd walked more than a block, through a variety of hallways, rooms and even green spaces, before Jane finally stopped.

"Ta da." She made a dramatic sweep of her arm and pointed to a quote written in light above the doorway: "In nature, as an organism evolves it increases in complexity and it also becomes a more compact or miniaturized system. Similarly a city should function as a living system."—Paolo Soleri

I didn't get it, and from Piper's raised eyebrows, it looked like I wasn't the only one.

"Eureka Towers was one of the first successful attempts at arcology," Jane explained. "I just wanted to share that with you."

"Arcology?" Piper asked.

"Like a blend of architecture and ecology?" I asked.

Piper nodded. "I'd never thought about it, but it makes sense."

We continued walking until Jane stopped beside a portly man who worked with an equally rotund woman at a virtual architectural model. As the couple entered new equations, features on the model adjusted from angular to curved, from wood to stone.

"One of the benefits of arcology is shared resources," Jane said.

"Everyone can use the tools these architects have or those of any other trade."

As we walked into the adjoining agriculture section, Jane waved at a group of women and children. "Some people, like these, prefer to come to the gardens and greenhouses to select their food, but most of us rely on the vending machines."

Smells wafted toward us on the humid air from vast kitchens visible through the transparent walls. A steady stream of harvesters carried fresh produce into the prep area.

I gave Piper a lop-sided grin. She lagged behind, looking positively green at the smells of cooking food. Jane didn't seem to notice, but she didn't know Piper was a mooneater. For all I knew, nobody here except the suneaters believed such people existed.

"The idea was to preserve as much of the area as possible surrounding the Tower by consolidating our living and work areas," Jane said, "but in the end, our main contribution was saving one redwood tree."

"And creating a model for the other towers," Piper added.

"I can't imagine what it was like before," I said, "but I've always heard the towers kept people in our cities from starving during the Black Days of the early 21st Century. Those who relied on older food distribution models were all but wiped out."

We kept walking, and my anxiety rose. "Jane, we've been gone quite a while, and Margie told us to stay close."

"Not to worry," she said. "I've been taking a circular route. We're not as far from where we started as you think. In fact, you can see the way back to the main tower from here."

I looked in the direction she pointed. We were still half a block away, but close in terms of the distance we'd walked. A doorway at the end of the hall opened and Margie waved frantically to us.

"Hurry!" she said. "They can't hold them off much longer."

Piper, Jane and I ran toward Margie, but we were still twenty feet away when the outer wall of the hallway exploded. We fell to the ground, instinctively protecting our heads from the debris that fell around us.

"Stop!" Margie yelled.

My heart raced at the sight of Margie struggling with Con Squad troopers, who dragged her through the jagged hole in the wall. They'd taken her, just like they'd taken my mother.

Piper grabbed my hand as we scrambled to our feet. "You can't help her," she whispered. "You'll only get us all caught."

The other troopers hadn't spotted us, but it was only a matter of time. How could I just leave Margie? It was like a vid replay, one where I let down people who cared about me.

Piper crawled closer to Jane. "Which way should we go?"

Jane pressed a hand against her right temple and moaned. Blood seeped between her fingers.

I edged closer, too. Piper pulled Jane's hand away, revealing a three-inch cut. It looked superficial, but Jane was dazed.

"C'mon," Piper hissed at me, tilting her head toward the corridor we'd taken earlier. We each grabbed an arm and dragged Jane a few feet past where the hallway split and into the darkened, dust-filled hallway. It was like walking into a cave.

"If we can make it to the arcology or agriculture section, we can use the tools as weapons," Piper said. We helped Jane to her feet and moved quickly down the hall, staying against the wall where the shadows were deepest.

A siren screamed, adding to the crashes, shouts, and clanging metallic sounds of the battle in the hallways behind us, and drowning out any noise we made. I wanted to put as much distance between us and the Con Squad as possible. Jane was more lucid by the time we reached the first green space. She motioned us toward a room on the far right.

Before we closed the door behind us, I heard running footsteps approaching.

"They're coming!" Piper hissed.

I followed Jane and Piper, who had crouched behind some large crates stacked in one corner. Moments later, the door opened. Someone stomped across the room and opened a closet on the opposite side of the room.

I closed my eyes, waiting for our discovery. The door to the closet slid shut. A moment passed, then another. I felt someone staring at me and squinted one eye open. A muscled figure stood silhouetted against the fading sunlight filtering into the room; he blocked the way out.

23
─────

ARI

"When will you see Natisha again?" I tried to act like I thought any guy's friend would, but it took a lot of imagination since I'd never known other men. And my turbulent feelings for Carl were hard to hide. It confused me why I should feel attracted to him. I wanted him to be happy, but it made me angry that he liked someone else. I was miserable that he wanted me to enjoy someone else's company. I wanted to look good for him, but I also wanted him to like me for who I was, whether Aaron or Ariadne. I guess that was too much to ask. He was usually so preoccupied. The few times we'd been together, our conversations had been superficial or awkward.

"I tried to get hold of her again tonight, but she wasn't available," Carl said. "I have to work until mid-afternoon tomorrow, so we'll get together then. You should be back from your first meeting before I go. I hope you made as good a choice as I did."

It puzzled me that Carl couldn't tell me much about Natisha, yet he felt they were well-suited. The male psyche was more of a mystery to me than I was to myself. When I thought of the young woman I chose, prickles of fear danced along my spine and my stomach cramped. It was almost like stage fright. I hoped she was a talker. Otherwise, I didn't know if I could pull it off. Acting wasn't my strong suit, and I was already straining the limits of my abilities.

It was almost eight, and I could tell without looking the moon would be rising soon. "Why don't we go on the balcony a while? I don't tire of looking at the redwood."

"I know. Let me finish one thing and I'll be with you." He disappeared into his bedroom. When he returned, Carl stopped at the Nadux dispenser and got us each a drink.

"What's this?" I took the cold, tall glass of amber liquid.

"It's called beer," he said, "a type of fermented beverage made from grains. Nathan introduced me to it earlier today and I thought you might want to try it, too."

I took a sip and frowned. "It's bitter." I took another sip. "But not bad."

"That's what I thought...the taste kind of grows on you," Carl said. "I rather like it."

The moon was beginning its arc across the cloudy sky. I pointed. "It looks beautiful framed by the branches."

"I still can't believe this is a redwood," he said.

I nodded. "I never saw one except in class vids."

"Me neither—and I didn't really think I ever would." Carl hesitated, then said, "You know how our past is hazy?"

I gave a chin bob.

"Well, sometimes I get flashes of things, of memories that don't really match what we're experiencing here," he said. "From what you've said, I take it you do, too."

"Oh?" I wanted to say more, but made myself wait.

"I probably shouldn't say anything, but when you questioned Nathan about the way women are treated here, I was glad." Carl looked over at me. "I can't really say why it doesn't seem right. It's little things —like the way they list them by number, and how you don't even get to socialize with more than one female at a time. It's just...artificial."

I smiled at him. "I'm glad to hear it's not just me. I felt really stupid and ashamed that I didn't know things I should've learned in orientation."

"No, don't feel bad about that," Carl said. "I guess we'll get used to all of this with time." He paused. "But maybe we shouldn't."

"You may be right," I added. "The mating protocol almost seems like a system that once had meaning, but doesn't any more. Does that make sense?"

"Like the panels Nathan showed us in the lobby when we first came in, about the Founders' goals?" Carl said. "And then we find out there's a giant redwood behind those panels that wasn't even mentioned."

"Exactly!" I said. "It's like something is hidden or forgotten, but everyone accepts things the way they are because they don't know a better way—they don't see behind the panels."

"Even though it's certainly not perfect, Nathan is right about one thing," Carl said. "At least some of the women find it better here at Eureka Towers than outside. Natisha told me some awful stories about the Con Squad."

"Really?" I said. "Like what?"

"Apparently people live under their total control, without any recourse if they get accused of being a mutant," Carl said. "That's worse than a death sentence, because it condemns your family and friends, too."

I thought about the two compounds I'd seen—one Eve and one Adam—and the Cain city between. In a fair world, the Cain city would be a place of moderation, somewhere in between our two extremes. Instead, New Humboldt seemed to have picked up the worst qualities from both systems, and doubled the paranoia.

"Why would anyone get accused of being a mutant who isn't one?" I hated to use the term "mutant," but didn't know how else to describe them.

"It's a very structured society, and it's especially hard on women," Carl said. "Natisha said her friends have been accused on all counts—from virgin birth, to being immortals. One accused of being a suneater starved to death after being left in a sun-filled cell without food."

"But why?" I asked again.

""It's all about control, I think," Carl said. "The Con Squad was given extensive powers because of fear, and now they're the ones to fear."

"So, Natisha's friends weren't mutants?"

"No, only people who someone thought was different." He raised his eyebrows. "Not so unlike here, even though we're suneaters among our own kind. I feel incredible pressure to fit in with the other Eurekans, so I can imagine how you must feel with a less successful orientation," he said. "I'm not supposed to tell you, but Nathan has already contacted someone about a reboot for you."

Who would Nathan have contacted—the Elder? Fike? If he contacted the Elder, how long would it take him to figure out one of the Towers' newest recruits was the Eve who Fike let escape? I tried not to look alarmed, but I felt like rushing out the door to find Piper. We should leave before the Elder had time to reach the Towers, but I had no idea how to find her. Then I thought of Seldon. He would know how to reach Piper.

"You're awfully quiet," Carl said.

I stood and paced. "I just remembered something I was supposed to tell my supervisor, but I can't get back to the twenty-fourth floor without a riser key."

"Maybe you can send him a message online," Carl said.

I followed Carl to his room and watched as he called up a directory. He pulled up my profile and clicked on the link labeled "work status." Above my title—Research Assistant, Lunar Astrophysics and Physiology Lab—was a link to my "Supervisor" and above that, "Director."

"I'm amazed at how easily you navigate the network," I told Carl.

"I've always had a gift for understanding programs. This system is different from what we used before, but I couldn't say exactly how." He shrugged. "Like everything else, it's shadow memory." He waved the keyboard in front of me. "Are you doing audio or manual?"

I grinned and drew the virtual keypad toward me. "I make fewer enemies when I slow down and write it out."

He left the room, calling out behind him, "Want another beer?"

"Sure," I said. "Be there in a minute." I stared at the blank screen. The cursor flashed, waiting for me to begin. Maybe straightforward, with just a little subterfuge, would work best. "Have time-sensitive data Re: lunar issues, please contact me," I typed.

I returned to the balcony with Carl and watched as lights came on and went off in the rooms across the atrium from ours. Seldon's room remained dark. I hoped he would get my message soon. Maybe I was overreacting, but I didn't think we had much time.

"Why don't we go to the lobby and see if anyone's got a card game going?" Carl said. "Or how about some billiards?"

"I'll be down in a few minutes," I said. "I don't want to be in the middle of something if Seldon gets back to me."

"Well, I hope he sees it soon," Carl said. "When you're working full-time, you won't have many nights to get to know the rest of the guys. I could introduce you to my work group."

After he left, even the thrumming of moonsong wasn't enough to calm my jangled nerves. I kept replaying Seldon's warning about an army of Adams invading the Towers, and imagined them hunting me down. Piper would have to return to the Matron without me—telling her I'd become nothing more than a lab rat.

But the Adams might not stop with me, if Seldon was right. They might take the opportunity to further restrict all the women, so Piper would be trapped, too. Without access to the moon, she would starve, just like Natisha's friend.

I told myself to stop borrowing trouble and tried to think about solutions rather than problems. Eurekans could generate high-powered infrared radiation, after all. Although I hadn't tried to feed on it, I had a hunch it would work well as an alternative food source for Eves like me.

And now I knew more about sunlight and how it might work within the Adams' bodies via Vitamin D. I'd been remembering other things—bits and pieces really—from conversations among the full-moon women about how much longer they'd been able to stay in the sunlight when they were young. They'd blamed their decreased resilience on overexposure to the Sun, but I wondered if it was something else. As they grew older, most grew stouter, too, developing the full breasts and hips characteristic of full-moon women. Perhaps their changed metabolism or higher body fat was somehow responsible for amplifying the Sun's effects. What made me almost certain this was true was Nathan's comment about needing less time to feed since he'd gotten older. If Eves could tolerate less Sun as they grew older, and Adams needed less time to feed, there must be a common reason having to do with aging.

I went out to the balcony. Although the rays were not yet of full feeding strength, I basked in the moonlight while watching for Seldon's lights to go on, or for Piper to show herself on the balcony like she had the night when Seldon spotted her.

But nothing happened. It was so quiet it was unnerving. I waited in the growing dark, with only the moon to keep me company. Usually, that would be more than enough, but not tonight. I felt restless and more than a little anxious. It didn't look like either of them were going to show, so I might as well go find Carl.

I had just turned to walk back inside when sirens blared.

24

BLAIR

"Time to go." The glow of the emergency lighting made a red streak on the man's face as he leaned forward and held out his hand.

"It's you!" I laughed with relief. I took Terence's hand and scrambled to my feet, then took Jane's elbow to steady her as she stood.

"What a nice surprise," Piper added. "I figured it was the Con Squad." She brushed off her tunic and peered behind Terence, but no one had followed him into the room. "How did you get here so fast with troopers all over the place?"

"I came from the other direction. I was almost to the arcology section when I heard the explosion and backtracked," he said. "I saw you duck in here."

I quickly sobered. "Then you didn't see ... they took your mother."

He pressed his lips into a thin line. "Are you sure?"

"She was standing right next to where the explosion went off," Piper said

"Why would they take her?" His scrunched-up face looked like someone had hit him in the gut.

"Well, she did kind of attack them," Piper said. "The distraction allowed us to get away."

He let out his breath. "That sounds like something she'd do." His voice lowered to a whisper. "Was she hurt?"

"I think she's all right," Piper said. "She put up quite a fight."

I looked down at the floor. "I'm sorry we couldn't help her." Shame burned my cheeks.

Terence twisted around and pounded his hand against the wall. "They have no right!" He took a few deep breaths before turning back toward us. "But you did the right thing. If they catch us, the whole Tower will be held responsible. There's no telling what they would do to make an example of us."

I heard the regret in his voice, but also the conviction behind his words. It helped ease my feelings of guilt.

"The best thing we can do is leave." Terence paused, taking a closer look at Jane. "What happened to you?"

"The explosion. Some of the debris caught me." Her fingers drifted to the cut on her temple, which had crusted over with dried blood.

"Need a hand?"

She shook her head, wincing at the motion. "I'm better now, just a little woozy."

We moved toward the door. "We need to go as fast as possible," he said.

We stood with our backs against the wall as he opened the door. Terence peeked out, checking both directions. "It's clear." He waved for us to follow and slipped into the hall.

Dust still hung thickly in the air. The sounds of conflict had grown more distant, closer to the main part of the building. I kept looking behind, expecting to see troopers emerge from the dust in pursuit. Why did they blast into the corridor if they were already inside the building? Nothing made sense.

"Where are we going?" I asked.

"There's an emergency exit to the alley," Terence said. "I'd just finished getting everything together when the building alarm sounded. I didn't know what was going on, but assumed the Con Squad was involved in some way. I figured they would want to seal off any obvious escape routes, so I took our car out of the garage."

"Good thinking," I said.

He led us across a green area and into the arcology section. It was deserted, but tools still hummed with power, like everyone had left in a hurry.

When we reached the agricultural section, Piper picked up a baton-sized laser tree trimmer. "Just in case," she said. With a quick flick of her wrist, a red beam lashed out toward a misshapen tree. A moment later, a branch two inches wide lay on the floor, cleanly severed from the trunk.

Jane and I exchanged glances. "Wow," Jane said.

"Here." I grinned at Jane and handed her a trimmer before grabbing one for myself. We sprinted after Terence, who was already nearing the end of the next hallway.

Instead of going through the kitchen, Terence turned the opposite direction. About halfway down the corridor, he stopped beneath a red "Emergency Exit" sign.

"Guess this is where we say goodbye for now," Piper said.

"Aren't you coming with us?" I asked. "I mean, with the troopers here and all?"

"It's tempting, but I can't leave yet." She raised her eyebrows and stared at me.

I finally realized what she meant–Piper didn't want to leave without Aaron, but she didn't want to talk about it in front of the others.

"Be careful!" I reached out and squeezed her hands.

Piper's blank expression made me think she felt a little awkward, but she squeezed back and mumbled, "You, too."

"Stay out of sight until the siren shuts off," Terence said. "Things should be back to normal soon."

"You remember your way to the kitchen, right?" Jane pointed down the hallway.

"Sure." Piper nodded.

"That's where I would go," Jane said. "It'll be the first place people gather, so you can find out what's going on before you head back."

Old-fashioned hinged doors with a manual push bar had large signs warning that an alarm would sound if opened. With the siren still blaring, the added noise when Terence shoved the doors open was almost imperceptible.

We emerged in a narrow alley. It took a minute for my eyes to adjust to the dark. In less than a week, I'd gone from being a fugitive on the run from the Con Squad, to being a captive in Eureka Towers. Now I'd made it back on the street, even if I was still on the run. I didn't know whether to rejoice at my regained freedom or to be fearful of the exposure.

"This way," Terence said.

Scuttling clouds passed over the moon. The sidewalks and road were wet from a recent rain, and the dank air smelled like rotted vegetables.

Jane grabbed my hand, and together we sprinted after Terence. He stopped in front of a white Shell car with a few dings in the side. The doors opened and we all piled in. Moments later, he gave his ID code and selected a route. "It's already programmed," he explained, "but it's a navi system separate from the city GPS. They shouldn't be able to track us right away."

"Oh, that's right. You've had a lot of practice keeping off their radar on your raids to find women." Remembering our last trip through the city in a car much like this one, I didn't try to keep the sarcasm out of my voice.

He grunted, "What set you off?"

"Just thinking about this mess I'm in because of you."

Terence raised his eyebrows and bit his bottom lip. "Surely I don't get all the credit."

I looked away. Maybe it was unfair to take my frustration out on him. But if he hadn't shown up when he did, would the lawyer Dina found have helped me to find my mother? Now I'd never know.

He sighed. "Anyway, I'd never travel with a couple of newbies like you if I had a choice."

My temper flared with renewed fury. "Jane wouldn't be a newbie if she'd been given the same opportunities as you to go into the city."

"Is that what you think, that this is an opportunity?" He laughed and shook his head. "I put my life on the line to safeguard Eureka Towers, to protect Jane and everyone else. We are the ones the outsiders like you fear, the ones you'd destroy if given the chance."

"Outsiders like me?" My jaws clenched. "All I ever wanted was to be left alone. But someone tampered with the water supply, and mutants became my enemy. You're no different from the Con Squad!"

"Don't ever say that!" he spat. "I'm nothing like them. We're simply trying to preserve our kind."

"At the expense of the women whose lives you control." I tilted my head toward Jane. "Maybe it is dangerous, but I'm glad she's here with us. At least she'll have a taste of freedom."

Jane smiled timidly at us both as the Shell car pulled away and sped onto the adjoining street.

Terence turned away from us, but kept his face shielded from other vehicles and pedestrians, as if that was second-nature. I did the same.

Behind us, barricades blocked the street. Dozens of troopers milled around the building. Flashing blue and red lights reflected off their mirrored face shields and the wet pavement.

I kept checking behind, feeling somewhat surprised our escape hadn't drawn any attention. Having Jane along did make me feel less conspicuous than traveling as a couple.

"Where are we headed?" I asked.

"To the North Side," Terence said. "A safe house we've used before."

"That's my home turf." My anxiety ratcheted up a notch. "People may be more likely to recognize me there."

Terence looked at me and snorted. "I don't think there's much danger of that. You don't exactly look yourself."

I tried to take it as a compliment, or at least as confirmation that my disguise was effective, but his words stung. "Yeah, and I don't hang out with biker dudes, either."

It took about thirty minutes to weave through the city to the North Side. All the while, Jane took in everything, from the moving walkways to the towering buildings. "It's so different from what I'd imagined."

"Really? I know you've seen vids." Terence said.

"It's all the sounds and smells—I didn't expect that. Like here it's not as noisy as it was near the Towers, but you can still hear the hum of people talking and the growl of traffic. And the air is fresher now—you can smell the rain, instead of that garbage when we were surrounded by high-rises. The deep corridors between the buildings must keep odors trapped or something."

"I hadn't thought of that," Terence said, "but you may be right."

"Inside Eureka Towers, I didn't realize what it would be like to stand outside in its shadow, or to feel the wind rushing in the canyon between the buildings," Jane said.

I only half-listened to their conversation, paying more attention to the neighborhoods we passed. By the time we reached the North Side, I felt better. At least I wasn't on my own anymore.

Terence had a network of people who could help us. Although I chided myself for thinking it, maybe he would consider me more than just a liability now that Margie was a prisoner. Terence and I shared a common goal–to find and free our mothers. It didn't seem as hopeless any more.

The car pulled behind a one-story white-frame bungalow and into the single garage. Interior lights came on automatically, and the door closed behind us.

"We're here," Terence said. "Home sweet home."

I moved to get out, but Terence blocked my way with his arm. "Let me go first...just in case."

"In case?" Jane asked as Terence disappeared through the doorway.

"I don't know," I said. "I guess in case it's been compromised?" Suddenly, I didn't feel quite as confident. The enormity of what we were up against slammed home. By now, I was sure my Reservist unit had been mobilized, and they knew me better than anyone except my mom. Would they recognize me through the disguise? What could the three of us hope to accomplish against the likes of the Con Squad, even with the help of other Eurekans?

And we'd been marked as terrorists.

25

ARI

I was almost to the door when it slid open and Carl walked in. "Thought I'd see if you were still here," he said.

"What's happening?" My pulse raced as I conjured up possibilities —all bad—from a fire to a full-blown invasion led by the Elder.

"Didn't you get the text about a street-level explosion right before the alarm went off?" he asked.

Bands of anxiety grew tight across my chest. An explosion? I glanced at my handheld as he stepped back into the hallway. "I don't know how I missed it." I'd have to check the settings to see if the pulse alarm had gotten muted somehow. Had I missed Seldon's reply, too? I wanted to scroll to the next message, but things were moving too fast.

"C'mon. We need to get to the safe room."

I walked swiftly after him. *Safe room?*

The lobby was empty when we arrived. He walked past the billiard tables to a door on the wall behind the riser. "The guys said this leads to the safe room." Carl waved his pinky at the sensor, and the door opened into a hallway behind the riser shaft. At the end, we took a sharp left onto an enclosed stairwell.

I heard voices above and below us as we joined others making their way down.

"Some of the guys with Security connections said the Con Squad already did a routine sweep," Carl said, "so I don't know why they upped the ante like that."

I grunted in agreement, saving my breath for the sprint. Fourteen floors later, we passed through massive double doors made of wood and steel, flanked by guards in black jumpsuits. We entered a cool, windowless basement room three times as big as an archery range.

I sucked in a deep breath, trying to slow my panting. Carl was barely winded. The air smelled of earth, evergreen and cold stone. The redwood's trunk spanned the rear third of the gray, concrete room, giving the only hint of life. This was where it met the earth; a ring of dark soil surrounded it, with a brass rail protecting it from onlookers.

Carl grabbed a gray metallic chair from a stack by the door, and I did the same. We started a new row. Already a dozen rows were each filled with dozen men who'd made it here before us, and more came in after we did. My breath finally started returning to normal. Carl watched as I checked my handheld.

"Wonder how that happened." I reactivated the pulse alarm. When Carl turned back toward the doorway, I flicked to the earlier messages and saw Seldon had replied "Don't contact me" within minutes of when I texted him.

I bit my lip, drowning a wave of rejection, then let the anger rise. What gave him the right to say that to me? I joined Carl in watching the men enter the room, waiting for Seldon's arrival. I'd find a way to get him to talk with me afterward, even if it was inconvenient for him. Whatever his problem was, he needed to know about Nathan's comment, and I really needed to contact Piper.

At the front of the room, a bald-headed man with eyebrows like bushy black caterpillars stood behind a podium, testing the mike. "We'll give them another minute or two to make it from the top floors," he said.

Carl leaned over and said, "That's the Council chairman, Lucian. He works in the solar lab, too."

"I know you have a lot of questions, but let me assure you, this is nothing we can't handle." Lucian's voice was calm and confident.

I spotted Nathan in the third row, and nodded at Jed when he finally entered, looking red-faced and exhausted after his trek from the top floor. The speaker signaled the guards to close the doors. Now there were as many rows in back of us as there were in front.

Nathan came back and squatted in the walkway next to Carl. "Glad you made it. Hang tight afterward and I'll answer any questions," he said.

"Great," Carl said.

"Jed is the top-floor monitor," Nathan added, motioning toward the back of the room. "Now that he's here, the doors are sealed for the duration of the meeting."

As Lucian began to talk, Nathan returned to his seat. My anger at Seldon shifted to frustration. Where was he? Did he stay away simply to avoid me?

"As most of you know," Lucian said, "the Con Squad has been looking for two fugitives they claim were responsible for the Blue Death that claimed so many lives after the Westover waterworks contamination incident five years ago."

Holo images of Terence and Blair were projected behind him.

"You'll recognize one of our own, Terence, and a young woman he saved from the Con Squad while on his mission earlier this week," Lucian said.

"If you needed any proof that Terence wasn't The Covenant mastermind behind the terrorist attack, here's what he looked like five years ago when that incident occurred."

Like the others, I laughed at the holos of a skinny, wiry-haired teen about half the size of the man whose image had saturated Nadux news.

"Which brings me to the real reason the Con Squad is hunting Terence. He was sent as backup for a retrieval, providing a diversion so the newborn could be taken to safety. That was accomplished, despite two casualties, the mother and another Eve. Fortunately, no bodies were taken for examination."

This appeared to be news to most of the men, who leaned over to exchange a few words with whoever sat next to them. Lucian waited until the rumble died down. An older man stood up in the front row. "Then what led them here to us?"

"The usual precautions were taken with decoy cars, but this time the Con Squad was able to pinpoint our quadrant. We think they may have used new technology that let them compare routes taken on previous missions. Rest assured, ours was not the only tower they invaded today."

The older man was back on his feet. "This is a perfect example of why we need to take control. The Eves are putting us all in danger."

Shouts of support surrounded me. I didn't know what to make of it—how did they think Eves were putting them in danger when we were the only ones who died? I shifted in my seat, fighting the urge to run. What would they do if they discovered I was not only a woman, but an Eve?

"Order!" Lucian shouted, scowling at the man. "We all are well aware of your feelings on this matter. We are here to give the Councilmen and Security time to secure the building. The troopers have left, but they took one of our Eurekan women who was combative."

My heart sank. I hoped it wasn't Piper, but it sounded exactly like what she would do. No one else seemed to give the news a second thought.

A man in our row stood. "I thought the sweep was already done before the explosion."

"That's true," Lucian said. "It's only conjecture, but we believe the Con Squad may have an informant who pointed them toward that part of the Towers. Terence and the woman he saved were both there, but managed to escape."

It was like everyone had been holding their breath until they heard Terence was gone. Tension ratcheted down and several men who'd been sitting on the edge of their seats leaned back. The relief was short-lived.

The doors slid open and the siren's piercing tone from outside filled the room. Nathan's mouth dropped open. I turned toward the door and smirked when I saw it was Seldon. Until I saw who followed him. I shrank in my seat, trying to disappear. He escorted Fike and the Elder to the podium. Lucian looked as pale and shaken as I felt, but he quickly found his voice. "This is quite a surprise."

"I'm sure it is," the Elder said sarcastically.

Inside my head, I was screaming. *The Elder is here!* I had no doubt that finding me topped his to-do list, no matter what he told the others. He couldn't let me get away after I'd been at the compound.

Lucian stuttered, "We're honored, Patron, that you and the Elder could join us."

Fike acknowledged Lucian's greeting with a nod. "Ordinarily, we would have honored the seal, Chairman, but this is not a day to stand on formality. In the next few hours, we may be called upon to step outside tradition if we are to preserve the very core of both our societies."

The front-row heckler stood again. "You know what needs to be done, Patron," he said. "If you'd listened to the Elder, we wouldn't be in the Con Squad's crosshairs now."

Around me, more than half the men mumbled in agreement. My skin tingled from the rising tension.

"I've carefully considered your concerns, but taking over the Eves' compound is out of the question," Fike said. "We are not murderers or slavers, and that's what we're talking about here. Not only would it be immoral, but it's shortsighted. If all Eves who conceive a male child carry to term, within a generation all the mothers will be dead. Both our races will die."

"You don't know that," a man behind me snapped angrily. "We don't *know* that every male birth leads to the mother's death. It's just what they tell you—Eves lie, you know."

I wanted to turn around and slap him. What did he know about Eves, or about any women, for that matter? It was obvious his only concern was what he wanted, not the truth. He certainly had no proof that Eves could survive a male birth, but that didn't seem to matter.

He continued, "And so we have to put good men in danger to bring our sons to safety. It just isn't right."

"Yeah!" others in the crowd shouted. "He's right!"

I couldn't believe what I was hearing. Had any of these men considered what they would do if the situation was reversed? How many would choose to die so a female child could live, if that was their only choice? And now Fike said they wanted to force Eves to live under their control? The very thought was unimaginable, yet after my short time here, it wouldn't surprise me if the Eurekans tried it. The programming had taken away their respect for women; to them, we were little more than a means to an end. I knew somehow it all led back to the Elders. They were the ones who did the programming. I just didn't know what they stood to gain.

Another heckler rose. "If the Con Squad tracks us down—and they will, whether it's this time or next—then everything will be lost. Technology won't let us hide anymore."

Fike swallowed hard and looked down at his hands before resuming. "I'll be the first to agree changes must be made. But first, we have to survive today. Thanks to your leaders' foresight, Terence and the woman are no longer in the building. There's nothing here to raise the Con Squad's suspicions. You have agriculture and aqua farms so your ability to survive off sunlight is not apparent. And, after all, virgin birth has never been a big issue for us men."

Laughter rippled through the audience.

"Despite what some would have you believe, we are *all* taking this seriously." Fike gave the Elder a sidelong glance. "Some would have you believe the answer is simple, but it is not. We need to look at this problem from all sides as we move forward, not seek solutions based on our immediate desires."

The Elder stood as Fike took a seat on the other side of Lucian. "Patron would have you think this is a complicated matter, but it really isn't. If the Eves have been telling the truth about their deaths from bearing sons, we will help find a cure. It doesn't have to lead to the end of both our races as he suggests. We're better than that."

A murmur of approval wove through the crowd. Fike shook his head ever-so-slightly. He looked around the room with the drawn face of a man who's lost his best friend. Then our eyes connected. The sorrow he felt reached out to me in a palpable wave.

"We can have sons who are like us, who don't have to taint their bodies with food," the Elder said.

The men cheered.

"We can have sons who live as long as we do, so we don't have to watch them die," he continued.

The men stood and yelled. The man in the front row shouted, "Elder, make it happen!" He pumped his fist in the air and others followed.

After several minutes, the Elder motioned for the men to sit. When they'd grown quiet, he said, "That's what I'm here to do—to make it happen. I've invoked emergency powers to call a joint meeting of the Elders and the Eureka Council. I will see no more of our men put in danger to save the life of a newborn suneater."

The men jumped to their feet, again applauding and whistling.

"The next time the Con Squad follows one of our cars, we may not be so lucky. It could mean the end of everything, of all of us. I won't let that happen." The Elder sat. Fike's face was a stony mask.

My body had gone rigid, caught up in a storm of fear, anger and disbelief. My hands clenched the seat so hard they hurt. I was surrounded my enemies, and all I could do was try to act like one of them. To blend in. It made my stomach cramp.

Lucian stood and waited until the room was silent. "You are released. Remain in your rooms until the first morning shift. We will update you on the Nadux community channel as news becomes available."

The next few minutes passed in a haze. Carl and I followed Nathan back up the stairwell, not even trying to wait on the riser. It was a good thing, despite my burning thighs. I needed to work off all the trapped emotions and taking the stairs helped. It didn't do anything to solve the problems, though.

When we reached the door to the lobby on the thirteenth floor, Carl asked Nathan, "What's this all about?"

He shook his head. "I don't know what to tell you. Joint council meetings were held when Eureka Towers was first organized. It's been more than a century since the last one, and even longer since an Elder invoked an emergency meeting. This is big—really big."

"Is Eureka Towers in danger?" I asked, as we moved toward our room.

Nathan paused next to a billiard table, forehead wrinkled. "You know, I can't say. There's definitely been a lot more political wrangling going on than I knew about. With the mood of that crowd today, I'd say we're in for a rough ride. From what I know of the Eves, they won't take kindly to what the Elder's proposing."

He didn't know the half of it. I had to find a way to get to Piper, and fast. We had to tell the Matron what was coming her way.

26

BLAIR

A t the sound of heavy footsteps approaching, I motioned to Jane and hurried across the garage. We flattened ourselves against the inside wall, standing beside the door Terence entered several minutes before.

"Sounds like someone's chasing him," Jane whispered.

We held our laser tree trimmers up, with fingers poised above the "on" switch. My heart thudded in time with the running footsteps, which grew louder with each breath. I expected to see Terence, not the white-draped figure that burst through the doorway, screeching like a banshee.

Jane shrieked.

My finger twitched, sending a laser stream upward. It cut through a metal bracket on the other side of the door and a shelf fell, sending assorted boxes of screws, nails, and bolts skittering across the floor.

"What the...?" Terence jerked the sheet off his head, dodging the projectiles, and spun around to face us. "You could've killed me!"

I switched off the trimmer and slammed it to the floor. "You ...are an IDIOT!" I screamed. I covered my face and ran into the house. My insides still quivered when Jane joined me minutes later in the sparsely furnished living room.

"He's such a tool." Jane rolled her eyes. "But I bet he won't play any more pranks."

I smiled weakly and brushed angry tears away. "Point one for the girls."

"Seriously, I think he feels bad about scaring us," Jane said.

"Well, he should," I said. "Being on the run is crazy enough without playing stupid tricks on each other."

Jane gave me a squint-eyed look, and I knew I had to get my act together. Drama could wait. I walked toward the garage and yelled, "You can come in now, jerkwad. I'm over it."

The sheet, draped over my abandoned tree trimmer, preceded Terence through the door. "I surrender."

I smirked and grabbed the trimmer. "Surrender accepted." Despite the scare he'd given me, I liked his playful spirit. It helped me feel more positive about our chances for surviving, even if logic told me otherwise.

"Hey Terence." Jane tugged his shirtsleeve. "What does it take to get a tour of this place? It's my first real house, after all."

I snorted. "It barely qualifies." It was smaller than the tract house my mom and I'd shared, and a far cry from the glass-and-metal perfection of Eureka Towers. The tiny living room had poured concrete floors with a single, threadbare cotton rug in front of a faded blue three-cushion couch. If there'd been more furniture than a couple of folding wooden chairs, it would've felt crowded. Thick red drapes hid narrow windows that flanked a flimsy pressboard door.

On the other side of the room, two stools sat beneath a waist-high bar topped with red linoleum. It separated the living room from the kitchen, which was nothing more than a few cabinets hung above a sink and a food dispenser so old it had a separate disposal unit. I recalled the pristine vending machines at Eureka Towers and stifled a groan.

As we walked across the room, I got a preview of the bedrooms through cracks in the pre-fab walls where the seams didn't fit together well. We stepped up three steps and entered a hallway with scratched and stained bamboo floors. Each new room made my stomach clench tighter–there was no place to hide in this house. Closet-sized bedrooms straddled the most depressing excuse for a refresher I'd ever seen. And it was moldy.

Terence walked into the smaller bedroom, which was almost filled by yellow metallic bunk beds and a black five-drawer chest. I heard a "snick" as he slid his hand behind the lower bunk. He grabbed the metal railing as the bed swung away from the wall. "Ta dah!" He fitted his fingers into cracks between the floorboards and lifted a trap door.

"Oh!" Jane muttered and quickly disappeared through the opening.

I looked warily at the ladder descending into darkness, then followed. By the time I reached the bottom rung and stood in a hallway barely wide enough for one person, Jane had found a wall switch. A single light glowed about ten feet away in the direction of the living room, casting deep shadows.

Terence started down the ladder, then I heard another "snick." The trap door closed, shutting off the natural light. Above, I heard the bunk beds slide back into place with a heavy thump. In the cramped, dark confines, my heart raced. I swept my hand through my hair, imagining spiders, and tried to breathe. "Uh...how will we get out?"

"We have options," Terence said. I couldn't make out his features even though he stood only inches behind me at the base of the ladder. His breath tickled my ear as he spoke. "Give me your hand."

He slid his hand around my waist, then enclosed my fingers in his. He was strong. Comforting. No, it was more than that. His warm breath grazed the back of my neck, raising my internal heat and taking my mind off the fears that only moments before had overwhelmed me.

He guided my hand back to the concrete wall. Our fingers moved across the cool, rough surface until we touched a shoulder-height depression. A "snick" followed our firm push, and I heard the bed moving above. He pushed it again and the sound reversed as the furniture once again covered the trap door.

Heat rose to my face. I was glad he couldn't see it. He had only taken my hand to show me the button.

"I used the outside button to close it more quickly," Terence explained. "I could've just waited until I got down here."

Terence placed my hand on a lever next to the button and pressed down. Above, I heard something big and heavy slide into place with a metallic thunk.

"That's an inch-thick steel plate to block the entrance," he said. "You can open it by pressing the lever again."

I glanced over my shoulder. My face was less than an inch from his. I sucked in my breath, tempted to close the remaining space so our lips would touch. He leaned down so his face brushed mine. My heart thudded wildly.

"Hey, where does this go?" Jane asked.

Terence cleared his throat and pulled back. "Well, uh...what?"

"Geesh, you two." Jane rolled her eyes. "Focus! This tunnel. Where does it go?" She pointed toward the lit area.

"Let's start with where we are." He released my hand and rested his on my waist, gently guiding me forward.

I reluctantly stepped further from him and walked toward Jane's voice. I wanted to strangle the girl. Jane stood under a naked light bulb where the corridor took a sharp turn. It narrowed so much we would have to turn sideways to fit. That made my heart race even faster, but for a different reason. I'd never been fond of enclosed spaces.

"Right now, we're standing under the living room," Terence said. "It has an eight-inch-thick concrete floor, which thermal scanners can't penetrate."

Next to where Jane stood, Terence hit two wall switches. One turned off the light above us and the other flicked on a hanging bulb about twenty feet ahead. He led the way down the narrow corridor, stopping where a wider hallway dead-ended at the next light. I figured we were now beyond the garage.

"If the Con Squad gets this far, we have a few surprises for them." Terence pointed to levers positioned on each split of the hallway. "These control steel doors." He demonstrated, pushing down the lever on the hallway we'd just left. An inch-thick panel slid down, closing off the corridor. "It's like the one beneath the bedroom's trap door," he explained. Then he pointed at a narrow, knee-high indention in the wall. Terence knelt and reached deep inside, until his shoulder rested against the wall. He pulled out two laser handguns. "This is the final surprise."

"Sweet," Jane said.

I rested my hand on the jagged rock wall at the edge of a finished concrete section. "This is stone. It must've required some pretty serious equipment or blasting to make these tunnels."

"Yeah, but the hard part was already done," Terence said. "When homes were first being built here in the early Twentieth Century, they kept hitting bedrock and could only clear partial basements or foundations. I've heard it was quite disastrous financially for the builders."

"So, they just put up shoddy houses," I thought aloud.

Jane bobbed her head appreciatively. "Decades later, someone figured out the basements were pretty handy for avoiding the Con Squad."

"Right," I said. "But how did they get connected like this?"

"You'll find some of the passageways are really tight–those parts were dug out with hand tools as we linked the partial basements together," Terence said.

Like where they stood wasn't cramped? Or dark. Or stuffy. I choked a little. It felt more like we were in an underground cave than a city basement. I had to make myself focus on what he was saying.

"...and adding on extras like steel panels and thicker concrete slabs." Terence said. "We've been expanding the system for more than twenty years."

"How many houses are connected?" Jane asked.

"Oh, not very many here–maybe ten," he said. "But we have other safe houses around New Humboldt with underground systems. They've already saved me twice."

"How do you know where the safe houses are?" I asked.

"There's a pattern. It's pretty complicated until you've done it a few times." Terence released a slow breath. "You have to swear not to tell anyone."

We nodded.

"No." He glared at both of us. "I mean you have to swear."

Jane raised a hand to her forehead in salute. "I swear, sir."

"I swear." I grimaced, partly reacting to his theatrics and partly to my guilt. Terence wasn't holding anything back from us, but I didn't feel comfortable sharing Piper's directions on how to find the Eves' compound with him.

"Okay, then. Did you notice the street name when we exited the ramp?" he asked.

"It was Udan or Uton—something like that," I said.

"Good enough. Utan Road," he said. "You were paying attention after all."

I considered telling him not to patronize us, but decided to let it go this time.

"And this house is at..." I began, then Jane joined me: "...246 Ann Arbor." We grinned and Jane made the two-finger victory sign.

Terence gave an eye-roll. "Can you guess the pattern?"

"Uh, the street number is divisible by two?" Jane offered.

He snorted. "Half the properties in the world have even-numbered addresses."

"It has something to do with the names of the streets," I guessed.

"Of course, or I wouldn't have asked you to name them," he said.

I put a hand on my hip. "You know, Terence, I've had it with the snarkiness." I made a fist and punched his shoulder to be sure I had his full attention. "You can cut the crap."

His eyes darted between us, as if taking our measure.

"Yeah, we're not stupid," Jane said. "Women didn't get briefed like men did at Eureka. That's no reason for you to be cocky."

He grunted. "Fine. I only thought you might want to know about the code."

"We do," I said. "But you can't blame us for not knowing what we weren't told."

"All right, I hear you," Terence looked at his feet.

"Are we straight?" At least he acknowledged our viewpoint.

"Sure." He sounded bored.

I gave an internal shrug–it had to be said. "Back to the code?"

"The first exit was a street that began with a U and the next street started with E—the second and fourth letters in Eureka," he continued. "The code I was given was 2466–a doubled number means a doubled letter, in this case double As for Ann Arbor."

"How did you know to turn left or right when you left the Towers?" Jane asked.

"Even numbers indicate right." He'd started walking again, heading down the wider corridor so we didn't have to scoot along with side steps.

I finally felt like I could catch my breath, even if we did still have to walk single file. We passed two wider areas with ladders before he stopped and climbed to the top. He listened for several minutes before putting his finger to his lips. He motioned for me to push the button to unlatch the trap door. It popped open, leaving a sliver of light around its border. Terence pushed it up a half-inch at a time.

For several minutes, he held it open to observe the room and listen. When he was satisfied the house was empty, he slipped his hand out and pressed the button to swing the furniture aside. In this house, I soon discovered, a chest of drawers with a hollowed out bottom sat atop the trap door instead of bunk beds.

Something seemed strange, though I couldn't place it at first. I swallowed hard when I realized what it was. When we'd entered the house on Ann Arbor, I'd heard street noise and screeching sounds from a nearby elevated railway. Now there was only the railway and what sounded like muffled voices.

Terence's forehead knotted, and I knew he must have had the same thought. He walked toward the window and carefully pulled the drapes back just far enough to see. He let them drop quickly, but I saw the flashing red and blue lights outside. "Shit!" he said. "What are they doing here?"

27

ARI

Nathan left us at the door to our room and hurried down the hall. I paused only a moment, then ran after him.

"Nathan, wait!" I yelled.

He spun to face me, his eyebrows furrowed. "Yes?"

"What will happen to the woman they took?" I couldn't shake the image of Piper being led away by the Con Squad. It made me weak-kneed, and I grasped for reassurance that things were better than they seemed.

He widened his eyes as if expecting me to explain why I cared. "As I understand it, the Con Squad seldom gives up people they take into custody."

"But she's a Eurekan," I protested, my hopes dashed by his aloofness. "Surely we don't let them invade the Towers and not defend our people."

Carl walked up and stood beside me. I was glad we'd talked earlier. At least I knew he shared some of my concerns.

"Natisha isn't answering my messages," he told Nathan.

"As you both should know from orientation, the women are not really Eurekan in the same sense you are," Nathan lectured. "As fond as we may be of them and our children, our primary duty is to those who share our heritage. That is the purpose of our way of life, and what we defend. You'd best remember that in the days ahead, if you don't want to be on the wrong side of events. But to answer your question, Natisha and the other women are safe." He turned on his heels and entered his rooms without a backward glance.

We exchanged wide-eyed stares. Carl recovered first. "What was that all about?"

I exhaled. "Guess we hit a sore spot."

"But it still doesn't answer the question of what's going on with the women," Carl said.

"Let me try calling." I used my handheld to call the only number I knew—the woman I was supposed to meet in a few hours—but got voice mail. "Just checking to see how you are. Call me," I said.

Carl shook his head. "This doesn't make sense."

The door slid open. "I wonder what he'd do if his mate or one of his kids got snatched by the Con Squad," I snapped as my fear morphed into anger. I stomped into our room.

"Doesn't sound like he'd care, does it?" Carl threw himself down on the couch with a huff. "I don't get it."

"It seems backward." I sat, then stood and paced a few minutes, then sat again. "Do you think the women and children have a safe room of their own? Maybe that's where Natisha and the others are." I stood and nodded toward the door. "Let's go check it out."

"But where would we start?" Carl propped up on one arm, looking drained of energy. "Eureka Towers is a big place."

I grinned at him. "Just follow me."

Carl reluctantly peeled himself off the couch. Minutes later, the riser doors swished shut as I punched the button. "When I met my supervisor here before my shift began, he escorted a couple of women back to the third floor."

"Women were on our floor?" Carl said.

I shrugged. "I think they have to be escorted."

The riser doors opened to the third floor. It was quiet—too quiet. I jumped to the worst-case scenario and imagined all the women had been taken by the Con Squad. I shook my head and my whole body shivered, trying to dislodge the morbid thoughts. Surely it couldn't be that bad.

Plush sofas and chairs on one side of the narrow room were a drab orange in the yellowish glow of dimmed overhead lights. Reflections of the multi-colored lights on the vending machines splashed across glossy black tabletops. Everything seemed in order, except no one was there.

"Now what?" Carl asked.

I didn't have a clue. "Try one of those rooms?" I kept my voice low and gestured toward the hallways that flanked the vending area. Evenly spaced doors made me think it was a residential area like our floor.

I wasn't prepared for the ear-splitting buzz that sounded when he stepped from the tiled entryway onto the carpet. He jumped back with a yelp, bumping into me, as the lights brightened to full power.

"Are you okay?" I asked. We both put our hands over our ears.

"Yeah," he mouthed, the words drowned by the buzzing alarm. His mouth gaped and eyes bulged, much like I expected mine did. Minutes passed. The noise made my nerves jangle but despite all the commotion, no one showed up to investigate.

"They can't be on this floor or someone would be here by now," I yelled. "This is crazy!"

We stood there for a few more minutes before Carl pushed the riser button. "I can't take any more of this noise!"

When the riser doors closed behind us, I breathed a sigh of relief. "Whew!"

Carl leaned against the wall and bent over with his hands on his knees. "That sound got me in the gut," he said.

By the time we reached the thirteenth floor, more color returned to his face. "Better?" I asked.

He nodded. "How about you?"

"Yeah, it was just really irritating." Had it affected him more because he was male? I was glad the women had some protection, even in a society like this.

When we got to our room, Carl went straight to the Nadux Room and returned with two beers. "Any other bright ideas?" he asked.

I shook my head. "I guess we'll have to wait for Natisha or my lady friend to reply to our messages."

"If we don't hear anything before then, we'll try again in the morning," Carl said.

I hoped we had that much time. I wondered what Fike and the Elder were doing now.

Being cut-off from Seldon was a huge problem. The women could've told us if the Con Squad took Piper, but that hadn't worked out. I needed to leave the Towers before the Elder found me, but without her, I didn't know where to go. And there was no telling what the Con Squad would do with Piper if she was simply abandoned by the Eurekans.

"I don't understand what's happening," Carl said. "I may not remember everything from before, but I clearly recall thinking this would be a place where I could have a more normal life – with a family. No offense, but living here with you doesn't seem quite like that."

"No offense taken," I said. "I feel the same." At least he wasn't pretending to be something he wasn't. That thought jarred something in my mind as I absentmindedly watched the Nadux continuously replay the holo of Terence and Blair. The woman seemed vaguely familiar, though I couldn't imagine why. I hadn't seen any women since coming here except the photos we'd looked through and when Piper joined me by the riser.

That's when it hit me– Blair, the other woman with Seldon and Piper! I paused the holo and tried to picture the woman on the Nadux with mousey brown hair instead of blonde, and with shapeless clothes that hid her youthful curves. Could it be? Had Piper left the riser with the woman the Con Squad was hunting?

Now I was more convinced than ever the Con Squad captured Piper while she was helping Blair escape. Sorrow and fear battled with anger and reckless determination to do something, anything, besides sitting here cowering. But I needed an ally. We'd seen Nathan's true colors, and Seldon was with the Elder and Fike. That only left Carl.

I had to find a way to motivate Carl to break his brainwashed obedience and seek out something far less comfortable—the path of a rebel. If I had lots of time, it probably wouldn't be too difficult. I could bring up things from the past—even the few things I knew about their compound and political structure might be enough of a trigger. Electric shock could work, but tasering him didn't seem like a good way to get him on my side.

Would it do any good if he knew who I really was, or was I just tired of the charade? If I was honest with myself, I knew the orientation made it more likely he would surrender me to Nathan than do something heroic to support me. He didn't know me well enough for that.

It had to be something that pulled at his heartstrings. Whenever I looked at him, I couldn't forget the image of how he guarded the newborns as the Con Squad pursued us. If I could tap into his protectiveness for them, I bet I'd be able to break his conditioning.

Piper had taught me something about this, the hard way, and we were both experiencing its unexpected consequences. What I learned was you couldn't simply stop a pattern, you had to replace it.

She thought I had an issue with curfews. It was really about freedom and authority; as the leader of the crescent-moon women, Piper had the authority, and I had no freedom. I had never needed much sleep, but that didn't matter to her. In the crescent-moon barracks, you were to remain in your bunk until the conch sounded at noon.

The third time Piper caught me in the nursery after curfew and took away my entertainment credits as punishment, I started sneaking outside the compound. Soon I recognized my forbidden forays to the field as something more basic—a call to freedom, not merely the wanderings of an insomniac. Yet it was all about breaking one pattern and replacing it with another. Maybe that rebel spirit was inside Carl, too, and just needed to be kindled.

28

BLAIR

"The Con Squad?" Jane asked, her eyes round with alarm.

"Hurry, get back down!" Terence pointed to the trap door. "Maybe we can lose them before the next safe house."

I rushed after Jane. What was going on? It had to be more than coincidence that the Con Squad was at the house we just left, but things were moving too fast to make sense of anything. Before Terence had closed the metal plate, Jane crouched beneath the second light and pulled two laser guns from their ground-level storage. She offered one to me and slipped another into her waistband.

I pushed it back. "I don't know how to use it." Truth was, Mom always told me not to carry a gun unless I was prepared to kill someone with it. Otherwise, it could easily be used against you. Although the last few weeks had made me question my resolve, I found I still wasn't committed to taking someone's life, but I kept a firm grip on the tree trimmer. My pocket taser was in my backpack.

Terence joined us and took the weapon I'd refused. I looked from him to Jane. "Hey, I'm not really comfortable with this. The Con Squad would probably be less likely to shoot at us if we aren't armed."

"Tell that to the others who've died in these tunnels," Terence snapped.

Jane gave me a sheepish smile. "I feel better with something that gives me a little distance from an attacker."

Terence flicked a lever behind us to put a second steel plate at our back. With the corridor to the Ann Arbor house still blocked, only one narrow hallway remained open.

We followed Terence, squeezing through side-first. We inched along in single file, our bodies pressed against the cold stone. The rapid pounding of my pulse from knowing the Con Squad was in pursuit made our pace seem even slower. Jane yelped and pointed at a particularly sharp ridge right at chest level. "Watch that one!"

When we finally reached another ladder, Terence and I exchanged worried looks in the dim light. Jane was breathing so fast I was afraid she would hyperventilate.

"Hey." I put my hand on Jane's shoulder. "Take a deep breath and let it out really slowly, like this." I demonstrated my best yoga breath, and repeated it a few times as Jane joined me.

Terence cleared his throat. "C'mon, we gotta go. Blair, you lead, and I'll cover the rear."

"Can't we stay here?" Jane asked.

Reading the answer in the tightness of his eyes and lips, I started up the ladder as soon as he pressed the button to unhinge the trap door. I did as he had done earlier–pushing the door up slightly so I could see into the room without giving our location away. I stayed that way for a couple of endless minutes, but heard nothing. I reached out and pressed the button to swing something massive away from the trapdoor. When I scrambled out, despite our desperate situation, I grinned at the sight of an ancient upright piano—the kind from before virtual keyboards. The abused brown monstrosity had missing keys and splintered posts. It reminded me of one my grandmother had taught me to play "chopsticks" on when I was little.

Like in the Ann Arbor house, heavy red drapes covered the windows. I headed across the kitchen and opened the door a crack as the sound of the piano swinging back in place filled the room. I crossed the empty garage with Jane and Terence at my heels, and opened the outside door a sliver. I was relieved to see the flashing lights still on the far side of a six-foot hedge, and none closer.

I quickly got my bearings in relation to the Ann Arbor house and began walking. I led them between the houses until we reached a house where a dog barked as we passed and lights came on inside.

"That's not good," Jane whispered, her voice carrying in the otherwise still night.

I motioned toward the tree-shaded sidewalk. It was more exposed but less likely to set off alarms or make guard dogs restless.

"Let's spread out so we're not so obvious," Terence whispered. "Remember to start with the fourth letter, E. Then go to a street starting with A. I'll see you there." Before I could reply, he crossed the street and disappeared behind a tree. Jane started breathing faster again.

"Guess he's right."

Jane reached out, gripping my hand. "Don't you leave me, too!" Her face was ashen even in the dark. It took me a minute to realize what had her so upset. A suburban landscape with yards, fences, roads, sidewalks and open spaces would be foreign to someone raised within the confines of tall buildings connected by courtyards and hallways.

"You know, I think Terence forgot we're women." I squeezed Jane's hand. "It would be stranger for us to be seen walking alone than together. Let's go."

We reached East Bay Avenue –only two streets down –then Adirondack Court two blocks to the right of that. Few cars passed, and there was no sign of the Con Squad. From the crossroads, we saw a jogger and a dog-walker, but neither paid us any attention.

I easily located the house–246 Uptown University St.–and walked to the side of the house by the garage to wait. A few minutes later, Terence hissed, "It's me," before he emerged from the shadows. If he knew we'd walked together, he didn't say anything about it. He entered 2466 into a keypad next to the garage door, and we entered. It was another abandoned house, much like the others. He motioned to the food dispenser, then disappeared into the bedroom.

Jane and I punched the green lights and grabbed the packaged food it spat out. I tore open a protein bar and gave half of it to Jane. "We better eat something while we have the chance."

Jane popped it into her mouth in one bite, then scrunched up her face. I soon discovered why–it was like eating lemon-flavored cardboard.

Terence returned as we took the last water packets from the dispenser. I frowned as he jammed another laser gun into a zip-pocket at his waist. Was he preparing for a shootout?

As the door slid shut behind us, Terence said, "Let's put more distance between us and them. I'll stay here a few minutes to see if anyone's following us."

"Let's stay together." I hated the pleading tone in my voice. "You're the only one who's done this kind of thing before."

"And that's why you need to do as I say," he said firmly. "You know the way to the next safe house, right?"

I pressed my lips together, fighting the urge to lash out at him but knowing it wouldn't do any good. What did I know, anyway?

Perhaps, like me, Terence suspected someone told the Con Squad our location. Maybe a hacker tapped into the car's programming, or an informant leaked the 2466 code. For all I knew, the Con Squad continuously monitored all the safe houses and only showed up when the prize was worth it. Terence and I would certainly fit the bill.

"What happens if you find out someone *is* following us?" Jane asked.

"I'll lead them away," he said. "If I'm not at the safe house in one hour, you'll know there's a problem, so get out quick."

"But you may need help," I said.

Terence looked away. "I can move faster without you."

My mouth fell open. "Well, yes, I guess you can." I spun around and started walking. "C'mon, Jane. Let's not waste any more of his time."

Jane straggled behind for a few steps, then ran after me. "You know he's just trying to protect us."

"Think what you like." To me, it sounded like he didn't want to be saddled with two women. Terence made no bones that he was used to traveling with men who knew what they were doing, and even then, he'd had some close calls. I wasn't sure if he'd show up even if no one was following us. "Let's find this safe house and hope they don't know how to find us there, too."

From Abigail Street, Jane and I went five blocks to Una Blvd. Entering 246 East End Ave., once again we plundered the food dispenser. We might be here for only an hour, but it could be much longer if Terence showed up. I didn't want to chance giving our location away because we had to leave our hideout to get more food.

This time, the trapdoor was located in a slightly larger bedroom. A queen-sized bed on a simple wooden frame filled more than half the room, giving barely enough space for the trap door to open when the bed swung aside. Jane went down first; I handed her some of the food packets, then went back for more. After a third trip, the immediate danger overrode my long-term survival instincts, and I joined Jane below.

I closed the trap door but didn't shut the steel door. Below, Jane placed the food and water packets on a narrow ledge that ran the length of the wall below the stairs. We worked together in the light of a single bulb, with darkness all around.

Abruptly Jane sat down, right in my way. "I need a break."

"Yeah, I'm really tired, too." Now that I'd quit moving, I noticed how much my legs ached. "How far do you think we ran?"

"Miles and miles." Jane rubbed her calves.

My stomach growled. Jane laughed when our hands collided as we both reached for food packets at the same time. Mine offered a tasteless mixture of chopped carrots and green peas, but it was better than cardboard.

Jane squinted her eyes and puckered her mouth. "What is this stuff?"

I looked at the packet. "Pickles. I haven't had those in years."

"Take them." She stuck her tongue out and made a retching noise. "You can't convince me they're edible." She pulled out another protein bar. "Who knew that food with no taste could be better than some flavors?"

Although I was still hungry, I stopped eating after I finished Jane's very sour dills. This food might have to last a couple of days.

"How long has it been?" Jane asked.

I had already checked my handheld at least a dozen times, and each time I was surprised only another minute or two had passed. "Only thirty minutes since we left Terence."

"Oh," Jane said. "Seems like a lot longer."

"Yeah, I know." Despite my anxiety, or maybe because of it, I felt exhausted. I didn't think I could stand another minute, but reconsidered after sitting a few minutes on the chilly, concrete floor. I'd never thought of myself as skinny, but it felt like I was sitting right on my bones with no padding in between.

After the earlier rush to get away from the Con Squad, time had slowed to a crawl, giving my mind ample opportunity to wander. What if the Con Squad captured Terence, or found us in the safe house? What if we couldn't find our way to the mooneaters' compound or weren't allowed to enter? What if I never saw my mother again?

I felt like curling into a ball and blocking everything from my mind. The thought of never seeing my mother had haunted me every day and night since they'd taken her, with my despair growing stronger each day. I wasn't any closer to finding her than on the first day; in fact, now I was a fugitive whose face had been on every Nadux in the country, so my chances were probably a fraction of what they had been. I was afraid to find out if my disguise would work or if I could find the Eve's compound, yet the alternatives were even worse. And what about Terence? If he was with us, he couldn't go near the compound.

I checked my handheld again. Another five minutes had passed.

"Blair?" Jane asked.

I turned toward her voice. Although Jane's face was in shadow, I made out her frown. "Was this how it was for you before Terence brought you to the Towers?"

I paused. "Only since the Con Squad took my mother. I knew it wasn't safe to go back home, and I couldn't trust my friends. A safe house like this would've been a step up."

"But it's so ..." Jane's shoulders twitched and she shuddered.

"Dirty?" I said. "Worn down? Depressing?"

"All of that, but especially depressing," Jane said. "And I thought I had it bad at the Towers because I wasn't allowed to leave. All I was missing was this?" She gestured at the darkened basement.

"You can't really make a comparison," I said. "Before the Con Squad entered our lives, things were really pretty good for Mom and me. Sure, the news was filled with all sorts of alarms and confrontations with dissidents or suspected mutants, but for the people I knew, it was work and play as usual. We had the latest organic designer food dispenser, and I could order tailored clothes delivered overnight to my door."

"You could go wherever you wanted?" Jane said.

"Yes," I slurred the word into a question. "Kind of. We were always being warned about being in the wrong place—how dangerous it was to be out after dark or to wear red in a certain part of the city where the gangs were. Mostly we stayed in our small chat groups...usually online, although I'd wander out each day to meet some of my friends at a teahouse or virtual link parlor."

"What about class?" Jane asked.

"Schoolwork was almost always easier to do online, unless it was physically interactive, like lab work," I said.

Jane's foot made a soft, staccato tapping against the floor.

Minutes passed. I tried to make myself ignore the growing tightening in my gut. Where was he? Terence should be here by now if everything was okay.

Jane wriggled, repositioning on the hard floor. "You weren't kept from doing things because you were a woman?"

"No." I patted Jane's hand, just like Mom used to do in our girl-to-girl talks. "A lot of things were wrong—are wrong—but women still do pretty much what they want. Of course, we are much more likely to fall under the suspicion of the Con Squad because of virgin birth allegations and such. Seems like women have always had to confront a double-standard to some degree."

Jane fidgeted some more. "How long has it been?"

I didn't have to look. I knew. "An hour and five minutes. He's late."

Jane grunted. "I thought we'd been down here a long time."

"We never should have split up," I said.

"Then the Con Squad might already have us all instead of just Terence," Jane said.

"It's odd how they kept showing up," I said. "Like they had someone on the inside."

Jane put her palms to the floor and pushed to stand. "We should leave—" Something upstairs screeched. A door? Jane froze in place, with her mouth still open.

I put a finger to my lips. The ceiling creaked as someone walked across the room above. A thunderous sound filled the basement as the bed moved away, exposing the trap door.

Jane reached for my hand, mouthing "Terence?"

I shrugged, trying to look calm, but my muscles tensed, ready to run. I stood and reached for the double light switch, then froze. What if I hit the wrong switch? While slamming the steel door shut was tempting, I didn't want to block Terence. We should've come up with some way to signal each other, like stomping in Morse code. I left the single light glowing as we tiptoed into the darkness on the other side of the room.

The trap door creaked as it popped open; fresh air flowed downward. The ladder groaned with someone's weight. My grip tightened on the tree trimmer. I backed further away from the entry, drawing Jane along with me. Jane raised her gun, but I shook my head and pressed her hand down. Accidentally firing at Terence was still fresh in my mind, and a gun could do a lot more damage than a tree trimmer.

The ladder groaned again.

29

ARI

Carl sat on the couch, looking toward me with unfocused eyes as he slowly sipped his beer. It wasn't long until morning. I didn't know if they'd try to resume work as usual, or if we'd be told to stay in our rooms a little longer. I couldn't help but wonder if more outsiders —from the Adams' compound or the Con Squad—were somewhere in the building, searching floor to floor for me. I jumped at every whoosh from the air handlers and each tiny creak the building made, expecting someone to rush in and take me captive.

Despite my escalating paranoia, it seemed unlikely I'd have a better chance than this to undo Carl's orientation. Should I start by asking if he'd ever known someone named Tibor? His own name certainly should have some resonance. Or would it be better to ask about the twins—what did he think of the names Rayson and Laylan?

When the door chime sounded, I cursed under my breath. Why now? As I walked toward the door, a lump lodged in my throat—had my captors arrived? Somehow I hadn't imagined them announcing their presence in such a civilized way. When I found Fike looking back at me through the privacy screen, it was like my prayers had been answered. If anyone could get me out of here and help me find Piper, it was him. Carl's re-orientation would have to wait.

"Aaron!" He gave my hand a firm shake and looked past me toward the living room where Carl stood watching us. "And you must be Carl."

With three brisk steps, he covered the distance and shook Carl's hand.

"Patron, what an honor," Carl said.

"Please, call me Fike." His voice was cool and formal. "I hope you both don't mind, but Nathan suggested meeting here."

"No problem," Carl said.

While I wondered what it was all about, my more immediate concern was how Fike could act like he'd never met "Carl." While we were at the compound, I had the impression he'd raised Tibor from the time he was Rayson's age. I fought the urge to pull Fike aside, frantic to know who was caring for the twins in his absence. Would I ever hold Rayson again? Could he help me find Piper so we could warn the Matron?

Fike took a seat next to Carl. "The conference room we've been using is too hectic for a private conversation, and this is kind of midway for both of us."

I didn't like Fike's distant tone of voice, or the way he kept avoiding my eyes. When Nathan entered a few minutes later, my discomfort felt like bats fluttering in my already-clenched stomach.

"Fike." He gave the older man a cold, expressionless nod.

Fike pressed his lips together in a straight line. He dipped his chin in acknowledgement and motioned toward the chair on his right. "Seldon said you had something to tell me."

Carl started to stand, but Nathan gestured for him to sit and glanced at me. "I think this may concern you, too."

Fike frowned, but remained silent.

"Obviously, the last person I want to ask for help is you, Fike, but Seldon said everyone else is under the Elder's control," Nathan said.

"You should know," Fike said. "You are one of his top minions, after all."

Nathan took a deep breath. "That may be, but it doesn't mean I know why he does what he does. Or agree with it."

"Let's cut to the chase—is it true your daughter is spying for him?" Fike asked.

"Wha—?" Nathan sputtered. "How did you know about that?"

"I had hoped it was just a rumor." Fike shook his head. "Your own daughter!"

"It's not like that. Jane wanted to leave the Towers." His voice cracked and his eyes darted away from Fike's. "I planted tracking devices in her clothes...and I let her go." Nathan stared vacantly toward the wall.

"You did what?" Fike yelled.

"The Elder said we needed to flush out the infiltrators so they would lead us back to their compound," Nathan answered in a flat voice.

"Why did he think that?" Fike asked.

"I don't know," Nathan said. "He asked if I'd seen anyone wearing a white scarf, and I remembered Margie escorting two women with white scarves. He's holding one of them downstairs, but he made sure Blair—the other one—managed to escape with my daughter and Terence."

Another woman with a white scarf? The Elder had Piper! My relief was quickly replaced with a sense of dread. Was the Elder better than the Con Squad, or worse? He knew more about our kind, and could use that to his advantage to get to me. I gave Fike a sideways glance, but he wouldn't meet my eyes.

"The Elder said it was like in the beginning, when the Eves decided to leave Eureka Towers. Except this time, the exodus would be reversed—instead of leaving here, the Eves want to take over Eureka Towers, and we'll be forced to return to the compound and the way of life we left behind."

"And you believed it?" Fike said. "You dumb bastard. When will you ever learn?"

"He said Eves already had spies in our midst, so we had to get inside their compound, too," Nathan said.

"Why are you telling me this?" Fike's voice stretched thin with stress and weariness.

Nathan winced. "Rather than let Eureka Towers revert to the Eves, the Elder joined forces with the Con Squad."

"No!" Fike slammed his hand on the couch and jumped to his feet. "That makes no sense. Cains have no interest in helping us."

"They do now," Nathan said. "The Elder can make Cains into suneaters like us. The ones who control the secret will be the most powerful and live twice as long as other Cains."

"You can't turn Cains into suneaters. It's not possible." Fike shook his head. "I'd like to believe what you're saying, but I would've heard about something this big. Somehow he's convinced everyone, but it just isn't true."

Nathan bit his lower lip. "I saw two Cains transformed into suneaters. We kept them under observation for a week."

Fike turned his hands palms up and sighed. "He's tricked all of you, Nathan. And whatever happens, the Cains won't simply go away and leave us alone after this incident is behind us."

"That's why I'm here," Nathan said. "He went too far. After my daughter left with Terence and Blair, I learned he was having the Con Squad track them. She's caught right in the middle of all this."

Fike looked out at the balcony, where the first rays of sunlight made it glow pink, then spun to face Nathan. "Do you have any idea what you've done?"

Nathan stood with his arms dangling at his sides and head downcast. "Besides putting my daughter in danger?"

"You've certainly done that," Fike said, "but so much more. If the Con Squad follows them and Blair goes where I think she will, it's all over. This time, you haven't just killed our pureblood sons, but everyone. Our entire way of life!"

Carl and I exchanged puzzled glances. What was Fike talking about? I'd seen nothing to give me a clue. At the same time, I realized things were more complex than anyone could understand in a few days. Although Nathan clearly had priorities different from mine, he didn't seem like a killer to me.

Nathan's face paled even more. "Maybe I deserve that, but it doesn't help anything. Fike, we haven't had any use for each other since those times, and for good reason. We're very different people. But now I'm begging you to help me undo what I've done and save my daughter. Please! I don't know what else to do, or who else to ask."

Fike studied the floor before asking, "Why did you want to meet here?"

"Seldon suggested it," Nathan said. "I thought we might need help, and he figured the two newest residents were the least likely to be among the Elders' fans."

Inwardly, I sighed with relief. I thought he was going to say I was the spy they'd been hunting, but it had been Seldon's plan to get Fike here, not the Elder's.

When Fike didn't comment, Nathan walked onto the balcony and Carl followed.

Fike paced from corner to corner. "They won't remember any of it." He brushed a hand through his silver hair. "It will be just like before. The Elder will get away with whatever he's planning, and no one can stop him."

"The orientation drug?" I asked.

He nodded. "A form of it, like what I administer to the workers on the Eve compounds."

Somehow, the Elder had used the drug to convince at least some of the Con Squad and his own men he could convert Cains to suneaters. When his power play ended, he could alter their memories again just as easily. The question was, what was really behind the Elder's actions?

The more I thought about everything that had happened, the more suspicious I became. At the compound, why had Tibor been so convinced the Elder wanted to banish me, when the Elder now seemed equally intent to brand me as a spy?

I had stumbled into the middle of something already in the works, and was only a problem because I'd made my way inside Eureka Towers without orientation. I figured it hadn't taken the Elder long to see a silver lining. He knew the Matron wasn't as rigid as Tibor thought and decided to use me as bait. Now he had Piper, who knew the way to the Eve's new compound, but perhaps he didn't realize that yet. Still, it was only a matter of time until he'd find me and take care of the loose end—my memory.

"What are you going to do?" I asked.

"I don't know," Fike said. "It may have gone too far already. If Blair made it to the Eves' new compound, there may be no way to protect them from the Elder or the Cains."

By the time Nathan came back inside a few minutes later, I was tired of dealing with both of them. "Look, we asked you earlier, where are the women?" I said.

He turned his eyes to the ceiling. "Why are you back on that? We need to focus on stopping the Elder."

"Why don't you just tell us?" Carl asked impatiently.

I gave him a grateful smile, then turned a hardened face toward Nathan. "And where's the woman who was with Blair?"

"They are all in the same place—on the nineteenth floor," Nathan said.

That was the floor where Carl had taken Natisha, I recalled, a floor with locks for privacy.

"With the Elder," he added.

30

_____

BLAIR

When the steel plate slid into place beneath the trap door, I knew it was Terence even before his worn boots and tight jeans came into view. When he reached the bottom of the ladder, Jane and I stepped out of the shadows. His scowl was unmistakable even in the dim light; anger radiated from him like heat.

"I told you not to wait more than an hour!" he whispered forcefully. "Why don't you ever do as I say?"

Jane cowered behind me.

I waved the tree trimmer at him. "We were just leaving."

Terence jumped back. "Watch it!"

"I am, but I don't like what I see," I snapped. "Come on, Jane." I crossed the room and loaded my pockets with food and water packets, and Jane did the same. Terence watched us from the base of the ladder.

Jane grabbed my tunic as I turned to leave. "Wait," she said timidly. "Please, wait." She turned toward Terence. "Why were you late?"

"The Con Squad. They were at the last safe house, too." He frowned accusingly at me. "There's no question they're following us."

I took a step back, surprised at his tone and frightened at the news.

"What I don't know is if the barriers we placed between us will matter at all." His eyes strayed to the food packets. "Are they following the same code, 2466, or is it something else?"

Jane caught his gaze and handed him one of her protein bars. "What else could it be?"

He swallowed the contents in one gulp. "They could be tracking us." She handed him another.

"But you didn't want us to know that?" My voice rose an octave.

"I wanted you to get away," Terence snapped. "From them, and from me."

I recoiled, again stung by his words.

He flexed his jaws and stared into my eyes. "The thought crossed my mind that one of you might not be quite what she seems."

"You think I'm one of them!" I said.

"Well, I've thought a lot about it, and it doesn't make sense why you were waiting outside the riser doors when everyone else fled," Terence said. "And once we took you into Eureka Towers, the Con Squad accused you and me of being with The Covenant—the Westover waterworks terrorists. They attacked the Towers, and now I've led them straight to our hiding places."

"You really believe that?" I shouted. "You kidnap me and get my face all over every Nadux in New Humboldt so I can't possibly find my mother, but somehow it's my fault?"

Terence looked up at the trap door. "Quiet!"

"Which is it?" I hissed. "If I'm a turncoat, I should shout at the top of my lungs, not cower here with you."

His shoulders hunched in an almost imperceptible shrug. "What else am I supposed to think? They never attacked the Towers before you came, and they've been right behind us every step of the way since we left."

I didn't understand it either. Now even Terence was against me. All the uncertainty I'd had while he was gone came rushing back. How was I going to get out of this and find my mother?

In the silence, a new sound drew my attention. Jane sat on the floor beneath the row of food and water packets, holding a round silver object and sobbing.

"What's wrong?" I stepped forward, but Terence was closer. He knelt beside Jane and held out his hand. "Where did you find this?" He glared at me.

Jane's tear-streaked face looked up at his. "Is it what I think it is?"

He turned the disk over, checking to see how solid it was. He nodded.

She sobbed, then blurted, "I didn't know!"

He put his hand on her shoulder and repeated, "Where did you find it?"

"It was sewn into the hem of my pants," she said. "I snagged them on bush when we were running. When we stopped to eat a few minutes ago, I saw something silver poking out the hole."

Terence looked away, breathing deeply as if he was counting to ten.

Irritated by his silence, I poked Terence's shoulder with my forefinger. "Was Jane bugged?"

He held out the coin-sized device and sighed. "Guess I owe you an apology."

I heard the words but wasn't ready to accept them. Then there was Jane. I didn't know whether to feel betrayed, or sorry that Jane had been used.

Terence wrapped his arm around Jane's shoulders and pulled her close. Her body heaved with sobs. "I guess that explains why your parents let you come with us without more of a fight," he mused. "I did wonder about that. Nathan's not known for giving women more freedom, even his own daughter."

Jane pulled away to wipe the tears from her cheeks and laughed bitterly. "Yeah, it was my mom who said it was too dangerous for me to go. I thought he'd finally decided it was wrong to keep me trapped in the Towers. But he wasn't thinking about me at all, was he?" Fresh tears fell onto her cheeks.

My gut twisted in sympathy, knowing what it felt like to want a father's love so much every cell in your body hurt. My father's absence had been a constant source of sorrow and disappointment, but I thought it might be even worse if your father used and betrayed you.

"I don't understand," Jane said. "Why would my dad help the Con Squad?"

My eyes met Terence's and I knew he shared the same thought— understanding "why" wasn't at our top priority. We simply needed to leave. Now. The Con Squad couldn't be far behind, and we needed to take advantage of the knowledge Jane's discovery gave us.

"It's going to be all right, Jane." Terence gave her another hug, then nudged her gently toward me. "We'll figure it out. Let Blair check the rest of your clothes, and you check hers."

I cocked a brow at him.

He pointed to a supporting pillar on the dark side of the room. "I'll hand my clothes out so you can check them, too. We could all be bugged."

The process took only a few minutes. I found another disk sewn into the pocket of Jane's blouse, but Terence and I were both free of tracking devices.

"I think we should leave them here and move on as quickly as we can," Terence said.

I put the two disks on the floor.

Terence led the way out through a tight walkway. At one point, he had to fish a food packet from his pockets and hold it until he squeezed through the narrow opening. He closed a steel plate behind us when they reached the next basement, and continued up the next ladder. He cautiously entered the safe house, then motioned for us to follow. He was out of sight when I emerged moments later.

Terence made a low whistle, guiding us further into the house. Jane moved ahead and I stayed in the rear, stopping long enough to shut the trap door and press the button to swing a heavy wooden dresser back over it. I didn't want to leave any clues we'd passed this way.

Outside, sounds of early-morning suburbia reassured me—barking dogs, cars humming past, a few indistinct voices. It took me a moment to locate Terence and Jane where they waited in the building's shadow. I locked and gently closed the kitchen door behind me and joined them. Terence started to move away, but I grabbed his bare arm. "Where are you heading?"

"There's a place not too far from here where we can stay," he said.

"Another safe house?" I asked.

"No, it's a place I found on my own. It'll be okay." He turned, but I didn't release his arm.

Although I still felt emotionally raw from Terence's earlier accusations, my sense of self-preservation screamed at me to take whatever advantage I could get. Terence knew ways to get around the city I'd never imagined, but with Jane's dad in cahoots with the Con Squad, it severely limited our options. "I have another idea."

He shifted back around so he faced me; Jane warily watched us both.

"Can you get us near the building where you found me?" I had to bite back the word "kidnap," which had first come to mind. Now was not the time for that conversation.

"Well, sure," he said. "It's really not too far from here. But getting there in the daylight is risky."

"Riskier than staying near here?" I asked. "The Con Squad isn't far behind us, and they'll expect us to lay low until dark. Does Nathan know what you look like now?"

Terence ran a hand over his bald head. "No, only the women on the third floor saw me after Abigail and my mom did all this."

Abigail had been busy. "Okay, then we'll see how well our disguises work. Tell me how to get to the building from here, and we'll meet you there."

Terence did a double-take. "We're splitting up?"

I sighed and grudgingly admitted, "Okay, I think you had the right idea earlier. If we keep switching up how we travel, we'll be harder to catch."

"True, and if Nathan's involved, he won't expect two women to strike out alone," Terence said. "But that's right in the middle of the city."

"I know that. I'm a city girl, remember," I said impatiently. "They won't expect us to be that stupid, so maybe today, it's a smart thing."

Jane's mouth curled in agreement.

"What's bothering me is how to avoid people who've seen my face on Nadux and think I'm a terrorist," I said.

Terence smirked. "You forget how you look."

I sneered at him, but Jane giggled.

"Yeah, it would be best to get far away from here before they discover we're gone," Terence said.

"I think I can help with that," I said. "If it's still where I left it, no one should be looking for us in a car like mine."

He cocked his head.

"You'll find out." I grinned.

He gave us instructions, pointing toward skyscrapers silhouetted against the rising sun. "It looks farther away than it is. You can be there in less than an hour—two hours tops, even if you're backtracking and trying to be hard to follow."

"Not a bad idea, but like you, I think it's more important to put as much distance as possible between us and where the Con Squad expects us to be," I said. "The car is in the Buckeye Garage on Ninth Street—fourth floor. We'll meet by the riser."

He nodded. "If you're not there in an hour, I'll check back twice at half-hour intervals. Then you're on your on."

"Okay." I swallowed hard, realizing I was responsible for what happened next. From detective shows on the Nadux, I knew it wouldn't take long for facial recognition software to see through our disguises. I wished I still had Dina's cream to help confuse the scanners with moiré patterns. We needed a break, and I hoped Nathan's collusion with the Con Squad had accidentally given it to us. With some luck, today the Con Squad would focus its resources on the safe houses instead of its usual surveillance of the city scans.

Terence gave us a mock tip-o-the-hat. "See you in an hour."

Jane returned the gesture, and I smiled. "In an hour."

Terence headed north and we went south. Within a few blocks, Jane and I turned east. As the day brightened, I had conflicting emotions as more cars sped by and people joined us on the sidewalk. We walked about a mile before the suburban houses gave way to scattered shops; soon only businesses with screen fronts reflected our passing images or the day's news. We paused at one of the popular storefronts, where a half dozen people sipping hot chai or orangina freezes watched the latest paparazzi vids of Great Britannia's royal dog, Pepi.

Soon only multi-storied buildings lined the street, blocking out much of the sunlight. We'd gone another mile when Jane balked at the sight of a moving walkway.

"Follow me. You'll like them." I guided her by the elbow for a few steps, then walked confidently onto the ramp with Jane close behind. It was wide enough we could stand side by side without blocking other pedestrians, whose focus was on their personal conversations or handhelds. We switched walkways a couple of times, and each time the crowds thickened as we went deeper into the heart of the city.

Once the hairs on my neck prickled, alerting me to watching eyes. A sideways glance revealed two boys about Jane's age. I chuckled and leaned closer so Jane could hear me over the waking city's cacophony. "You have some admirers."

Jane's gaze followed my head tilt. Her face flushed, and she gave them a shy smile before turning back toward me. "It doesn't even matter if they pick me—I can choose!"

If nothing else good came from all this, at least Jane had this taste of freedom. I gave her a quick hug and said, "Take a right at the next stop."

On Ninth Street, we watched from across the street as cars pulled up to the ramp at Buckeye Garage. After the passengers left, the turnstile rotated and the hovering car disappeared into the garage.

Jane watched another car enter the queue. "That's crazy."

"It's totally automated," I said.

"How does it work?" On the street side, a truck arrived in front of waiting pedestrians, who piled into the double cab.

"Beats me—some combination of levitation, GPS, and robotics," I said. "All I know for sure is the system responds to this." I pointed to the flesh-colored wristband.

"You've been wearing it all this time?" Jane asked.

"Yep," I said. "They're made to be inconspicuous. My mom's friend said people used to lose their keys all the time, so they just started wearing these instead. Of course, if it's your personal car, it's not an issue anyway."

Jane cocked her head.

"Retinal scanners or print pads," I explained.

"That makes sense." Jane checked her handheld. "We're right on time."

I led the way, exiting the stairs on the fourth floor just as the riser door opened and Terence walked out. He smiled. "I love it when a plan comes together!"

"Wait until you see this!" I pressed my fingers on both sides of the wristband and held my breath, willing it to work. Moments later, the doors opened to our red-and-white-checkered ride.

"A pizza delivery car?" he said.

31

ARI

I lowered onto the couch. Could this get any worse? Not only was the Elder holding Piper captive, but all the other women, too. "And Seldon?"

"He's there, too." Nathan closed his eyes and curled his hands into fists. "I'm the only one the Elder trusts."

"I see," Fike said. "And what does he think you're doing?"

"He sent me to check the third floor and reset the sensors." Nathan cut his eyes toward Carl and me. "*Someone* set off the alarm."

Carl snorted and shook his head. "*Someone* was actually concerned about the women and wanted to be sure they were okay."

My mind raced. I had to get Piper away before anyone—especially the Elder—figured out she was an Eve. Seldon would be doing what he could, but it didn't sound like he could get her free. We needed someone inside working with her. A woman? I looked up and saw Fike staring at me. He shook his head slightly. I reached to push my hair back from my face, forgetting for a moment it was no longer there. I cleared my throat uncertainly. "Nathan, what if you brought back a woman and said you found her hiding on the third floor?"

"What?" Nathan laughed and rolled his eyes. "You think you can play dress up and fool the Elder? Boy, you don't look a thing like a woman."

I turned away from him, unable to keep the corners of my mouth from turning up. Having the Elder think I was male was the least of my worries. Instead, I was afraid he would see through whatever disguise I could improvise and recognize me as the woman who'd escaped from the Adams' compound.

"Besides, what would you do once you got there?" Nathan ranted. "The doors on the thirteenth floor lock, you know. Those women aren't going anywhere until the Elder releases them."

"Unless someone else sets them free," Fike said. "*Someone* the Elder trusts."

"It's not that simple," Nathan said. "You heard those men downstairs. The Elder was listening, too, and he put those loudmouths on guard duty."

Fike shook his head. "What possible use could the Elder have for the women?"

Nathan's shoulders hunched. "Leverage. If the Eves do attack, he figures they won't allow the women to be hurt."

"He'd harm women to coerce the Eves to surrender?" Fike's voice rose indignantly. He stepped toward Nathan with his chin jutted out and fists clenched.

Nathan held up a hand defensively. "You knew this, Fike. Women have no value to him. But you're not blameless. You didn't stop him from making the orientation how it is today, now did you?"

Fike lowered his fists and slumped within his clothes. "The choices were never good ones—somehow he always made it seem like standing up for women was harmful to our sons. I had to pick my battles."

"Yeah, I did what I had to do, too." Nathan grunted. "And the cost was too high. Now my mate's imprisoned by woman-haters and the Con Squad's hunting down my daughter."

Carl walked over and stood between the two men. "There must be some way we can help. Can we get into where the women are being held without being noticed? Maybe we could create a distraction?"

Nathan shrugged. "If we work together, I guess it's possible someone could get into the room without being seen, but I have to ask again—then what?"

"Then we find a way to get the women out," Fike said.

"Even though you don't see it now, Nathan, I bet I could pass as a woman," I said. "I just need to get some clothes and a wig. Once I get inside, I'll blend in."

"There's a back way in?" Carl asked.

Nathan nodded. "Part of the emergency system. Each floor has two lobbies that can be reached by the riser or stairs. Since most common areas were built to showcase the redwood, the back lobbies are seldom used. As you'd expect, the Elder kept the better rooms near the tree for him and his men."

"Perfect!" Fike said. "We could draw their attention to the main lobby."

"You'd also have to put at least one guard out of commission before he has a chance to warn the others," Nathan said.

Fike looked at the ceiling and held his chin as he thought. "It's common knowledge about the alarm going off on the women's floor, isn't it?"

Nathan nodded.

"Well, if you escorted Aaron in through the back lobby and turned 'her' over to the guard, wouldn't he just assume she was the one who set it off?" Fike asked.

"Probably," Nathan said.

"Then what would happen?" Carl asked.

"He'd probably stick her in with the others."

"He wouldn't have to tell the Elder?" Fike asked.

"He would, unless I tell him I'll do it," Nathan said. "But what good does that do? Then they'll just have one more captive."

"I could tell the women what's going on," I said. "When you create a distraction, we'll make our escape down the back stairs."

Nathan's back straightened. "No, not down the stairs. Up!"

"Up?" the three of us said together.

"On the twenty-first floor, the back lobby connects with Lovers' Lane—the walkways through the redwood's top branches." Nathan's eyes were bright. "Privacy is part of the courtship ritual. None of the guards would think to go up the stairs, and I doubt the Elder has ever considered how to access the walkways."

"But the women can't go out on Lovers' Lane—they'd be in plain view!" I said.

"Let me put it this way, if you make it to the twenty-first floor without being seen, you can disappear." Nathan gestured and made a "poofing" sound. "No one's going to be thinking about a trip to Lovers' Lane in the middle of a crisis. And there'd be no other reason to go up those access stairs since that's the only place they go."

"That's great, but they still have to get out of a locked room and past the guard," Carl said.

Fike thumped his forefinger on his chin, his eyes turned upward. "I'm sure I could create a diversion that would keep the Elder occupied." He turned to Nathan. "If we timed it right so you were still by the guard, you could send him to check out the disturbance while you watch the women."

"And I'd let them out." Nathan nodded. "Yes! It could work."

"But after they disappear from the locked rooms, they'd still be trapped in the stairwell," I said.

Nathan grimaced. "If the diversion lasts long enough, we could get them across Lovers' Lanes and down the stairwell or riser on the other side. For now, though, I think we should focus on getting the women away from the Elder."

"And taking away his leverage," Fike said.

It wasn't going to be easy, but at least I could see some possibilities. The air surrounding me seemed to grow lighter, lifting a burden from my shoulders. "Sounds good to me, too. I'll need a few minutes to get ready."

Nathan focused on Fike. "Maybe I'll check in with the Elder after I drop her off, but return to the guard before the disturbance begins?"

Fike nodded.

Carl asked, "What do you think we should do as a distraction? We could blow up something."

Fike pursed his lips and tilted his head. "That seems like a bit much."

Carl snorted.

"Smoke always gets your attention," Fike said, "and I happen to know a great way to generate lots of smoke without fire."

I turned to Nathan. "Any ideas on where I could find a wig and some women's clothing? I didn't see those kind of options on the Nadux."

He raised his eyebrows. "The beauty salon would be a good bet for a wig—Abigail's always offering the women plenty of options. And Margie usually keeps some spare clothes since she often hosts newcomers."

"The first thing is to get the alarm turned off," Carl said. "There's no way we can do anything until it's disabled."

"I reset it once, so doing it again is no problem," Nathan said.

When we reached the lobby, Fike said, "Carl, I could use some help." We entered different riser cars. Nathan pushed the button for the third floor. When we arrived, he opened a panel behind the riser button and flicked a switch. I winced as he stepped into the hallway, but the alarm remained silent. I released the breath I'd been holding and followed him. He pushed the door chime but didn't wait for an answer before he entered.

"Margie," he shouted as the door slid open. "Margie?"

We walked into an apartment much like the one I shared with Carl, except for the wall art, which gave it a woodlands feel. "Try the guest room." Nathan pointed to the left.

I checked through the built-in drawers beneath the bunk bed and found some blue leggings and a white tunic in much the same style as the ones I'd worn when I left the compound with Layla. I placed my sandals into the Nadux recycler and selected a pair of spike-heeled boots in my size.

Nathan waited for me in the hallway. We headed toward the lobby. On the other side, we entered a shop with three swivel chairs facing mirrors on one side and built-in bench seating along the walls. He pointed at a beaded curtain covering a doorway at the back of the room. "That's where Abigail says she does her 'makeover magic.'"

I took a few steps toward the door. "I'll be back in a minute."

Nathan avoided my eyes and rushed out of the shop. I had a hunch he wanted to check his mate's room. It seemed strange that I didn't even know her name.

The beaded strands slipped through my fingers as I went through the doorway into the salon's back room. A swivel chair and mirror took up one side, but nine small doors from waist-height to the ceiling filled the opposite wall, with drawers below in the same pattern of three across and three deep. I opened the middle door and found an assortment of hair clasps in a variety of colors, and even a tiara. As I explored behind each door and opened every drawer, I found fake eyelashes, eyebrow pencils, lash dye, tweezers, depilatory ray pencils, contact lenses, cheek pads, makeup, wrinkle freeze, and hairpieces of all kinds and colors — falls, switches, wigs, extensions.

Remembering the picture Carl chose, I grabbed a shoulder-length blonde wig and popped in pale turquoise contacts. I looked ridiculous, and nothing like Natisha. Even though my skin tone was lighter than usual due to all the sunlight I'd been getting, the contrast with the honey-colored hair was comical. The contacts were stunning, but not on me. They stared out from the mirror with a riveting appeal as startling as the famous Afghan Girl cover of an ancient National Geographic magazine I'd seen in class—not the reaction I wanted.

I heard the front door slide open and gingerly parted the beads. Nathan wandered aimlessly around the shop. "Back here," I called. "It will take me a few more minutes. I just found what I wanted."

And that was true. I carefully secured a chin-length blonde wig that hung in spikes, framing my face. Black roots and streaks helped it look more natural with my skin. I popped in green contacts that let some of my eyes' natural blue show through, and thinned and lightened my eyebrows. I added some makeup—a touch of blush and lip stain.

I stepped out of the jumpsuit and unwound the scarf from my chest. I could breathe for the first time in days. I slipped into the clothes I'd picked up at Margie's. They were a little tight for my taste, particularly after wearing shapeless jumpsuits. I didn't realize how much difference the clothes would make until I stepped in front of a full-length mirror. My curves were back. Smirking, I stepped into the room with Nathan.

He took one look and stumbled back into one of the stylist's chairs. "You're a...woman?"

32

BLAIR

J ane giggled as Terence spluttered, "Really, Blair? Pizza delivery?"
I entered the car and began pushing buttons to program our
route. "C'mon," I motioned. "We can discuss it on the way."

Jane pushed aside a blanket lying on the cracked red vinyl seat
and crawled in beside me. Terence edged inside the door, which slid
shut as soon as he was seated. "I don't get it. Why do you even have a
car, much less this car?"

"I usually use the walkways and the tube," I said, "but *this* is more
than just a car."

We exited the garage onto the street and picked up speed to
merge into traffic. By the time I finished programming it, we were
approaching the SuperFlex.

"Wait." Terence scooted to the edge of his seat. "You can't link to
the chain—it's too easy to track and almost impossible to escape if
the Con Squad initiates a lockdown."

"It'll be okay," I said.

"You don't understand, I was caught in a lockdown," he insisted.
"All traffic on the SuperFlex was literally frozen in place. Fortunately
for me, the troopers' car-to-car search yielded that day's fugitive
before they reached me."

I nodded. "Usually you'd be right. But look around you. Really look." I gestured widely, commanding their attention. "You can't turn in any direction without seeing pizza or Chinese delivery cars."

Terence grunted and Jane whistled under her breath. He cringed at the metallic snap of a new link fastening. "Okay, but that's not going to help us if there's a lockdown." We were now the middle of a five-car chain.

"Of course it will. That's my second point—nobody really sees these delivery cars anymore," I said. "They might as well be invisible, like the food dispenser in your flat."

"Did you steal it?" Jane asked.

I laughed. "No, it belongs to my mom's friends. Apparently, it's a salvage vehicle they bought on the black market for use in circumstances like this. Hiding from the Con Squad isn't as rare a thing as I thought." I saw Terence's jaw tighten as we sped up another level on the SuperFlex. I hoped the theory about our invisibility was sound. I reached up and blacked the windows, shielding us from view but letting us see outside. "How about a little privacy?"

"You can't drive around with your windows blacked out!" Terence jumped to his feet. "The traffic monitors will be all over us."

I grinned and pointed at one of the passing delivery cars. Its windows were opaque, covered with red and white daily specials overlaid with flashing yellow and black sale prices. "The pizza delivery union has one of the strongest promotional lobbies. It's amazing how they get advantages no one else gets—privacy comes at a price, and today it's a two-for-one special."

Jane laughed out loud.

Terence smirked. "A two-for-one special? Guess that's one way of looking at it. I have to hand it to your mom's friends. This is a great idea."

I smiled. We cruised onto the SuperFlex's highest twist, which gave us a panoramic view of New Humboldt as we headed southwest. Terence nudged Jane and pointed east toward a group of skyscrapers. "Eureka Towers is over there."

She nodded and rested her chin on her hands, keeping her eyes riveted on the sights. "It's a big city." Another ten minutes passed before we neared the edge of the sprawling metropolis. "Why are pizza and Chinese food delivered instead of vended, when they would be fresher?"

"Ah," I sighed. "We outsiders don't have the high-end vending machines you have at Eureka Towers."

"You mean those awful food packets weren't just old?" Jane asked.

I shook my head. "That's about as good as they get."

Jane grabbed her throat and made gagging noises.

"Now you understand why there are so many delivery cars!"

Jane nodded.

I punched in a code, and we slowed into a downward spiral through the loops of the SuperFlex.

"What now?" Terence's back stiffened. "Is there a problem?"

I sighed. "Not exactly. But the rest of my plan for escaping the Con Squad requires help."

"Here we go again," Terence said.

"You could act like you trust me, even if you don't," I said. "It's not like your plan at the safe houses worked very well."

He frowned at me, then at Jane, who blushed.

"There's no way Jane's dad could know about this." I reached over and squeezed Jane's hand, which felt cold in mine. "In fact, it involves meeting people I never knew existed until yesterday."

"What do you mean?" Terence asked.

"I mean mutants."

"Mutants?" He snorted. "We're trying to get away from suneaters."

"That's not who I meant."

He frowned when I paused, but Jane leaned forward with blinking eyes, eagerly awaiting my next words.

"I met a mooneater."

Jane tilted her head. "You mean someone who lives off moonlight, not food, like Terence's dad lived off sunlight?"

"A mooneater?" Terence scoffed and shook his head.

"Yes, and she can't get out of Eureka Towers with all the heightened security," I said. "She needs to get a message to her people. It seems the suneaters at the Towers led by the Elder are planning to attack them."

Jane gasped, but Terence's face remained unchanged. Although I'd hoped otherwise, this wasn't news to him.

"She gave me this." I held out the white scarf. "When other mooneaters see it, they will guide us to their compound." I bit my bottom lip and faced Terence. "I should say, they'll help Jane and me.

It's strictly prohibited for males to come near the mooneaters' compound—you'd be killed before you even got close."

"They'll approach any woman who wears a white scarf? Sounds like a lot of malarkey to me," he said.

"There's more to it than that," I agreed. "I just thought you'd like to know the gist of it since we'll need to split up again. I owed you for getting me out of jam with the Con Squad, so now we're even."

"I don't know how you figure that." Terence rolled his eyes. "But whatever."

"You're going to leave him?" Jane asked.

I shrugged. "We don't have much choice. And he's made it pretty clear he'd be better off alone."

Jane's chin quivered. "That was before we found out about the tracking devices."

I sucked in a deep breath. "Don't worry about it yet. First, we have to get closer to where they live, and then one of the mooneaters has to spot us. We have a little more time to see if there's a better way."

"What makes you think you're going in the right direction?" Terence asked.

"I programmed the car to look for apples. Have you noticed those?" I pointed at a holo sign, which blipped into our vision for a quarter-minute, then disappeared. Soon another appeared.

"Genesis Apple Orchard?" Jane giggled.

"You've gotta be kidding!" Terence slapped his hand on the seat and guffawed.

"I know," I said. "But that's what I thought about pizza delivery, too. Turns out, it's so obvious, it's invisible."

"Next thing you'll say is that we have to kiss a snake," Terence said.

I chuckled. "Believe me, I'll work on that for you." Growing serious, I pulled the crescent-moon pendant from my neck and showed it to them. "Whoever approaches us should have an amulet like this, but with a full moon. If not, there's something wrong, and we need to leave."

"Sounds like they've been infiltrated before," Terence said.

"Maybe so." I slipped the pendant back on. "We just have to be careful."

The car unlinked from the SuperFlex and maneuvered suburban streets much like the ones we'd traveled on foot the night before.

Finally, it pulled up to an open air market beneath a flashing holo of a snake's head bobbing for apples, promoting the Genesis Apple Orchard "one mile east—-follow the signs. Kiddie playground and spiced cider."

I selected a three-spoon-rated teahouse from the screen and within minutes, the car slid to a stop next to another pizza delivery car. "Guess you have to eat something besides pizza sometimes," I joked.

Terence got out and we followed him, blinking in the bright sunlight. "You really think this scarf-thing is going to work?"

I kicked a brown pebble that had found its way onto the concrete walkway. "I know it won't work if we don't try, and we don't exactly have a lot of other options."

Inside, the teahouse was low-budget cozy. The ornate light fixtures and ruffle-skirted tables contrasted with geometric wall paintings and sharp-edged counters. Earthy scents of tea and aromatic spices filled the air, and a display of scones and sandwiches made my mouth water.

"Let's grab something decent to eat while we can." Jane's eyes were riveted on an orange scone.

"Don't you want another food packet?" Terence teased.

She shot him a piercing look. "I'll save them for you."

We'd finished eating and were getting ready to leave when a young woman about Jane's age bumped into the table, splashing tea onto my back.

"I'm so sorry." She reached for a napkin.

"It's quite..." I looked up and faced the knotted ends of a white scarf. "...all right." I stared at the woman's blue eyes and dark hair. She looked a lot like Piper. "Don't I know you from somewhere?"

The woman smiled. "I don't think so, although you look familiar to me, too."

A flush heated my neck and face as I thought how badly this could go if the woman meant to turn us over to the Con Squad. I steeled my nerves and said, "White is the color of the moon."

The woman nodded and glanced to the side. I couldn't see who she consulted, but a moment later, the woman reached under the scarf to display a pendant just like Piper's. A knot formed in my stomach—it was a crescent moon, not a full moon, and it was on a golden chain.

A moment passed as I wrestled with what to do. If the pendant and chain were wrong, Piper said to leave.

Terence stood and handed me a napkin. "Looks like no damage was done."

Jane took the cue and checked her handheld. "We really must be going." She rose, grabbing my elbow as she did.

I reached back and dabbed the wet spot with the napkin. I smiled apologetically. "If we pass this way again, maybe we can figure out where our paths have crossed."

The wooden chair scraped against the concrete floor as I stood and followed Terence and Jane out. A woman I'd never seen before leaned against our car, blocking the door.

"Here goes nothing," Terence mumbled barely loud enough for me to hear. "Be ready to jump in when I get her out of the way."

He stepped forward and reached out to grab the woman, but stopped when she held out a pendant engraved with a full moon. She turned to face me. "White is the color of the moon."

I displayed Piper's crescent-moon pendant. "White is the color of the moon."

Behind us, the teahouse door slid open. The woman with the crescent-moon pendant stepped out, accompanied by two men.

I brushed past the woman with the full-moon pendant to open the car door. We all hastily entered. As the car door slid shut behind Jane and Terence, the woman who'd spilled tea on me called out, "There they are."

Terence slapped his hand against the seat in frustration. "Just another minute and they wouldn't have seen us."

"Don't worry." The woman handed me some coordinates. "They won't be able to follow us for long."

I hesitated a moment, then entered the codes. We joined a stream of traffic and the teahouse fell out of sight. We'd left so quickly, I hadn't even seen what kind of car the other woman had.

I activated the ad screens and hoped our pursuers wouldn't be able to identify this particular pizza delivery car among so many others. Jane and Terence kept watch behind us as I focused on the woman with the full-moon pendant. She pulled out a white scarf that had been hidden beneath her tunic.

"I was afraid you'd fall for her ruse," the woman said, "but we were ready either way."

"Who was she?" I said. "For that matter, who are you?"

The woman laughed and brushed her shoulder-length black hair away from her face. "As you guessed, I'm a Daughter of the Moon. She was an imposter, perhaps with the Con Squad, but that's not really their style."

"Do you have a name?" Terence asked.

I blushed at his rudeness, but the woman chuckled. "You can call me Night."

The car had taken a series of loops and now headed back toward the city. "Where are you taking us?" I asked.

"Someplace safe, where we can talk," Night said.

"There's no time for that," I said. "I have an important message for the Matron."

The car pulled into an industrial park on the outskirts of New Humboldt. Even at midday, the shadows between the boxy multi-story warehouses and shipping docks gave it an eerie feel. Jane slipped her hand into mine and scooted closer to Terence as an oversized corrugated metal door slid open, and the building's dark maw swallowed the car.

Night opened the car door and gestured for us to exit. Terence ducked his head and stepped out, followed by Jane. As I moved to follow, handcuffs snapped shut on my wrist. Someone gave my other hand a hard jerk and snapped on the second cuff, pulling my arms tight behind me. From the corner of my eyes, I saw Terence and Jane were in a similar predicament. Our captors stood behind us, and a dozen or more women waited in the shadows flanking the entrance. It had only taken a second to make us prisoners.

"Things are often not as they seem," Night said. "We can't afford to take chances."

33

ARI

H e spluttered. "How...?"

I winked. "Let's just say that Abigail must know a thing or two about makeovers. She had all the supplies I needed." I laughed and gave Nathan's shoulder a playful jab. "So, now do you think I can fool the Elder?"

Nathan swallowed hard. "I'd never have recognized you. You look like a real woman."

As we walked to the riser, I wondered if he now suspected who I was. Just as quickly, I discounted that idea. If the Elder had mentioned his search for a woman who escaped from the Adams' compound, surely Nathan would've figured out what had happened before now. He already knew "Aaron's" orientation was faulty.

My gut clenched as the door to our apartment slid open. How would Carl react? Part of me wanted the disguise to work so well he'd be as flummoxed as Nathan—and would find me as attractive as Natisha. Another part wanted my new look to rekindle his memories so he would remember me—the real me. My stomach sank when we entered the apartment and found Fike waiting alone.

He blinked twice, then said, "My, my. You certainly don't look like yourself."

I grinned at the double meaning and felt layers of tension slip away. "That's what I wanted to hear." If I didn't look like Ariadne to him, perhaps I had a chance of fooling the Elder.

"Where's Carl?" Nathan asked.

"He's gathering a few more supplies," Fike said. "We knew you needed to get back upstairs as soon as possible so the Elder wouldn't get suspicious, but I wanted to confirm our plans before you left."

Nathan and I were back on the riser a few minutes later. We'd soon know if our hastily conceived attempt to free the women would work. We hadn't had time to come up with a back-up plan, so it was now or never. The rapid beat of my heart thudded in my ears louder than the riser's metallic whirr.

* * *

I stood with my back against the locked door, uneasy under the gaze of about thirty frowning women who obviously didn't know what to make of a stranger joining them in captivity. I hadn't yet caught my breath, which I'd been holding since the riser doors opened a minute or so ago onto the back lobby of the nineteenth floor. After a tense moment when the guard first saw me, things had gone so smoothly it was unnerving.

No explanation had been needed. Nathan merely pushed me forward with a terse, "Found the problem," and the guard shoved me inside this room. I could hear them still talking in the hallway, but couldn't make out the words. If things continued to go as planned, I only had a few minutes to get the women on my side.

"My name is Ari." I looked around the crowded room, searching for Piper. "Some of the men are trying to free you. We'll only have a minute or two, so you need to be ready."

"We don't have any women at Eureka Towers named Ari," said a gray-haired woman in an old-school black sheath dress. "I know every name and every face, and you're not one of us."

I cleared my throat to give myself a moment to think. I couldn't let her doubts get in the way of what I had to do. That's when I spotted a familiar face. I hurried over and grabbed the arm of a woman on the second row. "Natisha! Tell them how Carl's been trying to reach you."

She gave me a puzzled look, but stepped to face the group. "Yes, she's right. Before our handhelds were taken, he'd tried to contact me several times." She turned back to me. "But who are you?"

"I'm working with him," I said. "Carl sent me to take you and the other women to a safer place. The Elder is planning to use you as hostages to make the Eves give in to his demands. He wants to make them have more male children."

The women gasped. "Won't they die?" Natisha asked.

"Yes." Tears threatened to spill onto my cheeks. Where had that come from? "We can't let that happen," I said in a choked voice. I sucked in a breath and shoved away my fears for the Eves—for all those like me.

"But what can we do?" she asked. "The door is locked."

"There's going to be a distraction. If things go right, the guard will leave Nathan here while he goes to investigate," I explained. "When the door opens, we have to be ready to run."

"Why?" asked a redhaired woman about my age. "We can't even get off this floor without a male escort. We certainly won't be able to hide in a hallway."

I bobbed my head in acknowledgement. "I have a plan. It may not work, but it's our only chance. I know it's a lot to ask, but just trust me." I turned back to Natisha. "Gather up the women who've been to Lovers' Lanes. They'll lead the way."

While she chose the women, I hunted for Piper. About a third of the group assembled a few minutes later. Exasperated after a fruitless search, I asked, "Have you seen a new girl named Piper? She may have been with a woman named Margie."

Several looked away.

"What is it?" I asked, my nerves taut. "What happened?"

Natisha rested a calming hand on my arm. "I don't know about Piper, but the Con Squad took Margie."

"Oh no!" I said.

"Right after the explosion," the gray-haired woman added. "Margie was helping her son and that girl disappear."

"Blair," Natisha said. "The ones you saw on the Nadux terrorist alert."

"Then where is Piper?" I hated the pleading tone in my voice, but I was panicked. I had to find her.

Natisha shrugged. "In one of the other rooms?"

That's when I realized one thing we'd overlooked in our planning. The rooms on the nineteenth floor were designed for intimate rendezvous, not to hold dozens of people. "How many rooms are there?"

The women looked at each other, some with a palms-up gesture. "Three other rooms, if they're like this one," the gray-haired woman said. "Last count, there were 120 of us, including crones like me and the youngsters."

I looked away and pressed my lips together, fighting the urge scream. Why couldn't things be simple for once? Was it too much to ask?

"Ari," Natisha said. "You said we only have a few minutes—tell us what to do."

"Right," I said. "Since there are other rooms, we'll have to split the leaders into teams. It will take a little more time to explain what we're doing while we're making the escape, but we should still be able to make it work." I hoped that was true, but either way, we had to try.

I had just finished briefing them when I heard shouting in the hallway. Natisha and six of the leaders gathered at the front with me, and the other women crowded close behind us. When the door slid open, I grabbed Nathan and pulled him toward the next room as I explained the problem. He waved his pinky at the scanner and the door opened. Natisha and one of the other women went inside to lead the women to the stairwell, and Nathan and I hurried to the next room.

"Stay with him," I told two of the women when Nathan stopped by the next door, and motioned for the other three to follow me. I didn't know if it would work, but when I reached the next door, I swept my pinky at the scanner. Nothing happened. *It should work. Why didn't it work?* I breathed deeply and looked over at Nathan for guidance, but he was briefing the women from the other room. I gave a frustrated huff and tried again. The women gasped and stepped back from me when it opened.

"It's a long story." I grinned, glad I'd gotten permissions to this floor even if I hadn't had my rendezvous yet. The last of the leaders and I rushed to the fourth room, where Nathan met us. I hoped the gray-haired woman was right and we'd now freed all the women. We couldn't risk going any further. Each room had taken us closer to the other lobby where the Elder and his men were. Billowy white smoke blocked any view beyond this room, but shouts were getting louder and the sound of running footsteps coming closer.

I searched the women's faces as they followed our group toward the stairwell. No Piper. How had I missed her? As we reached the corner, I looked back over my shoulder and saw a form emerging from the smoke. I ducked out of sight. "Faster," I whispered. "They're coming."

We rushed up the stairs to the twenty-first floor, then dashed across the hall toward a black door next to the riser—the access to Lovers' Lanes. The women before us had done a good job of leaving room and we had no problem entering the crowded stairwell. I put a finger to my lips and the muttering ceased in a collective intake of breath. I gazed with dread, expecting the old-fashioned push door to swing open at any moment. I heard shouts as the men reached the empty rooms two floors below.

"They're gone!"

"Dammit, find them. Now!"

Heavy footfalls passed outside our sanctuary several times before it grew quiet again. In a way, that was even more chilling. Where were they? Was a sentry waiting for us to step into the hallway?

Natisha made her way to my side. "We're just supposed to wait?" she whispered.

I nodded. This part of the plan would be more difficult than I thought. The stairwell allowed standing-room only for more than a hundred frightened women and children. A few whimpers from the youngest threatened to spread. It wasn't going to be easy to remain here quietly.

"I need to find Piper." I motioned up the stairwell with my eyes.

"Go ahead," Natisha said. "I'll stay here by the door. The other women know me, so they'll be less likely to challenge my authority."

I squeezed her hand. "Thanks." I pressed upward with muttered apologies. I pushed past the young woman whose picture I had chosen, but she didn't recognize me as Aaron with my blonde hair and blue eyes.

When I reached the twenty-fourth floor, I had no doubt. Piper wasn't here. I tried to not let my imagination run wild, but I kept thinking of all the stories we'd been told about what happened to Eves outside our compound. Was she being tortured or raped? Was she even still alive?

34

BLAIR

"Sorry," I told Jane and Terence. "I didn't see this one coming."

"That's what you get for trusting someone you just met," Terence grumbled.

I barked a laugh at him. "Yeah, it seems like I would've learned by now. But I didn't exactly have a lot of choices."

He looked away.

Night walked over to me, pulled the crescent-moon necklace over my head and examined it carefully. "Where did you get this?"

"We have important information for the Matron," I said. "Or maybe you're not interested because I should have trusted the other woman at the teahouse, after all."

Night frowned at me. "It can't hurt for you to give me a name. If it's someone I recognize, perhaps I'll help you reach the Matron. Now who gave this to you?"

I glanced at Jane and Terence. Both shrugged. "Piper."

Night gave an almost imperceptible nod, then tipped her head toward Terence. "Why are you traveling with him?" Her voice relayed contempt and suspicion.

"Well ..." I halted, unsure if mentioning we were fugitives would help anything. We'd gone to a lot of trouble to not be recognizable, but if these were Eves, I had to trust them. I hoped the truth would work to our advantage. "If you've seen any Nadux reports lately, you know the Con Squad is hunting two alleged Covenant terrorists."

"Yes, the ones responsible for the Blue Death," Night said.

I snorted. "It's all lies."

"Blair." Terence stepped toward me, but the woman next to him grabbed his cuffed hands and jerked him to a stop. "Don't do this."

"Well, what do you want me to do?" I snapped at him. "If the truth doesn't get us to the Matron, it won't matter anyway." I tossed my head back defiantly. "We're the ones the Con Squad is looking for, but we had nothing to do with contaminating the waterworks."

Night's forehead furrowed. She pulled up her handheld. A few taps on the screen later, she said, "Hard to believe. Now that I know to look beyond the surface, I can see your true features." She nodded toward Jane. "What about her?"

"Part of the misdirection—traveling as a threesome rather than a couple," I said.

"Why didn't Piper come with you?" Night asked.

"Piper said she had to meet up with someone before she could leave," I said. "With all the security, she was afraid they wouldn't be able to escape."

"You mean she's a prisoner?" Night's voice rose.

My thoughts raced. I wanted to be truthful, but for Terence's sake, maybe it wasn't the best time to talk about how the men at Eureka Towers treated the women. "Not exactly. With all the security alerts, they don't want to call attention to the building. All travel is restricted."

"But you're here."

"Everyone agreed we had to leave," I said. "It would be a disaster for the whole community if the Con Squad found us there."

Night faced about a dozen women standing in the shadows at the side of the room. "The pendant is authentic. I think she can be trusted, although she's still hiding something."

An older woman wearing a loose-fitting orange robe quietly approached. "Uncuff the women's hands."

"What about me?" Terence said. No one responded.

When Jane and I were freed, I rubbed my wrists and glanced at Terence. As I suspected, his face and neck were red, and he pressed his lips tightly together. I understood his frustration, but getting mad wasn't going to make our captors want to release him sooner.

Night and the other women dipped their heads as the older woman passed them. She stopped in front of me. "I'm the Matron," she said.

My heart fluttered with relief. We'd made it after all.

"I apologize for these precautions, but it's how our kind has survived over the millennia," she said.

If I'd learned one thing in the past few days, it was my ideas about the world were far from the reality. I'd gone from believing in mutants, to thinking they were a fabrication. Could this woman truly be an immortal?

"Piper sent a message for me?" Matron asked.

"Yes." I wished I'd asked Piper to describe her. I had no way to know if this woman was the Matron, but the other women clearly deferred to her. I met her piercing blue eyes. "Piper learned an attack on your compound is planned."

Matron smiled. "Piper is easily alarmed. No one could possibly know our new location."

"But they do!" I insisted. "And the Elder has gotten everyone stirred up about the way—I don't know a good way to say this—uh, how Eves won't carry male babies to term."

"Won't?" Matron's eyes crinkled. "Actually, we can't. We'd die."

"They don't believe that," I said. "He's convinced the men they'd be safer if they controlled you like they do the other women." I winced. I really hadn't meant to say that last part either, but now it was out.

Night grunted and glared at Terence. Angry murmurs rose from the women standing in the shadows. The Matron held up her hand and silence returned. She pointed to Terence, "Is that what you think —that we should be under your control?"

He clenched his jaw and straightened, then replied slowly. "Eureka Towers provides a safer place for women, free from the threats of the Con Squad."

Another murmur arose, and the Matron frowned. "Go on."

"Children born to women who mate with suneaters—like Jane and me—require food for sustenance," Terence said. "We're not suneaters, like those born to your kind. Your offspring are the only sons who matter to some suneaters, like the Elder. It's the only way they can continue to survive."

"Even if it kills us," Night snapped.

The Matron put a calming hand on Night's shoulder. "He's just the messenger."

Night stepped back.

"Why would men from the compound care, since they've already chosen a different way of life?" the Matron asked.

"To help the suneaters avoid capture by the Con Squad, men from the Towers help retrieve the newborns from the city by providing diversions and other resources." Terence pointed to me. "That's how our pictures ended up on the Nadux. She was just in the wrong place at the wrong time, standing by the riser when I accompanied a suneater and an Eve out of the building with two newborn Adams."

"Then the Con Squad brought out a body on a gurney," I said.

"I created a diversion, but it was the closest they've come to capturing some of us," Terence said.

"They have a body?" Night's voice was low and hesitant.

"It disappeared," I said. "The woman with the infant aimed a gun of some sort at the gurney as they were driving away, and then the gurney was empty."

"Thank goodness," Night said softly.

"What did this woman look like?" the Matron asked.

"Well, she looked a lot like all of you do—black hair, blue eyes, brown skin," I said. "I recognized her in a picture one of the women was showing around at the Towers. Piper said her name's Ariadne."

"So, Ari's being held at the Towers, as I was told," the Matron said.

"It's not quite like that. She's disguised as one of the suneaters—as a male." I grimaced, not daring to look at Terence and Jane. I hadn't shared this information with them.

"I see," the Matron said slowly. "Yet you easily recognized her."

"Only because of her eyes," I said.

The Matron took a deep breath. "This is a lot to consider." She turned back to Terence. "I'm still not clear on how the Elder could convince the men at Eureka Towers to go along with his plan to enslave us. Because that's what you're really talking about, isn't it?"

Terence shifted his weight. "Like I said, we endanger ourselves and our families every time there's a birth and we have to do a retrieval. The Elder says this will be a better way for all of us, even your kind."

"I'm sure he is concerned for our wellbeing," the Matron said sarcastically. "So, I'll ask you one last time, what do you think of his plan?"

Terence sighed. "I don't like it, but I don't see another option that allows suneaters or those of us at Eureka Towers to survive. We can't continue to do newborn retrievals and avoid the Con Squad—their surveillance techniques improve faster than our ways of subverting them. We lose too many men. Now they've attacked the Towers looking for Blair and me. It's only a matter of time before they realize suneaters live there."

The Matron motioned to Night. "Take him to the guardroom."

"Wait." I stepped forward, trying to stall them but unsure what to do. My feelings for Terence ran the gamut. He had protected me, but his defense of the women's treatment at the Towers infuriated me.

"We aren't going to harm him, just keep him out of the way," the Matron said.

"The Con Squad would've captured Ariadne and me if it hadn't been for him," I said. "He didn't have to be there for us."

"And then he enslaved you." The Matron turned to Terence. "You're a young man, so I can see how you would be swayed by someone as persuasive as the Elder. Perhaps you'll see things differently after you've tasted the life your women lead—with no freedom."

Night grabbed Terence's arm to lead him away when Jane blocked the way. "It's true things need to change, and not the way the Elder wants. But Terence isn't the enemy. He stuck with Blair and me, even when he suspected one of us was an informant and after he found the tracking devices."

Night whirled to face the oversized doors where they'd entered. "You're being tracked?"

"The Con Squad always knew where we were," Jane continued.

Night's voice rose. "So, we've led them here, endangering Matron?" Other women scattered into defensive positions around the room, and two flanked their leader.

"No," Jane said hurriedly. "We found the trackers and got rid of them before we went to the teahouse."

Night studied each of them. "And the informant?"

"It was me," Jane whispered. "But I didn't know anything about it. I just wanted to leave the Towers. I wanted to help. Someone planted the bugs in my clothes."

The Matron asked Terence, "The Con Squad is working with the Elder?"

"I can't explain it." He shrugged. "It's not something they discussed when I was around. There must be some connection, though, since Jane's clothes had the devices, and the troopers showed up at every safe house."

Night shook her head. "Matron, we must leave here immediately. We can't take a chance that they're not still being tracked, even if they believe they aren't."

The Matron studied my face. "They trusted us, and I'd like to do the same. But search them and their car to be sure they didn't miss anything."

Night motioned for some of the other women to begin the search and turned to leave with Terence.

"You're going to need him when we go back to Eureka Towers," Jane declared.

"You can be our guide," the Matron said.

"I don't have access to all the places he does," Jane said.

"What makes you think we're going to the Towers anyway?" Night said.

"Well, I don't think you'd leave two of your women in the Elder's clutches," Jane said.

The Matron smiled at Jane, then faced Terence. "And will you?"

"Help you?" He paused.

I put my hand on his shoulder. "They're just trying to protect themselves, not harm anyone."

"I can see that," Terence said, "but if we go back, it puts everyone there in danger again."

"After we get Piper and Ari out, you can leave with us," the Matron said.

"We can stay with you?" Jane asked.

"We'll find someplace safe for you," the Matron said.

"And him, too?" Jane asked.

The Matron nodded and waited for Terence's answer.

"Yes, I'll do what I can to help you at the Towers," he said.

The women who'd been searching the pizza delivery car and patting down their clothes gave Night a thumbs-up signal. "Good," she said. "No tracking devices."

"Then let's get started," the Matron told me. "It's high time we taught the Elder a lesson or two about strategy."

35

ARI

W hen I heard the commotion below, I first thought the Elder had discovered our hiding place. Then a "shooshing" command filtered up through the women to where I had been standing for the last fifteen minutes. I was still trying to wrap my mind around Piper's absence—what it meant for her, me, and the rest of the women.

I didn't want to dwell on what she might be facing when there was little I could do to help her. And without her help, I couldn't get to the new compound, so the Matron would be caught unaware by the alliance of the Adams and the Con Squad. Unless we found a way to join forces with the Eves, it was only a matter of time before the Elder recaptured the Eurekan women.

I soon spotted the cause of the disruption—Nathan. He pushed through the crowd on the stairs below and stood at my side. "What are you doing up here? We need to go while they're searching the other floors."

"We can't leave yet." I said. "One of the women is missing."

He tilted his head and gave me a puzzled look. "We can't endanger all the women for the sake of one."

"You just came from the Elder's rooms, right?" I nervously twirled a strand of blonde hair around my finger.

He nodded.

"Could he have her?"

"Didn't see any women," Nathan said tersely. "Now c'mon. It won't take them long to walk through most of the living spaces. Then they'll come back here to secure this area. We need to be gone before then."

"You don't understand. It's Piper who's missing." I grabbed his sleeve and whispered, "And Piper's an Eve."

Nathan grew very still, then leaned closer. "A what?"

"Piper's an Eve—a mooneater." I kept my voice low and calm even though my heart was racing. I really didn't want to tell him this, but I didn't know what else to do. "You have to find out where she is—if the Elder or the Con Squad are holding her prisoner."

Nathan slowly met my eyes, his face inches from mine. Barely restrained anger contorted his features and turned his skin red. "What makes you think she's an Eve?" he hissed.

Before I could reply, a hand rested gently on his shoulder. He turned toward the woman. Their glance exchanged more than words —affection, concern, support. I figured she must be his mate. .

"What is it, Nathan?" Her voice was soothing.

"She says an Eve is here at Eureka Towers," he replied through gritted teeth. "Looks like the Elder's right. They've already started to infiltrate."

My mouth fell open. "It's not like that at all!" How could he jump to that conclusion?

The woman held a finger up, urging my silence. "I agree it's suspicious, but if she's right about the woman being an Eve, surely there are other possibilities."

Heedlessly, I blurted, "She was hunting for something."

The woman sighed at me, and Nathan grunted. "Oh, that makes a lot of sense. What could we possibly have that would interest an Eve? There's only one explanation. It's like the Elder said—things are getting too risky now at the compound, so the Eves think living at Eureka Towers would be safer."

Nathan took a step away, and the woman's hand slid from his shoulder. "I need to let the Elder know it's already begun."

"What about our daughter?" the woman asked, her voice pleading.

"Don't you see? This changes things," he said.

"No, I don't see," the woman replied. She pressed her lips into a thin, hard line. "You said you'd look after Jane, and the Eves are her only hope of escaping the Con Squad."

"What do you think will happen if the Eves turn all of us out of the home we've built here?" he asked, his voice harsh. "Despite the Elder's little scheme, do you think we'd fare any better with the Con Squad?"

"They already have Margie," the woman said. "We can't give up on Jane. You know the Elder doesn't care what happens to any of the women, including me." She paused. "Are you just going to forget about that?"

Nathan's shoulders slumped as he took another step down. "Look, I tried."

The woman turned away from him, her face twisted like she was in pain.

"Wait." I pushed forward and grabbed his arm. "Piper wasn't part of any scheme. She was looking for someone."

He sighed and shook his head as he pulled away. "Get your story straight—she's looking for someone or something? Either way, it's only some made-up excuse."

Fear squeezed the breath from my lungs, and my heart froze. I had to tell him. "She was looking for me," I said through clenched jaws, "because I'm also an Eve."

I could feel all the women's faces turn my way, but I locked my gaze on Nathan's eyes. "I was at the last retrieval. The infants' mother was a friend of Layla, the Eve whose body disappeared from the gurney. I didn't know what was going on or where we were—it was my first time out of the compound. When the Con Squad came, Layla provided cover while I helped Tibor escape with the infants. He took us back to the Adams' compound."

I could almost see thoughts speeding behind Nathan's eyes, but I couldn't guess what they were.

"The Elder was furious with Tibor for bringing an Eve to the compound," I continued. "I escaped when they exiled him here as punishment, but I never went through the orientation. That's why I didn't know the things I should've known."

"So, Tibor is Carl," Nathan stated, his voice even. "And you're an Eve who's been disguised as a male, but now you're posing as a woman? I'll hand it to you, Aaron—or whatever your name is—you have a good imagination."

"But it's true," I said. "You have to believe me."

He sighed. "Look, even if you are an Eve, that doesn't explain why another Eve would come here looking for you. As a male, it would be a lot easier for you to slip away than for one of the women to escape the Towers unnoticed."

His mate cut her eyes at him and frowned at his casual reference to her captivity, but she didn't comment.

"I can see that," I agreed, "except for one thing. The Eves just moved to a new compound, and I don't know where it is. The Matron knew that. I can't find my way back on my own."

"They just moved?" His head jerked back and he squinted at me, as if trying to bring my image into focus. "But that doesn't make any sense."

"Our new compound wasn't quite finished, but an incident with the Cains made the Matron move up our relocation." I pressed my eyes shut, trying to block the images of how this all started. It seemed like a long, long time ago. "The important thing is the Eves didn't come here," I sighed. "They went somewhere else."

"I don't think the Matron would move the Eves twice in such a short timeframe," his wife said, clearly taking my side. "Surely once is dangerous enough when the Con Squad is watching every move."

Nathan sucked in a long breath. He looked at his mate, then covered his face with both hands for several moments. "I don't know whether to believe you or not, but for now we'll go ahead with the plan." He raised his head and stared at me. "Who else knows you're an Eve—Carl? Fike?"

I'd been dreading this question. Should I admit Fike helped me? Surely that would be obvious, but it didn't feel right to expose him when Nathan hadn't decided what his next steps would be. Although Fike and the Elder were clearly on opposite sides, if the Elder had proof Fike aided an Eve, it might enrage the already combatant Eurekans he had enlisted to help him subdue the women. "You'd have to ask them," I said.

"Thanks a lot," Nathan snorted. "I'll do that."

I only hoped I got to Fike and Carl first. I hated that my plans to help Carl remember who he was had been interrupted, or that I hadn't just told him the truth, but I couldn't do anything about it now.

The next part of the plan called for us to split up again. By now,

Carl and Fike should be back in our room on the thirteenth floor. Natisha and I would lead half the women there, while Nathan and his mate would take the others down the hall to his room. We'd go through the back lobbies to enter the thirteenth floor. Then came the part I now dreaded— to maintain his cover, Nathan was to return to the Elder.

"I'll take the first group," he declared, leaving no room for argument. He and his mate headed down the steps. I followed them, joining Natisha at the landing of the twenty-first floor as the first half of the group left. We waited anxiously, listening for any shouts or running footsteps to indicate they'd been discovered.

Five minutes later, we were ready to make our move when I thought I heard someone outside. I motioned to Natisha, who nodded. She'd heard it, too. Someone whispered again, loud enough so I picked up the words this time: "Wait here while I check it out."

Natisha motioned upward and the group moved silently up the stairs, past the turns of the stairwell so we were invisible if anyone opened the door on the twenty-first floor. Natisha went to the top, where I stood earlier, and I waited on the landing of the twenty-second floor behind the last of our group.

We all heard the slightest creak of the door below at the same time. My gut clenched and I pressed my lips together. Above, Natisha opened the door to Lovers' Lanes and walked onto the exposed walkways.

36

BLAIR

Night led the way, followed by the Matron. Now uncuffed, Terence joined Jane and me to form a third row, which was flanked by three women on either side, walking single file. I wasn't sure if it was for our protection or intimidation.

We passed groups of dark-haired, dark-skinned women armed with bows. Stories I'd read about Amazons must have been written about women like these, or perhaps these very ones. They loaded laser guns and other supplies onto shimmering circular vehicles, each large enough to carry a dozen troops.

"They're wearing Nano Armor." Terence whispered, awestruck. "It's the strongest and most versatile substance made. It can withstand any weapon—from microscopic Nanobots to nuclear explosives."

Night passed through a retinal scanner and doors slid open to an empty, all-white room. As we walked down the center, our shoes clattered on the floor's glasslike surface. Holographic panels activated on either side. Our escorts dropped off to manipulate controls hovering in the air at waist height.

The holographic images showed real-time views of the city. Some of the controllers spun in for close-up views of buildings or even rooms within buildings, while others pulled out for distant views. It had to rival the Con Squad's surveillance network. The effect was dizzying. The Matron pointed to one of the panoramic views, which showed Eureka Towers from the other side of the SuperFlex.

"As you suspected, Jane, we will retrieve Ariadne and Piper from Eureka Towers," she said. "But in doing so, we need to disarm the Elder in such a way that other Adams or Cains aren't tempted to follow the path he's chosen."

"You aren't going to attack the Towers, are you?" Jane's eyes brimmed with tears. "My mom's there, and all my friends."

"That's not our way." The Matron reached over and squeezed her hand. "As you can see, we're capable of protecting our own. We could pull off an assault, but I've always found it more effective to offer hope instead of harm. It was only a matter of time until the Elder tried to form an alliance with the Cains. Now that he's taken that step, it will be his undoing."

"But how could you know?" Terence said.

"It's what I would've done in his place," she said. "How else could he coerce us to do his bidding?"

My admiration for the Matron grew.

"We haven't been able to overcome the deaths to our kind that result from bearing sons, but we have found a way to use genetics to bring the Cains over to our side," the Matron continued. "It's not exactly immortality, but they can live three times as long with the vigor of youth."

The Con Squad had always claimed mutants were immortal—it was an attribute they both envied and feared. I replayed mental images of their anxious search for the body that disappeared from the gurney in the riser lobby where Terence had found me. The key to immortality was a prize that had evaporated that day before the Cain scientists could unlock its secrets in their laboratories.

"That's amazing," I said. "But how is offering the Cains longer lives going to help you overcome the Elder?"

The Matron smiled. "Just wait and see."

We didn't have long to wait. I watched as the vehicles deployed in different directions throughout the city, their Nano Armor concealed by ad screens. The warehouse soon appeared on the main console as a glowing hub at the center of dozens of white spokes, which tracked the vehicles.

"For centuries, we've sent full-moon women into the cities," the Matron said. "My scientists have worked side-by-side with Cains on many projects, helping them make advancements they otherwise wouldn't have made. We've also watched the Elder's movements. Earlier this week, Night learned he had convinced some Cain leaders he could make them into suneaters. That is, of course, not possible—any more than I could make you a mooneater. Our bodies are too different."

I tried to imagine all this, but it was a lot to take in.

"He used a mind-altering drug, like what he uses to clear the minds of suneaters who choose to raise families at Eureka Towers," Night explained. "After I told the Matron, we put our plan into motion."

We continued at a steady pace toward a circular conference room behind clear glass panels in the center of the white room. My heart raced with fear when I saw the three men who waited inside, and a quick glance at the wide-eyed expressions on Jane's and Terence's faces assured me they recognized them, too. Why would the Matron bring them here—the ones responsible for hunting us down?

When we reached the center of the hub, it settled over us like a ceiling of light. The Matron acknowledged the top leaders of the Cain government with a dip of her head, which the men returned. She motioned for Terence, Jane, and me to take seats along the outside of the glass-walled room. She and the men continued walking to a glass-topped table at the middle of the room. That was fine with me—I wanted as far away from them as possible. My stomach cramped with anxiety, and I had to force myself to sit and not bolt through the nearest doorway.

"Ready?" the Matron asked.

"Yes, Matron," the president replied. The Con Squad Commander touched his wrist monitor. The head of the Mutant Studies Institute smiled and said, "This is a generous gift, Matron, one that will change the course of history."

Six holo screens on either side of the walkway now displayed a picture of the conference room with a superimposed countdown timer. Night stood near the door, by one of the hovering control panels. "A statement of national importance will commence in five minutes," she said, broadcasting the message across all Nadux channels and repeating it as the minutes counted down.

When the last minute expired, the Matron stood.

37

ARI

Walking among the redwood's branches was something I'd longed to do ever since I'd come to Eureka Towers days ago and discovered its secret. Now I couldn't enjoy the leisurely stroll I'd imagined. Instead, I had to be as quiet and inconspicuous as possible. As I stepped onto the walkway, it took only one quick glance to realize looking down was a very bad idea. Vertigo washed over me, leaving my vision blurry and my stomach in my throat. Adrenaline from the pursuit kept me moving forward, and after a few seconds I began to feel better.

Natisha led four dozen women at a run through the maze of crisscrossed wooden walkways that wove downward through the thickening branches. She had told me we'd aim for a series of platforms on the twenty-second floor, guessing they would be less likely to be seen by the Elder's men on the nineteenth floor, but not too close to the entrance to the Lovers' Lanes on the twenty-fourth floor.

I brought up the rear. Natisha's pace sent the walkways swinging, and we all had to grip the guide ropes tightly to keep from falling. Keeping pace, I looked back over my shoulder every few minutes, imagining the door behind us opening.

It had only taken us a few minutes to cross the atrium, partially shielded from potential onlookers by fragrant, thick green needles and the reddish bark of limbs that—even at this height—were as big around as my thighs. Sounds of our running feet echoed, bouncing off the balconies that opened onto the atrium. I kept imagining a male's alarmed shout, calling attention to our flight. But it never came.

I dashed onto a partially enclosed platform. I couldn't believe our luck—we'd made it across without a problem. Women huddled together, kneeling or sitting so their heads would be lower than the waist-high panels of woven wooden strips that enclosed the area beneath the handrails. The other side was a series of secluded bowers designed for lovers, with vines draping across a half-dozen entrances.

Natisha motioned me over. "We made it!" I whispered, and hugged her. She smiled but glanced nervously over my shoulder toward the walkways we'd just crossed. We'd come out through the only entrance to Lovers' Lanes, which meant we were stuck here.

I was pretty sure Nathan would keep to the plan since he knew about the Eves' new compound. With any luck, he would connect with Carl and Fike before he reported back to the Elder. I hoped he'd let them know about Piper. Maybe it wouldn't take them long to figure out something had gone wrong and find a way to get us out of here without raising the alarm.

At any rate, we weren't going anywhere for a while. I'd just begun to relax when I heard voices coming toward us from the direction of the access door. I turned to the women next to me and put a finger to my lips. They did the same, sending a silent warning through the adjoining platforms.

"Someone would've seen them if they'd come this way," a man said in a frustrated tone. "Besides, it's not like that many women can move quietly."

A younger voice said, "They could be further down on the Lanes."

"C'mon, what would you know of such things?" the other man jeered. "This is your first time up here, isn't it, boy? I'm telling you, we'd know if they was here."

Silence followed. Had they gone? Time passed. I peered down the walkways. I jerked my head back when I caught the muffled sound of footsteps. Someone was headed our way.

I glanced back at Natisha and my face must have said it all. She turned pale. The women grew still as my panic transmitted to them. The footsteps neared, but our only exit was cut off. We'd done the best we could, but we'd walked into a trap of our own making—we couldn't go forward or backward. I jumped when a deep male voice called out, "Hey, you need to come right away!"

"Way to blow my cover, asshole!" the younger voice replied angrily.

He was so close, chill bumps covered my arms. My back was against the vine-covered wall, and he was on the opposite side. The vines ended less than a foot away. If we each reached out our hands, they would touch. I closed my eyes and cringed, trying to make myself smaller.

"I'm almost to the platforms." He sighed.

Loud footsteps crossed the walkway and stopped. If either man took one more step, they'd see me. I pressed my lips together and breathed as quietly as possible. Across from me, two women slipped further back under the vine cover.

"Look, do what you want, but all Nadux channels have been blocked for an announcement by the top Cain officials," the older man said. "I don't think you'll want to miss it."

The young man sighed again. "What can be so blasted important as all that?"

"Dunno," the other man said. "I gotta give you points for trying, but even the women aren't stupid enough to hide in an exposed area like this. I mean, you could see these walkways from any balcony."

Their footsteps retreated, leaving only quiet. The women emerged from their hiding places. Their faces relaxed, showing a cautious sense of relief. Natisha swept her hand across her forehead and pursed her lips to mime "whew."

I gave the men enough time to reach the door below, then rushed back to the stairway. I couldn't relax yet. After closing the door behind me, I listened. Soon my eyes adjusted to the hallway's relative dimness, and I tiptoed down to the landing on the twenty-second floor and looked below. The rest of the stairwell was empty, too.

Back at the top of the stairs, I opened the door and motioned to Natisha. While the men watched the announcement would be our best chance. I returned to the stairwell and hurried down to the twenty-first floor. I listened, then opened the door to the hallway. Empty. I gave an inward sigh of relief.

I quickly led the women down the hall to the stairwell entrance in the back lobby, then hurried down eight floors. When we reached the thirteenth floor, I told Natisha, "Keep everyone here while I check out my room. If I'm not back in five minutes, send someone to Nathan's room and see if it's safe there. And if that doesn't work..." I shrugged and threw my hands up; I didn't know what we'd do.

The room Carl and I shared was around the corner and halfway down the hall where the over-sized fish tank filled one wall. As I passed Nathan's room, I was tempted to check it out. But if he'd been compromised or changed his mind, I could walk into a trap. I decided to keep to the plan.

The hall was eerily quiet. Was everyone in their rooms in front of the Nadux, or had they called another meeting down in the basement assembly room? I hesitated outside our door for just a moment, then brushed my hand in front of the scanner. The door slid aside, and I heard a woman's voice coming from the living room. It sounded strangely familiar. I walked in, keeping as close to the wall as possible to see if I could get a view of the room before I was spotted.

The room was empty except for Carl and Fike, who sat on the sofa, totally focused on the Nadux. With a gasp, I walked trancelike to the center of the room. I had indeed recognized the voice. I couldn't imagine how the leader of our secretive group had come to be the focus of every Adam and Cain, but there was no denying the fact.

"Matron!" I said with disbelief, and lowered onto the sofa to sit beside a very startled Carl.

38

BLAIR

From my vantage point just outside the glass-walled room, I looked from the live event to the larger-than-life holographic images on either side of the table. The projections had some advantages. When the camera zoomed in for close-ups, I could see their faces better. The men had bland expressions, but a slight smile animated the Matron's face as she rose to speak.

The Matron's blue eyes focused on me, and me alone. It was an eerie feeling. Did everyone watching have the same reaction?

The Matron's smooth, dark skin glowed under the lights, picking up peachy highlights from her ankle-length orange robe. An inch-wide band of cream-colored lace on the neck and salt-and-pepper tendrils wafting down from her bun softened her face's strong lines. If I had met her on the street, I would've guessed her age at forty—fifty, at the most.

"Greetings." The Matron smiled wider, and my heart lightened. "The gentlemen here with me need no introduction. They are your society's top leaders—responsible for your safety, science and social services. They are here with me to officially announce an agreement that will affect all our lives.

"I am the Matron, leader of a race of women you call the Eves. Some may know us as the mooneaters, since we do not require food, or as immortals who procreate through virgin birth.

"Our differences have sparked fear, and fear breeds violence. Tonight, we will set a different course that builds on our shared heritage and offers a peaceful path forward.

"After centuries of work, our scientists recently made a breakthrough that will make your lives better and bring a brighter future to those yet unborn. Your lifespan can triple. You can live centuries without debilitating diseases or the infirmities of old age you now suffer after only a few decades.

"This is possible only because we share the same genetic lineage. We have always lived alongside you. You see us at the office and in the grocery store. We are scientists and lawyers. We are your friends and neighbors. We are not the monsters some say we are—those stories are rooted in secrecy, misunderstanding, and greed.

"Today I will tell you the truth about how our histories are woven together. For eons, Eves had thriving cities and a peaceful, enlightened society. We were all of one kind—females who conceived our daughters without a partner. Then a genetic mutation occurred.

"I was less than a century old when the first male was born to an Eve. That was ten millennia ago.

"We did not know what to make of the child we called Adam; he was so different from all others. We did not know why his mother died. Up to that point, only accidents or wild beasts had taken a life.

"More of these strange children were born and their mothers died. We called them our "suns" because they were nourished by the Sun's rays instead of the moon's. Eventually, we learned to identify these pregnancies early. Some Eves chose to proceed with the birth and die so their suns could live. Most thought the price was too high and chose to abort. It's a terrible decision to make, and most of us face it many times in our immortal lives.

"When the first suns reached adulthood, they had a sexual drive much like other species. Some mated with Eves. The children conceived were larger at birth, and many of those Eve mothers died in childbirth.

"We now faced threats from within our own bodies and from our suns. With sad hearts, we retreated into remote compounds to avoid all contact with our suns. Our cities became theirs. Fewer and fewer suns of Eves were born, but over time, their numbers grew because they, too, were immortal.

"As time passed, hybrid males and females paired. Their offspring became your race—the Cains. Unlike your forebears, neither sunlight or moonlight nourished your race enough to sustain you without consuming food. Even though you live only a short time, your higher fertility rate led to a population explosion. Some of us found ways to live among you, but rumors of immortals who thrived on sunlight or moonlight led to a ruthless hunt to discover our secrets. That hunt ends now.

"As your living ancestors, we are gifting you the secret to a true Fountain of Youth. All we require in return is for you to honor the sanctity of our way of life and our privacy.

"To that end, your leaders have agreed to the following conditions:

"First, the Con Squad and Mutant Studies Institutes will be disbanded, and no further attempts will be made to capture or study Eves."

The men sitting next to her nodded their assent as she glanced toward each.

"Second, all women currently held by the Con Squad or their associates will be released unharmed to us before sunrise tomorrow.

"And third, the Cains will be our allies if our suns—the so-called mutants you know as Adams or suneaters—attempt to force Eves to carry pregnancies to full term."

She paused to look again at the men beside her. The president stood and offered his wrist to her in acknowledgement of the pact. The Matron touched her wrist to his, and continued.

"We are the mothers of all humankind, but our future is perilous. Forcing us to bear more suns would bring extinction to Eves and Adams. Even now, some who doubt such consequences would force us into captivity like breeding animals. That cannot be allowed to happen—now or ever."

Behind the Matron, the Con Squad Commander fidgeted with his handheld on the glass table in front of him. I suspected he knew what was afoot at Eureka Towers.

"Eves who choose to bear suns will no longer have to fear being hunted down by the Con Squad when they go into the city, and those who come to retrieve the infants will travel in safety, without pursuit," the Matron continued. "I call upon our suns to hear the truth of what I'm saying, and to ignore those who try to cloud their judgment. I ask you to join us in finding a way for your mothers to survive. Their deaths are a loss too painful for us all to bear."

When the Matron sat, the president again stood, but I couldn't concentrate on his words. What of the armored troops already deployed throughout the city? Would the Con Squad really release all the innocent people like my mother and Margie who'd been branded as mutants?

39

ARI

"Who are you?" Carl said, jumping to his feet. "And how did you get in?"

His rapid-fire questions took me by surprise. I forgot I'd gone with Nathan before Carl saw my disguise. I didn't have time to explain. Something was terribly wrong if the Matron was on the Nadux.

"It's just me—Ari ... Aaron. Remember?" I said, softening my voice. "Your roommate, in disguise." So much for thinking he might recognize me as Ariadne.

"Aaron?" he said, doing a double-take at the Nadux. "How do you know the Matron?"

"Shh," I said. "I don't want to miss what she's saying."

Fike smirked—he'd already seen my new look—then we all turned our attention back to the projection.

"I ask you to join us in finding a way for your mothers to survive so you can know these women who loved you so much they were willing to give up their lives," the Matron said. "They are the special ones, and their deaths are a loss too painful for us to bear."

"I remember her now—the Eve who bore the infants we named Rayson and Laylan," he told Fike, his voice husky with stress. "She died so they could live."

Fike put a hand on Carl's shoulder. "Yes. Your memories are coming back. Do you remember your real name now?"

He nodded. "Tibor."

The Matron's words struck home with me, too. I thought how different things might have been if the Con Squad hadn't pursued us. Layla would still be alive, and I'd be with her in our new compound instead of stranded here with no way home.

"What did I miss?" I asked.

"The Matron offered the Cains a way to live longer," Fike said, "and they've agreed to disband the Con Squad and to return all Eves to us by sunrise."

My heart leapt. If I turned myself in to the Con Squad, could I trust them to honor the agreement and return me to the Eves? First, I'd have to get past the Elder, and I didn't see that going well.

As if reading my mind, Fike said, "I know the Elder too well. After spending a lifetime hating the Eves, this pronouncement won't change his heart. He will never trust the Matron, and he will never be satisfied until he has total control over the Eves."

My gut told me he was right. All I could deal with now was this one Adam I'd come to care about. "Tibor, do you remember me now?" I pulled off the blonde wig. "I was with you. We rescued the infants together."

"Ari?" he said.

I nodded. "I tried to find a way to tell you who I was, but—with the brainwashing and all—I was afraid you'd turn me over to the Elder."

"So, what am I doing here?" he asked Fike.

"The Elder was furious with you for bringing her to the compound." He tilted his head toward me. "He exiled you here."

"How did he get so much control?" Tibor asked. "These men have lost sight of what Eureka Towers was supposed to be about. How did I become one of them?"

"It's a long story, with lots of mistakes made on both sides. But right now, we have to worry about what Nathan's doing," Fike said, turning to face me. "Have you seen him?"

"He and his mate were supposed to lead half the women to his apartment," I said. "Then he was going back to the nineteenth floor so the Elder wouldn't get more suspicious. I'd asked him to tell you they have Piper."

Fike's eyebrows scrunched together in a questioning look.

"The Matron sent Piper to find me," I said. "She's an Eve."

Fike groaned. "Just what we need—another Eve for the Elder to hold hostage."

"Hey." I glared at him. I still couldn't believe Piper had been the one to try to rescue me after all the differences we'd had in the past. "We'll get Piper, and the two of us will warn the Matron about the pact between the Elder and the Con Squad. For all I know, they still plan to attack our compound. If they tracked Nathan's daughter there, they may already be on the way."

Fike frowned. "I hope you're not too late."

I protectively clutched my hands to my elbows as my mind ran through all the scenarios. If I was honest with myself, I knew it was at least as likely we wouldn't be able to escape Eureka Towers, or—if the Elder went ahead with his plan—we would arrive at the compound after the Eves were all enslaved. I couldn't let my thoughts go down that path, though; I had to keep moving forward, acting as if things would turn out for the best. An involuntary shiver shook my body.

Perhaps guessing where my thoughts had wandered, Fike glanced at Tibor and changed the subject. "I wonder what happened to Nathan."

"Maybe he's still down the hall," I suggested, though I didn't really believe it. "I told the rest of the women to wait in the stairwell, then go to Nathan's apartment if I didn't return in five minutes."

"You'd better get going, then," Fike said. "Bring them here, and I'll check Nathan's apartment. Tibor, you stay and monitor the Nadux. We'll need to know as much as we can about what's happening outside the Towers."

On the Nadux, the president was still talking. I put on the blonde wig as Fike and I walked toward the door. "What do you think the Elder's going to do?"

"He's going to feel trapped," Fike said. "He'll come out fighting."

The door slid open to chaos. The women who'd been with me were lined up against the wall in single file. Some were crying and others were yelling at a half-dozen men, who were jerking the women's wrists into plastic cuffs. A tall, angry man I recognized from the meeting that morning grabbed Fike's arms and shoved him into Natisha. She yelped and moved away, covering her bloodied face with her hands. A sleeve was torn off her blouse.

"Take the women back to the nineteenth floor, and double the guards," he told two burly men. "This time, we'll make sure they don't go anywhere." He pointed at Fike and Natisha. "The Elder will want to see these two troublemakers," he told a stout, redhaired man. He poked Fike's chest with his finger. "Looks like we're finally going to get you out of the way, old man."

The tall man turned back toward me and shoved me against the fish tank's thick glass wall, causing the fish on the other side to scatter from the impact. "Nathan told us about you," He lowered his face to within inches of mine. "So, Aaron—or should I call you Eve?—where are the rest of the women?"

I turned my face away and grimaced, but he grabbed my chin and jerked my face around so I couldn't avoid his gaze. His breath stank of meat.

"I said, where are the others?" he yelled.

I couldn't think straight. How had they discovered the women hiding in the stairwell but not the ones in Nathan's apartment?

"We got separated," I began, stalling for time.

He pressed me against the glass wall. "No tricks." With his hand on my throat, I had to struggle to breathe.

"We were up on Lovers' Lanes," I sputtered.

"Told you," said a freckle-faced teen. I recognized his voice as the one who'd been on the walkway a few minutes ago.

A black-haired man shook his head. "I can't believe they were that stupid."

"Huh," the teen said. "Smart enough we didn't find them until Nathan tipped us off."

The tall man frowned at the teen, then back at me.

"Half of us got out before we heard someone coming," I said. "I really don't know what happened to the others. For all I know, they're still there—at Lovers' Lanes." It could've happened that way, and in fact, I didn't know where the other women were—just where they were *supposed* to be. And back at Lovers' Lanes was the least likely place they'd have gone. Were Nathan's mate and the other women in his apartment, or had they gone somewhere else? I let the uncertainty fill my voice.

"All right, you two." The tall man pointed toward the teen and the black-haired man. "Go search every inch of Lovers' Lanes—move every vine, check all the bowers and platforms. If they're there, I don't want a single woman to escape."

"We're on it," the teen said. They took off at a run to the stairwell we'd come down.

"I'm personally escorting this one up to the Elder," he called after them.

I had ten minutes, at most, before their return. What would they do to me when they found no one there?

"You're going against the terms of the new accord the president just announced," I said, grasping for something to say.

The tall man scowled and pushed me ahead of him, toward the lobby. "You mean the propaganda on the Nadux?" He huffed. "Just a stalling tactic. They've got the Matron right where they want her."

A chill settled in my stomach. "The Con Squad's been disbanded. You're supposed to turn over all Eves to the Matron before sunrise."

"Yeah, or what?" He sneered. "If they come to Eureka Towers looking for an Eve, they're not going to find one."

I swallowed hard at the threat.

"Surely you aren't naive enough to think they'll disband the Con Squad to live a few centuries more when each of us could become Adams—immortals living off sunlight? The leaders of the Con Squad know what they're doing, all right, and this deal with the Matron's just a decoy."

I wanted to think he was bluffing, but the assurance in his voice made it seem like an all-too-real scenario. As we walked, one question played in a loop in my mind: Why had Nathan told the Elder about me when he knew the Eves already had a new compound?

When we arrived on the nineteenth floor, the Elder waited by the riser, his lips in a thin, sinister smile. A pair of silver handcuffs dangled from his hand.

40

BLAIR

Terence moved closer behind me and whispered, "This isn't adding up. What about the troops?"

I nodded. "The Matron must not trust her new allies. As she said, that's how she's survived all these years."

Jane leaned in, too, her face bright with excitement. "So, everything's going to be okay!"

Terence and I exchanged a guarded glance. "The Matron has it all under control," I said.

When the broadcast ended, Night escorted the three Cain officials from the glass-walled room. She secured blindfolds over their eyes before leading them to waiting cars.

"Surely this isn't necessary," the president protested. "We're on the same side now, after all."

With a hint of mischief in her voice, Night said, "I'm sure Matron would agree, if you show us to your headquarters. Are you asking us to accompany you there?"

"Uh, well, no," the president stammered.

"Okay then." The blindfolds remained in place.

I walked over to the table and asked the Matron, "What happens now?"

"We've given the head of the Mutant Studies Institute a serum that will do exactly what I said it would—it is truly a Fountain of

Youth," she said. "Once he confirms to the public it's real—and we'll be there to be sure that happens—no one can stop the demand for it. No longer will people have to live in fear of being called a mutant."

"But what about those the Con Squad already has?" I said. "My mom. And Terence's."

"I don't mean to make it sound like all our problems will be solved by this drug." The Matron glanced at Jane. "But we've taken away the government's power to claim it's for the common good to drag people out of their homes because they're different—because they're mutants."

"Do you know where our mothers are being held?" Terence said.

"We know enough," she said. "By sunrise, those who aren't voluntarily turned over to us will be freed by other means. As you see," she pointed to the glowing hub above, "our warriors are positioned throughout the city, ready to move at a moment's notice."

"But you didn't ask the Con Squad Commander to release the Cains they have in custody—just the Eves." My voice quivered.

"No, I didn't ask," she agreed. "I demanded—just not on the Nadux broadcast. The agreement spells out the details completely, including names. It will take some time—not long, I think—for people to get used to the idea that fearing mutants was all a sham."

I gave it a moment to sink in: I'd finally found an ally to help me find my mom. Even so, I knew I wouldn't be able to relax until Mom was safely away from the Con Squad.

"How did you get the names of their captives?" Jane asked.

"From our full-moon women," the Matron said. "As I mentioned, many women have chosen to live at least part of their lives outside the compounds. They frequent the teahouses and workplaces where people discuss who's been taken by the Con Squad."

"So, we just wait?" I said.

The Matron laughed. "I wish it was that simple." She looked at Terence. "Night needs to get into Eureka Towers without being noticed."

He sucked in a deep breath, then nodded. "Only Night?"

"For now. We'll have to rely on the element of surprise to get our two cadets away from the Elder," the Matron said.

"I can take her through the arcology unit," Jane said.

The Matron gave Jane a kindly smile. "You can give her directions, Jane, but I need you and Blair here to help if the other women aren't returned by sunrise. Even full-moon women like me can only be out in the daylight for short periods of time without losing our strength."

Terrence glanced nervously at Night, who grinned impishly at him. "C'mon, it'll be fun," she taunted. "Or I could lock you up."

I laughed at Terence's cowed expression. "She makes a good point. Think of it as penance for how women are treated at the Towers."

"I'll do what it takes to get my mom back," he said reluctantly. "Take care of Jane."

"I will." I pulled the off the wristband and handed it to Night. "It's not a bad way to get around town." I watched as Terence and Night drove out of the warehouse in the pizza delivery car. It was going to be a long night of waiting.

* * *

"Time for us to go," one of the Matron's aides said, waking me from a dreamless sleep.

I rubbed my neck, sore from being propped at an odd angle against the wall. How had I fallen asleep? Jane, still asleep in the chair next to mine, rested her head on my shoulder. "Is it morning?"

"Not quite," the woman said. "The Matron wants to speak with you."

I gently eased Jane's head back against the wall. I stretched, rubbed my eyes, and then followed the woman across the mostly darkened warehouse. Only a few women moved around the huge building—some checking equipment and others riding small carts loaded with boxes.

The woman stood aside and motioned toward a door open to the outdoors. Tinges of pink lightened the gray sky. The Matron stood in the doorway, silhouetted against the dim light.

"We'd hoped for the best, but not surprisingly, the Con Squad is trying to out-fox us," the Matron said. "They've only released a fraction of those being held."

I looked up, hoping one of those was my mom, but the Matron shook her head.

"Eves are vixens at heart, so we're prepared," she said. "Will you act as our spokesperson?"

"Me?" I said, taken aback. Earlier I thought the Matron might want me to run errands, not act in any official capacity. "I doubt anyone will listen to someone my age."

"They will listen because you represent me," the Matron said. "And because you'll explain the consequences of not listening." She handed me a round device with two buttons. "The green button is the incentive." She motioned for me to press it.

An image sprang up in front of us showing small structures dotting the city. "We're providing self-serve kiosks to dispense the serum. They're already operational, as we will announce at dawn."

She pushed the red button. "This is to let the Cain authorities know I mean business." Another map of the city showed the glowing streaks of light where troops had been deployed. "My warriors are waiting outside every Con Squad officer's home, every government building, and of course, outside the president's mansion. We will take our own hostages unless they release the rest of the so-called mutants."

I swallowed hard, impressed. "What about Piper and Aaron?"

"I knew the Elder would never voluntarily release an Eve." She shook her head. "Terence and Night are inside the Towers. They've made contact with Abigail, who's always been a friend to the Patron and me. It's only a matter of time before they find a way out."

41

ARI

The Elder pulled the wig off my head. "So, it's true—you've been hiding here at the Towers. It doesn't take a genius to guess the mastermind behind that scheme."

Fike's expression remained calm despite the Elder's glare. I tried to step back, but the tall man's grip on my shoulder held me in place. I flinched in pain, but he only squeezed harder. Across the room, one of the burly men stood behind where Fike and Natisha sat. My stomach knotted in fear. We were trapped.

"I wouldn't put it past my old friend Fike to have tipped off the Matron to your whereabouts," the Elder said. "I guess we'll have to make sure you're not here if anyone checks."

"What about the agreement?" I said. "The top officials endorsed it; you'll be going against the Cains, as well as the Eves."

The Elder shook his head. "Don't believe everything you see on the Nadux. We make our own rules, without any help from the so-called authorities."

A redhaired woman brought in a tray of drinks and set them on a table. It was Abigail! Even though she was also captive, it gave me hope; maybe she could tell Tibor. The knot in my stomach eased a little. As Abigail turned around to leave, she winked at me, as if reading my mind, then hurried out of the room.

"For now, though, take a seat," the Elder said. "I have a few loose ends to tie up before we leave for the compound."

The compound? After all he'd done to ensure I was kept away from there, now he was taking me back? While I relished the thought of holding Rayson again, somehow I didn't think that was what the Elder had in mind. I reached for a glass of water as I sat down next to Natisha.

"Hey, that's not for you," one of the burly men said, taking the glass from my hand.

As I withdrew, I checked the tray to see if Abigail left a message for us. Nothing. That was disappointing, but it would've been risky. I shrugged and gave Natisha what I hoped was a reassuring grin. "Guess they don't want to waste water on us."

The other guard roughly tapped my shoulder. "No talking."

I sighed, then turned my attention to the Elder and the tall man. I tried to overhear what they were saying as they left the room, but their voices were too low. The Elder unlocked a door on the left. As it slid open, I saw bare windows along the wall that bordered the balcony. It was almost dawn.

A dark-haired woman sat with her back to us. Her head slumped forward. Despite her unnaturally pale skin, I recognized her immediately, sending all my senses into panic mode. Piper. How long had she been in that room yesterday before the sun set?

Fear lodged in my throat as I remembered how drained I'd felt from the short time I'd spent in the sun-filled lobby when we first arrived and I was trying to pass as a suneater. The nausea and weakness had been debilitating after less than thirty minutes' exposure.

Fike sighed. Maybe he realized who she was, too.

The Elder looked back at me and smiled, then told the tall man, "Bring that chair over here, next to hers. I wouldn't want to keep old friends apart."

I really didn't want to go in that room. I yelled "no!" as I jumped up and ran toward the door, but the tall man caught my arm and jerked me toward the room. My shin bumped hard against the wooden tea table, toppling the two remaining glasses on the tray, and splashing me and floor.

"Why are you doing this?"

Ignoring my protests, he pushed me onto a chair and fastened the handcuffs tightly around my wrists and legs, matching those Piper wore. Despite the commotion, she didn't stir. My chest tightened, as if someone grabbed my heart in their fist and squeezed. She had to be all right—she had to be!

"Now, you do whatever it takes to get that blonde to tell us where the others are," the Elder said, "while I make sure our old friend Fike finds accommodations suitable to his new position."

I glanced back over my shoulder, alarmed at the Elder's tone. Fike stood and followed without complaint. Our eyes met briefly before the door slid shut. From his dull expression, I feared the Patron had lost hope. I couldn't see Natisha, but I heard her yelling, "Don't touch me," and "Stop," as her voice and sounds of struggle grew more distant.

I pulled against the restraints, wanting to go to her aid, then gasped as the cuffs dug deeper into my skin.

Streaks of light already stretched across the balcony. Before long, the whole room would be bright.

"Piper," I said. "Are you all right?"

Piper didn't move. I struggled against the restraints, trying to get closer, but her fingers hung limply, wrists dangling, and too far away to reach. The sound of her breathing was all that told me she was still alive.

As minutes passed, I watched the sunlight creep toward us. Our chairs were positioned so close our knees almost touched the glass walls. It didn't take long for the rays to reach our toes. Then our legs. Then our bodies.

I tried to think about something else—to come up with a plan— but energy drained from my body as it warmed in the sunlight.

"Piper, stay with me," I called, noticing her breath growing more shallow.

I knew the Matron would be looking for us, but time was our enemy. The Eves couldn't move as freely around the city in the daylight, and I doubted the Matron knew where the Adams' compound was located.

As my skin grew warm and pale, my thirst grew, and also the nausea. Piper gagged, startling me, but still she didn't rouse.

"Piper, talk to me," I pleaded. Her dry lips didn't move.

Behind me, the lock clicked, and I braced myself. The door slid open and locked again.

"It's me," Seldon said, taking quick strides across the room.

"Thank goodness," I said. Every muscle that had tightened in futile flight-or-fight instinct now unclenched with relief. "How did you get away long enough to change?"

"Years of practice have made me an expert at that," he said. "But I only have a minute. I'll get you out of here soon."

"How long has Piper been here?" I asked.

"The Elder's men found her hiding in the back lobby stairwell soon after the alarm sounded," he said. "I think she was trying to make it from the women's quarters to my room upstairs. It didn't take the Elder long to figure out sunlight sapped her strength...and what that meant."

"She's so...pale," I said.

"I know." His voice sounded as troubled as I felt. "Here." He handed me a key. "When I come back, we'll need to move fast. Just hang on until then, okay?"

He put his hand on my shoulder. Something about it made the tears rise, though I held them back. He was there for me...for us. This was a world I'd never imagined during my years as a crescent-moon cadet, safe inside the compound walls. And now I realized what the Matron had said was true about my claims of being a prisoner. All my life, other Eves had protected me and the other cadets. And now this stranger I'd met only days ago was willing to go against men he'd known all his life to help us. It was a humbling thought.

I started to open the cuffs when I thought I heard someone approaching. I didn't think Seldon would be back so soon, so I slid the key beneath me. The door slid open.

"My dear, you look a bit peaked," the Elder said with a sarcastic lilt to his voice. "And your friend's complexion is absolutely ashen. Don't you watch the Nadux ads? You must take more care to avoid the sun's damaging rays." He laughed.

"Such a brave man—can't even face Eves without keeping them in handcuffs!" I yelled.

He smirked.

I shuddered with suppressed anger. I wanted to claw out his eyes.

"You two," he called, and a couple of young men entered. "We'll be ready to move them in about ten minutes. Get the Shell car ready—the one with the privacy screens."

The door hissed shut. Minutes ticked by. Once I thought I heard the lock, but it was just my imagination. Where was Seldon? My temples throbbed. I gripped the key in my sweaty, shaking hand, afraid I'd drop it as I struggled to get it at the right angle to unlock the cuffs on my left wrist. When the door slid open, I hastily put my hands back behind me. I breathed a relieved sigh to see Seldon, not the Elder.

"Hurry," Seldon said as he entered and locked the door behind him. "They've gone to get the car."

I unlocked the other cuff and within seconds freed Piper, too. My wrists and ankles were raw, but hers were bleeding.

The sound of raised voices in the room outside warned us that the tall man had returned. "Where's the Elder?" he yelled. "That lying Eve was just stalling."

Seldon motioned for me to be still.

The man stomped across the room, heading away from us, and a door hissed as it slid open. "There weren't no women on Lovers' Lanes, and she knew it."

Seldon nodded at me, and we each took one of Piper's arms and carried her over to the wall by the door so we wouldn't be seen if it opened. Then I held her up while Seldon unlocked the door. He peered out, then nodded. When we were out, he paused long enough to lock the door behind us, then we ran as fast as we could with Piper weighing us down. About halfway down a long hallway, we entered a room on the left. We lowered Piper onto the floor behind a couch, and knelt behind it as we talked.

"Stay here for now," Seldon said. Panting, he added, "I have to go back and keep them off track a little while longer. The Matron sent someone for you—she's hiding upstairs until we can come up with a plan."

"But what about Piper?" I said, as I struggled to catch my breath. "We can't take her out in the sunlight. She's too weak now."

He pursed his lips and shook his head. "What else can we do? If we try to stay here until moonrise, the Elder will catch us. Don't think going to the Adams' compound is going to help either of you, now or in the long-term."

"I know," I said. "We can't let him use us as pawns, or keep us for his breeding program. But it seems like there should be something we could do for Piper."

I rested my hand on her face. Piper was as close to dead as anyone

I'd seen. Seldon rose. "Stay here. It's not great, but there's no reason anyone should look for you here. I'll be back."

When the door locked behind him, I scooted over until my back was against the couch and cradled Piper's head on my lap. I remembered our constant bickering, and wondered why I'd never thought of her as I did now—as my big sister. Who had the Matron sent after us? I hadn't thought to ask Seldon. Guilt washed over me—another Eve was in danger because of me.

My thoughts played a constant loop of guilt, hopelessness, and scheming. What could I do to help Piper? How could we escape? Tibor was still free, as far as I knew, but he was so new to the Towers, I doubted he'd be able help much with an escape plan. Surely he'd heard the noise in the hallway, so he must have realized it would be best to act like his conditioning was still working. Perhaps he'd even join with the Elder's men to prove his allegiance and track us down.

And then, there were the other women. Nathan's mate must be behind his change of heart about me, though nothing about that scenario made much sense. Unless he was trying to protect her or their daughter by giving me up.

Something kept niggling at the edge of my memory about the talks Tibor and I had about our new jobs. My eyes rested on a watercolor painting of the moon above a field, and I had it—the experiments they'd been doing to amplify moonlight. It was a longshot, but what if the machine that had no effect on Adams would actually revive an Eve? I stroked her hair, and had a sense of actual pain in my heart when I looked at her face, which was even paler than before. We had to at least try the moonlight simulator—it could very well be Piper's only chance.

42
___

BLAIR

At dawn, the Matron walked back to where we'd broadcast from hours before, and I joined her. Another Eve voiced a countdown, which again overrode all other Nadux programming.

"Citizens of New Humboldt," the Matron began. "Your leaders have once again put their own desires above your well-being. They did not abide by the terms of our agreement, but I will not penalize you for their short-sightedness. Self-serve kiosks have been installed at key intersections, hospitals, and elder care facilities. With the serum, you can begin your new lives today."

On cue, I pushed the green button, and the image displayed on camera.

"I encourage you to give first preference to those who are ill and elderly, who will see immediate relief," the Matron continued. "Instructions are provided when you enter. Because of years of propaganda, I can understand if some think this a trick. I assure you, it isn't, and to prove the point, I will now demonstrate.

"My warriors are situated at strategic points throughout the city for one purpose—to ensure our demands are met in a timely and complete manner. I am prepared to take as many hostages as are still being held, and those will come from the highest ranks of government and their families."

I pushed the red button, and the illuminated city map sprang to life.

"I have positioned a kiosk outside the president's mansion so you could see the results he experiences from the serum. My aim is not to give him preferential treatment, but to allow your leader to lead."

The Matron motioned, and the view shifted to a single kiosk. The president—flanked by two Eves wearing head-to-toe Nano Armor—stood at the kiosk's entrance. They pushed him inside.

"His treatment will take about five minutes—that's average for a healthy, middle-aged person," the Matron explained. "While we wait, I'd like to introduce you to Blair. She changed her appearance to avoid capture, but you may recognize her as one of the so-called terrorists recently sought by the Con Squad."

The image that had been broadcast of Terence and me running from the office building appeared behind us. I looked wistfully at my shoulder-length blonde hair and green eyes, knowing how mousey I looked now. By contrast, mentally comparing Terence's bad-boy bald head, tats, and piercings to the fresh, wholesome face on the holo made me want to giggle.

"Blair and Terence are not members of the Covenant or any other subversive group," the Matron continued. "Nor did they have anything to do with the contamination of the Westport reservoir that caused the Blue Death. Five years ago, they were barely in their teens. But I'll let Blair tell you why they become hunted."

Totally shocked, I snapped my head up to look at the Matron. We hadn't discussed this. Until five minutes ago, I'd never considered speaking on the Nadux. I instantly decided it was about as intimidating as bungee jumping from the top of Westover Falls. What did the Matron expect me to say?

"Truthfully, Matron, I don't know why the Con Squad is hunting me, except I was in the wrong place at the wrong time. I was there to see a lawyer, hoping he could help me find my mother. The Con Squad took her forcefully from our home, claiming she was a mutant."

The Matron nodded. "So, you were just trying to find your mother?"

"Yes, and later the Con Squad invaded the Towers where Terence lived and took his mother, too."

The Matron held up a finger. "We'll continue in a moment." She tapped the console to change to a street view in front of a huge home. "The president's treatment is complete."

We watched the Nadux screen as the kiosk door slid open and the president emerged. His white hair was now dark brown, and his wrinkled skin was smooth.

"I hope this demonstration shows you some of the benefits of this Fountain of Youth," the Matron said.

The president moved easily toward his wife and two children, who were being guarded by Eve warriors. He smiled and nudged his wife toward the kiosk. Although the sound from the site wasn't transmitted, when the warriors refused to let her pass, the president grew agitated and yelled at them. He jabbed his finger into one warrior's shoulder, but she didn't budge.

"Until our people are released, none of the other top government officials or their families will receive the serum," the Matron said. "But you have the free choice to benefit from this gift, or to live in fear and reject it." She turned to me. "Please continue with your story."

"Ah, sure." I was still trying to process what I'd just seen. I turned from the monitor to face Matron. "As I entered the lobby of the lawyer's office building, a man and woman carrying infants rushed out, followed by a third man. I didn't think much of it, but when the other riser doors opened, Con Squad troopers carried a body bag. Then troopers searched through the crowd for the couple carrying the infants—suspected suneaters.

"That's when the third man—Terence—returned. He told me to follow him or I'd be restrained by the Con Squad as a mutant. So, I did.

"You can imagine my surprise when Terence and I were labeled as terrorists and blamed for the Blue Death." I pulled out my blue armband and held it in front of the camera. "Like so many others, I joined the CS Reserves because of the Blue Death attacks. I thought it was my duty to help hunt down mutants who threatened our society. But so-called mutants aren't the problem. The Con Squad fosters fear to keep us powerless. We deserve better."

When I stopped, Matron said, "If the hostages are released, as I hope they soon will be, Blair will be available to greet them. She is a Cain, like you, so I believe she is the perfect spokesperson to act on my behalf while I tend to other matters."

The broadcast ended, and the Matron rose. "My warriors will be here to assist you, but their armor can only protect them from sunlight for an hour at a time. To the extent possible, we must reserve that protection in case we are attacked."

"You mean here or at the new compound?" I said.

"Both are a concern," Matron said. "This building has extensive sun shielding, but our compound has relatively little. And few warriors are left there to protect our home. It would be mostly up to the cadets, and they don't have Nano Armor. This is a very critical time, and much depends on whether Ariadne and Piper can avoid falling into the Elder's hands. Take care, Blair, and thanks for bringing us Piper's message."

"Of course," I said. "I can't thank you enough for what you're doing for my mom ... for all of us. It really is going to change everything."

The Matron nodded. "A new chapter ... And Blair, I expect you to introduce me to your mother when I return."

I swallowed hard, excited at the prospective of reuniting with my mother, but afraid to hope it would soon become a reality. I followed two warriors to a room along the building's outer perimeter, where other Eves monitored street surveillance cameras. Outside the kiosks, people lined up. Many escorted the elderly. Near the hospitals, excited people pushed gurneys and wheelchairs. Some had concerned expressions as they waited for their loved one's turn, viewing with a cautious expectation the jubilation of others whose friends and family experienced miraculous cures.

I found the Children's Hospital line spellbinding. An emaciated, bald-headed boy was carried in, then he skipped out minutes later, unaided, with a healthy smile and thick black hair. A teen on crutches with a bandaged forehead went in, and walked out with no sign of trauma; he held up his crutches in a salute to those waiting. Story after story unfolded on the screens. And I knew the Matron had been right—for most, this gift of hope would overcome the tyranny of fear.

But I also knew the Con Squad troopers were a breed apart. They wouldn't easily give up the power they'd taken.

As the sun rose higher in the sky, more of the Matron's warriors returned to the warehouse. Some exchanged their Nano Armor for fresh suits and returned to their posts, but others rested. By midday, I was getting fidgety. I paced the halls and kept looking outside every few minutes to see if anyone was coming. Waiting made me feel useless.

Night and Terence had been gone long enough to reach Eureka Towers. Were they inside the building? Had they located the two Eves yet? I had hoped they would check in, or that the Matron would let me know her plans, but neither happened. Instead, I heard a knock on the warehouse door. Puzzled, I checked the holo screen.

With a scream of delight, I opened the door. "It's you!" I shrieked. "It's really you."

"Honey, I've been so worried about you," Mom said. "I'd almost given up hope that we'd ever be together again!" She reached for my face. "You look ... older."

"It's a long story." I stepped back and took a moment to really look at Mom's disheveled hair, dirty clothes, and bruised face. "What have they done to you?"

Mom tried to cover needle tracks on her arms with her hands, but it only drew my attention to them.

"Those bastards drugged you?" My anger flared at the thought of the Con Squad subjecting her to addictive or hallucinogenic substances. "I'll kill them."

"No, no," Mom said. "It's all behind us now. They didn't drug me—much—since it didn't work." She pulled her sleeve down over the worst of the marks. "You're not wearing your armband any more?"

I chuffed. "After watching you get dragged out of our house, and then being hunted down as a terrorist? No, I'm not a Reservist anymore."

She hugged me. "I've been so worried that you would totally disown me to keep from being associated with a mutant. I know how much you wanted to belong."

"I should've thought for myself instead of just listening to their lies." I looked away, not wanting to meet her eyes. "Mom, they came after you because of me."

"What do you mean?"

"They arrested one of my classmates, so I went to Headquarters to see if I could be of help. Instead, the trooper decided to look into my background. She found something 'irregular' that caused them to come after you."

"Ahh, I see," she said. "They claimed I had you by virgin birth and was an immortal. They wanted me to turn over the others. Of course, I was of no help, which made them pretty frustrated."

"I'm so sorry, Mom," I said. "I can see how hard they were on you —I bet you've lost ten pounds."

"That was another test—to see if I could survive without food," she said. "It's a good thing this revolt happened when it did."

A lump rose in my throat when I thought of how close I'd come to losing her. I took Mom's hand. "I'm so glad we're together now. I want to hear everything, but first, let's go find you some food and clean clothes."

"Well, actually, the Matron set up some sort of treatment for us," she said. "The warriors said it's like a Fountain of Youth?" She laughed. "Frankly, I'd settle for a hot shower and a cup of tea."

I beamed. "You can have that, too, but of course they're right. We need to get you to one of the kiosks. That will be the best thing for you. I've been watching miracles happen all day."

Mom smiled. "Then let's go join the others. They're waiting outside. Your friend Margie's been asking about you."

43

ARI

After a while, I started tracking time by counting. "One alligator, two alligators..." I counted sixty alligators sixty times, and figured more than an hour passed, but Seldon still didn't return. I slipped Piper's head off my lap and grabbed a sofa pillow to put underneath it. She remained unconscious but seemed no worse.

The living area adjoined a bedroom twice the size of mine on the thirteenth floor. It had a mirror on the ceiling above the bed, and the adjoining oversized refresher had reflective walls and a padded bench long enough to recline upon. Although the Nadux Room was smaller, the refreshment console had a variety of different wines and cheeses, in addition to the more standard fare. I retrieved a cup of water and then examined the Tailor. Instead of only jumpsuits, it had shorts and tees for men, and lacy garments for women. This was definitely a place designed for courting couples, but something about it seemed wrong.

What did I know, though? The ambiance was far outside of what I'd seen in the culture I'd grown up in, which meant it both intrigued and intimidated me. I still hadn't come to grips with my feelings for Tibor. Would I be willing to take those feelings to the next level if he tried to kiss me or touch me in an intimate way? The thought made warmth rise deep in the center of my body. Like most crescent-moon cadets, I had experimented with a few partners. I knew something about how to pleasure another Eve, and what it was like to be pleasured. Would it be the same with him?

I'd just finished recycling my water bottle when the Nadux came on in the living room. My heart jumped. Had someone come in without my hearing them and turned it on? Then I heard the countdown and figured it must be another priority announcement from the Matron. Instead, the young woman on the holo screen identified herself as Blair. Next to her stood two women—one looked enough like Blair to be her sister.

"It's my pleasure to announce the hostages taken by the Con Squad have now been released, thanks to the efforts of some concerned citizens. I'm happy to report my mother was among those rescued." She wrapped an arm around the woman with curly hair, then reached for the other woman. "And this is my friend, Margie. They have all been given priority treatments in the kiosks to reverse the ill effects of their questioning and captivity."

I walked over and sat on the couch. I could see the Matron's plan like tiles in a mosaic. The first tile was her offer of a long and healthy life to the millions of Cains in New Humboldt. The second tile was when she freed the Con Squad's prisoners—the so-called mutants—erasing the fear that had kept Cains subservient. The third and fourth tiles were further steps to engage the Cains in reclaiming their loved ones and then their own destiny. The next tiles in the Matron's pattern must have something to do with the compounds.

"If your loved ones were taken, tell the Eve warrior at the nearest kiosk, and we'll expedite your reunion with those who survived, or we'll advise you where to find your loved one's remains. We will keep you posted on future developments."

In the silence that followed, I listened carefully for any sound of approaching voices. Still, I heard nothing. I continued exploring the apartment. On the wall opposite the Nadux Room, I found a small nook with a computer. I hesitated a moment, then logged in. Above my name, links to various chat screens flashed. Did I dare? I could be giving away my location. I looked over at Piper's prone body and decided I had to try. I had to find a way back into the lab and to the moon simulator.

First, I tapped Tibor's link. When I got no response, I tried Seldon's. What if Seldon had switched back into his Abigail persona and not been able to change back? Piper needed help now. I wasn't really sure I could trust Jed, but I felt I had to try.

Immediately, I got a reply, "Aaron?"

"Have you seen Seldon?" I asked.

"Not since dawn," Jed replied. "But some other people have been asking about you."

"I'm in some trouble," I admitted. "And I desperately need your help, but I think I can help you, too."

I held my breath. I was asking a lot of him—his whole society was tumbling down around him and a "newbie" like me claimed to be able to help him? It was almost comical, if I wasn't so desperate. Though he was Seldon's friend, I had no clue if Jed was still under the control of the Elder's programming. I just had to trust my instincts.

"What can I do?" he asked.

I let out my breath. "I know the timing is weird, but I think I've figured out a way to make your enhanced moon spectra experiment work."

"That would be amazing," he said.

"But I don't have a key to the riser, so I need an escort."

"Where should we meet?" Jed asked.

I hesitated a moment, knowing this could be a huge mistake. "I'm on the nineteenth floor, in the room to the left of the riser in the front lobby. I'll need help moving some supplies for the experiment, so bring an enclosed gurney of some sort. A big one."

"I'm on my way," he said.

"Oh, and Jed," I said, "if those people who asked about me come back, I'd appreciate it if you don't mention we talked."

"All right," he grumbled, "but I'm going to need an explanation. There's more craziness going on today than I've seen in my entire lifetime. All this cloak-and-dagger stuff. Next thing I know, the Matron's going to come on the Nadux inviting us all to a ball, or some such nonsense."

I smiled at the thought. He might not be as far off as he thought. I went back to the Tailor and dialed around until I found a forest-green jumpsuit. I ordered Piper's a size larger than mine. With great difficulty, I got both of us changed and recycled our other clothes and shoes, then knelt in back of the couch next to Piper. Moments later, the door slid open.

"Aaron?" Jed asked.

Recognizing his voice, I stood. "Here."

He recoiled slightly. "Well, I wasn't expecting you to be playing hide and seek." He pulled in a cart with two large shelves. "Hope this will do. It's the biggest I could find. I didn't take time to unload it, though."

"It's perfect," I said. "Jed, I don't want to get you in trouble, but the Elder hurt my friend, and your experimental moon spectra simulator is her only hope."

Jed looked down at Piper, his mouth a thin line, and shook his head. "What's this all about?"

"She's an Eve," I said. "The Elder trapped her in the sunlight, and it depleted her life-force. I don't think she'll make it until moonrise."

He lifted one of her wrists, noting the bloody marks from the handcuffs, then frowned when at the raw circles around mine. "What happened to you?"

I sucked in my breath. It wouldn't do any good to deny it. "The Elder handcuffed me in the sunlight, too, because I'm also an Eve. Piper came here to rescue me." I waited for a reaction, but he just stood there.

Finally he said, "Guess that explains why you didn't mind working nightshift."

"I'm so sorry I had to mislead you. But please help me save her!"

For a moment, I thought he was going to say no. Then his face softened, shifting to a hard-jawed determination. He knelt beside Piper and gently picked her up. "Pull that crate off the lower shelf and open it."

I did. He lowered her carefully into it. It was empty except for some bubble wrap, which popped under her weight. We closed the lid and slipped our fingers into handholds on each side, then lifted the wooden crate back onto the lower shelf. He motioned to a crate about half the size on the top shelf. "Think you can squeeze into that?"

With a boost from Jed, I climbed onto the cart. I lifted the crate's lid and stepped in. I hugged my knees to my chest and curled my head over so the lid would close. It was a tight fit, but we only had to go up the riser.

Jed let out a huff and the cart jerked forward. "You're heavier than you look," he growled. Then we were out of the room and moving down the hall. He stopped to unlock a door, and we were moving again. The cart passed from carpeted to slick floors, then stopped.

"Where you headed, Jed?" a man asked.

"Taking some supplies back to the lab," he said. "Those techs down here never return anything they borrow."

"That's the truth," the man answered. "I hear Nathan's mate and some other women are missing. If you spot them, give me a call."

"I'll sure do that," Jed replied. "Not," he growled under his breath. Then we were moving forward again, and my stomach lurched as the riser sped upward. When we exited, the wheels clattered loudly over the mesh grating. He opened another locked door. The next time we stopped, he tapped on the lid of the crate. "You can come out now."

As I reached to push the lid up, I imagined the Elder outside waiting for me. I slowly raised it and was relieved to find only Jed there. He gave me a hand as I stepped out of the crate and jumped off the cart.

"Thanks, Jed," I said.

"Don't thank me yet," he replied. "Let's see if this simulator can help. Seldon said we might have some excitement around here, but I had no idea. If we can get the Elder out of the way, though, I'm in."

My joints ached, and my feet had gone to sleep from lack of circulation. I helped Jed lift Piper and carry her to the reclining leather chair near the vacuum chamber.

"I can't do this alone," he said. "I'll need Seldon's help."

I nodded. He walked into his office, leaving us alone in the gleaming white laboratory. Minutes later, Jed returned smiling. "He'll be up soon. You wouldn't believe how excited he was to find out you were here."

Excited probably wasn't quite the right word. When Seldon arrived, at first I wasn't sure if he planned to hug or hit me.

"What were you thinking?" he said. "I told you to stay there, and what do you do?" He turned to Jed. "I can't thank you enough for this."

Jed bobbed his chin. "Aaron, or whatever her name is, thinks the moon spectra simulator may help her friend."

Seldon sighed. "We can try, Ari," he said, "but our studies show it doesn't work."

"We have to do something," I said. "If we don't, you know as well as I do, Piper won't make it."

He nodded, and Jed joined him at the control panels. The lights on the holo screens lit up. Soon a bright beam of blue-white light covered Piper. "She'll need to stay here at least thirty minutes," Seldom said.

"It would probably be safer for everyone if you waited somewhere else," Jed told me.

"She can stay with me."

I turned to see Tibor waiting in the doorway. "How long have you been there?" I asked. My body buzzed all over.

"Long enough to know you're a crazy person," he said. "You know what the Elder will do to you if he catches you again."

Thoughts of the sun-filled room flashed through my mind, but in my gut, I knew that was only a taste of what the Elder was capable of doing.

"They're looking everywhere for you," Tibor continued.

"Except where they've already checked," I said.

44
_____

BLAIR

"It's happening!" yelled one of the Eves monitoring the holo screens. A whoop went up around the room.

It took me a moment to realize what I was seeing on the various monitors.

"The Matron was right—the Cains are rebelling against the government." An Eve pointed at one of the monitors. "That's Con Squad headquarters."

"And the courts building," another said.

"That's where I was held," Mom said, pointing to a ten-story concrete building with no windows on the ground floor and an orange CS insignia on a blue banner above the massive doors.

Outside each of these buildings and dozens more, crowds jeered and brandished signs that read: "No more fear," "Mutant like me," and a red circle with a diagonal line over "CS."

"We've got an incoming. Someone's overriding the Nadux," one of the warriors said, switching to a live feed. The set was familiar— announcements from the president and other high government officials were always held in this blue-draped room with a bigger-than-lifesize Con Squad crest on the wall. Three men I didn't recognize sat at a desk with microphones in front of them.

"My name is Lucian," said the bald-headed man with bushy eyebrows. "With me are some of the new leaders of the Cain and

Adam communities. Our coalition was responsible for the release of the Con Squad's hostages Blair announced earlier.

"We pledge to make this transition a smooth one. No longer will we tolerate the regime of fear that has taken good people from their families and friends. Just as the treatment freely given to us by the Eves will make our lives better and longer, we pledge to give the Matron and Eves the privacy and respect they deserve.

"We will ensure that the Con Squad and Mutant Studies Institute are disbanded, and that no further attempts will be made to capture or study Eves. We have joined forces with the Matron's warriors outside the government offices and the homes of the top officials. We will stand beside them wherever troops are needed because this is *our* city, and it is time for power to be returned to the people."

With the end of the announcement, the monitors returned to their normal scanning mode. Crowds of people thronged in the streets.

Mom pointed out a tall, gray-haired woman waving a sign. "There's Dina!"

"I'll have to tell you all she did for me, Mom," I said. "She's amazing."

Reporters interviewed those who'd been released, some of whom had waited to take the treatment until they could document the broken bones, sunburnt skin, scars, and emaciated bodies they'd suffered at the hands of the Con Squad.

"I never thought I'd see the day when we didn't have to worry about the Con Squad," Mom said. "We gave up too much—our rights, our freedom—in the name of safety."

"And what we got in return was tyranny," Margie said.

"We can't let the fear-mongers take control again," I said.

"Things will be different now," Mom said. "These women—warriors?—will make it better."

Jane, who'd been following their interchange, walked over to me. "Can we go to Eureka Towers now? I'd really like to make sure my mom's all right, too. And Margie wants to see Terence."

"I'll check." I walked over to the Eve who'd been my liaison since the Matron's departure. "When can we return to Eureka Towers?"

"We'll connect you with our contact as soon as possible, but for now, we can only wait," she said. "I don't think it will be long. Lucian was one of our liaisons, so the situation at the Towers must be under control."

"The women at Eureka Towers weren't allowed to do anything without supervision by the men," Jane complained to my mother. "I'd never even been outside the compound. I think the Matron should lock all the men up for a year just to show them how it feels."

Mom laughed. "I know exactly how you feel."

"Whoa, Jane," Margie said. "They weren't all bad. At least Terence didn't abandon you when he found out why you were being followed."

"Fine," Jane said. "Six months will do for him."

Margie and I laughed.

"I think Night shared your opinion about Terence," I said. "We'll see if she's had a change of heart when she gets back."

"Yeah, well, they can throw away the key when they lock up my dad," Jane said. "What kind of man uses his own daughter like that? I thought he wanted better things for me, but all along, my mom was the one trying to look out for me. I see that now."

"It was a terrible thing for him to do," Margie said, "but we don't know why he did it. We know the Elder could make the Con Squad believe things that weren't true. He may have tricked your father, too."

"I don't care," Jane said. "Some things you just don't do, and using your daughter—without her knowledge—to betray her friends is one of those things."

I gave Jane a hug. "We know it wasn't your fault, Jane. And it all turned out okay."

The Eve who'd been my liaison walked up. "A message is coming in for you from Eureka Towers."

As we approached the holographic screen, full-sized images of Terence, Seldon and Nathan materialized in front of us.

45

ARI

"We'll watch over her," Seldon said. "Jed's right. You should go with Tibor."

I took another long look at Piper. Though I was reluctant to leave, I knew it probably would be safer. Having us all in the same place was courting disaster.

"One minute," Jed said. When he returned from his office, he held out a key. "I planned to give this to you on your next shift."

"For the riser?" I asked, as I took it.

He nodded. "Be sure to use the back risers or the stairs. They're less traveled, but still dangerous, of course. If you're not careful, you can get trapped."

I swallowed hard. Trapped meant captured, and captured meant things I didn't want to think about. "Thanks, Jed. We'll be back soon."

Tibor tapped my shoulder. "We should leave."

"Follow me," I said. I gathered my courage before opening the door to the back stairwell. On the landing, we listened. All was quiet. After a quick glance, we raced down two flights of stairs to the landing below. Again we listened, repeating the process until we reached the twenty-first floor.

I bent over, winded, and said, "Okay, this is it. Ready?"

"In a minute," Tibor said, breathing deeply.

I cracked open the door so we could hear better, then opened it just wide enough to see both ways down the hall. "Coast is clear," I said, dashing across the hall to the entrance and opening the black door. Tibor followed me and we clattered up the next flights of steps to where the walkways of Lovers' Lanes began.

As I reached to open the door, Tibor grabbed my wrist.

"Ouch!" I said, jerking back.

"I'm so sorry," he said, examining the marks on my wrists.

"It's nothing." I hid them from view.

"I can't seem to get this right." Tibor put his hands on my shoulders and pulled me close to him. "I've been so worried about you, ever since I remembered how we met and what you did for the babies."

I trembled under his touch—a feeling so powerful and unlike anything I'd experienced before that I couldn't control it. I wanted him to hold me closer, but it confused me. Was something wrong with me for desiring an Adam? My senses registered the heat of his body, the scent of sunlight and fresh air, the electricity of his skin on mine. Then he leaned over.

Tibor's lips touched mine so softly I thought I might be dreaming it. Then he pulled me closer, sliding one hand behind my head, guiding our kiss to a deepness I felt at my core. His tongue traced my lips, then thrust inside my mouth. Surprise gave way to desire—I wanted more. I pressed my body against his, straining for every inch of our bodies to touch.

He pulled back and smiled. He brushed a hand through my hair and caressed my face. "We need to take this slow."

It was all I could do to concentrate on what he was saying. His mouth looked full and kissable. With his arm around my waist, we slid down the wall to sit on the floor. He pulled me closer so my head rested on his shoulder.

"We'll wait here instead of going onto the walkway," he said. "There'll be less chance of being spotted. But one day, I want to walk with you among the branches."

"I want that, too," I said. "But you're right; here is safer."

His body pressing against mine made my heart beat louder and faster. Then I thought about Natisha. Had he held her like this when they met on the nineteenth floor? Suddenly feeling hurt and confused, I pulled away.

"What's wrong?" he asked.

"Did you and Natisha do...this?" I asked, motioning at the two of us entwined together. "Did you kiss her?"

"Ah," Tibor stammered.

"You kissed her!" I said.

"I didn't KISS her," he said, shaking his head. ""It wasn't the same. Not at all."

I twisted around so my back was toward him.

"I wouldn't have kissed her at all if they hadn't taken away my memories." He placed a hand on my shoulder. "Really, Ari, when my memories came back, I kept getting flashbacks of you protecting Rayson as we ran from the Con Squad. I even adored that you didn't want to leave the nursery. Although it got us in huge trouble with the Elder, I knew you stayed because you cared so much for the baby. An Adam, just like me."

My eyes brimmed with tears, then anger swelled. I shoved his hand away. "Yeah, that's why you picked someone who looked as different from me as possible."

"Aw, Ari," he said softly. "I would never intentionally hurt you."

"Obviously, I'm not your preferred type of woman." The words continued to spill out, despite an inner voice telling me to stop. To listen. "If you had to date, why couldn't you want someone who looked like me?" *Or see through my disguise, and recognize me?*

"Ari, I love the way you look," Tibor said.

"I look like a boy," I said,

Tibor toyed with the fringes of hair at the nape of my neck. I shivered.

"We were roommates, and you were my best friend," he said. "It would've looked strange if I'd chosen a woman who looked like you."

"But you thought about it?" I asked.

He nodded. "Of course." Tibor pulled me closer. "Natisha's a very nice woman, but it's you I care about." His eyes met mine with a gaze that held nothing back. I knew he was sincere.

As my anger faded, I berated myself for being so shallow. Here I was, upset about their brief time together, when I could still hear in my mind Natisha's desperate cries as the Elder's men took her away.

"I wonder where Natisha is," I said. "She was screaming for help. We need to find her and Fike."

"We will, Ari," he said, "and the other women, too. But first, you and Piper need to get out of here and warn the Matron. The rest of us will take care of the Elder and his men."

My emotions warred—I never wanted this moment of being close to Tibor to end, but I wanted to rush to Piper and see if she was okay. I loved his touch on my skin and longed for more, yet desperately wanted to be gone from here, back to the Eves' compound and simpler times. No matter how this day ended, I knew none of our lives would ever be the same.

"Time to go," I finally said, rising to my feet.

Tibor looked at me with sad eyes. "I wish we had longer, but you're right. We need to go." He led the way down the stairs, and checked the hallway before we dashed across to the stairwell. Wordlessly, we agreed not to chance the riser, though I patted the key in my pocket for reassurance that we could, if needed.

I held my breath as I put my pinky up to the scanner, then sighed with relief as the lock clicked open. Apparently the Elder hadn't thought to disable my access. We entered. The room was eerily quiet, which made our footsteps seem even louder. No one was around. Even the area near the vacuum chamber where we'd left Piper was deserted.

"Where is everyone?" I whispered, my gut clenching more with each step.

Then a figure rushed at me from a dark corner of the room. I jumped back, prepared to run, until I saw it was Piper. She was still pale, but steady on her feet.

"Ari!"

She hugged me so tight I thought my ribs would break. "Ow! I see you've got your strength back. And I thought you were going to die."

"I would've without this simulator," Piper said. "Jed told me you were the one who figured it out."

"Bravo, Ariadne," a dark-haired, blue-eyed woman dressed in shimmering armor said as she emerged from the shadows.

"This is Night," Piper said, introducing the woman.

"The Matron sent me to escort both of you to the new compound," Night said.

I checked to see Tibor's reaction, and did a double-take. His attention was focused on a bald man with a lip piercing and tats who stood behind us.

Seeing my distraction, Night said, "Terence acted as my guide."

"Terence?" The name was familiar. "The guy who left with Blair and Jane?" I squinted to examine his features more closely, but he still didn't look like the man I'd seen on the Nadux.

"Yes, that's the one," Night said. "And the women are safe."

"Praise the moon," I said. "We were so worried when we found out Jane's father had her tracked by the Con Squad. It's part of the Elder's plan to find the new compound. We were trying to get out to warn the Matron."

"She suspected as much," Night said. "She's taken precautions, but we can't leave any Eves here to be used as hostages. We need to go. Do you have riser access or will we need Terence's help again?"

"I can do it," I said. "Just give me one minute."

I walked over to Tibor as Night and Piper moved toward the riser. "We're leaving now," I told him.

Tibor took my hand. "Whatever it takes, I promise we'll meet again soon."

"Be brave," Seldon added.

Not trusting my voice, I pressed my lips together and gave a quick bob of my head as my fingers slipped out of Tibor's grasp. Night's lifted eyebrows made me wonder what she thought about my relationship with Tibor. I didn't have time to worry about it now, though. I sprinted over to the riser and waved my pinky at the scanner.

"Hit the express button," Night said, pointing to an X-button at the lower right of the panel. "Terence said that keeps it from stopping on other floors. Go to the basement. We came up from there, and only ran into a few stragglers."

I raised my eyebrows at Piper, which she mimicked. What had Night done to those stragglers? As if reading our minds, Night handed each of us throwing stars and readied her bow.

When the riser doors slid open minutes later, we had already positioned ourselves with our backs to the walls so the car would appear empty at first glance. As Night said, no one was in sight, though I could hear voices further down the corridor. We'd have to move fast to keep from being seen.

Night tilted her head to the right and ran. We followed silently, as the bowmaster taught us. "You must learn to move as swiftly as a thought and as quietly as a shadow," Layla always said, her voice now a ghostly echo in my mind.

"Check over there," a male voice called out from around the next corner. "I'll take this side."

We rushed to the inside wall next to a set of double doors. I waved my pinky at the scanner, and the doors slid apart. We'd barely entered when the footsteps rounded the corner before I could close the doors.

"What the...?" the man muttered. "Hey, over here!" One of the search party stood in the hallway, right outside the room.

Before I realized what was happening, a throwing star whizzed past my face. I heard a gurgling sound, then a thump. By the time I turned back around, Night was dragging him by his feet into the room.

"Close it!" she hissed.

We exited through another door. Night moved even faster than before down the hall, with Piper and me close behind. We had almost reached an intersecting hall when another voice called out behind us, "Intruders!"

She turned and released an arrow. The man fell, hands gripping the shaft piercing his throat.

Maybe it was the rush of adrenaline or because of all that had happened since I left the compound, but the sight of blood didn't faze me except for a twinge of regret. I stayed focused on our escape.

"We're almost there," Night said.

We turned the corner. On one side, rubble was all that remained of the wall, which was covered by a tarp.

"That's where the Con Squad entered the Towers," Piper said. "It's where they captured Margie."

"This way." Night lifted the tarp. On the other side, two men's bodies were mostly hidden behind some shrubs.

On the sidewalk outside the building, we passed a few startled Cains, but kept moving quickly until we reached a parking garage. Night toyed with a flesh-colored wristband. Moments later, a red-and-white checkered Shell car appeared.

"A pizza delivery car?" I laughed.

"It's Blair's," Night said as we settled in. "It actually is quite clever —no one pays attention to pizza and Chinese delivery cars, even the Con Squad."

46

BLAIR

"Mom!" Terence smiled broadly as their conference connected. "We wanted to come after you when the Con Squad took you, but I was afraid it would only make things worse since we were the fugitives they were hunting."

Margie replied, beaming, "You did the right thing, son. I'm proud of what you've done—keeping Jane and Blair safe. And I'm fine now. Just fine."

"Did Night leave with Piper and Ari?" I asked. Jane, Margie and I stood beneath the holographic transmitter so the three men could see their images.

Terence chuckled. "Yes, they are on their way to the Eve's compound in your pizza delivery car."

I grinned. I wished we were together in person, but at least we could catch up in relative safety.

"Jane, honey, I'm so glad you're okay," Nathan butted in. "I've been so worried..."

"Yeah, so worried you sent the Con Squad after me," she said coldly, hands on hips. "You're not my father anymore."

"It's not what you think," he said. "At first, I thought the Elder was trying to keep us all safe. By the time I learned better, he already had the Con Squad tracking you. I went to the Patron to get his help, then

I found out Eves had already infiltrated our building. Still, I had decided to not say anything, until the Elder threatened your mother."

"Is Mom okay?" Jane shrieked.

"She must be." Nathan pulled nervously on his chin. "But we haven't been able to find her or the women who were with her when we left Lovers' Lanes."

"Margie, Blair—we have to find my mom," Jane pleaded. "We have to go to the Towers. I may know where she is."

"Then tell me," Nathan said, his voice weary and frustrated.

Jane glared at him. "I'm done trusting you! The women can handle this without your so-called help."

"Can we go?" I asked the warrior.

"The Elder and his men have left the Towers," she said. "I'll arrange transportation."

Minutes later, the four of us were traveling to Eureka Towers, escorted by two of the Matron's warriors.

"Over there," Jane said, pointing toward a side entrance of the massive building. One of the warriors walked ahead of them, following Jane's instructions. "We'll turn right at the Arcology sign," she said.

In a green space bordering the area, Jane walked up to a trellis of flowering vines, then disappeared.

"Where'd she go?" Even when we examined the trellis, we couldn't see a latch or doorway. Then I heard a click and half the trellis disappeared, revealing a door where Jane and her mother stood.

"It's something we've been working on for theatrical productions," Jane explained proudly. "A combination of touch simulation and regular holo projection."

"A stage prop?" I said. "Fascinating."

"Come here, you," Margie said to Jane's mom. As they embraced, the other women emerged from the hidden room. "It's all over now," Margie told them. "And things are going to change. Let's go find my boy."

We reached the riser in the main lobby as the door slid open.

"Mom!" Terence yelled. His hug lifted Margie off her feet. "I was afraid I'd never see you again."

"I had my doubts, too." She caressed his face.

Nathan's mate stepped toward him. "Jane said you told the Elder about Ari to save me." She shook her head, then reached out for his hand. "When will you ever learn? It was the wrong thing to do, Nate, but I'm glad to know you care."

"Someday I hope you'll forgive me," he said. "And you, too, Jane. I promise to try to make it up to you."

Jane rolled her eyes. "I'll never understand grown-ups." She stomped into the riser car and jabbed the button. "I'll be in my room."

As the riser door slid closed, Terence walked over to me. "I saw you on the Nadux, and not as a fugitive this time."

I grinned. "Yeah, that was the kind of attention I can do without."

"And this is your mother?" He offered his wrist to her.

"Terence." She spoke coldly but touched his wrist with hers. "We might not be here together now if it hadn't been for you—I have to give you credit for that–but I'm not forgetting you kidnapped Blair."

He lowered his wrist and bowed his head. "I didn't want the Con Squad to harm her just because she was in the wrong place at the wrong time, but I see now that I didn't appreciate the bad position I put her in." He turned to me. "I'm really sorry."

I bit my bottom lip. "Yeah, well, I was way too trusting. I definitely think my survivor skills have improved a lot since then. It's been a crash course!"

"Maybe we could start over?" Terence said.

Ignoring my mother's frown, I nodded. We had been through a lot together and, in the end, he'd done what he could to make things right. "I must be out of my mind, but I like you."

Terence grinned.

Seldon gave Terence a reassuring slap on his shoulder. "That's a start, boy."

"Have either of you seen Abigail?" Margie said. "And I had hoped Natisha and Fike would be here, too."

"Jed and Tibor are checking out the rooms on the nineteenth floor now," Seldon said, "but I know where Abigail is."

"She's okay?" Margie asked.

I whispered to Terence, "She's not going to like this."

Margie spun around. "What do you mean? Is she hurt?"

"No, nothing like that," Seldon said, frowning. "You see, I'm Abigail."

Margie snorted and narrowed her eyes at him. "And I'm Mother Moon. That's not even funny, Seldon."

"He's telling the truth," I said.

Seldon placed his hand on Margie's shoulder. "I didn't want to deceive you, my friend, but I had to."

Margie's mouth fell open, reminding me of a goldfish.

"You mean all these years – *ALL* these years — you've been living a double life?" Margie said, her voice rising. "You didn't trust me—when I shared all my secrets with you—but you told these girls you've only known a few days!" She wrenched away from him and went to stand by Terence, who squinted at Seldon, as if trying to picture him as the redhaired woman.

"It's not like that," I said. "Piper found out first, then I learned when I went with her to Seldon's apartment to meet Aaron."

"Carl's friend?" Margie said.

I nodded.

"I remember seeing his image on one of the girls' handhelds." Margie paused, then looked suspiciously at me. "Why were you girls in a man's room?"

"It's pretty complicated, Margie," Seldon began.

She held up her hand to Seldon. "It's too late for you to try to explain anything to me about this. Blair, go on."

I grimaced and gave Seldon a defeated look. "You see, Aaron is one of the Eves who infiltrated the building."

"That's why I put Aaron on the night shift with me," Seldon said.

Margie scowled fiercely, and he took a step back. "Wait," Margie said. "Aaron is an Eve who was disguised as a man?"

"Yep," I said. "The new girl—Piper—is also an Eve. She was sent here to help Aaron—actually, Ariadne—escape and find her way to the new Eve compound."

"That's when things got even more complicated," Nathan interrupted. "I took Aaron up to the nineteenth floor—dressed as a woman—so we could help the women escape. That's when I learned Aaron was actually an Eve, and that Piper was missing."

Margie put her hands to her face and rubbed her temples. "Okay, I think I've got it. But is anyone else not who they seem to be?"

I shook my head.

"For now, we need to focus on finding Natisha and the Patron, but later," Margie glared at Seldon, "you better believe we're going to have a long talk about all this."

"Of course." He gave her a contrite and hopeful smile. "Let's see if Jed and Tibor have had any luck."

When the door opened on the nineteenth floor, Jed and Tibor were waiting to get on. They held a stretcher between them, with Fike lying unconscious on it.

"Fike!" Seldon rushed to the older man's side. Fike didn't respond. His head and hands were bandaged, and his skin looked gray.

"He's lost a lot of blood," Tibor said. "The Elder roughed up him and Natisha pretty bad. We're taking them to one of the kiosks for treatment."

Behind Jed, a young man with blonde hair wrapped an arm around Natisha's shoulders, supporting her as she hobbled toward the riser with her right leg in a makeshift splint. Her left eye was swollen shut and her lip was cut.

"Natisha," Margie cried. "What did they do to you?"

"Nothing that won't mend," she said. "I'm just glad Ari was able to get Piper out of that room before it was too late. I guess we showed them, eh?"

Margie laughed, relieved, and said, "You sure did."

47

ARI

The car accelerated, reaching the SuperFlex in minutes. It jostled slightly as we connected to the chain, then our speed tripled.

"Sit back and relax," Night said. "The new compound is on the outskirts of town, and we'll have to travel off the SuperFlex about half the way, which will take longer."

With a sigh, Piper leaned back on the cracked red-vinyl bench seat. "Wish it was a full moon tonight, but I guess I'll have to make do."

I nodded, grateful she was doing well enough now to make it until moonrise. "I heard you spent most of the day in that room."

"Yes, they caught me right after the siren went off."

"Why didn't you leave with Blair?" I asked.

She shook her head and grinned at me. "Do you really have to ask?"

I looked down at my lap, secretly pleased, but embarrassed at my selfishness. Had she really stayed there for me?

"Blair wanted me to go with them, but I wasn't leaving without you," she said.

She actually said it; Piper didn't leave because of me. I looked up and caught her gaze. For a moment, our heartbeats must have been in sync. I put a hand on her shoulder. "That means a lot to me."

Piper looked away and wiped her cheek. When she turned back

around, she smirked and said, "Besides, I couldn't let you have all the fun, being out of the compound for the first time and all that."

With mock disgust, I sighed. "Yeah, well, I'm looking forward to a hundred years or so of boredom to make up for all this fun."

"That I'll believe when I see it," Piper said. "I have a feeling things are going to be different, even for the crescent-moon cadets like us. It sounds like the Matron is ready to work with the Adams instead of acting like they don't exist."

I hoped she was right. Tibor, Fike, and the infants were important to me. I knew forgetting them wasn't an option.

"Look for signs for the Genesis Apple Orchard," Piper said.

"What?" Then I recalled what Fike had told me about returning to their compound.

"Yeah, that's how you know the way." She grinned.

Sure enough, I soon saw one sign, then another. One was at the ramp where we exited the SuperFlex, and still another where it turned from pavement to gravel. When I closed my eyes, the sounds of the road were familiar. I was pretty sure we'd come down a road like this when we left the Adams' compound.

We continued another fifteen minutes until I saw a built-up area back from the road. I recognized the multistory buildings. "That's the Adams' compound!" I said. "Fike said our new compound was nearby."

Twenty minutes later, we turned at a sign for Genesis Apple Orchard. Apple trees lined the dusty road. Up ahead, men and women thronged outside the tall walls of a compound. Spires of three circular buildings rose behind the walls—I knew they would be for each of the groups, with the largest for the full-moon women.

Night stopped the car fifty yards away from the crowd.

"What's happening?" Piper said.

"It looks like the Elder and his men made it here before the Matron," Night said. "We need to find her."

I followed Night and Piper at a run. We kept behind the cover of the apple trees, with Night circling the compound to get a better feel of what was happening. Just outside the compound walls, about a dozen injured men and women lay on the grass. Most had bandaged limbs or heads; some were unconscious.

"That's not good," Night said.

Her tone made tendrils of fear rise within me.

"What do you think happened?" Piper asked.

"The Eves are keeping the Adams outside the compound," Night said. "If they get inside, we lose our only sanctuary."

"But why are all the injured men and women together?" I asked.

"We may be barbaric in many ways, but the Adams share with us a common respect for those who are injured or noncombatants," Night said. "At least, that's always been true up until now."

I figured the nervous edge to her voice was due to the scene unfolding as we approached a large group of about a hundred Adams on one side, and as many Eves on the other.

In the center, the Matron and the Elder stood facing each other. Both had shed their full-length robes—the Matron for a sleek microfiber tunic over black leggings and the Elder for loose-fitting silk pajamas.

"Oh no," Night said. "I had hoped she wouldn't do this."

"Do what?" I said.

"It's the only way to keep a confrontation in check—to have champions fight the battle."

"You mean, if she loses, the Elder decides what happens to us?" Piper said.

"We could become the Adams' slaves? Their breeders?" I asked.

"The Matron is the best leader we've ever had," Night said. "And the best warrior. But they aren't permitted to use weapons."

The last words trailed off. She sounded worried, which didn't reassure me. Somehow I figured Night was the Eves' best warrior. Even so, I felt confident the Matron's brains could overpower the Elder's brawn.

Then the Elder attacked. He sidestepped, then swung his leg in an arc that swept the Matron off her feet. Before she could recover, he pulled a hidden throwing star from the cuff of his sleeve and drew back his arm to sling it at her face.

I gasped; in such close quarters, he couldn't miss. At the last second, the Matron jerked her head aside. The star slammed into the dirt, sending a divot into the air. I held my breath, willing the Matron to recover.

She arched her back and sprang to her feet in an acrobatic leap. It was nothing short of a miracle.

The Elder laughed. "Well done, but all for nothing." Another throwing star slid into his hand.

An angry murmur rose from the Eves, which the Matron quietened with a gesture. "I expected better of you," she told him.

He held up the star, taunting her. "There's no honor in dying." He circled her one full turn. Her focus never left his face.

I stared at the gleaming blades of the deadly throwing star and twitched each time the Elder raised or lowered his hand even a fraction of an inch. When he began circling the Matron a second time, the flash of another star from his left hand caught me by surprise. As the star drove into the Matron's left shoulder, a collective cry went up—the Adams in jubilation and the Eves in despair.

Reeling from the impact, the Matron used the momentum to spin toward the Elder. Before he could release the other star, the Matron drove the heel of her right foot into his chin. With a loud pop, he went down. His body sprawled on the grass with his neck at an impossible angle. His eyes stared vacantly.

The Matron stood quietly above his body for a moment, then motioned to one of the warriors. She took the Disruptor, which I'd first had seen in the field outside our other compound, and twice swept the beam over the Elder. His body disappeared.

It had all happened so fast, I couldn't believe he was really dead. The stunned faces of the men surrounding us showed they were having an even harder time accepting it. As the shock wore off, a spark of hope grew inside me—and pride. The Matron had defeated him without resorting to cheating.

"Your leader agreed to the rules of combat," the Matron said. She pressed her right hand firmly against the injured shoulder to slow the bleeding as she addressed the Adams. "But if you have another champion, now is the time for him to come forward." She waited as the men talked among themselves. The tall man who'd taken me to the Elder glared at me, but no one stepped up to answer her challenge. "Then it's settled. Your true leader—the Patron—will arrive soon. Together we will forge a new alliance."

Night, Piper and I followed the Matron through the gates of our new compound. I recognized the architectural style as similar to that at the Adams' compound, except for pergolas with sun-screening covers that extended over most of the courtyard. Even so, the Sun tapped our energy; we needed to get inside soon.

In front of each tower was a circular fountain. Rising from the center of the fountains were white marble sculptures of an Eve holding the moon in one of its phases—new, crescent, and full. Behind us, the full-moon women carried the injured Eves inside the compound. Cadets of all ages ran to and fro, carrying bandages, water, and other supplies wherever they were needed.

The Matron leaned on Night as we neared a cottage that looked identical to her home at the old compound. The door opened and Myranda ran to the Matron. "You're injured!" She scowled at Night. "What happened?"

Night took a step back, releasing the Matron, who laughed softly. "Everything is all right now." She wrapped her uninjured arm around Myranda's shoulders and kissed her. "I'm so grateful to have you to come home to."

"Was it the Elder again?" Myranda said. "I knew you would overcome him—as you have so many times."

"He's dead," the Matron said sadly. "I killed him."

Myranda sighed. "I know that's not what you wanted, but it should've been done long ago."

She motioned for us to enter as she guided the Matron to a cushioned chair on a covered porch facing a center atrium. We'd been there only a few minutes when someone knocked on the door.

Myranda opened it. "Patron! I've been expecting you. Please, all of you, join us."

Fike pulled a chair onto the sunny side of the porch, flanked by Blair and her mother, Terence, Margie, and Seldon. Piper moved over to let Tibor sit between us.

My spirits lifted, taking my mind off the weariness that weighed down my body. I was watching history being made—not only were Adams in our compound, but Cains, too. I glanced at Piper and smiled. From her awed expression, I figured she also recognized the importance of this gathering.

"We have much to discuss," Fike began. "But first, thank you for inviting us here, and for what you did today. You placed your life on the line for us, again, and it won't be forgotten."

The Matron smiled. "My friend, you would've done the same for me."

"This time, the old fox trapped me." He shook his head. "I've gotten too soft."

"Not at all," the Matron said, reaching out for his hand. "You're exactly what the Adams need—someone who is compassionate and fair. But the Elder was right about one thing—we must find a way so more Adams can be born. That can only happen if we work together to find a way for Eves to survive male births. From what Ariadne says, the scientists at Eureka Towers may have a start on finding the answer."

"The results so far aren't very promising," Seldon cautioned.

"But Piper's recovery shows what I suspected is true," I said. "Eves respond differently than suneaters to infrared and visible light rays."

"The challenge is finding out why—exactly how our body chemistry is different," Tibor said.

"I think we'll find it has something to do with the way we age—either metabolism changes or body fat," I said.

"With the help of your scientists, Matron, we'll have a much better chance of success," Seldon said.

"We can work out the details later, but this must be a top priority," the Matron said. "Until it's resolved, our two cultures can never truly be at peace."

"Yes, but having the Con Squad out of the way will help us all," Fike said.

Blair squeezed her mother's hand and nodded at the Matron. "That's certainly true! Speaking on behalf of those you call Cains, sharing the healing kiosks with us has defused the Con Squad's fear tactics."

Matron smiled at them. "We all have much to do,"

"We've already started deprogramming the men at Eureka Towers," Fike said.

"Once the men realize how they've mistreated the women, I'm sure my good friend Margie will have no trouble establishing fair representation for women's concerns," Seldon added.

"The trick will be keeping the women from locking up the men and throwing away the key," Blair whispered to her mother.

"I heard that," Margie said. She winked at Terence, who squirmed uncomfortably. Returning her focus to Seldon, she continued, "I'd like to think the change would be automatic, but reversing years of mistreatment will probably take ongoing efforts on both sides for quite some time."

He nodded. "But together, I know we can do it."

After we decided the next steps to be taken, the others said their goodbyes to the Matron. Tibor and I lingered by the door.

"On the way over, Fike said he'd like you to visit Rayson and Laylan whenever you want," Tibor said.

"I'd love that!"

He reached over, lifted my chin and leaned down. I closed my eyes in anticipation, then Piper grabbed my upper arm and dragged me halfway out the door.

"What!" I screeched, trying to pull away from her viselike grip. "Stop that."

When I looked back at Tibor, he stood with his eyes wide and mouth gaping open.

"Well done, Piper," the Matron said. She looked at Tibor, then me, and laughed. "You two should try a little discretion in front of your elders."

Fike chuckled. "Time to go." He escorted Tibor past us with a two-finger salute to Piper and me.

I returned the gesture, but my eyes were locked on Tibor's until he rounded the side of the cottage. He and Fike were gone.

"C'mon, dweeb, time to see our new temp quarters," Piper said.

"One moment, Piper." I swallowed hard and turned back to face the Matron. After all that happened, I wanted her to know I finally understood. "You were right. I was never a prisoner. What matters most to me are all of you here, my friends. Being free comes at a price, and I didn't appreciate that as soon as I should have."

The Matron smiled. "Well said, Ariadne. But you showed me I was also wrong. Fifty years doesn't seem like much time to someone like me, but it's too long for a young woman to be confined to a compound when there's a whole world waiting beyond the walls. Things are different now, and I'd like both of you to help me decide how to make some changes for our cadets."

Piper nodded, and I did, too. Immediately, I started thinking of ways we could join forces with Tibor and some of the younger Adams.

"And Ari?" The Matron gave me a look I couldn't decipher.

"Yes, Matron?"

"Keep some time open to go to New Humboldt. Jed and Seldon will need to work closely with our scientists, and I told them you would be our liaison."

I tried to find the words to express how honored I was, but all I managed to stutter was, "Yes ... and thank you!"

Piper latched onto my arm. "We better leave now before Ari's head's too big to fit through the doorway."

The Matron smiled and gestured for her to take me away.

* * *

When the bell sounded that night, I was lying on my bunk in the new dormitory, remembering the feel of Tibor's touch. When would I see him... and the babies... again?

As I rose, I looked around the room, which was much like our dorm in the old compound. Yet, I felt so different. The rest of the girls didn't know what to expect from me after my escapade, but I knew it wouldn't be long until their curiosity would overpower their shyness.

We went outside into the moonlight. I stood next to Piper in the circle. Unfettered by clothes, I raised my face and palms toward the sky. My body fed on the moonsong, its tones shifting subtly as the moon climbed higher in the cloudless sky.

ACKNOWLEDGMENTS

Moonblood began with a dream. A woman and her daughter stood nude in a shadowy field lit only by moonlight. I felt the woman's desperation, her fear for the child. I knew she was not quite human, even though she looked it. She was immortal, but not invincible. And they were in danger.

I awoke wondering about this woman. What would it be like to live alongside "ordinary" humans, yet be so different? How would her immortal race be perceived by mortals? The moonlight that bathed the dreamscape conjured up thoughts of how women's creative lifeforce —their moonblood—is also tied to moon cycles. What if women could create life on their own, without sex, like some species do?

It's been a long journey since those early forays into this near-future world. Eight years ago, I submitted a 22-page story entitled "Moonblood" to my long-time critique partners—Brad R. Cook and Cole Gibsen. My heartfelt thanks to them for helping me turn that story into a novel, and to Jennifer Lynn, who joined our group before the final chapters were critiqued two years later.

I shared the revised novel with an online critique group led by Terri Bruce, a friend from Broad Universe. My thanks to her and to critique partners Jeremy Hughes, Leann Orris, Anna Priemaza, Angi Shearstone, and Aimee Hyndman for their valuable insights.

I also appreciate the excellent feedback and encouraging responses from my Beta readers - Al Gritten, Janet Bettag, Marguerite Devers Green, Terri Bruce, and Karen Kraft. Special thanks to Karen for her editing prowess.

I'd also like to acknowledge my husband, family and friends, who encouraged me to pursue my passion, and Soul Song Press for giving *Moonblood* a home.

And a huge "thank you" to all my amazing readers for your time and interest. You make it all worthwhile!

ABOUT THE AUTHOR

T.W. Fendley is an award-winning author whose published works include *Zero Time*, a historical fantasy novel for adults, and *The Labyrinth of Time,* a young adult contemporary fantasy novel. Teresa's short stories are available on Kindle and Audible.

She fell in love with ancient American cultures while researching story ideas at the 1997 Clarion Science Fiction and Fantasy Writers' Workshop. Since then, Teresa has trekked to archeological sites in the Yucatan, Peru, and American Southwest.

She began writing fiction in 2007 after working more than 25 years in journalism and corporate communication. When she's not writing, Teresa explores the boundaries of consciousness through remote viewing and shamanism. She currently lives near St. Louis with her artist husband and his pet fish. Learn more at https://twfendley.com

***

T.W. Fendley hopes you liked *Moonblood*. If you did, please consider leaving a review online. Even one or two sentences can help future readers decide if it's a book they'd also enjoy. The author appreciates your support!

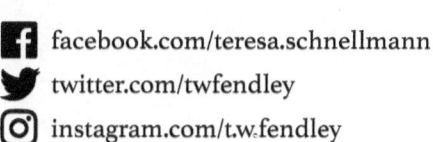

facebook.com/teresa.schnellmann
twitter.com/twfendley
instagram.com/t.w.fendley

ALSO BY T.W. FENDLEY

Zero Time Chronicles:

Zero Time

Jaguar Hope

The Mother Serpent's Daughter

Young Adult:

The Labyrinth of Time

Short Stories:

Solar Lullaby

The Mentor

And I Feel Fine

The Fourth Treatment

Audiobooks:

The Labyrinth of Time

Jaguar Hope

The Mother Serpent's Daughter

Solar Lullaby